THE BIG BOOK OF SCIENCE FACTS

by

Brian Alchorn, Catherine Chambers,

David Dalton, Dougal Dixon, Ian Graham,

Colin Hynson, Steve Parker, Dee Phillips,

Clint Twist, and Richard Walker

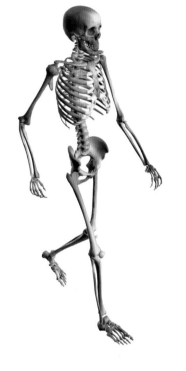

WITHDRAWN

Tick Tock Books

North American edition copyright © *TickTock* Entertainment Ltd. 2010
First published in North America in 2010 by *TickTock* Books Ltd.,
814 North Franklin Street, Chicago, Illinois 60610
www.ticktock-books.com

ISBN: 978-1-84898-173-7
Tracking Number: 3339LPP0110

Printed in China
9 8 7 6 5 4 3 2 1

Picture credits (t=top; b=bottom; c=center; r=right; l=left; OFC=outside front cover; OBC=outside back cover):
Adidas: 91tr. Alamy: 30tl, 36c, 51b, 115t, 123b, 124cr, 137c, 142l, 143c, 152b, 154c, 156cr. Ancient Art and
Architecture: 73tc. Bridgeman Art Library: 110–111 (all), 112c, 112b (both), 113 (all), 131t, 135c, 139t, 144c.
Corbis: 68b, 70b, 71t, 78tc, 79t, 80b, 83tl, 83bl, 83bc, 85t, 85bc, 88b, 89c, 97tl, 97cl. Fujitsu Limited: 100b.
George Eastman House: 77b. Image Select: 82t, 82b, 83tc, 84b, 87t, 87c. Kobal Collection: 127b. Louvre Museum, Paris:
72. Mediscan: 40b. NASA: 109tr, 109cl, 109c, 112tr, 114–115c, 114b (all), 115br, 116–117c, 118–119 (all),
120–121 (all), 122 (all), 123t, 123c, 124tl, 124cl, 124b (both), 125 (all), 126 (all), 127t, 128 (all), 129 (all),
130 (all), 131c, 131b, 132 (all), 133b, 134 (all), 135t, 135b, 136 (all), 137t, 138 (all), 139c, 139b, 140 (all),
141 (all), 142t, 142b, 143tl, 143b, 144bl, 144br, 145 (all), 146–147 (all), 149 (all), 150–151 (all), 152c (all),
153 (all), 155 (all), 156l, 156cl, 156b, 157 (all), 158t, 158b, 159 (all), 160 (all), 161 (all). PhotoAlto: 20cl.
Pictor: 56cl. Primal Pictures: 22b, 22cr, 24t, 24c, 26t, 26bl, 27br, 29tl, 29tr, 33t, 35t, 38c, 38b, 41br, 42br, 43, 44b,
53tc, 53tr, 53br, 62cl, 63t, 63cr, 64bl. Roslin Institute: 71b. Sandia National Laboratories: 101. Science & Society Picture
Library: 76c, 82c. Science Museum, London: 97bl. Science Photo Library: 17 (hormonal system), 19t, 23t, 26c, 28t, 31t,
36b, 39b, 42t, 45, 49t, 52cr, 54b, 55t, 56b, 59t, 59bc, 60br (embryo), 61bl (fetus), 63cl, 78bc, 79bc, 103br, 109bl.
Shutterstock: OFC (all), 1, 11bc, 47b, 92b, 96t, 164tl, 165br, OBC (all). Sony: 100c. Tony Stone: 20b, 23b, 28bl, 44c,
46b, 49b, 55b, 61 (new baby). U.S. Fish and Wildlife Service: 24b, 63br. Welcome Photo Library: 50 (all from week 1)

CONTENTS

HOW TO USE THIS BOOK

THE BIG BOOK OF SCIENCE FACTS is an easy-to-use, quick way to look up facts about the amazing world of science and scientific discoveries. Every page is packed with cutaway diagrams, charts, scientific terms, and key pieces of information. For fast access to all the facts, follow the tips on these pages.

FACT BOXES
An at-a-glance look at a more specific topic.

INTRODUCTION TO TOPIC

TWO QUICK WAYS TO FIND A FACT:

1 Look at the detailed **CONTENTS** list on page 3 to find your topic of interest.

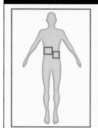

Turn to the relevant page and use the **BOX HEADINGS** to find the information box you need.

2 Turn to the **INDEX,** which starts on page 168, and search for keywords relating to your research. The index will direct you to the correct page and where on the page to find the fact you need.

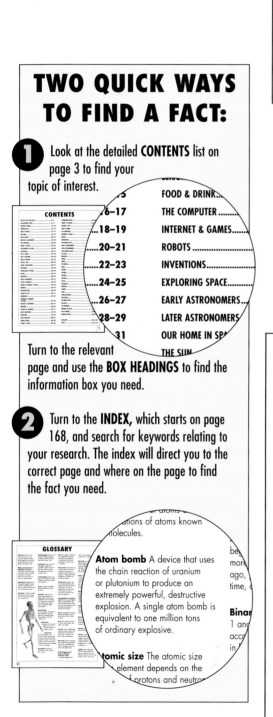

GLOSSARY

...ations of atoms known
...molecules.

Atom bomb A device that uses the chain reaction of uranium or plutonium to produce an extremely powerful, destructive explosion. A single atom bomb is equivalent to one million tons of ordinary explosive.

tomic size The atomic size ...element depends on the ...f protons and neutro

Binar
1 and
acco
in

WHERE IN THE BODY?

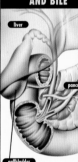

The liver is in the upper abdomen, behind the lower right ribs. The pancreas is in the upper left abdomen, behind the stomach.

LIVER & PANCREAS

Your body cannot digest food with just its digestive tract (passagewa which is made up of the mouth, gullet, stomach, and intestines. T liver and pancreas are also needed. These organs are next to the stomach, and they are digestive glands, which means they make powe substances that break down the food in the intestines. Together with t digestive tract, the liver and pancreas make up the whole digestive sys

WARM LIVER

The liver is so busy with chemical processes and tasks that it makes lots of heat.

- When the body is at rest and the muscles are still, the liver makes up

up to one fifth of the body's total warmth.

- The heat from the liver is not wasted. The blood spreads out the heat all around the body.

See pages 44–45 for information on the circulatory system.

THE LIVER'S TASKS

The liver has more than 500 known tasks in the body — and probably more that have not yet been discovered. Some of the main ones are:

- Breaking down nutrients and other substances from digestion, brought directly to the liver from the small intestine.

- Storing vitamins for times when they may be lacking in food.

- Making bile, a digestive juice.

- Breaking apart old, dead, worn-out red blood cells.

- Breaking down toxins or possibly harmful substances, like alcohol and poisons.

- Helping control the amount of water in blood and body tissues.

- If levels of blood sugar (glucose) are too high, hormones from the pancreas tell the liver to change the glucose into glycogen and store it.

- If levels of blood sugar (glucose) are too low, hormones from the pancreas tell the liver to release the glycogen it has stored.

Alcohol is a toxin that the liver breaks down and makes harmless. However, too much alcohol can overload the liver and cause a serious disease called cirrhosis.

GALLBLADDER AND BILE

liver

pancr

gallbladder

The gallbladder is a small storage bag unde the liver.

- It is 3 in. (8cm) long and (3cm) wide.

- Some of the bile fluid ma in the liver is stored in th gallbladder.

- The gallbladder can hold u to 1.5 fl. oz. (50mL) of

- After a meal, bile pours fr the liver along the main k duct (tube), and from the gallbladder along the cyst duct, into the small intest

- Bile helps break apart or digest the fats and oils in foods.

- The liver makes up to 2 pt. (1L) of bile each da

52

BOX HEADINGS
Look for heading words linked to your research to guide you to the right fact box.

JUST THE FACTS
Each topic box presents the facts you need in short, quick-to-read bullet poi

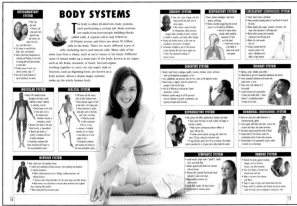
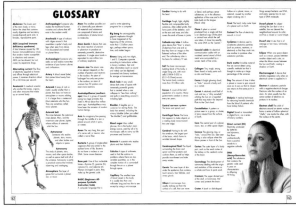

16–17 Body Systems

162–167 Glossary

HOW THE PANCREAS WORKS

...ty foods, such as French ...es, are broken apart by enzymes made in the pancreas.

...he pancreas has two main ...obs. One is to make ...ormones; the other is to ...make digestive chemicals ...alled pancreatic juices.

...hese juices contain about ...5 powerful enzymes that ...reak apart many substances ...n foods, including proteins, ...arbohydrates, and fats.

...he pancreas makes about ...3.2 pt. (1.5L) of digestive ...uices daily.

...uring a meal these pass ...along the pancreatic duct tubes ...nto the small intestine to ...attack and digest foods there.

• See page 62–63 for information on hormones.

WHEN THINGS GO WRONG

...llowish tinge to the ...and eyes is known as ...dice, and it is often a ...of liver trouble.

...ly the liver breaks down old ...ood cells and gets rid of the ...ng substance in bile fluid.

...mething goes wrong, the ...ng substance builds up in the ...and skin, causing jaundice. ...itis, an infection of the liver, ...ause jaundice.

UNUSUAL SUPPLY

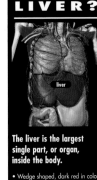

liver

One of the liver's main functions is to break down nutrients for the body. This means the liver has a unique blood supply.

• Most body parts are supplied with blood flowing along one or a few main arteries.

• The liver has a main artery, the hepatic artery.

• The liver also has a second, much greater blood supply. This comes along a vessel called the hepatic portal vein.

• The hepatic portal vein is the only main vein that does not take blood straight back to the heart.

• This vein runs from the intestines to the liver, bringing blood full of nutrients from digestion.

• See pages 46–47 for information on blood.

BABY LIVER

Most babies and young children have big abdomens (stomachs). This is partly because their liver is much larger in proportion to their body's overall size when compared to the liver of an adult.

• An adult's liver is usually 1/40 of their body weight.

• A baby's liver is closer to 1/20 of their body weight.

By the time a baby becomes a toddler, their liver is not such a large proportion of the total body weight.

WHAT IS THE LIVER?

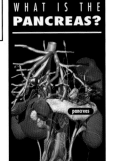

liver

The liver is the largest single part, or organ, inside the body.

• Wedge shaped, dark red in color.

• Typical weight 3.3 lbs. (1.5kg).

• Depth at widest part on right side 6 in. (15cm).

• Has a larger right lobe and smaller left lobe.

• Lobes separated by a strong layer, the falciform ligament.

WHAT IS THE PANCREAS?

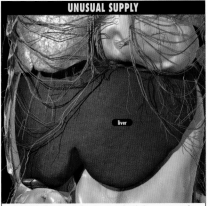

pancreas

The pancreas is a long, slim wedge- or triangular-shaped part.

• It is soft and grayish pink in color.

• Typical weight 0.21 lbs. (0.1kg).

• Typical length 6 in. (15cm).

• Has three main parts: head (wide end), body (middle), and tail (tapering end).

53

EXTRA INFORMATION

The black box on the right-hand side of the page explains a new aspect of the main topic or provides a timeline.

LINKS

Look for the purple links throughout the book. Each link gives details of other pages where related or additional facts can be found.

• See pages 46–47 for information on blood.

GLOSSARY

• A glossary of words and terms used in this book begins on page 162.

• The glossary words provide additional information to supplement the facts on the main pages.

PICTURE CAPTIONS
Captions explain what is in the pictures.

AN AMAZING STORY . . .

Ever since Stone Age people invented simple tools for digging and cutting, inventions have changed the way humans live. Throughout history our natural curiosity about the world around us has led us to search for more information about our planet and our ancestors. The timeline on these pages tracks the past 250,000 years and looks at some of the groundbreaking moments in human history.

What secrets are still to be discovered about our planet and our ancestors?

250,000 B.C.
STONE TOOLS
Paleolithic (early Stone Age) humans make simple stone tools, such as hand axes, by flaking a piece of flint from a large stone, then chipping away smaller flakes to create sharp edges for cutting.

A flint hand ax, c. 250,000 B.C.

C. 30,000 B.C.
BOW AND ARROW
Cave paintings that date from 30000 B.C. onward show late Stone Age humans using bows and arrows to hunt animals. Hunters also use a wide variety of snares and traps to catch their prey.

THE FIRST CLOCKS

Long before there were clocks people relied on regular natural events to keep track of time. They worked, ate, and slept according to the rising of the Sun. Over time, people invented many ways to track the passing of time.

c. A.D. 100—Water clocks
Water ran through this ancient Chinese clepsydra, or water clock, over a set period of time. As each section of the staircaselike timepiece emptied, people knew an exact amount of time had passed.

A clepsydra, or water clock

c. A.D. 800—Candle clocks
When candles were used for telling the time, they were often divided up into sections. Each of these sections took an hour to burn.

Sundials
For hundreds of years people have used sundials to tell the time. The sundial's gnomon (pointer) casts a shadow onto the scale marked on the flat base. The scale shows the hours of the day.

Pendulum clocks
In the 1650s there was a great breakthrough in timekeeping when a Dutch scientist, Christiaan Huygens, built the first pendulum clock.

Huygens designed a mechanism that used the swing of a pendulum to control the rotation of weight-driven gearwheels inside the clock. This use of the pendulum had originally been thought of by the Italian mathematician Galileo Galilei.

A model of a Mesopotamian wheeled vehicle, c. 2000 B.C.

C. 3000 B.C.
WRITING
The Sumerians of southern Mesopotamia invent writing. These Mesopotamian texts, still in existence today, range from simple lists of goods to complex stories and the laws that governed the Sumerians' society.

A.D. 200
CENTRAL HEATING
The Romans build villas and public baths using central heating systems called hypocausts. Heat from fires is drawn into an open space under the floor; the heat then rises through the floor into the walls, heating the building.

1400
CANNON
In Asia, bamboo-tube guns are produced that use gunpowder to shoot arrows at the enemy. By 1400, metal cannon that fire stone cannonballs are in use in countries across Europe.

1608
TELESCOPE
Hans Lippershey invents the telescope. Italian scientist Galileo Galilei builds his own telescope in 1609 and makes many new astronomical discoveries—the future for Lippershey's marvelous invention is secured!

Toolmaking dates back even farther than this timeline, to *Homo habilis* ("handy man"), who lived two million years ago.

9000–7000 B.C.
FARMING
People discover that domesticating animals, such as sheep and goats, gives a more regular meat supply than hunting. Cultivation of crops, such as wheat and barley, begins.

C. 7000 B.C.
MAKING FIRE
Neolithic people discover how to make fire. They create simple tools for producing friction and use flints struck against rocks called pyrites to cause sparks.

C. 3500 B.C.
WHEEL
Wheels are first used in Mesopotamia (modern-day Iraq) as a turntable for making pottery. By 3500 B.C. there are vehicles in use that have solid wheels made by joining two or three wooden planks together in a disk shape.

C. 2500 B.C.
GLASS
Glass is made by heating sand with limestone and wood ash. The method for making glass is probably discovered by accident. Ancient Egyptian glass beads have been found from around 2500 B.C.

C. 2000 B.C.
CHARIOT
On the southwestern fringes of the Asian steppes the lightweight two-wheel, two-horse chariot is developed. Chariots quickly become prestige war vehicles used by civilizations such as the ancient Egyptians.

An ancient Egyptian wall carving showing a chariot

C. 1000 B.C.
GREEK ALPHABET
The ancient Greeks use a 24–letter alphabet adapted from the Phoenician alphabet. Each symbol in an alphabet represents a sound rather than a word. This is quicker to learn and easier to use than earlier pictogram writing systems.

A cannon and cannonballs

1455
PRINTING PRESS
German craftsman Johannes Gutenberg develops movable type and designs and builds the first printing press. In 1455 Gutenberg prints his first book, a Latin Bible.

A page from the Gutenberg Bible

THE ATOMIC CLOCK
The atomic clock was invented by English physicist Louis Essen in the 1950s.

- Atomic clocks use the energy changes that take place in atoms to keep track of time.

- Atomic clocks are so accurate that they lose or gain no more than a second once every two or three million years!

The NBS-4 atomic clock in the U.S.

1756
CARBON DIOXIDE
English scientist Joseph Black discovers the gas carbon dioxide when he notes that a substance in exhaled air combines with quicklime in a chemical reaction that can be reversed by the application of heat.

1772–1774
OXYGEN
Two scientists working independently discover oxygen—the Swedish chemist Carl Wilhelm Scheele in around 1772 and the English chemist Joseph Priestley in 1774.

1770s–1780s
STRUCTURE OF WATER
French chemist Antoine-Laurent de Lavoisier discovers that water is a chemical combination of two gases that are found in air—hydrogen and oxygen.

The idea of forming sheets of paper from macerated tree bark, hemp, rags, and fishnets was conceived in China around 100 B.C.

Without the invention of paper and printing, it would not have been possible to produce this book!

c. 1770 B.C.—Minoan printing
The Minoans invent the first known printing method. They use a writing system of 45 symbols that are punched into a disk of clay before baking it. Only palace scribes could read and write, so Minoan printing was probably used only for tax lists and royal propaganda.

c. 200 B.C.—Punctuation
Early Greek writers did not even use spaces between words. Aristophanes of Byzantium, the librarian at the Library of Alexandria, is the first person to use punctuation in around 200 B.C. He adds it to Greek text.

c. A.D. 350—First books
Books with pages, known as codices, become the standard way of storing words.

600—Block printing
Paper is pressed onto blocks on which text has either been carved or handwritten.

Korean King Htai Tjong has the first true metal typeface made—100,000 bronze characters are cast.

1455—First movable type
German Johannes Gutenberg invents a technique for mass-producing individual metal letters. The text is assembled letter by letter to make up a page, an oil-based ink is applied, and paper is then pressed against it to make a print. The type is then reassembled for the next page.

1464—Roman type
German printer Adolf Rusch, in 1464, then Konrad Sweynheim and Arnold Pannartz in 1465, seeking to avoid the heavy, spiky letters of early types, first uses a roman font—the forerunner of the type that this book is printed in.

c. 100 B.C.—Invention of paper
Cai Lun (T'sai Lun), an official at the Chinese royal court, is credited with the invention of paper.

• See page 76 for information on Johannes Gutenberg.

1794

COTTON
In the U.S., engineer Eli Whitney patents his invention, the cotton gin, a machine that combs the seeds out of cotton after it has been harvested.

Slaves work at a Whitney cotton gin.

The *Locomotion* pulled 28 coal-filled wagons on the new Stockton and Darlington line.

1838—1839

CELLS
From 1838 to 1839, German scientists Matthias Schleiden and Theodor Schwann conclude that all plants and animals are made from tiny building blocks called cells.

1900

FINGERPRINTING
British scientist Francis Galton and police officer Sir Edward R. Henry devise a system of fingerprint classification, which they publish in June 1900. The Galton-Henry system is used in the U.K. for criminal identification from 1901 onward.

A fingerprint

Wilbur and Orville Wright

1908

MODEL T
The first Model T car is produced by the Ford Motor Company. Revolutionary production methods will see 15 million Model Ts role off the Ford assembly line over the next 19 years.

1927

EXPANDING UNIVERSE
While studying recently discovered galaxies outside the Milky Way, Edwin Hubble discovers that the galaxies seem to be moving away from the Milky Way. This leads to the discovery that the universe is expanding.

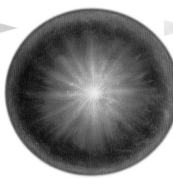

An expanding universe

1796 ▶

VACCINATION
British doctor Edward Jenner discovers the process of vaccination and successfully vaccinates a small boy against smallpox, a devastating disease during this period. The number of smallpox cases falls rapidly in the years following Jenner's discovery.

1822 ▶

MECHANICAL COMPUTER
Computer pioneer Charles Babbage, an inventor and professor of mathematics, conceives the first mechanical computer. However, the technology to build it will not be available for many years.

1824 ▶

BRAILLE
Frenchman Louis Braille invents an alphabet that can be written and read by the blind. The alphabet has 63 characters.

1825

RAILROAD
The Stockton and Darlington Railway, the first railroad in the world to carry freight and passengers using steam traction, begins operation in England on September 27.

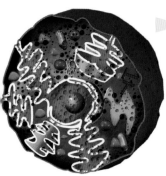

An animal cell

1876 ▶

TELEPHONE
In March 1876, Scottish–American inventor Alexander Graham Bell is granted what is often said to be one of the most valuable patents ever—U.S. Patent No.174465 for the development of a device to transmit speech sounds over electric wires.

1877 ▶

PHONOGRAPH
The first sound recording is made on a machine called a phonograph. American inventor Thomas Edison records himself reciting the nursery rhyme "Mary Had a Little Lamb."

1882

POWER PLANT
American inventor Thomas Edison supervises the installation of the world's first power plant in New York. The power plant becomes operational in September 1882.

1901 ▶

MARCONI'S MESSAGE
Italian physicist Guglielmo Marconi creates a worldwide sensation when he succeeds in sending a radio message across the Atlantic Ocean on December 12. The message is dot dot dot, which is Morse code for the letter "S."

1903

FLIGHT
The Wright brothers achieve the world's first powered flight with their Flyer biplane on December 17. The flight covers 120 ft. (36.5m) and lasts just 12 seconds.

1913 ▶

ATOMIC STRUCTURE
Danish physicist Niels Bohr proposes his theory of atomic structure—that an atom consists of a nucleus that is surrounded by a cloud of orbiting electrons arranged in a series of concentric outer shells.

1926

TELEVISION
British television pioneer John Logie Baird gives his first public demonstration of a television system. He presents moving pictures of a face. The pictures are fuzzy, but amazing at the time!

1941 ▶

PLUTONIUM (Pu)
The synthetic radioactive element plutonium is made in Berkeley, California, by a team of scientists using a cyclotron. Plutonium is used as an ingredient in nuclear weapons and as a fuel in some types of nuclear reactors.

1943

COLOSSUS
During World War II, Alan Turing and a team of British scientists secretly build Colossus (one of the first electronic computers) to decipher top-secret messages created by the German Enigma coding machine.

TIMELINE: INVENTION OF PHOTOGRAPHY

Thanks to the invention of photography, this book is packed with photographs of inventors and their inventions.

1826—First photograph
In France, Joseph Niepce produces the world's first true photograph (as opposed to shadowgraph). The exposure time is about eight hours.

1839—Daguerreotype system
In France, Louis Daguerre demonstrates his daguerreotype system, which produces a single positive image on a sheet of copper. Exposure time is 30 minutes.

1841—Negatives
In England, William Talbot patents his calotype process, which produces a negative image from which numerous positive copies can be made. Exposure time is 2–3 minutes.

1851—Glass plates
In England, Frederick Archer introduces glass plates for photography. Exposure time is a few seconds.

1874—Roll film
In the U.S., George Eastman develops roll film. He first uses paper, then later transparent celluloid. Exposure time is less than one second.

1888—Kodak camera
Eastman launches the Kodak camera, which produces circular images.

1941—First color film
In France, Auguste and Louis Lumière produce the first film for color transparencies.

1942—First color prints
In Germany, the Agfa company produces the first film to make color prints.

1946—Instant prints
In the U.S., Edwin Land introduces a camera that makes instant prints—the Polaroid.

A daguerreotype camera (1839)

• See page 77 for information on George Eastman.

Archaeologists can figure out the age of this Egyptian mummy by using Willard F. Libby's discovery of the carbon-dating process.

CARBON DATING

American chemist Willard F. Libby discovers that the unstable carbon isotope C14 decays over time to the more stable C12. This means plant matter or the body of an animal can be dated by the proportions of C14 and C12 left in it.

TRANSISTOR

Three American physicists, William B. Shockley, John Bardeen, and Walter H. Brattain, invent the transistor— a device that will advance electronics and allow for the eventual miniaturization of computer circuitry.

NUCLEAR POWER

Fission

Fission is the process by which the nucleus of an atom is split in two, releasing an enormous amount of energy. The fission of uranium atoms was first observed under laboratory conditions in the late 1930s.

Chain reaction

On December 2, 1942, a team of scientists led by Italian Enrico Fermi achieved the first controlled nuclear fission chain reaction. Fermi realized their discovery could be used to build an atom bomb.

Manhattan Project

During World War II a team of scientists in the U.S. worked on the top-secret Manhattan Project to design and build atom bombs. The first bomb was tested at Alamogordo Air Field, New Mexico, on July 16, 1945. During the following month, two atom bombs were dropped on the Japanese cities of Hiroshima and Nagasaki.

Nuclear power

Uranium fission can be contained and controlled inside a nuclear reactor to produce heat for generating electricity. The first atomic power plant making electricity for homes and businesses began operation in 1956 at Calder Hall in England.

SUPERSONIC AIRLINER

On March 2 the Concorde, a passenger aircraft capable of flying at twice the speed of sound, makes its first test flight piloted by chief test pilot André Turcat. Concorde was a joint achievement between French and British engineers.

Concorde

HIV VIRUS

HIV, the virus that causes AIDS, is identified by French scientist Luc Montagnier and a team working at the Pasteur Institute in Paris.

DNA PROFILING

English scientist Alec Jeffreys invents a method of analyzing DNA to produce a set of characteristic features that are unique to each individual. The process is called DNA profiling and can be used to identify criminals or eliminate innocent crime suspects.

Alec Jeffreys, inventor of DNA profiling

1996—Dolly the sheep is born.

HUMAN GENOME

The Human Genome Project completes the task of reading in sequence all of the "letters" in the human genome (the set of instructions to build a body that is contained inside every body cell).

1952

DNA DISCOVERIES

American biochemists Alfred Hershey and Martha Chase demonstrate that DNA is the means by which genetic information is transmitted. In 1953, Francis Crick and James D. Watson discover the structure of DNA.

DNA

1967

HEART TRANSPLANT

On December 3 a team of 20 surgeons, led by South African heart surgeon Christiaan Barnard, perform the world's first heart transplant at the Groote Schuur Hospital, Cape Town, South Africa. The patient, Louis Washkansky, lives for 18 days.

1974

LUCY

Professor Donald Johanson and his assistant, Tom Gray, discover the most complete Australopithecus skeleton ever found during excavations in northern Ethiopia. Nicknamed Lucy, this early hominid lived 3.2 million years ago.

1975

MICROSOFT

Bill Gates and his friend Paul Allen start Microsoft. The company creates the operating systems MS-DOS and Windows. These programs will be used on almost every PC in the world.

Bill Gates

1991

WORLD WIDE WEB

The World Wide Web is launched to the world via the Internet. It was invented in 1989 by British computer scientist Tim Berners-Lee for use at the scientific research facility at CERN in Switzerland.

www — the World Wide Web

1996

DOLLY THE SHEEP

A team of scientists working in Scotland at the Roslin Institute succeed in producing the first-ever cloned mammal. Dolly the sheep is born on July 5.

2000

DRAFT HUMAN GENOME

A first draft of the human genome is published after more than ten years of intensive effort. It consists of some three billion pairs of nucleotide bases divided into thousands of separate genes.

2004

A NEW DWARF PLANET

On March 15 NASA announces the discovery of a new dwarf planet at the farthest boundaries of our solar system. The dwarf planet, named Sedna, has a diameter of 992 mi. (1,600km).

2006

PLUTO

Seventy-six years after its discovery in 1930, Pluto is demoted to a dwarf planet, along with Eris and Ceres.

2008

LHC

The Large Hadron Collider (LHC), the world's largest and highest-energy particle accelerator, is launched on September 10, but operations are suspended nine days later owing to a fault.

Pluto is now classed as a dwarf planet.

DEVELOPMENTS IN MATHEMATICS

Place value
The use of "0" for zero probably dates from c. A.D. 500. This marks the emergence of the decimal system we use today.

Decimal fractions
Though used in China in around A.D. 200, decimal fractions were not developed in other parts of the world until the 1300–1400s.

Algebra
The word *algebra* comes from a book by Al-Khwarizmi, an Arab mathematician who lived around A.D. 780–850. The most famous algebraic equation is that of Albert Einstein:

$$E=mc^2$$

Imperial measures
Standard imperial units of distance (for example, the mile) were set under England's Queen Elizabeth I in 1592.

Metric measures
The meter, liter, and gram were adopted by the French in 1795.

Pythagorean theorem
Pythagoras lived c. 580–500 B.C. His theorem says that the square drawn using the longest side of a right angle triangle is equal in area to the sum of the areas of the triangles on the other two sides. This theorem is used for navigation, maps, building, and land measurement.

This diagram shows Pythagoras's theorem.

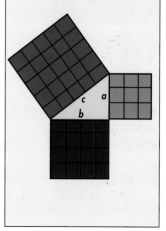

Humans have always wanted to know more about their origins and the planet on which they live. Today we know our planet is 4.5 billion years old, not the 74,832 years proposed by the French scientist Georges Buffon in 1778. Paleontologists have identified the first animals that lived on Earth, and anthropologists have studied the fossils of our earliest ancestors. Scientists have discovered that all plants and animals are made from tiny building blocks called cells, and we now know that DNA within our body cells makes us who we are.

Fossil hunter William Buckland (1784–1856)

DISCOVERING THE DINOSAURS

DINOSAUR FOSSILS
- In the 1820s Englishwoman Mary Anning began a career as a professional fossil collector on the shores of Lyme Regis, England. Anning supplied the greatest scientists of the period with their material, and during her career she discovered fossils of plesiosaurs, ichthyosaurs, and the first pterosaur in Great Britain.

This illustration of an *Ichthyosaurus* is based on fossil finds.

A *Megalosaurus* jawbone

THE FIRST DINOSAUR
- Fossils of a jawbone and teeth were found in Oxfordshire, England, in around 1815.

- William Buckland, of Oxford University, studied the fossils, and he deduced that they were from a large meat-eating reptile.

- In 1822 Buckland's colleague James Parkinson named the creature *Megalosaurus* ("big lizard").

INVENTING DINOSAURS
- In 1842 English scientist Sir Richard Owen invented the term *dinosauria* to describe the *Megalosaurus* and two other fossil animals, *Iguanodon* and *Hylaeosaurus*, found at the time.

THE FIRST BIRD
In 1860, 1861, and 1877 the fossils of a single feather and two birds were discovered in the same Jurassic limestone quarry in Solnhofen, Germany. The bird was named *Archaeopteryx*. It seemed to be at a transitional stage between dinosaurs and birds.

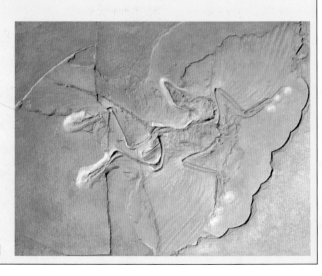

An *Archaeopteryx* fossil

CHARLES DARWIN

- During an expedition English scientist Charles Darwin (1809–1882) was intrigued by the variety of bird species that he observed when visiting the Galápagos Islands.

- When, in 1837, ornithologist John Gould showed that, despite their differences, the Galápagos Islands birds' were all closely related finches, it led Darwin to suggest that the various forms had evolved from a single species.

- In 1859 Darwin published *On the Origin of Species*, a book presenting the theory that animals and plants have not always looked the way they do today, but have evolved from earlier forms and are still evolving.

HOMO ERECTUS

The discovery:
The remains of a skull and some teeth with features similar to those of both apes and humans. Found in caves in Java (Indonesia). Nicknamed Java man.

Discovered by:
Dutch paleontologist Eugene Dubois in 1891.

Homo erectus skull

Discovery fact:
The first known fossils to be discovered of Homo erectus.

> • See page 11 for the discovery of Lucy (1974).

CONTINENTAL DRIFT

- In 1912 German meteorologist Alfred Wegener proposed that the world's continents were once joined together in a single large landmass. He called this continent Pangaea.

- Over millions of years, the individual continents had drifted apart, but it is still possible to see how they fitted together.

Africa

South America

- Wegener's discovery of "continental drift" was finally accepted by the world's scientists in the 1960s.

TIMELINE

1902—Chromosomes
American surgeon Walter Sutton discovers the chromosome theory of inheritance. He deduces that Mendel's features were controlled in living cells by structures called chromosomes. The chemical messages encoded in the chromosomes are the genes.

1909—Burgess Shale
American paleontologist Charles Walcott discovers the Burgess Shale fossil site in Canada's Rocky Mountains. Dating from the Cambrian period, it contains thousands of fossils of marine animals.

1927—Birth of a universe
Belgian priest Georges Lemaitre proposes a forerunner of the big bang theory: that the universe began with the explosion of a primeval atom.

1953—Age of Earth
Fiesel Houtermans and Claire Patterson use radiometric dating to date the age of Earth at 4.5 billion years.

1963—Plate tectonics
Fred Vine and Drummond Matthews discover ocean-floor spreading. This leads to the understanding of plate tectonics.

1964—The big bang
Arno Penzias and Robert Wilson detect cosmic radiation (radiation coming from space) and use it to confirm the big bang theory.

1980—Dinosaur extinction
Luis and Walter Alvarez put forward the asteroid impact theory of dinosaur extinction.

1985—Ozone depletion
Scientists of the British Antarctic Survey discover the depletion of ozone in the upper atmosphere.

1991—Asteroid impact
Chicxulub crater in Yucatán is pinpointed as the site of the asteroid impact that caused the extinction of the dinosaurs.

> • See the glossary for explanations of many of the scientific terms used in this timeline.

THE STORY OF DNA

1869—DNA discovered
Swiss graduate chemist Johann Miescher identifies a particular substance—deoxyribonucleic acid (DNA)—in the nuclei of white blood cells. The importance of this discovery goes unnoticed for more than 50 years.

1929—DNA molecule
In the U.S., Russian-born chemist Phoebus Levene establishes that the DNA molecule is composed of a series of nucleotides that are each composed of a sugar, a phosphate group, and one of four bases: thymine (T), guanine (G), cytosine (C), or adenine (A).

1950—Base pairs
In the U.S., biochemist Erwin Chargaff discovers that the bases are arranged in pairs and that the composition of DNA is identical within species. However, it differs between species.

1952—The genetic code
Two American scientists, Alfred Hershey and Martha Chase, conduct an experiment proving that the DNA molecule is the means by which genetic information is transmitted.

1952—DNA analysis
In England, scientists Maurice Wilkins and Rosalind Franklin analyze the DNA molecule using x-rays.

1953—The shape of DNA
Wilkins' and Franklin's results enable the shape of the DNA molecule to be determined by Francis Crick and James Watson.

1965—Cell proteins
American biochemist Marshall Nirenberg deciphers the genetic code through which DNA controls the production of proteins inside body cells.

1983—Polymerase chain reaction
American researcher Kary Mullis invents the polymerase chain reaction (PCR), a laboratory process that enables scientists to duplicate small sections of the DNA molecule many millions of times in a short period of time.

> • See page 79 for information on Francis Crick and James Watson.

HUMAN BODY

DISCOVERY TIMELINE

200 B.C. — Claudius Galen
Greek-born Roman doctor Claudius Galen describes the workings of the body. Galen's work is often based on animal dissections. His findings, many incorrect, remain unchallenged until the 1500s.

1543 — Vesalius's anatomy
Flemish doctor Andreas Vesalius publishes the first accurate description of human anatomy (structure), *De humani corporis fabrica libri septem* (The Seven Books of the Human Body). It is based on Vesalius's dissections of human cadavers.

1614 — Santorio
Italian physician Santorio Santorio completes 30 years of research, experimenting on his own body to see how it works.

1800 — Cells
French doctor Marie-François Bichat shows that organs are made of different groups of cells called tissues.

1889 — Neurons
Spanish physiologist Ramón Santiago y Cajal discovers that the nervous system is made up of neurons (nerve cells) that do not touch.

1905 — Hormones
British physiologists William Bayliss and Ernest Starling invent the term *hormone* to describe the newly discovered "chemical messengers" that control many body activities.

1912 — Vitamins
Polish–American biochemist Casimir Funk invents the term *vitamin* to describe nutrients required by the body in tiny amounts to make it work properly.

1970s — Natural painkillers
It is discovered that natural painkillers called enkephalins and endorphins are produced by the body.

- See pages 56–57 for information on DNA.
- See page 71 for information on genetic engineering.

Most body activities, including how we move or digest food, are now well understood thanks to discoveries made in the past 500 years. The earliest anatomists studied the structure of body parts such as the heart and kidneys. Later, physiologists discovered how these organs worked. Today there are still things to learn. For example, the Human Genome Project, having "read" the DNA in our cells, is now identifying the instructions that are needed to build and run a human being.

Anatomist Andreas Vesalius (1514–1564)

TIMELINE: BLOOD DISCOVERIES

1628—Blood circulation
British doctor William Harvey proves through experiments that blood circulates around the body, pumped by the heart along blood vessels.

1658—Red blood cells
Red blood cells are first observed and identified by Dutch naturalist Jan Swammerdam, using an early microscope.

1661—Blood capillaries
The existence of blood capillaries (tiny blood vessels that link arteries to veins) is discovered by Italian microscopist Marcello Malpighi.

1884—Action of white blood cells
Russian zoologist Elie Metchnikoff describes how white blood cells surround and devour bacteria and other germs.

1901—Blood types
The existence of blood types is discovered by Austrian-American doctor Karl Landsteiner. The four blood types are later named A, B, AB, and O. Blood transfusions will work only if the right type of blood is given, so Landsteiner's discoveries pave the way for the safe transfusion of blood.

1959—Hemoglobin structure
Austrian–British scientist Max Perutz discovers the structure of hemoglobin, the substance inside red blood cells that carries oxygen and makes the cells red.

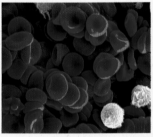

Blood cells

THE HUMAN GENOME PROJECT

- In the late 1980s groups of scientists around the world began an unprecedented research project — to produce a map of the human genome (human genetic code).

- Several anonymous donors provided DNA for the project. The map will be typical of all human DNA.

- In 2000 scientists released a "rough draft" of the human genome, showing all of the three billion or so base pairs in human DNA.

- In April 2003 the Human Genome Project completed the map, giving scientists the ability, for the first time, to read a complete genetic blueprint for building a human.

- It will take decades to understand what all of the 25,000 to 30,000 human genes do, but scientists hope that new treatments and earlier diagnosis of diseases will be among the many benefits of this vast and pioneering project.

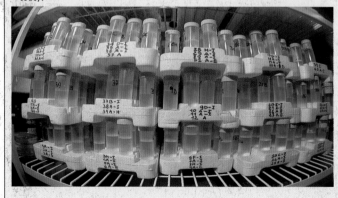

The human body is made up of 100 trillion cells of 200 different types. It has taken hundreds of years to understand how it works, and there are still more discoveries to be made.

EAR

The ear was first described in detail by Italian anatomist Bartolomeo Eustachio in 1562. He gave his name to the eustachian tube that connects the air-filled middle ear to the back of the throat.

BRAIN

Part of the left side of the brain, called Broca's area, controls speech. It was first described in 1861 by French doctor Pierre Paul Broca. He made his discovery while treating a brain-damaged patient.

PITUITARY GLAND

In 1912 American doctor Harvey Cushing described the pituitary gland and how it works. This raisin-sized gland, at the base of the brain, is vitally important, releasing nine hormones that control growth, reproduction, and many other body activities.

VEINS

Veins are blood vessels that return blood to the heart. In 1603 Italian anatomist Hieronymus Fabricius showed that veins have valves. These prevent the backflow of blood away from the heart.

LUNGS

In the 1600s British doctor John Mayow discovered that "breathing in" happens when the chest gets bigger, making the lungs expand to suck in air. He experimented with models of the chest made from bellows.

PANCREAS

Made and released by the pancreas, the hormone insulin controls levels of glucose in the blood. Insulin was first isolated in 1921 by Canadian scientists Frederick Banting and Charles Best.

KIDNEYS

In 1842 British doctor William Bowman described the microscopic structure of the kidney. Two years later, in 1844, German scientist Karl Ludwig discovered how the kidneys make urine.

STOMACH

Digestion in the stomach was first described in 1833 by American doctor William Beaumont. He experimented by dangling food into a man's stomach through a hole in his side that had been produced by a shooting accident.

LIVER

In the 1850s French physiologist Claude Bernard was the first person to investigate what the liver, the body's largest internal organ, does. We now know the liver performs over 500 vital functions.

FEMALE REPRODUCTIVE SYSTEM

In 1672 this system was described in detail by Dutch anatomist Regnier de Graaf. Earlier, in 1561, Italian anatomist Gabriello Fallopio described the fallopian tube that links the ovary to the uterus.

MUSCLES

How muscles contract (get shorter) to pull bones and move the body was independently discovered in 1954 by British scientists Andrew Huxley and Hugh Huxley.

BONE

Bones are hard and strong because they contain rigid microscopic cylinders that lie in parallel to each other. These are named Haversian systems after Clopton Havers, a British doctor who described bone structure in 1691.

INTEGUMENTARY SYSTEM

- Skin, hair, and nails.
- Protects soft inner parts from physical wear and knocks, dirt, water, the Sun's rays, and other harm.
- Skin keeps in essential body fluids, salts, and minerals.
- Helps control body temperature by sweating and flushing to lose heat, or turning pale with goose bumps to retain heat.
- Provides sense of touch (see sensory system, page 17).
- Gets rid of small amounts of waste substances via sweat.

BODY SYSTEMS

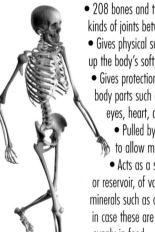

The body is often divided into body systems, each performing a certain job. Body systems are made from microscopic building blocks called cells. A typical cell is only 0.0012 in. (0.03mm) across, and there are about 50 trillion cells in the body. There are many different types of cells, including nerve and muscle cells. Many cells of the same type form a tissue, such as nerve tissue or fat tissue. Different types of tissues make up a main part of the body, known as an organ, such as the brain, stomach, or heart. Several organs working together to carry out one major task or function, such as digesting food, are known as a body system. About a dozen major systems make up the whole human body.

MUSCULAR SYSTEM

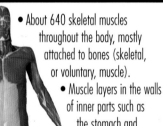

- About 640 skeletal muscles throughout the body, mostly attached to bones (skeletal, or voluntary, muscle).
- Muscle layers in the walls of inner parts such as the stomach and intestines (visceral, or involuntary, muscle).
- Muscle in the walls of the heart (heart muscle, or myocardium).
- Muscles get shorter, or contract, to produce all forms of bodily movement.
- Sometimes combined with bones and joints and known as the musculoskeletal system.

SKELETAL SYSTEM

- 208 bones and the various kinds of joints between them.
- Gives physical support to hold up the body's soft, floppy parts.
- Gives protection to certain body parts such as the brain, eyes, heart, and lungs.
- Pulled by muscles to allow movement.
- Acts as a store, or reservoir, of valuable minerals such as calcium, in case these are in short supply in food.
- Sometimes combined with muscles and known as the musculoskeletal system.

NERVOUS SYSTEM

- Brain, spinal cord, and peripheral nerves.
- Controls and coordinates all body processes, from breathing and heartbeat to making movements.
- Allows mental processes such as thinking, recalling memories, and making decisions.
- Sensory nerves bring information from the sense organs and other sensors.
- Motor nerves carry instructions to muscles about movement and to glands about releasing their products.
- Works along with the hormonal system.

SENSORY SYSTEM

- Eyes, ears, nose, tongue, and skin make up the five main sets of sense organs.
- Also sensors inside the body for temperature, blood pressure, oxygen levels, positions of joints, amount of stretch in muscles, and many other changes.
- Gravity and motion sensors in the inner ear contribute to the process of balance.
- Sometimes included as part of the nervous system because the main sense organs are in effect the specialized endings of sensory nerves.

RESPIRATORY SYSTEM

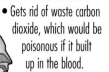

- Nose, trachea (windpipe), main chest airways, and lungs.
- Obtains essential oxygen from the air and passes it to the blood for distribution.
- Gets rid of waste carbon dioxide, which would be poisonous if it built up in the blood.
- Useful extra function is the ability to make vocal sounds and speech.

CIRCULATORY (CARDIOVASCULAR) SYSTEM

- Heart, blood vessels, and blood.
- Heart provides pumping power to send blood all around the body.
- Blood spreads vital oxygen, nutrients, hormones, and many other substances to all body parts.
- Blood collects wastes and unwanted substances from all body parts.
- Blood clots seal wounds and cuts.
- Closely involved with the immune system in the body's self-defense and ability to fight disease.

DIGESTIVE SYSTEM

- Mouth, teeth, throat, esophagus (gullet), stomach, intestines, rectum, and anus make up the digestive passageway, or tract.
- Liver, gallbladder, and pancreas, plus the tract, make up the digestive system.
- Breaks down, or digests, food into nutrients tiny enough to take into the body.
- Gets rid of leftovers as solid wastes (bowel movements, or feces).
- Nutrients provide energy for all life processes and raw materials for growth, maintenance, and repairing everyday wear and tear.

URINARY SYSTEM

- Kidneys, ureters, bladder, and urethra.
- Filters blood to get rid of unwanted substances and wastes.
- Forms unwanted substances and wastes into liquid waste, or urine.
- Stores urine, then releases it to the outside.
- Controls amount and concentration of blood and bodily fluids, ("water balance") by adjusting amount of water lost in urine.

REPRODUCTIVE SYSTEM

- Only system that differs significantly in females and males.
- Only system that does not work at birth, but begins to function at puberty.
- Male system continuously produces millions of sperm cells per day.
- Female system produces ripe egg cells, about one every 28 days, during the menstrual cycle.
- If egg cell joins sperm cell to form an embryo, the female system nourishes this as it grows into a baby inside the womb.

HORMONAL (ENDOCRINE) SYSTEM

- About ten main parts called endocrine, or hormone-making, glands.
- Some organs with other main tasks, such as the stomach and heart, also make hormones.
- Hormones spread around the body in blood.
- Closely linked to the nervous system for coordinated control of inner body processes.
- Closely linked to the reproductive system, which it controls by sex hormones.

LYMPHATIC SYSTEM

- Lymph vessels, lymph nodes ("glands"), lymph ducts, and lymph fluid.
- Gathers general bodily fluids from between cells and tissues.
- One-way flow channels fluid through lymph network of nodes and vessels.
- Helps distribute nutrients and collect wastes.
- Lymph fluid empties into blood system.
- Closely linked to immune system.

IMMUNE SYSTEM

- Defends the body against invading dangers such as bacteria, viruses, and other microbes.
- Gets rid of debris in tissues from normal wear and tear.
- Helps in recovery from disease and illness.
- Helps in repair of injury and normal wear and tear.
- Keeps watch for problems and disease processes arising inside the body such as malignant (cancerous) cells.

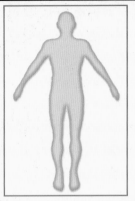

The skin is a tough but flexible layer that covers the entire body. It helps control temperature and protects internal organs from damage.

THE SKIN

When you look at yourself in the mirror, most of what you see is dead! Your skin, hair, and nails are not living. But just underneath this dead surface, skin is very much alive, and very busy, too—as you see and feel if you are unlucky enough to scratch or cut yourself. Skin is the body's largest single main part, or organ. It has at least ten main tasks, which include providing your sense of touch. Skin wears away every month—but it replaces itself every month, too.

SKIN MICROPARTS

An average patch of skin 16 sq. in. (1cm²) (the size of a fingernail) contains:

- 5 million microscopic cells of at least 12 main types.

- 100 tiny holes, or pores, for releasing sweat.

- 1,000 microsensors of about six main shapes for detecting various features of touch.

- 100 plus hairs.

- About 3.3 ft. (1m) of tiny blood vessels.

- About 19.5 in. (50cm) of micronerves.

- About 100 of the tiny glands that make sebum, a natural waxy-oily substance that keeps skin supple and fairly waterproof.

TOUCH

Your sense of touch, or feeling, is more complicated than it seems. It's not just a single sense detecting physical contact. It's a "multisense" detecting:

- Light contact, such as a brush from a feather.

- Heavy pressure, such as being pushed or squeezed hard.

- Cold, like an ice cube.

- Heat, such as a hot shower or bath.

- Movement, including tiny fast back-and-forth vibrations — your fingertip skin can detect vibrations that are too small for your eyes to see.

- Surface texture, such as rough wood or smooth plastic.

- Moisture content, from dry sand to wet mud.

By wearing warm clothes in winter we protect our skin from feeling the cold.

DANGEROUS SWEAT

A person can lose 5.3–8.5 qt. (5–8L) of sweat before their body will suffer from the loss of important salts and minerals.

EXTRA SENSITIVE

- Skin on the fingertips has more than 1,170 microsensors per square inch (7,600cm/cm²), providing the most sensitive touch.

- Fingertips have a lot of sweat glands, making a thin layer, or film, of sweat on the skin that helps you grip better.

- Fingertip skin also has tiny ridges, or swirls, to give even better grip. These form the pattern of your fingerprints.

- Every set of fingerprints for every person around the world is different — even those of identical twins.

A thin layer of sweat on the fingertips will help you grip better. Try thoroughly washing your hands, drying them well, then picking up a paper clip.

SWEAT FACTS

Total number of sweat glands	**3–5 million**
Total length of tubes in all sweat glands stretched out straight and joined end to end	**31 mi. (50km)**
Amount of sweat on an average day	**0.32–0.53 qt. (0.3–0.5L)**
Amount of sweat on a cold day	**0.07 qt. (0.07L)**

LAYERS OF THE SKIN

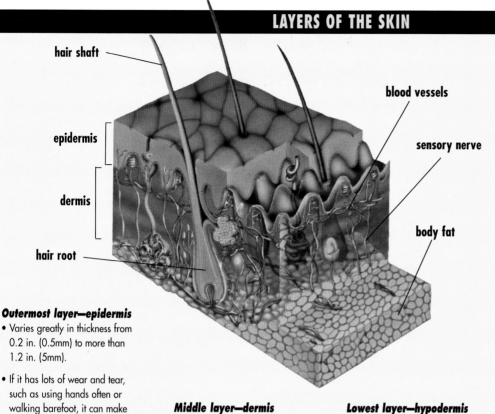

hair shaft

blood vessels

epidermis

sensory nerve

dermis

body fat

hair root

Outermost layer—epidermis
- Varies greatly in thickness from 0.2 in. (0.5mm) to more than 1.2 in. (5mm).
- If it has lots of wear and tear, such as using hands often or walking barefoot, it can make itself twice as thick as normal for extra protection.
- Microscopic cells at its base multiply fast, fill with the tough substance keratin, move outward, become flatter and die, and form the surface layer that is continually rubbed away.

Middle layer—dermis
- Contains sweat glands, hair roots (follicles), most of the microsensors for touch, and tiny blood vessels called capillaries.
- Also contains fibers of the substances collagen (for strength) and elastin (for stretchiness).

Lowest layer—hypodermis
- Mostly contains body fat, which acts as a cushion against knocks and pressure.
- Works as an insulator to keep in body warmth.

• See pages 44–45 for information on blood circulation.

• See pages 44–45 for information on blood circulation.

MAIN TASKS OF THE SKIN

Protection
- Providing protection from knocks and bumps
- Keeping out dirt, germs, and liquids such as water
- Shielding the body from the Sun's dangerous rays (especially UV, or ultraviolet), perhaps by getting darker (getting a suntan)

Fluid retention
- Keeping in valuable body fluids, minerals, and salts

Touch
- Providing a sense of touch

Temperature control
- Cooling the body if it gets too hot
- Keeping heat inside the body in cold conditions

Vitamin D
- Producing an important nutrient, vitamin D, that keeps the body healthy

Waste removal
- Removing some waste products (in sweat)

Antigerm layer
- Producing germ-killing substances that form a layer on the skin

MICROSENSORS

- The largest touch microsensors are called Pacinian corpuscles. They have many layers, like tiny onions, and are up to 0.2 in. (0.5mm) across. They detect hard pressure.
- The smallest microsensors are 100 times tinier and feel light touch.

SHEDDING SKIN

- Each minute about 50,000 tiny flakes of skin are rubbed off or fall from the body.
- This loss is natural and is made up by microscopic cells at the base of the epidermis that multiply rapidly.
- This happens so fast that the epidermis replaces itself about every month.
- Over a lifetime the body sheds more than 88 lbs. (40kg) of skin — enough to fill two typical garbage bags.

SIZE OF THE SKIN

Area
A typical adult's skin, taken off and ironed flat, would cover some 2.4 sq. yd. (2m²)—about the area of a single bed or a small shower curtain.

Weight
The weight of the skin is about 6.6–8.8 lbs. (3–4kg) for a typical adult—twice as heavy as the next-largest organ, the liver.

SKIN THICKNESS

Skin makes itself thicker where it is worn or rubbed more. On average:

• See pages 32–33 for information on the eyes.

- Soles of feet 0.2 in. (5mm) or more
- Back 0.12–0.16 in. (3–4mm)
- Palms of hands 0.8–0.12 in. (2–3mm)
- Scalp on head 0.6 in. (1.5mm)
- Fingertips 0.4 in. (1mm)
- Average over body 0.4–0.8 in. (1–2mm)
- Eyelids 0.2 in. (0.5mm)

0.20
0.16
0.12
0.08
0.04

HAIR & NAILS

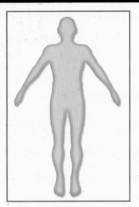

Hair is found almost all over the body. Nails grow at the end of each toe and finger.

Hair and nails, like the outer layer of skin (epidermis), are dead. The human body has hairs all over apart from a few places, such as the palms, the sides of the fingers, and the soles of the feet. However, some hairs grow thicker and longer, so we notice them more. These are the hairs on the head (scalp), eyebrows, and eyelashes. As we grow up, hairs also appear under the arms (axillary hair) and between the legs (pubic hair).

WHY HAVE EYELASHES AND EYEBROWS?

Eyelashes and eyebrows draw attention to our eyes. They also perform some useful functions.

Eyebrow hairs
Help stop sweat from dripping into the eyes.

Eyelash hairs
Help whisk away bits of windblown dust, dirt, and pests such as insects.

NAIL GROWTH

- Most nails grow about 0.02 in. (0.5mm) each week.
- In general, fingernails grow faster than toenails.
- Nails grow faster in the summer than in the winter.
- If you are right-handed, nails on your right hand grow faster than those on your left.
- It is the other way around if you are left-handed.

EYEBROWS AND EYELASHES

in. of hair growth per month

Scalp hair — 0.48 in.
Eyebrow
Eyelash

(y-axis: 0.48 in., 0.40 in., 0.32 in., 0.24 in., 0.16 in., 0.08 in., 0 in.)

- Scalp hairs grow 0.012–0.016 in. (0.3–0.4mm) each day, which is about 0.40–0.48 in. (10–12mm) each month.

- Eyebrow hairs grow slowly, only 0.006 in. (0.15mm) per day, usually reaching a greatest length of 0.40 in.(10mm).

- Eyelash hairs grow at a similar rate to eyebrow hairs, but usually stop growing at 0.28–0.32 in. (7–8mm) long.

• See pages 32–33 for information on the eyes.

THE THICKNESS OF A HAIR

- Most scalp hairs are around 0.002 in. (0.05mm) thick, so 500 in a row would measure 1 inch.
- Fair or blond hairs are usually thinner than dark or black scalp hairs.
- Eyelashes are thicker, up to 0.003 in. (0.08mm).

NAIL PARTS

There are many technical words to describe the fingernails.

Nail plate
The main flat part of the nail.

Free edge
The end of the nail that you trim, which is not attached to the underlying finger or toe.

Nail bed
The underside of the nail plate that is attached to the underlying flesh but slides slowly along as it grows.

Lunula
The pale "half-moon" where the youngest part of the nail emerges from the flesh of the finger or toe.

Eponychium
The cuticle fold where the nail base disappears under the flesh of the finger or toe.

Nail root
The growing part of the nail, hidden in the flesh of the finger or toe.

HAIR STRUCTURE AND THICKNESS

- Hairs are glued-together rods of dead, flattened microscopic cells filled with the tough, hard body substance called keratin.

- A hair grows at its root, which is buried in a pocketlike pit in the skin called a follicle.

- Extra cells are added to the root, which pushes the rest of the hair up out of the skin.

- The part of the hair above the root is called the shaft.

• See pages 18–19 for information on the skin.

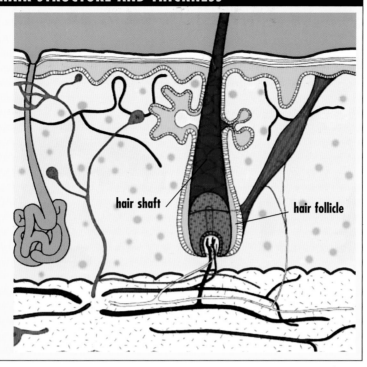

hair shaft

hair follicle

• See pages 18–19 for information on the skin.

HAIR GROWTH

Different kinds of hairs grow at different rates.

- Because most scalp hairs grow for only 3–5 years, their maximum length is 19.5–31.2 in. (50–80cm) before they fall out and are replaced.

- However, some people have unusual hair that falls out much less often and can reach lengths of 23–26 ft. (7–8m).

Hair growth in thin, fair hair is slower than in thick, dark hair.

NUMBER OF HAIRS

The number of hairs on the head varies according to the color of the hair. In a typical adult the number is:

Blond	130,000
Brown	110,000
Black	100,000
Red	90,000

• See page 61 for information on signs of aging.

• See page 61 for information on signs of aging.

HAIR LIFE CYCLES

Most types of hairs grow for a time, slow gradually down in growth rate, then "rest" and hardly grow at all.

- After this "rest" they usually fall out and are replaced by new hairs growing up from the same follicles (pits) in the skin.

- This means, on average, about 100 hairs are lost from the head every day.

- In eyebrow hairs the life cycle lasts about 20 weeks.

- In eyelash hairs it lasts around ten weeks.

- In scalp hairs this life cycle lasts up to five years.

FASTER HAIR GROWING

- Hair growth is faster at night than during the day.

- Hair growth is faster in the summer than in the winter.

- Hair growth is faster around the ages of 15–25 than before or after.

HAIR
WHY HAVE IT?

Hair was probably more effective at its jobs millions of years ago, when it was longer and when we looked more like our closest cousins, the apes (chimps and gorillas).

Protection
- Scalp hair protects against bangs and bruises.

- It also shields the top of the head and the delicate brain inside from the sun's fierce heat or icy cold weather.

Warmth
- Body hairs stand on end when you're cold, each pulled by a tiny muscle attached to its root called the erector pili muscle.

- This "hair-raising blanket" around the body helps trap air and keeps in body warmth.

Safety
- Our hair can also stand on end when we feel frightened. When our body hairs were longer, in prehistoric times, the "hair raising" also made us look bigger and more impressive to enemies.

NAILS
WHY HAVE THEM?

A nail is a strong, stiff dead flat plate made of keratin, the same dead substance as hairs. Each nail acts as a flat, rigid pad on the back of the fingertip.

Touch
- When you press gently on an object, the fingertip is squeezed between it and the nail.

- This makes it easier to judge pressure and the hardness of the object. Without a nail, the whole fingertip would bend back.

Scratching
- You also use nails to scratch, get rid of objects on the skin—and maybe pick your nose!

MUSCLES & MOVEMENT

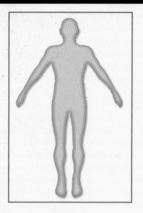

Every move you make, every breath you take, every song you sing . . . Muscles power all of your body's movements, from blinking to leaping high in the air. Muscle actions are controlled by messages traveling to them from your brain along motor nerves. Muscles are the body's biggest single system—a group of main parts that all work together to carry out one or more vital tasks.

• See pages 30–31 for information on the brain.

Muscles are found throughout the body. They help us move, from walking to making twists and turns.

SAVE ENERGY— GIVE A SMILE

• All muscles need energy to work. Energy is carried by the blood in the form of blood sugar (glucose).

• You use about 40 facial muscles to frown, but only half as many to smile. So save your energy by smiling more!

• See pages 46–47 for information on blood.

TYPES OF MUSCLES

The body has three main types of muscles: skeletal, visceral, and cardiac.

• Skeletal muscles are mostly attached to the bones of the skeleton, pulling on them to make you move.

• Skeletal muscles are the ones we normally mean when we talk about "muscles."

• Skeletal muscles are also called voluntary muscles because you can control them at will (voluntarily when you wish) by thinking.

• Skeletal muscles are also called striped, or striated, muscles. Under a microscope they have a pattern of stripes, or bands.

• Visceral muscles form sheets, layers, or tubes in the walls of the inner body parts (viscera) such as the stomach, intestines, and bladder.

• Visceral muscles are also called involuntary muscles because you cannot control them—they work automatically.

• Visceral muscles are sometimes called smooth muscles because under a microscope they lack any pattern of stripes.

• The third type of muscle is cardiac muscle, which forms the walls of the heart.

• See pages 42–43 for information on the heart.

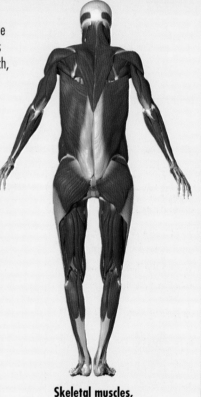

Skeletal muscles, seen from the back

MUSCLES THAT MAKE FACES

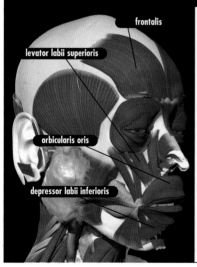

frontalis

levator labii superioris

orbicularis oris

depressor labii inferioris

We use our muscles to communicate and send information—and not just by speaking, which uses around 40 muscles. We also use muscles to "make faces," or create facial expressions. Here are some of the 60 or so facial muscles and what they do.

Muscle name	Site	What it does	Expression
Frontalis	Forehead	Raises eyebrows	Surprise
Procerus	Between the eyes	Pulls eyebrows in and down	Concentration
Auricularis	Above and to side of ear	Wiggles ear (only in some people!)	
Buccinator	Cheek	Moves cheek	Blowing, sucking
Risorius	Side of mouth	Pulls corner of mouth up	Grin
Depressor labii	Under lip	Pulls lower lip down	Grimace

Facial muscles allow us to make a huge range of expressions.

INSIDE A MUSCLE

A muscle is a bundle of fibers. These bundles are called fascicles. Within each fiber is a group of fibrils. A single fibril contains myosin and actin filaments. These slide past one another to shorten the muscle.

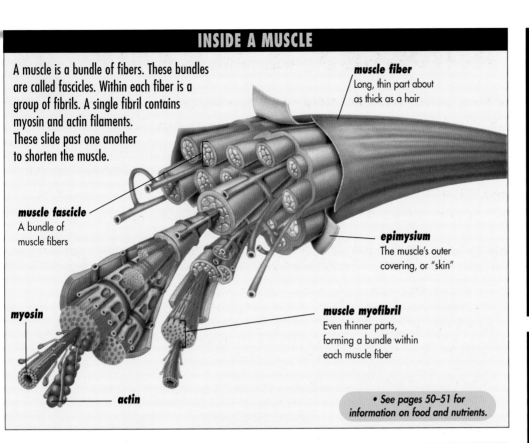

muscle fiber
Long, thin part about as thick as a hair

muscle fascicle
A bundle of muscle fibers

epimysium
The muscle's outer covering, or "skin"

myosin

muscle myofibril
Even thinner parts, forming a bundle within each muscle fiber

actin

• See pages 50–51 for information on food and nutrients.

MUSCLE POWER COMPARISON

This list shows the power of the body's muscles compared to various machines, in watts (the scientific unit of power).

Laser-pen pointer	**0.002 W**
Heart by itself	**2 W**
All of the body's muscles working hard	**100 W**
Family car on a highway	**100,000 W**
Space shuttle	**10 billion W**

INDIVIDUAL VARIATIONS

• Some people have very small versions of certain muscles or none at all — owing to the natural variations between different people.

• For example, a few people lack the thin sheetlike muscle in the neck called the platysma.

HOW MUSCLES WORK

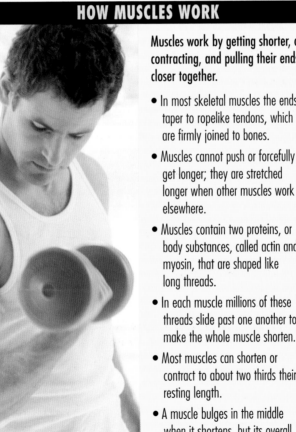

Muscles work by getting shorter, or contracting, and pulling their ends closer together.

• In most skeletal muscles the ends taper to ropelike tendons, which are firmly joined to bones.

• Muscles cannot push or forcefully get longer; they are stretched longer when other muscles work elsewhere.

• Muscles contain two proteins, or body substances, called actin and myosin, that are shaped like long threads.

• In each muscle millions of these threads slide past one another to make the whole muscle shorten.

• Most muscles can shorten or contract to about two thirds their resting length.

• A muscle bulges in the middle when it shortens, but its overall size or volume does not change.

Exercise can increase the size of muscles, but it has no effect on the actual number of muscles or the number of muscle cells — these stays the same.

MUSCLE
R E C O R D S

• There are about 640 main skeletal muscles.

• Muscles form about two fifths of the body weight in adult men and slightly less — about one third of body weight — in adult women, girls, and boys.

• Plenty of exercise and activity makes muscles grow bigger and stronger, so they form up to half of our body weight.

MUSCLE
R E C O R D S

Bulkiest

Gluteus maximus, forming most of the buttock. It works when you pull your thigh back to push your body forward when you walk, run, and jump.

Smallest

Stapedius, deep in the ear. When the ear detects very loud noises, it pulls on the body's smallest bone, the stirrup (stapes), to prevent it from moving too much, which could damage the delicate inner parts of the ear.

Longest

Sartorius, running from the side of the hip down across the front of the thigh to the inner side of the knee.

Most powerful for its size

Masseter, which runs from the cheekbone to the lower side of the lower jaw; bulges when you chew.

Busiest

Orbicularis oculi, better known as the eyelid muscles— they work up to 50,000 times each day as you blink and wink.

Biggest tendon

Calcaneal tendon, which joins the calf muscles to the heel bone. It takes the strain when you stand on tiptoe and is often called the Achilles tendon.

THE SKELETON

Your skeleton consists of all the bones in your body—more than 200 of them. It is like an inner framework that supports the softer, floppier body parts such as the intestines, nerves, and blood vessels. Your skeleton is not fixed and stiff. It is a moving structure that muscles pull into hundreds of different positions every day.

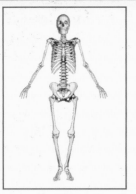

Bones are found throughout the body. Flexible parts of the body, such as fingers and toes, have more bones.

BONES NOT JOINED TO OTHER BONES

There are three bones in the body that are not joined to any other bone.

Hyoid
A U-shaped bone in the front of the upper neck, near the throat and the base of the tongue.

Kneecap, or patella
This is inside a muscle tendon and slides over the front of the knee joint, helping protect it.

SIZE AND VARIATIONS

Our bones provide a strong inner framework that holds up the soft inner parts of the body.

- There is no truth in the old belief that men and women have different numbers of ribs. Both have 24—12 pairs.

- However, the total number of bones varies slightly as part of the natural differences between people.

- For example, about one person in 20 (man or woman) has an extra pair of ribs, making 13 pairs instead of the usual 12.

- There are more bones—more than 300—in the skeleton of a baby than in that of an adult.

- As the baby grows some of its bones enlarge and join or fuse together to make bigger single bones.

- The skeleton forms about one seventh of the body's total weight.

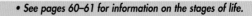
• See pages 60–61 for information on the stages of life.

TAIL END

The lowest part of the backbone is called the coccyx.
It is made of between three and five smaller bones joined or fused together into one, and it is shaped like a small prong. It is all that is left of the long tail that our very distant ancestors had millions of years ago, when they looked like monkeys and lived in trees.

Monkeys and humans are descended from the same distant ancestors.

WHAT ARE BONES LIKE?

Imagining our bodies as different everyday objects can help us understand how they work.

Levers
The long bones of the arms and legs work like levers, with their pivot, or fulcrum, at the joint.

A bicycle chain
The many separate bones, or vertebrae, of the backbone move only slightly compared to one another. But over the whole backbone this movement acts like the links of a bicycle chain, allowing the movement of bending over.

A cage
The ribs work like the movable bars of a cage. This protects the heart and lungs, yet gets bigger and smaller as the lungs breathe in and out.

An eggshell
The dome shape of the cranium around the brain is a very strong design, like an eggshell. Any sharp ridges or corners would weaken it.

• See pages 26–27 for information on bones and joints.

NOT ALL BONE

Most of a baby's skeleton is made of cartilage, not bone.

- Most bones of the skeleton begin not as real bone, but as a slightly softer, more flexible smooth substance called cartilage (gristle).

- In a developing baby the shapes of the eventual bones form first as cartilage.

- Then as the baby grows into a child the cartilage shapes become hardened into real bones.

- Even in an adult skeleton some bones remain partly cartilage.

- For example, the front end of each rib, where it joins to the breastbone, is made not of bone, but of a cartilage called costal cartilage.

- The nose and ears are mainly cartilage, not true bone, which is why they are slightly flexible.

SKELETON STRENGTH

Our skeleton is made of living bones that can repair themselves if broken.

- The bones of the human skeleton are stronger, size for weight, than almost any kind of wood or plastic.

- If the skeleton were made of steel, it would weigh four times as much.

- The thigh bone can stand a pressure of 0.47 tons per sq in. (3 tons per cm^2) when we leap and land.

- The skeleton can also repair itself, which no type of plastic or metal can.

NUMBERS OF BONES

A human skeleton contains, on average, 206 bones. They are divided up through the body as follows:

Skull

Cranium (braincase) 8

Face 14

Ear 3 tiny bones each

Total: 28 bones

Throat (hyoid bone) 1

Backbone

Neck (cervical vertebrae) 7

Chest (thoracic vertebrae) 12

Lower back (lumbar vertebrae) 5

Base of back (sacrum, coccyx) 2

Total: 26 bones

Ribcage

Ribs 24

Breastbone 1

Total: 25 bones

Arms

Shoulder 2

Upper arm 1

Forearm 2

Wrist 8

Palm 5

Fingers and thumb 14

Total: 32 bones in each arm (includes hand)

Legs

Hip 1

Thigh and knee 2

Shin 2

Ankle 7

Sole of foot 5

Toes 14

Total: 31 bones in each leg (includes foot)

SKELETON'S MAIN TASKS

The main tasks of the skeleton are to:

- Hold up the body, giving support to softer parts.

- Allow the body to move when pulled by muscles.

- Provide openings for the nose and mouth, for breathing and eating.

- Protect certain body parts, for example, the upper skull around the brain, the front skull around most of the eyes, and the ribs around the lungs and chest.

- Store many body minerals, such as calcium and magnesium, for times when food is scarce and these minerals are in short supply for other body processes such as sending nerve messages.

- Make new microscopic cells for the blood at the rate of three million per second. These cells are produced in the soft jellylike bone marrow found in the center of some bones.

The skeleton provides some protection for vital body parts, but it is wise to wear a helmet when you are doing activities that involve going fast.

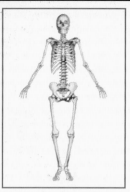

Joints allow the skeleton to move. They can be found all over the body.

PARTS OF A BONE

Periosteum
The outer covering, or "skin," wrapped all around the bone.

Foramen
Small hole in the bone where a nerve or blood vessel passes inside the bone.

Compact bone
Very strong, hard outer layer of bone, like a shell.

Osteons (Haversian canals)
Tiny "rods" of bone substance bundled and glued together to make compact bone.

Spongy, or cancellous, bone
Inner layer of a bone, under the compact bone, that has holes like a sponge.

Marrow
Jellylike substance in the center of most bones.

Red marrow
Found in all bones of a baby, but in an adult, only in the long bones of the arms and legs, ribs, backbone, breastbone, and upper skull. Makes new microscopic cells for the blood.

Yellow marrow
In adults, found mainly in smaller bones of the hands and feet. Contains fat for use as an energy reserve, but can change to red marrow if needed, for example, after serious bleeding.

The bones in your skeleton hold you up. But you would not be able to move if it was not for the joints that link your bones together. More than half of your body's bones—112 out of the total of 206—are in your wrists, hands, fingers, ankles, feet, and toes. So are more than half of your 200 plus joints. Your bones, muscles, and joints work so closely together that they are sometimes described as a single system—the musculoskeletal system.

BONE MAKEUP

- The name *skeleton* comes from an ancient word meaning "dried up." But living bones are about one fourth water. (Overall the body is two thirds water.)

- The main minerals in bone are calcium, phosphate, and carbonate.

These form tiny crystals that give bone its hardness and stiffness.

- Bone also contains tiny threadlike fibers of the substance collagen, which makes it slightly flexible under pressure, so it is less likely to snap.

- If a bone is soaked in a special acid chemical, all of the crystals of calcium phosphate and calcium carbonate are removed. It leaves only the collagen fibers, which are so flexible that a long bone such as the upper arm bone can be tied in a knot!

During long space flights, the lack of gravity means that bones are put under little pressure. They start to lose minerals and become weaker. Astronauts exercise regularly to keep their bones strong.

• See pages 50–51 for information on food and nutrients.

LIGAMENTS

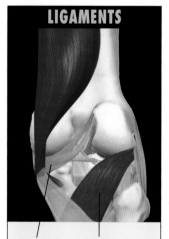

ligament   muscle

Bones are held together at a joint by stretchy straps called ligaments, which stop them from moving too far or coming apart. If the bones slip and come out of their usual position, this is called a dislocation.

YES AND NO

The two uppermost backbones (cervical vertebrae) of the spine have special joint designs. They allow the head to make important movements.

- The atlas (uppermost) is more like a ring. It supports and allows the head to turn, or rotate, to look to the side, as when saying "no."

- The axis (second uppermost) has a curved shape, like a saddle. It allows the head to tilt to the side and nod, as when saying "yes."

Nodding and shaking your head is only possible with two special joint designs in the backbone.

PARTS OF A BONE

Doctors have names for each part of a bone.

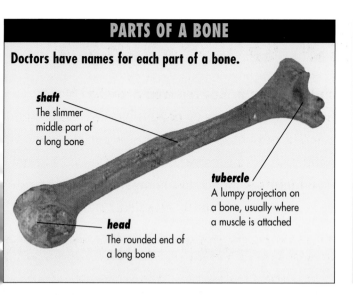

shaft
The slimmer middle part of a long bone

tubercle
A lumpy projection on a bone, usually where a muscle is attached

head
The rounded end of a long bone

BONE RECORDS

Longest
Thighbone (femur), forming about one fourth of total body height.

Widest
Hipbone (pelvis), forming the body's broadest part.

Smallest
Stirrup (stapes) deep inside the ear, a U shape just 0.32 in.(8mm) long.

Toughest
Lower jaw (mandible), used hundreds of times daily when chewing.

DESIGN OF A JOINT

The different designs of your body's joints are sometimes compared to machines and mechanical gadgets.

Hinge joint
Allows the bones to move only back and forth, not side to side (as in a door hinge).

Examples: knee, smaller knuckles of fingers.

Ball-and-socket joint
Allows the bones to move back and forth and also side to side, and perhaps twist (rotate).

Examples: hips, shoulders, larger knuckles.

Saddle joint
Shaped like a saddle for tilting and sliding.

Example: thumb.

Washer joint
Limited tilting with a pad, or washer, of cartilage between the bone ends.

Examples: joints between the backbones, where the cartilage pad is called the disk (intervertebral disk).

Fixed, or suture, joint
No movement at all, because the bones are firmly joined together.

Examples: between the bones of the cranium (upper skull) around the brain.

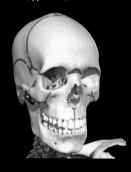

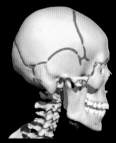

There are eight bones in the cranium. They are fused together to protect the brain underneath.

REDUCING WEAR AND TEAR

- Where the ends of a bone touch in a joint, they are covered with smooth, glossy cartilage to reduce wear and rubbing.

- The space between the bones is filled with a slippery liquid called synovial fluid that works like oil in a machine to reduce wear even more.

- The fluid is kept in place by a loose bag around the joint, the joint capsule.

- New synovial fluid is always being made by the inner lining of this bag, the synovial membrane.

Even a large joint like the hip contains only about a teaspoon of synovial fluid.

BIGGEST JOINT

Your single biggest joint, the knee, has an unusual design with extra cartilage and ligaments.

- As well as cartilage covering the ends of the thigh- and shinbones, it has two pieces of curved moon-shaped cartilage between these bones.

- The cartilage pieces are called menisci and help the knee "lock" straight so that you can stand up easily.

- When athletes have "torn knee cartilage," it is usually one of the menisci that is damaged.

• See pages 22–23 for information on muscles.

- The knee has two strong sets of ligaments, the lateral ligaments on the outer side and the medial ligaments on the inner side (next to the other knee).

- As well as these, it has two ligaments inside, keeping the ends of the bones very close together.

- These two ligaments form an Xlike cross shape and are called cruciate ligaments.

Playing sports can sometimes damage your knee joints. It is important to always warm up before exercising.

NERVOUS SYSTEM

You are nervous, I am nervous, everyone is nervous. That is, we all have a nervous system to control our every movement and action and every process that happens inside the body. Your nervous system is made up of your brain, spinal cord, and nerves. It works by sending tiny electrical signals called nerve impulses. Millions of these travel around the body and brain every second, like the busiest computer network.

WHERE IN THE BODY?

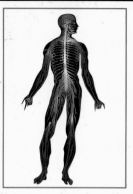

Nerves run throughout the body, carrying electrical signals from the brain.

MAIN PARTS OF THE NERVOUS SYSTEM

There are two main nervous systems within the body. The central nervous system is the brain's main control center. It sends nerve impulses to the rest of the body using the peripheral nervous system. We have conscious control over the central and peripheral nervous systems.

Central nervous system: Brain

Inside the top half of the head.

Spinal cord

The main nerve link between the brain and the body.

Peripheral nervous system: Cranial nerves

Connect directly to the brain rather than the spinal cord. They go mainly to parts in the head like the eyes, ears, and nose.

Spinal nerves

Branch out from the spinal cord to the arms, legs, back, chest, and all other body parts.

• See pages 30–31 for information on the brain.

SLOW TO HURT

When you hurt a finger, you probably feel the touch first, and then the pain starts a moment later. This is because the signals for touch travel faster along the nerves than the signals for pain.

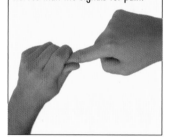

AUTOMATIC SYSTEM

• Some parts of the nervous system work automatically without you having to think about them.

• These automatic parts are called the autonomic nervous system. They control inner processes like heartbeat, digestion, body temperature, and blood pressure.

We have no conscious control over some parts of our body, such as the systems that control digestion.

NERVES AND NERVE CELLS

A nerve's outer covering is called the epineurium. Inside are bundles of nerve fibers, or axons, each too small to see without a microscope.

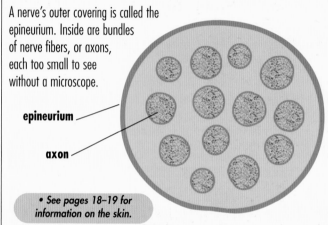

epineurium

axon

• See pages 18–19 for information on the skin.

NERVE SIGNALS

A nerve signal is a tiny pulse or peak of electricity made by moving chemical substances into and out of a nerve cell.

Average signal strength	$\frac{1}{10}$th of a volt
Average signal length	$\frac{1}{1,000}$th of a second
Average recovery time before another signal can pass	$\frac{1}{500}$th of a second
Slowest signals travel at	1.6 ft. (0.5m) per second
Fastest signals travel at	459 ft. (140m) per second

THICKEST NERVE

The sciatic nerve, in the hip and upper thigh, is about the width of its owner's thumb. This is thicker than the spinal cord, which is usually the width of its owner's little finger.

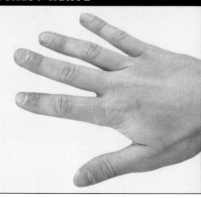

NERVES AND NERVE CELLS

Nerves are flexible but tough, so they can easily move at joints but withstand being squeezed by muscles around them.

- Each nerve fiber is the long wirelike part of a single microscopic nerve cell called a neuron.

- Usually found near one end, the nerve cell has a wider part—the cell body.

- Branching from the nerve cell body are even thinner spidery-looking parts called dendrites.

- Nerve messages from other nerve cells are picked up by the dendrites, processed, and altered as they pass around the cell body. They are then sent on by the axon (fiber) to other nerve cells.

- Most nerve fibers are 0.0004 in. (0.01mm) wide, so 2,500 of them side by side would stretch 1 in. (2.5cm).

- The fibers have a covering wrapped around them called the myelin sheath. It makes nerve messages travel faster and stops them leaking away.

A typical nerve looks like shiny wire or string.

SPINAL CORD

The spinal cord in the back is one of the most important parts of the nervous system.

- Joins the brain to the main body.

- Is about 18 in. (45cm) long in a typical adult.

- Has 31 pairs of nerves branching from it, both left and right.

- Is protected inside a "tunnel" formed by a row of holes through the backbone.

- Like the brain, has a layer of liquid around it, called cerebrospinal fluid, to cushion it from knocks and sudden twists.

NERVE JUNCTIONS

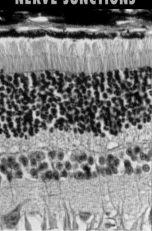

Synapses are so small that scientists have to use special electron microscopes to study them.

Each nerve cell receives signals from thousands of other cells and passes on signals to thousands more.

- Individual nerve cells do not actually touch one another where the ends of their dendrites and axons (fibers) come together.

- The ends are separated by tiny gaps at junction points called synapses.

- The gap inside a synapse is just 0.025 micrometers wide, which means 40,000 in a row would stretch 0.039 in. (1mm).

- Nerve messages "jump" across a synapse not as electrical signals, but in the form of chemicals called neurotransmitters.

- This chemical "jump" takes less than $\frac{1}{1,000}$ th of a second.

NERVE LENGTHS

- All of the nerves in the body, taken out and joined end to end, would stretch about 62 mi. (100km).

- The longest single nerve fibers, in the legs, are up to 3.28 ft. (1m) in length.

DIRECT TO THE BRAIN

Twelve pairs of cranial nerves join directly to the brain and link it to the following parts:

1. Nose
For smelling

2. Eyes
For seeing

3. Eyelid-moving and pupil-constriction muscles

4. Eyeball-moving muscles

5. Skin and touch
On forehead, face, cheeks, jaw muscles, muscles for chewing

6. Eyeball-moving muscles

7. Tongue
For taste, saliva (spit) glands, tear glands, facial expressions

8. Ear
For hearing and balance

9. Rear of tongue
For taste, swallowing

10. Swallowing muscles
Also lungs and heart in chest

11. Voice-box muscles
For speaking

12. Tongue muscles
For speaking, swallowing

NERVES EVERYWHERE

There are nerves in every body part, including the heart, lungs, and guts.

- The thickest ones near the brain and spinal cord are known as nerve trunks.

- The thinnest ones spreading into body parts are terminal fibers.

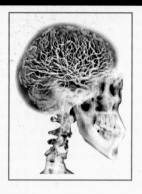

The brain is inside the cranium (the domed part of the skull), forming the upper half of the head.

THE BRAIN

Sometimes we describe a very clever person as having "lots of brains." But we have only one brain each. It contains more than 100 billion nerve cells, or neurons—about as many as there are stars in our galaxy, the Milky Way. The brain also contains perhaps ten times as many "support" cells called glia. It is not the size of a brain that makes it clever, nor the exact number of cells. It depends on how often its owner uses his or her brain and in how much detail—by looking, listening, learning, remembering, using imagination, and having ideas.

HUNGRY FOR ENERGY

- The brain consumes about one fifth of all the energy used by the body.

- But the brain forms about only $\frac{1}{50}$ th of the whole body.

- So the brain uses ten times more energy for its size compared to most other body parts.

- This energy is mainly in the form of blood sugar, or glucose, brought to the brain by its main blood vessels, the carotid and vertebral arteries.

- Average blood flow to the brain is 22.5 fl.oz. (750mL) per minute, about one eighth of the heart's total output.

- This flow is the same whether the body is at rest or very active.

- This is unusual because blood flow to other body parts changes greatly between rest and activity—for example, activity increases blood flow to the muscles by ten times and decreases flow to the stomach and guts by half.

- See pages 44–45 for information on the circulatory system.

CORTEX IN CONTROL

planning movement

making movement

speech

touch

hearing

vision

- The outer gray layer of the cerebrum, over the top of the brain, is called the cerebral cortex.

- Spread out flat, it would be the area of a pillowcase—and almost as thin.

- However, deep grooves called sulci mean it is wrinkled and folded into the space inside the upper skull.

- The cortex has about half the brain's total number of nerve cells, around 50 billion.

- Each of these can have connections with more than 200,000 other nerve cells.

- The connections are made by spidery-looking "arms" called dendrites and a much longer wirelike part of the nerve fiber.

- The cortex is the main place where we become aware of what we see, hear, smell, taste and touch—that is, what we sense.

- It is also the place where we plan movements and actions, known as motor skills, and get them started.

- Each of these sensory and motor processes takes place in a different area, or patch, of the cortex known as a center.

- The cortex is also the major site for thinking and our general awareness and consciousness—what we call our "mind."

- And the cortex is involved in learning and memory, although scientists are not quite sure how.

- See pages 32–37 for information on the senses.

- See pages 22–23 for information on muscles.

THE WEIGHT OF THE BRAIN

The weight of an average adult brain is 3.09 lbs. (1.4kg).

The largest accurately measured normal human brain is 6.4 lbs. (2.9kg).

BRAIN SIZE

- Bigger brains are not necessarily smarter, and there is no link between the size of a healthy brain and intelligence.

- The average female brain is slightly smaller than the average male brain.

- But the average female body is smaller, in comparison, to the average male body.

- So compared to body size, women have slightly larger brains than men.

MAIN BRAIN PARTS

cerebrum
The big wrinkled, domed part covering most of the top of the brain forms more than four fifths of the entire brain. It has a thin outer layer of "gray matter," which is mainly nerve cells, covering an inner mass of "white matter," which is chiefly nerve fibers.

thalamus
This is two egg-shaped parts almost at the center of the brain. It helps sort and process information from four of the senses (eyes, ears, tongue, skin) going to the cerebrum above.

hypothalamus
Just below and in front of the thalamus is the center for powerful feelings, emotions, and urges such as anger, fear, love, and joy.

cerebellum
A smaller wrinkled part at the lower rear, it looks like a smaller version of the entire brain. In fact its name means "little brain." It carries out detailed control of muscles so that we can move around, stay balanced, and carry out skilled actions.

brain stem
The base of the brain contains the main "life support" areas for heartbeat, breathing, blood pressure, and control of digestion. Its lower end merges into the top of the spinal cord.

HOLLOW BRAIN

- The brain has four small chambers inside it called ventricles.

- These are filled with a pale liquid called cerebrospinal fluid, CSF.

- CSF is found around the brain, between two of the protective layers called meninges that surround it. CSF is also found inside and around the spinal cord.

- The total amount of CSF inside and around the brain and spinal cord is about 3.8 fl.oz. (125mL).

- This fluid flows very slowly and is gradually renewed about three times every 24 hours.

- CSF is important, as it helps cushion the brain from knocks.

- The liquid also supports the brain within the skull, brings nourishment, and takes away wastes.

- If someone has epidural anesthesia, this is injected into the meninges and CSF around the lower spinal cord.

SLEEP

Even when asleep, the brain is as active sending nerve messages around itself as it is when awake. This is shown by recordings of its electrical nerve signals.

- Older people tend to sleep more hours overall, but often in several sessions, such as "cat naps" throughout the day.

- Usual sleep needs for most people every 24 hours:

Newborn baby	20 hours
10-year-old	10 hours
Adult	7–8 hours

LEFT AND RIGHT

- Nerve messages from the body cross over from left to right at the base of the brain.

- This means the left side of the brain receives signals from, and sends them to, the right side of the body.

- In most people the left side of the brain is more active in speaking and reading, scientific skills, using numbers and math, and figuring out problems in a step-by-step way.

- The right side of the brain is more

active in dealing with shapes and colors, artistic skills such as painting and music, having ideas, and "jumping" to answers without detailed thought.

- In a right-handed person the left side of the brain is generally dominant. In a left-handed person the right side of the brain is generally dominant.

A person may write with one hand but use the other to carry out everday tasks.

THE GROWING
BRAIN

The development of the brain happens quickly after conception. It continues to grow in size after birth and makes new nerve connections throughout childhood.

Inside the womb
- The brain is one of the first main body parts to form—just three weeks after conception it is a large arched bulge.

Four weeks after conception
- The brain is almost larger than the rest of the body.

20 weeks after conception
- The brain weighs about 3.5 oz. (100g).

At birth
- The brain is 14–17.5 oz. (400–500g), about one third of its final adult size. In comparison, a new baby's body is about ⅕th of its final adult size.

Growing up
- By the age of three, the brain is almost fully grown and weighs 2.4 oz. (1.1kg).

- The brain does not make any new nerve cells after birth.

- It does make new connections between nerve cells, perhaps millions every week, as we take in knowledge, develop skills, and learn new things.

From the age of about 20 years
- The brain shrinks by about 0.035 oz. (1g) of weight per year. This represents the loss of around 10,000 nerve cells each day.

- Certain drugs, including alcohol, can speed this cell loss and make the brain shrink faster.

• See pages 60–61 for information on the stages of life.

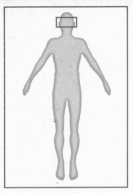

Each eyeball is in a bony bowl called the eye socket. It is formed by curved parts of five skull bones.

BLIND SPOT

There are no rods or cones at the place where all of the retina's nerve fibers come together to form the start of the optic nerve. This area is called the optic disk.

- Since light cannot be detected here, it is known as the blind spot.
- Normally we do not notice the blind spot because our eyes continually dart and look around at different parts of a scene.
- As we do this the brain guesses and "fills in" the missing area from what is around and what it has seen just before or after.
- The optic nerve contains one million nerve fibers—the most of any nerve carrying sense information to the brain.

FLOATERS

- Some people see spots, or "floaters," that seem to be in front of the eye.
- These are actually inside the eye, in the vitreous humor jelly that fills the inside of the eyeball.
- They are usually stray red blood cells or bits of fibers that have escaped from the retina.
- We cannot look straight at them because as we move the eyeball, they also move inside it.
- A few floaters are normal, but medical advice is needed if they suddenly increase in number.

EYES & SIGHT

For people with normal vision, sight is the most precious sense. Experts estimate that more than half of the information we have in our brains comes in through our eyes as words (like these), photographs, drawings, real-life scenes, and images on screens. Yet the eye does not really "see." It turns patterns of light rays into patterns of nerve signals that travel to the brain. The visual, or sight, center at the back of the brain is the "mind's eye," where we recognize and understand what we see.

WHAT AN INCREDIBLE SIGHT

As it goes dark in the evening what we see seems to lose color and "gray out." This is because the cone cells do not work as well, and we rely on the rods.

- The eye's inner lining, the retina, is where light rays are changed to nerve signals.
- The retina has an area about the same size as a large postage stamp (wider across than high).
- It has millions of microscopic cells that make nerve signals when hit by light rays.
- 125 million are rod cells, which work well in dim light, but they cannot see colors— only shades of gray.

- 7 million are cone cells, which see fine details and colors, but work only in bright light.
- Most of the cones are concentrated in a slightly bowl-shaped hollow at the back of the retina, the fovea, or yellow spot.
- This is where light falls to give us the clearest, most detailed view.

- See pages 28–29 for information on nerves.

COLOR CONES

Many people who are red-green colorblind can learn to tell colors apart by their shade, or hue, rather than the actual color.

- There are three types of light-detecting cone cells in the retina.
- They are called red, green, and blue cones.
- This is not because of their colors—they all look the same.
- They have these names because the three types of cones detect three different colors of light.
- The brain figures out the color of an object from the active cones.

- In some people not all of these cones are present or work properly.
- This is called colorblindness or, more properly, defect of color vision.
- Most common is when red and green appear similar.
- This often runs in families and almost always affects boys rather than girls.
- True colorblindness, seeing everything in shades of gray (like an old black-and-white movie) is very rare, affecting less than 1 in 10,000 people.

MAIN PARTS OF THE EYE

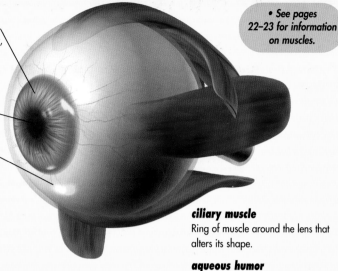

• See pages 22–23 for information on muscles.

iris
Colored ring of muscle that can alter the size of the hole (the pupil) within it, making it smaller in bright light to protect the delicate inside of the eye.

pupil
Hole in the iris through which light enters the eye's interior.

sclera
Tough outer layer, or sheath, around the whole eye apart from the cornea.

cornea
Thick clear dome at the front of the eye.

conjunctiva
Sensitive covering at the front of the eyeball, over the cornea.

lens
Pea-shaped blob about 0.4 in. (10mm) across that alters in shape to see and focus clearly, from looking at faraway objects to close ones.

retina
Inner layer lining the eyeball's interior.

choroid
Blood-rich layer between the sclera and retina.

ciliary muscle
Ring of muscle around the lens that alters its shape.

aqueous humor
Thin, clear fluid filling the space between the cornea and the lens.

vitreous humor
Thick, clear jellylike substance filling the main eyeball and giving it its rounded shape.

MOVING THE EYEBALL

Behind the eyeball are six small ribbon-shaped muscles that make it turn and swivel in its socket, or eye orbit.

Medial rectus
Moves the eye inward toward the nose.

Lateral rectus
Moves the eye outward away from the nose.

Superior rectus
Moves the eye upward to look at the sky.

Inferior rectus
Moves the eye downward to look at the ground.

Superior oblique
Pulls eye inward and downward.

Inferior oblique
Pulls eye upward and outward.

In total the eye can tilt as follows:

• look up by 35 degrees
• look down by 50 degrees
• inward toward the nose by 50 degrees
• outward by 45 degrees

IRIS SECURITY SCANS

Usually people with darker skin and hair have browner irises. People with lighter skin and hair have bluer irises.

• Each person has a different color and detailed pattern of marks on the iris.

• Photos or scans of the iris fed into a computer can be used like fingerprints for identification and security checks.

• Rarely a person has two different-colored irises, perhaps being born like that or as a result of injury or illness.

• Every person in the world has different fingerprints, which can be used for identification and security checks.

• The same applies to the colored part of the eye, the iris.

BLINKING AMAZING

• We spend up to 30 minutes of our waking day with our eyes shut during blinks.

• Blinking washes soothing, cleansing tear fluid over the eyes. The fluid clears away dust and helps kill germs.

• Tear fluid comes from the lachrymal gland, just above and to the outer side of each eye, under a fold of skin.

• On average:
Number of blinks per minute: 6
Length of a blink: 0.3–0.4 seconds
Total amount of tear fluid made in a day: 10 tsp. (50mL)

The numbers can triple if surroundings are dusty or have chemical fumes.

MEASURING THE EYE

The eyeball is almost a perfect sphere, or ball shape. Its measurements are as follows:

Side to side: 0.96 in. (24mm)
Front to back: 0.96 in. (24mm)
Top to bottom: 0.92 in. (23mm)

• The eyeball's overall weight is 0.88–1.05 oz. (25–30g).

• The eye is one of the body parts that grows the least from birth to adulthood.

20/20 VISION

The saying "20/20 vision" comes from describing how clearly a person can see.

• 20/20 vision means a person can see at a distance of 20 ft. (6.09m) what normal eyesight can show.

• The larger the second number, the worse the eyesight.

• Someone with 20/60 vision can see at 20 ft. (6.09m) what a normal-sighted person sees clearly at 60 ft. (98m).

• Shortsightedness (myopia) is due to the eyeball being too big for the focusing power of its lens, for example, 1.12–1.16 in. (28–29mm) across.

• Farsightedness (hypermetropia) is due to the eyeball being too small for its lens to focus, for example, 0.80–0.84 in. (20–21mm) across.

• Astigmatism is when the curve of the eyeball is not regular in all directions like a bowl, but curves more in one direction than the other like a spoon.

EARS & HEARING

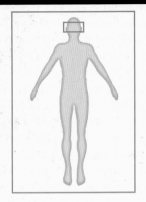

The outer ear is on the side of the head, usually level with the nose. The inner ear is deep in the temporal skull bone, almost behind the eye.

Sssh—can you hear that sound? Hardly anywhere is truly silent. We can usually hear some kind of sound, whether the roar of a jet plane, friends talking, or birds singing while the wind rustles grass. Most of the time we are not aware of sounds around us because they tell us nothing new. The brain blocks out frequent noise like humming machinery or distant traffic. Only when we hear something new, important, or exciting does the mind turn its attention to hearing.

OUTSIDE TO INSIDE

The ear is divided into three main sections:

Outer ear
Ear flap (pinna or auricle), ear canal.

Middle ear
Eardrum, tiny ear bones, middle ear chamber.

Inner ear
Cochlea, semicircular canals, and their chambers.

EAR BONES

- The body's six smallest bones, three in each middle ear.

- They were named long ago from items more common at the time having to do with horse riding and ironsmiths.

- Hammer (malleus) is attached to the eardrum.

- Anvil (incus) is the middle of the three.

- Stirrup (stapes) is attached to the oval window of the cochlea.

- *See pages 24–27 for information on bones.*

STEREO HEARING

- Sound travels about 1,082 ft. (330m) per second in the air.

- A sound from one side reaches the ear on that side more than 1,000th of a second earlier than it reaches the other ear.

- The sound is louder and clearer in the closer ear, too.

- The brain can detect these differences in time, volume, and clarity and figure out the direction a sound comes from. This is known as stereophonic hearing.

- Headphones and earphones copy these differences to give the impression of wide-apart sounds.

- Even sounds in front and behind can be told apart, whether they come from low down or high up.

- A sound from the floor directly in front causes some echoes and brings these mixed in with it.

- A sound from directly above has fewer echoes, and these reach the ears after the main sounds.

- *See pages 30–31 for information on the brain.*

SENSE OF BALANCE

In space there is no gravity to help give astronauts a sense of balance. The lack of gravity causes about one third of people to get space sick.

- The three semicircular canals are at right angles to one other.

- Each canal has a jellylike blob at one end in its widened part, or ampulla.

- Stuck in the jellylike blob are microhairs from hair cells.

- As the head moves, fluid in the canal swishes back and forth and moves the jellylike blob.

- This moves the hairs of the hair cells, which make nerve signals and send them to the brain.

- In the wider parts next to the canals, the utricle and saccule chambers, are more blobs with hairs on them.

- Gravity pulls these down, bending the hairs and making the hair cells produce nerve signals.

- The canals sense any movements of the head, while the chambers detect head position.

- However, balance involves much more, including information from the eyes about what is upright and level, from the skin about whether the body is leaning, and from inside the muscles and joints about strains on them.

- The brain uses all of this information to adjust muscles and keep us well balanced.

HOW WE HEAR

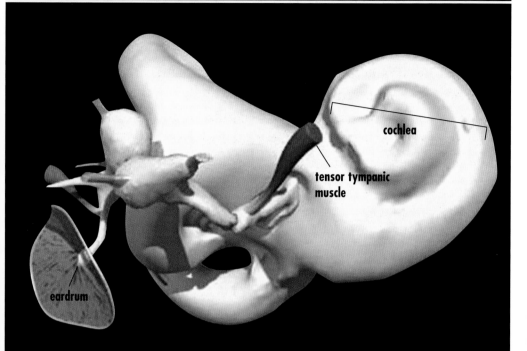

cochlea

tensor tympanic muscle

eardrum

1. Sound waves approach as invisible ripples of high and low air pressure.

2. Outer ear flap funnels sound waves.

3. Ear canal carries them into the skull.

4. Eardrum shakes fast, or vibrates, as sound waves bounce off it.

5. Vibrations pass along row of three tiny bones, or ossicles.

6. Third ossicle makes thin "window" of cochlea vibrate.

7. Vibrations pass into fluid inside cochlea, causing ripples.

8. Ripples shake 50–100 microhairs on each of 25,000 microscopic hair cells inside cochlea.

9. Hair cells make nerve signals when shaken.

10. Nerve signals pass along nerve fibers into cochlear nerve.

11. Cochlear nerve is joined by vestibular nerve from balance parts.

12. Both nerves form auditory nerve, which carries nerve signals to the brain.

DAMAGE CONTROL

Some sounds are too loud for us to hear comfortably. We put our hands over our ears to try to protect them.

- Sounds above 90 dB, especially if high pitched like whining or sawing, can damage hearing.

- Many places have laws controlling noise and limiting people being exposed to it, such as factories, airports, and music clubs.

PITCH

Sound reaches us as waves of vibrations of the air. Higher sounds make the air vibrate more quickly than lower sounds.

- Pitch is the scale of a sound — whether it makes the air vibrate at a high or low frequency.

- Our ears can detect sounds from 25 to 20,000 vibrations per second.

- Dogs can detect much deeper and higher sounds than this.

EAR MEASUREMENTS

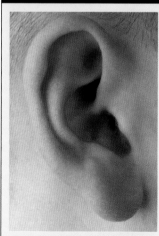

The ear canal leads from the outer ear to the eardrum. It is 0.8 in. (20mm) long and slightly S shaped.

Eardrum surface area 0.09 sq.in. (55 mm²) (about the size of the nail on the pinkie).

Stirrup less than 0.2 in. (5mm) long.

Cochlea spiral, like a snail, with two three-fourth turns.

Cochlea 0.36 in. (9mm) across at the wide end.

Cochlea straightened out would stretch 1.4 in. (35mm).

Semicircular canals each 6–8 in. (15–20mm) long, curved into a C shape (for balance), each less than 0.04 in. (1mm) wide.

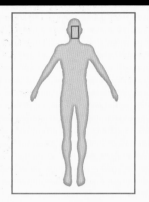

The nasal and oral chambers—nose and mouth—form the front lower fourth of the head, each shaped by the skull and jawbones around it.

NOSE & TONGUE

Smell and taste are called chemosenses. This means they detect chemical substances—tiny particles that are too small to see. Your nose reacts to particles called odorants that float in the air. The tongue does the same to particles called flavorants, which are found in foods and drinks. Both of these senses are very useful because they can warn us of danger—but they also give us plenty of pleasure.

FAST TRACK SIGNALS

Nerve signals about smell take a different route through the brain compared to signals from other senses.

Smell signals pass through a brain part called the limbic system, which is involved in feelings and emotions. This is why a strong smell brings back powerful memories and feelings.

- *See pages 30–31 for information on the brain.*

INSIDE THE NOSE

Nostrils
Two holes, each leading to one side of the nasal chamber.

Nasal cartilages
Curved sheets of cartilage (gristle) forming the "sticking-out" part of the nose.

Nasal chamber
The air space inside the nose, roughly below the inner sides of the eyes.

Septum
The flat sheet of cartilage dividing the two halves of the nasal chamber.

Turbinates
Shelflike ridges on each outer side of the nasal chamber.

Olfactory patch
Fuzzy-looking area inside the top of each half of the nasal chamber that detects smells.

LOCK AND KEY

Experts are still not exactly sure how smell and taste work in detail. The main idea is the "lock and key theory."

- Microscopic sense cells for both smell and taste are called hair cells, with many tiny hairs, known as cilia, sticking out.

- These hairs are probably coated with thousands of different-shaped receptors, or "landing pads."

A rose produces a particular smell particle that our nose can recognize.

- Each type of smell or flavor particle has its own particular shape.

- Particles try to fit in all of the receptors on the hairs, but they slot exactly only into certain ones of the same shape, like a key fitting into a lock.

- When a particle fits into a receptor, the hair cell sends a nerve signal to the brain.

- The brain figures out the smell or taste from the overall pattern of nerve signals it receives.

MICRODETAILS: THE NOSE

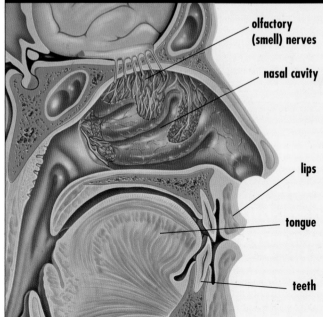

olfactory (smell) nerves

nasal cavity

lips

tongue

teeth

- The olfactory patch in the top of the nasal chamber is about the same area of a thumbnail.

- Each olfactory patch has ten million smell hair cells.

- Each smell hair cell has 10–20 microhairs sticking down from it.

- All of the microhairs from one nose, joined end to end, would stretch over 328 ft. (100m).

- The microhairs stick into the sticky, slimy mucus that lines the interior of the nasal chamber inside the nose.

- Odorant particles, floating in air, seep into the mucus coating the inside of the nasal chamber.

- The particles then come into contact with the microhairs.

- A single smell hair cell lives for about 30 days and is then replaced.

- Over many years some smell hair cells die but are not replaced.

- Younger people have a more sensitive sense of smell than older people.

MICRODETAILS: THE TONGUE

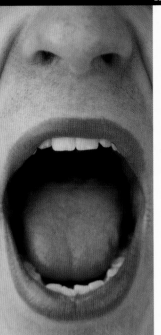

The tip, sides, and rear of the tongue have about 10,000 tiny taste buds too small to see.

- Most taste buds are around and between the little lumps, or "pimples," on the tongue called papillae.

- Each taste bud is shaped like a tiny onion and contains about 25 taste hair cells.

- Each taste hair cell has about ten short microhairs sticking up from it.

- The microhairs stick through a hole, called a taste pore, at the top of the taste bud, onto the tongue's surface.

- Flavorant particles in foods and drinks seep into the saliva (spit)

covering the tongue and come into contact with the microhairs.

- A single taste hair cell lives for about ten days and is then replaced.

- Over many years some taste hair cells die but are not replaced.

- Younger people have a more sensitive sense of taste than older people.

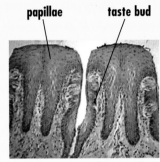

papillae   taste bud

A close-up view of a taste bud

HOW MANY?

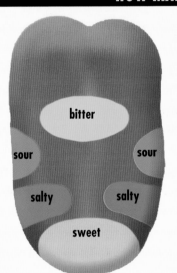

bitter

sour   sour

salty   salty

sweet

We sense different basic flavors on different parts of the tongue.

- The tongue can detect only four main flavors: sweet at the tip, salty along the front sides, sour along the rear sides, and bitter across the back.

- There are no taste buds on the main middle part of the tongue's upper surface or below it.

NOT ALL IT SEEMS

Food is less appetizing if we have a cold. The nose is full of mucus, our sense of smell does not work, and food seems less "tasty." In fact, it's less "smelly."

When we "taste" a meal, it is not only taste at work.

- Smells from food in the mouth waft up around the back of the roof of the mouth into the nose.

- Here they are sensed by the nose in the usual way.

- Touch sensors in the gums and

cheeks and on the tongue tell us about the food, too.

- These touch sensors detect if the food is hot or cold, hard or soft, rough with bits, or smooth like cream.

- Enjoying a meal involves taste, smell, and touch.

NOSE AND MEMORY

With practice most people could probably tell apart up to 10,000 different smells— odors, scents, and fragrances.

However, this depends on having a good memory as well as a sensitive nose.

SNIFF, SNIFF

The nasal chamber inside the nose makes up to 1 qt. (0.5L) of slimy mucus every day. Most we sniff in and swallow; some we blow out.

TONGUE TASKS

The tongue is the body's most flexible muscle.

It has 12 parts, or sections, of muscles inside it and goes from long and thin, poking out, to short and wide at the back of the mouth in less than one second.

In addition to taste, the tongue:

Helps in eating
- Moves food around inside the mouth so that it is all chewed well.

- Separates a smaller lump of food from the whole chewed mouthful, for swallowing.

- Licks pieces of food off the teeth and lips.

Touches the lips
- Moistens the lips to help them seal together well.

- Stops drooling.

Communicates
- Changes shape while speaking to make words sound clear.

- Helps make other sounds for communication, such as whistles, hisses, and clicks.

TONGUE TWISTER

Usually we do not have to think about talking—the words just come out of our mouth.

When we try to say a tongue twister, we realize how difficult it can be for the brain and the tongue to work together. Try these!

- Peter Piper picked a peck of pickled peppers.

- Which wristwatches are Swiss wristwatches?

- A skunk sat on a stump and thunk the stump stunk, but the stump thunk the skunk stunk.

WHERE IN THE BODY?

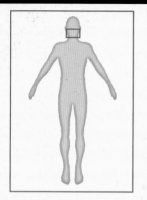

The two jawbones form the lowest parts of the face, including the chin and lower cheeks.

G ive yourself a smile in the mirror—and take a look at your teeth. Hopefully they are clean and shiny! Teeth are the hardest parts of the whole body. We use them hundreds of times each day as we bite and chew. But they are the only body parts that cannot repair themselves if they are damaged or diseased. So we must take care of them by brushing, flossing, and going for regular dental checkups.

WHAT TEETH DO

Bite small bits of large pieces of food

↓

Crush food into softer pieces

↓

Chew these into even softer, more squishy lumps

NUMBERS OF TEETH

Baby, or milk or deciduous:
8 incisors
4 canines
8 premolars
Total: 20 in full set
Baby teeth are important because they help the adult teeth grow into the correct shape.

Adult, or permanent:
8 incisors
4 canines
8 premolars
12 molars
Total: 32 in full set

• See page 60–61 for information on the stages of life.

TOOTH NAMES AND SHAPES

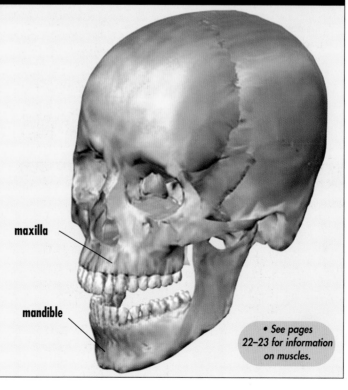

incisors
Thin and straight edged like tiny shovels, for slicing.

canines
Longer and pointed, for ripping.

premolars
Fairly wide and low, for chewing.

molars
Wide and low with lumpy surfaces, for crunching.

• See pages 24–27 for information on bones.

JAWS AND CHEWING

• The upper jawbone is called the maxilla.

• The lower jawbone is called the mandible.

• The mandible is the largest and strongest bone of the face.

• The mandible has some of the hardest, toughest bone in the body.

• One of the main chewing muscles is the temporalis, which runs from the temple (side of the head above the ear) to the lower side of the lower jaw.

• Another main chewing muscle is the masseter, which runs from the cheekbone to the lower side of the lower jaw.

maxilla

mandible

• See pages 22–23 for information on muscles.

TWO ROOFS

The roof of the mouth has two main parts.

• The front part behind the nose is called the hard palate.

• It is formed by a backward-facing, curved plate of the upper jawbone (maxilla) plus part of another skull bone behind this, the palatine.

• The rear part above the back of the mouth is the soft palate.

• This is made mainly of muscles, cartilage (gristle), and fibers.

• The palate can bend up as a lump of food is pushed to the back of the mouth for swallowing.

PARTS OF A TOOTH

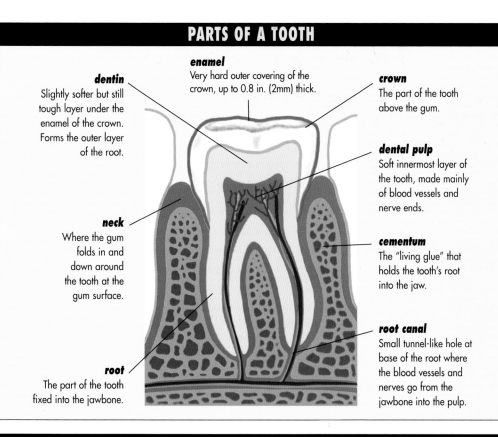

dentin
Slightly softer but still tough layer under the enamel of the crown. Forms the outer layer of the root.

enamel
Very hard outer covering of the crown, up to 0.8 in. (2mm) thick.

crown
The part of the tooth above the gum.

dental pulp
Soft innermost layer of the tooth, made mainly of blood vessels and nerve ends.

neck
Where the gum folds in and down around the tooth at the gum surface.

cementum
The "living glue" that holds the tooth's root into the jaw.

root
The part of the tooth fixed into the jawbone.

root canal
Small tunnel-like hole at base of the root where the blood vessels and nerves go from the jawbone into the pulp.

PLAQUE DANGER

- All mouths are full of bacteria, although not all bacteria are harmful.

- Without regular brushing, bacteria form on the hard enamel of the teeth.

- The bacteria multiply and form a film over the enamel. This is called plaque.

- Sugary foods help "glue" the plaque onto the tooth enamel.

- Sugar also makes the plaque produce acid, which eats into the tooth enamel.

- The acid makes tiny holes in the enamel. These get bigger and are called cavities.

- The tooth does not hurt until the acid reaches the nerves. By then the cavity is already there.

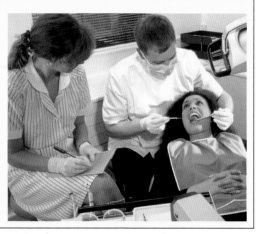

A dentist checks that your teeth are healthy and that no cavities are developing.

FALLING OUT, GROWING IN

Teeth	Time baby teeth appear (months)	Time adult teeth appear (years)
1st incisors	6–12	6–8
2nd incisors	9–15	7–9
Canines	14–20	9–12
1st premolars	15–20	10–12
2nd premolars	24–30	10–12
1st molars	–	6–7
2nd molars	–	11–13
3rd molars	–	18–21

FUNNY NAMES

- Canines are called eye teeth.

- Wisdom teeth are the rearmost molars, not appearing until a person is grown up and supposedly more experienced and wiser than a child.

- In some people the wisdom teeth never erupt, or grow, above the gum.

FACTS ABOUT SALIVA

We could not chew and swallow without saliva (spit). It would be very difficult to eat.

Chewing
- It moistens food so it is easier to chew.

- The moist food can be squashed into a lump that slips down easily when swallowed.

- Our taste sensors work less well when food is dry, so saliva gives dry food its taste.

Enzymes
- Chemicals called enzymes in saliva begin to digest the food as it is chewed, especially starchy foods like potatoes, bread, rice, and pasta.

Hygiene
- Saliva washes away small particles of food and helps keep the mouth clean.

- See page 48–49 for information on digestion.

HOW SALIVA IS MADE

Saliva is made in six salivary glands around the face.

- The parotid glands are below and to the front of each ear.

- The submandibular glands are in the angle of the lower jaw.

- The sublingual glands are in the floor of the mouth below the tongue.

- Together, the six glands make a total of about 1.6 qt. (1.5L) of saliva each day.

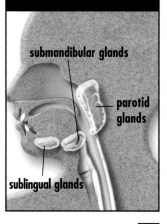

submandibular glands

parotid glands

sublingual glands

LUNGS & BREATHING

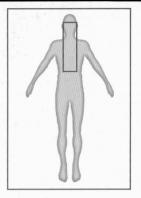

Air enters the respiratory system through the nose or mouth and travels down the windpipe (trachea) to the lungs.

Puff, pant, in, out, suck, blow . . . The body's breathing, or respiratory, system obtains the vital substance oxygen from the air around us. Oxygen is needed to take part in the body chemistry that breaks apart blood sugar (glucose), releasing its energy to power almost every body process and action. The main parts of the system are the lungs, reached by the series of airways leading down through the nose, throat, and windpipe, or trachea.

• *See pages 36–37 for information on the nose.*

SIZE AND SHAPE OF THE LUNGS

- Each lung is shaped almost like a cone.

- The upper point, or apex, reaches slightly higher than the collarbone across the top of the chest to the shoulder.

- The wide base sits on the dome-shaped main breathing muscle, the diaphragm, which is roughly level with the bottom of the breastbone but curves down to the bottom ribs around the sides.

- The left lung has two main parts, or lobes, and a scooped-out shape where the heart fits.

- The right lung has three lobes and is on average about one fifth bigger than the left lung.

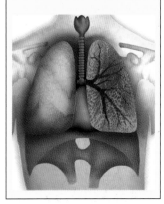

TOTAL BREATHING

- Volume of air passing through the lungs in a year: 1 million gallons (4 million liters).

- Number of breaths in a lifetime: about 500 million.

AIR SPEEDS

Air is expelled from our lungs at different rates.

Feet (meters) per second

Speed	
98 (30)	
82 (25)	
65.6 (20)	
49 (15)	
32 (10)	
16 (5)	
0	

Normal Fast Cough Sneeze

Normal breathing—
6.6 ft. (2m) per second

Fast breathing—
23 ft. (7m) per second

Cough—
65.6 ft. (20m) per second

Sneeze—
98 ft. (30m) per second

AIR AND BREATHING RATES

These are average volumes for an adult man. For women the amounts are about one fourth less.

All of the air in the lungs when fully breathed in	**6.4 qt. (6L)**
Air in the lungs left after breathing out completely	**1.3 qt. (1.2L)**
Air between breathing out normally and breathing out forcefully and completely	**1.0 qt. (1.0L)**
Air breathed in and out at rest	**0.53 qt. (0.5L)**
Extra air when breathing in very forcefully	**3.50 qt. (3.3L)**
Normal breathing rate at rest	**15 in and out per minute**
Breathing rate after great activity	**50 per minute**
Amount of air breathed in and out after great activity	**3.2 qt. (3.0L)**

- **The amount of air going into and coming out of the lungs varies from 8 qt. (7.5L) at rest to 159 qt. (150L) after great activity.**

• *See page 42 for information on the pulse rate during exercise.*

HOW AIR CHANGES

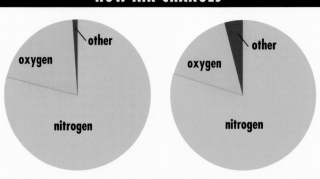

Fresh air breathed in
79% nitrogen
20% oxygen
0.03% carbon dioxide
0.97% other

Stale air breathed out
79% nitrogen
16% oxygen
4% carbon dioxide
1% other

Air passes through a series of chambers and tubes on its way deep into the lungs.

The total length of all the air tubes in the lungs joined end to end is 31 mi. (50km).

• See page 64 for information on the tonsils.

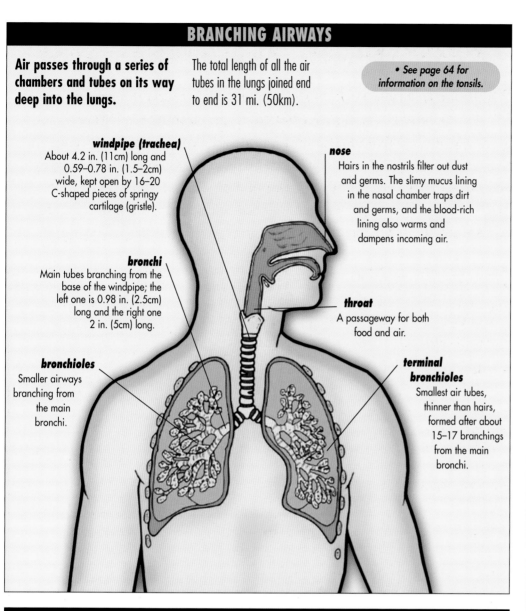

windpipe (trachea)
About 4.2 in. (11cm) long and 0.59–0.78 in. (1.5–2cm) wide, kept open by 16–20 C-shaped pieces of springy cartilage (gristle).

nose
Hairs in the nostrils filter out dust and germs. The slimy mucus lining in the nasal chamber traps dirt and germs, and the blood-rich lining also warms and dampens incoming air.

bronchi
Main tubes branching from the base of the windpipe; the left one is 0.98 in. (2.5cm) long and the right one 2 in. (5cm) long.

throat
A passageway for both food and air.

bronchioles
Smaller airways branching from the main bronchi.

terminal bronchioles
Smallest air tubes, thinner than hairs, formed after about 15–17 branchings from the main bronchi.

FAIR EXCHANGE

The places where oxygen is taken into the body are tiny bubble-shaped spaces deep in the lungs called alveoli.

• Alveoli are bunched at the end of the smallest airways, the terminal bronchioles.

• There are 250–300 million alveoli in each lung.

• Breathing not only takes in oxygen, but it also gets rid of the waste product carbon dioxide, which would soon poison the body if it collected.

Spread out flat, all of the alveoli from both lungs would cover a tennis court.

BREATHING AND SPEECH

Air passing out of the lungs has a useful extra effect—speech.

• There are nine pieces of cartilage (gristle) in the voice box, which is called the larynx.

• Front ridge of the thyroid cartilage forms the "Adam's apple," which males and females have, but which is more noticeable in males.

• About 19 muscles of the larynx alter the length of the vocal cords (vocal folds) to make the sounds of speech.

• The vocal cords are about 0.2 in. (5mm) longer in men than women, giving them a deeper voice.

• Average pitch of male vocal cords: 120 Hz (hertz, or vibrations per second).

• Average pitch of female vocal cords: 210 Hz.

• Average pitch of child's vocal cords: 260 Hz.

THE VOICE BOX

Above the voice box (larynx) is the leaf-shaped flap of epiglottis cartilage. When food is swallowed, this folds down over the entrance to the voice box to prevent food from entering the airway and causing choking.

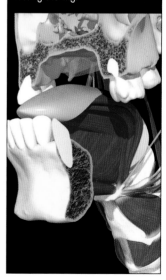

THE HEART

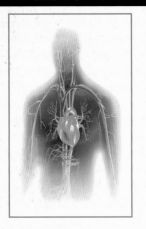

The heart is between the lungs. It tips slightly to the left side, which is why people think it is on the left side of the body.

In the center of your chest below a thin layer of skin, muscle, and bone sits your heart. This simple, yet essential, pump carries blood to and from your body's billions of cells, nonstop, day and night. During an average lifetime (70 years) the heart beats 2.5 billion times. Although your heart cannot actually control whether you will fall in love or if you are a big-hearted (kind) person, without the heart's second-by-second collection and delivery service, your cells—and your body—would die.

THE HEART'S JOB

The right and left sides of the heart work side by side like two pumps.

Every time the heart contracts, or beats, the right side pumps oxygen-poor blood back to the lungs to pick up oxygen, and the left side pumps oxygen-rich blood from the lungs out into the body.

PULSE RATE (HEARTBEATS) PER MINUTE

The number of heartbeats per minute is called the pulse rate. The resting heart rate changes throughout our lives. When we exercise, our heart needs to supply more oxygen to our bodies, so it pumps harder and faster.

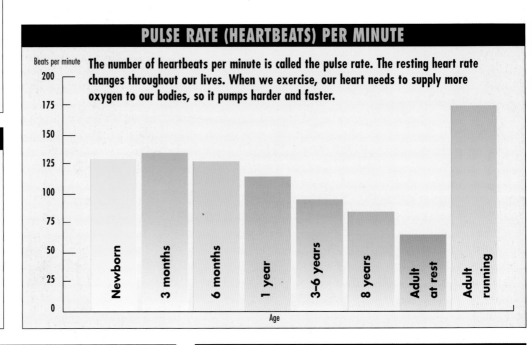

PHYSICAL CHARACTERISTICS

The heart is about the size of its owner's clenched fist. As you grow from a child into an adult, your heart grows at the same rate as your clenched fist.

Average heart weight—male **10.5 oz. (300g)**	Size: Length	**4.7 i n. (12cm)**
Average heart weight—female **8.8 oz. (250g)**	Width	**3–3.5 in. (8–9cm)**
	Front to back	**2.34 in. (6cm)**

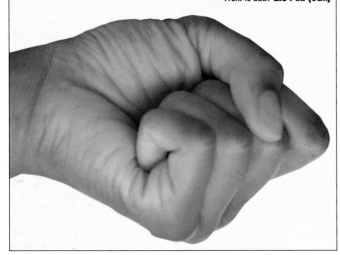

WHAT MAKES THE HEART BEAT?

At the top of the heart is a tiny area called the sinoatrial node. It sends out electrical signals that make the cells in the heart wall contract.

THE HEART'S OWN BLOOD SUPPLY

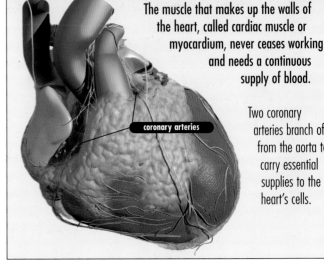

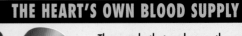
coronary arteries

The muscle that makes up the walls of the heart, called cardiac muscle or myocardium, never ceases working and needs a continuous supply of blood.

Two coronary arteries branch off from the aorta to carry essential supplies to the heart's cells.

THE HEART (VIEWED FROM THE FRONT)

superior (upper) vena cava

aorta

aortic valve

pulmonary artery

sinoatrial node

right atrium

left atrium

pulmonary veins

pulmonary valve

mitral valve

pericardium

tricuspid valve

septum

left ventricle

inferior (lower) vena cava

right ventricle

heartstrings

muscular wall of cardiac (heart) muscle

PARTS OF THE
HEART

Aorta
The largest artery in the body. It is about the diameter of a garden hose.

Atrium
One of the two small upper chambers in the heart that receives blood from the veins and passes it to the ventricles below.

Heartstrings
Cords that hold the valve in place between the atrium and the ventricle.

Inferior vena cava
A large vein that collects blood from the lower half of the body.

Pericardium
The tough outer covering of the heart.

Septum
The muscular wall that divides the left and right sides of the heart.

Superior vena cava
A large vein that collects blood from the upper half of the body.

Valve
A sort of door that opens only one way to let blood through, but stops it from flowing backward. The heart has four valves: tricuspid, pulmonary, mitral, aortic.

Ventricle
One of the two large lower chambers in the heart that receive blood from the atrium above and pass it out into the arteries.

HOW THE HEART WORKS

Dotted lines represent oxygen-poor blood

•••• 1) Blood flows in from the body to the right atrium through the superior and inferior vena cavae. It is known as oxygen-poor blood because the body has taken and used the oxygen that the blood was carrying.

•••• 2) The right atrium pumps the blood through the tricuspid valve into the right ventricle.

•••• 3) The right ventricle pumps the blood through the pulmonary valve into the pulmonary artery and out into the lungs.

Inside the lungs

4) As the blood travels through the lungs, it releases waste gases and picks up oxygen.

Dashed lines represent oxygen-rich blood

--- 5) The blood flows from the lungs into the left atrium through the pulmonary veins.

--- 6) The left atrium pumps the blood into the left ventricle.

--- 7) The left ventricle pumps the blood through the aortic valve into the aorta and then around the body.

CIRCULATORY SYSTEM

Something that circulates goes around and around, and that is exactly what happens to the blood inside your body. Pumped by your heart, your blood flows around a network of pipes and tubes called blood vessels on a nonstop, never-ending journey throughout your body. The blood vessels, together with the heart itself and the thick red liquid called blood, make up the body's circulatory system.

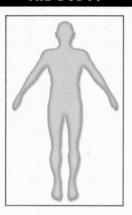

Blood vessels reach every tiny part of your body, from the top of your head to the tips of your fingers and toes.

- Some parts have much fewer blood vessels than others, such as the tough, tapering tendons at the ends of muscles, which have more than ten times fewer blood vessels than the muscle itself.

- Only a few small body parts have no blood vessels at all, for example, the lens of the eye.

DIFFERENT NAMES

The circulatory system is also called the cardiovascular system.

- "Cardio" has to do with the heart. It comes from the ancient Greek word *kardia*, which means "heart."

- "Vascular" has to do with blood vessels. It comes from the Latin word *vas*, meaning "vessel."

- The vessels leading to and from each body part are known as its vascular supply.

MAIN VEINS AND ARTERIES

Exercise pumps the blood around the body faster.

Veins
- The main vein bringing blood from the head, arms, and upper body back to the heart is called the superior vena cava.

- The main vein bringing blood from the lower body, hips, and legs back to the heart is called the inferior vena cava.

- Both of these main veins are about 1.2 in. (30mm) wide.

- Blood flows very slowly through them, at only 0.04 in. (1mm) per second.

- At any single moment these main veins contain one tenth of all the body's blood.

Arteries
- The body's main artery is the aorta, carrying blood from the left side of the heart to all body parts.

- The aorta is 15.6 in. (40cm) long and arches up, over, and down behind the heart inside the chest.

- The aorta's width is about 1 in. (25mm).

- The aorta's walls are 1.2 in. (3mm) thick.

- Blood surges through the aorta at about 11.7 in. (30cm) per second.

- *See pages 46–47 for information on blood.*

BLUE AND RED

Blood that has a lot of oxygen in it is red in color. When the body has used the oxygen, the blood becomes blue.

- Arteries carry blood from the heart, but not all of this blood is "red," or fresh and high in oxygen.

- The pulmonary arteries from the right side of the heart to the lungs carry "blue," or stale, blood low in oxygen.

- Similarly, veins carry blood to the heart, but not all of this blood is "blue," or stale and low in oxygen.

- The pulmonary veins from the lungs to the left side of the heart carry "red," or fresh, blood high in oxygen.

- *See pages 40–41 for information on the lungs.*

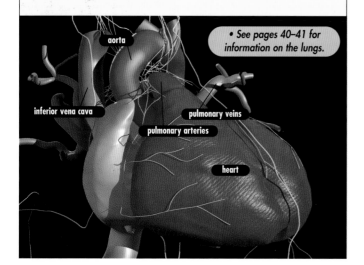

aorta

inferior vena cava

pulmonary veins

pulmonary arteries

heart

NAMING THE PARTS

Most arteries and veins are named for the body parts they supply.

cerebral vessels in the head

• See pages 30–31 for information on the brain.

• See page 48 for information on the stomach.

coronary arteries carry blood to the heart's muscular walls and are named because their branching shape looks like a crown ("corona") around the heart

hepatic artery and vein for the liver

renal artery and vein for the kidney

gastric artery and vein for the stomach

iliac artery and vein to the leg

TYPES OF BLOOD VESSELS

Arteries
- Carry blood away from the heart.
- Thick, muscular walls to cope with the surge of high pressure as blood is forced from the heart with each heartbeat.
- Take blood to the body's main parts, or organs.
- Divide and become thinner, forming arterioles.

Arterioles
- Smaller and shorter than arteries.
- Muscles in the walls can tighten to make the arterioles smaller or relax and make them wider to control the amount of blood flowing through.
- Divide and become narrower, forming capillaries.

Capillaries
- The smallest blood vessels, very short and too thin to see without a microscope.
- Walls are so thin (just one cell thick) that nutrients and useful substances can pass from the blood inside, through the walls, to cells and tissues around.
- Thin walls also allow wastes and unwanted substances to pass from cells and tissues into the blood to be taken away.
- Join together to form venules.

Venules
- Thin walled and very flexible.
- Collect blood from within each main body part.
- Join together, forming veins.

Veins
- Wide with thin, floppy walls.
- Have pocketlike valves sticking out from their walls to make sure blood flows the correct way.
- Carry blood from the main body parts back to the heart.

BLOOD VESSEL CHART

Blood vessel	Typical diameter across (in./cm)	Wall thickness (in./cm)	Typical length (in./cm)	Blood pressure inside (blood emerging from heart = max. 100)
Arteries	0.20/0.5	0.04/0.10	6/15	90
Arterioles	0.02/0.05	0.0008/0.002	0.2/0.5	60
Capillaries	0.00032/0.00081	0.00004/0.0001	0.028/0.07	30
Venules	0.0008/0.002	0.00012/0.0003	0.12/0.31	20
Veins	0.6/1.5	0.02/0.05	6/15	10

JOURNEY TIMES

The journey time from any tiny drop of blood depends on its route around the circulatory system.

- A short trip from the heart's right side to the lungs and straight back to the heart's left side can last less than ten seconds.

- A long trip from the heart's left side all the way down through the body and legs to the toes, then all the way back the heart's right side, can last more than a minute.

• See pages 42–43 for information on the heart.

LENGTH AND AREA

- If all of the body's blood vessels were taken out and joined end to end, they would stretch about 62,000 mi. (100,000km)—two and a half times around the world!

- If all of the capillaries were ironed flat, their surface area would be about half a football field.

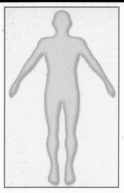

At any single moment, about one sixth of all the body's blood is in the arteries, almost three fourths is in the veins, and less than 1/20th is in the tiny capillaries inside the body parts, or organs.

HOW MUCH?

The amount of blood in the body depends mainly on body size.

- On average, blood forms 1/12th of the body's total weight. This is slightly less in women compared to men.

- Most women naturally have more fatty tissue than men, which has less blood supply compared to other body parts.

- Also most women naturally have less muscle tissue than men, which has more blood supply compared to other body parts.

- An average adult woman has 8.5–10.6 pt. (4–5L) of blood.

- An average adult man has 10.6–12.7 pt. (5–6L) of blood.

- For people of average weight and build, the volume of blood is about 1.07 fl. oz. per pound (79mL/kg) of body weight.

• See pages 22–23 for information on muscles.

Ouch, that cut hurts! And from it oozes a thick red liquid that every part of the human body needs to stay alive—blood. Pumped by the heart, it flows through tubes called blood vessels. Blood carries useful substances, such as oxygen and nutrients, to all the body parts. It also collects wastes and unwanted substances, and these are mainly removed by the kidneys. However, apart from this delivery-and-collection service, blood does much, much more.

BLOOD FLOW THROUGH BODY PARTS

In general, busier body parts need more blood supply.

- When a body part is active, changes occur in the blood vessels in order to supply it with more blood.

- The muscles in the walls of the small blood vessels, called arterioles, relax.

- This allows more blood to flow through the arterioles to the parts of the body they supply.

- The width of the arterioles is mainly controlled by signals from the brain sent along nerves.

- The hormone adrenalin also affects the width of the arterioles.

• See pages 44–45 for information on the circulatory system.

BLOOD TYPES

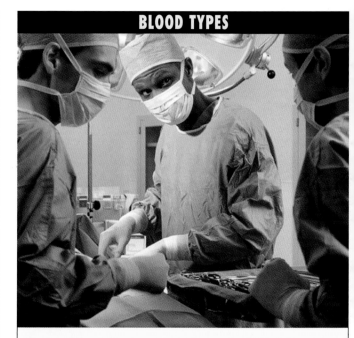

The four different blood types were discovered in 1900. Before this blood transfusions had a high rate of failure. Today we realize it is vital to know the blood types of the donor and patient so that they can be matched in order for blood to be used safely.

- Certain types, or groups of blood, when mixed together, may form clumps, or clots.

- Clots can be dangerous during a blood transfusion, when blood is given, or donated, by one person to be put into another person, the recipient.

- ABO is the system for testing blood for its group. A person can be either A, B, AB, or O.

- A person with group O is a "universal donor" whose blood can be given to almost anyone. A person with group AB is a "universal recipient" who can receive blood from almost anyone.

Blood type	Can donate blood to	Can receive blood from
A	A, AB	A, O
B	B, AB	B, O
AB	AB	A, B, AB, O
O	A, B, AB, O	O

RED BLOOD CELLS

Red blood cells carry oxygen around the body.

- Red blood cells are among the most numerous cells, with 25 trillion in an average person.

- They are also among the smallest of the cells—each one is just seven microns (0.003 in./0.008cm) across and two microns thick.

- Each red cell is shaped like a doughnut without the hole poked completely through.

- A red cell's color is due to the substance hemoglobin.

- Hemoglobin joins, or attaches, to oxygen and carries it around the body.

- Each red cell contains 250 million tiny particles, or molecules, of hemoglobin.

- Each red blood cell lives for three or four months and then dies and is broken apart.

- This means about three million red blood cells die every second—and the same number of new ones are made.

- Red blood cells, like white blood cells and platelets, are made in the jellylike marrow inside bones.

Our blood contains millions and millions of red blood cells.

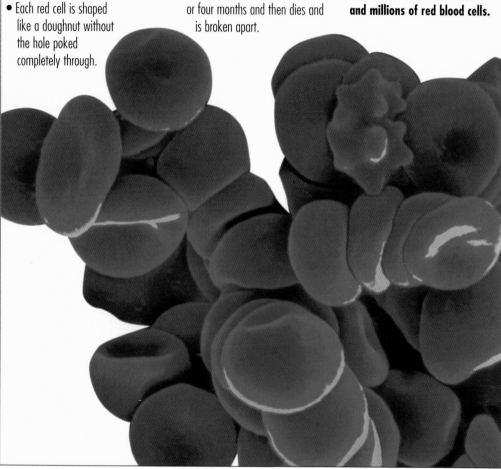

red blood cells 40–45%

other up to 5%

plasma 55%

Blood is mostly made up of plasma and red blood cells. White blood cells and platelets make up a tiny proportion of the total.

Plasma
- Forms just over one half of blood by volume.
- Pale straw color.
- Over nine tenths is water.
- Contains many dissolved substances such as blood sugar (glucose), hormones, body salts and minerals, unwanted wastes such as urea, disease-fighting antibodies, and dozens of others.

Red blood cells
- Form just under one half of blood.
- Also called erythrocytes.
- Carry life-giving oxygen from the lungs all around the body.
- Pick up waste carbon dioxide to take back to the lungs for removal.

White blood cells
- Form less than $1/100$ of blood.
- Also called leukocytes.
- Attack, disable, and kill invading germs.
- Engulf, or eat, waste bits such as pieces of old broken-down cells.

Platelets
- Form less than $1/100$ of blood.
- Also called thrombocytes.
- Are not so much whole living microscopic cells, but more parts, or fragments, of cells.
- Help blood clot (thrombose) to seal cuts and wounds.

BLOOD FLOW AT REST AND AT WORK

Part of the body	Flow in pints (pt./L) per minute	
	At rest	During hard exercise
Heart	0.53/0.25	1.6
Kidneys	2.54/1.2	1.27
Main muscles	2.12/1	25
Skin	0.85/0.4	4.24
Stomach, guts, etc.	4.16/2	1.27
Brain	1.6/0.76	1.6

Only the brain's blood flow stays the same however active the body is, from running a fast race to being fast asleep.

IN ONE DROP OF BLOOD

A pinhead-sized drop of blood contains:

- 5 million red blood cells
- 5,000 white blood cells
- 250,000 platelets

If a person is ill, the number of germ-fighting white cells in blood may rise from 5,000 to 25,000.

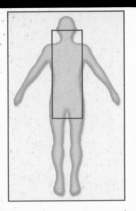

The digestive system starts at the mouth and ends at the anus. Most of its main parts, the stomach and intestines, are in the abdomen (lower half of the main body).

APPENDIX: A PUZZLING PART

The appendix is a finger-sized part of the body branching from the start of the large intestine.

- It is a dead end with its tip sealed, leading nowhere.

- It is hollow inside.

- It varies in length from 2–6 in. (5–15cm).

- It seems to have no important task in digestion (or in any other body function).

The appendix may swell up with "stuck" food and germs, causing appendicitis, with severe pain in the lower right abdomen.

DIGESTION

A car needs gas, a truck uses diesel, and a jet plane runs on kerosene. These are all fuels that provide the energy needed to make machines go. Your "body machine" needs fuel, too, and it gets it in the form of food. Food gives you the energy to move around, walk and run, and keep your inside processes, such as heartbeat and breathing, going. But food gives you more than energy. It provides nutrients for growth, making newer and bigger body parts, repairing old worn-out ones, and staying healthy, too. The parts of the body specialized for taking in and breaking down foods into tiny pieces are called the digestive system.

FOOD'S JOURNEY

Part of tract	Length in in./cm	Time spent by food
Mouth	4/10	Up to 1 minute
Throat	4/10	2–4 seconds
Gullet	10/25	2–5 seconds
Stomach	10/25	3–6 hours
Small intestine	226/574	2–4 hours
Large intestine	59/150	5–10 hours
Rectum	8/20	5–8 hours

RECYCLING

- The digestive system makes more than 21 pt. (10L) of digestive juices each day.

- Most of the water in these juices is taken back into the body by the large intestine.

- Only about 0.21 pt. (0.1L) is lost in the wastes from the system.

- The digestive system recycles $^{99}/_{100}$ of its water.

STOMACH

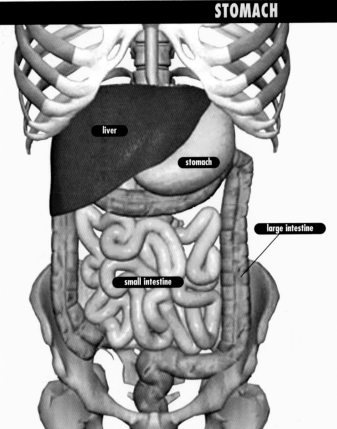

liver

stomach

large intestine

small intestine

The stomach is a J-shaped bag behind the left lower ribs.

- Measures about 12 in. (30cm) around its longer side.

- Has thick muscle layers in its walls that squirm and squeeze to mash the food inside.

- Average amount of food and drink contents is 3 pt. (1.5L).

- Lining makes about 3 pt. (1.5L) of gastric juices each day.

- Gastric juices include hydrochloric acid and digestive chemicals called enzymes — pepsin attacks proteins in food and lipase attacks fats.

- Takes in, or absorbs, few nutrients, including sugars.

- Lining also makes thick mucus to protect the stomach's gastric juices from digesting itself.

THE DIGESTIVE TRACT

The digestive system includes the digestive passageway, or tract, described here and also parts that work along with this, including the liver and pancreas. The digestive tract is the "tube," or passageway, for food.

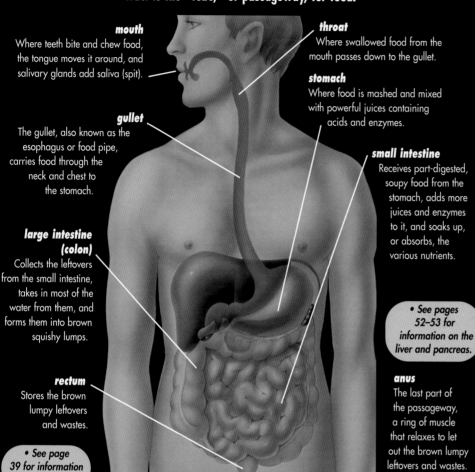

mouth
Where teeth bite and chew food, the tongue moves it around, and salivary glands add saliva (spit).

gullet
The gullet, also known as the esophagus or food pipe, carries food through the neck and chest to the stomach.

large intestine (colon)
Collects the leftovers from the small intestine, takes in most of the water from them, and forms them into brown squishy lumps.

rectum
Stores the brown lumpy leftovers and wastes.

• See page 39 for information on saliva.

throat
Where swallowed food from the mouth passes down to the gullet.

stomach
Where food is mashed and mixed with powerful juices containing acids and enzymes.

small intestine
Receives part-digested, soupy food from the stomach, adds more juices and enzymes to it, and soaks up, or absorbs, the various nutrients.

• See pages 52–53 for information on the liver and pancreas.

anus
The last part of the passageway, a ring of muscle that relaxes to let out the brown lumpy leftovers and wastes.

SMALL INTESTINE

- Average width 1.2–1.6 in. (3–4cm).

- Has three main parts: duodenum (10 in./25cm), jejunum (88 in./224cm), and ileum (117 in./297cm).

- Receives digestive juices from the pancreas and liver.

- Inner surface has many folds called plicae.

- On these folds are tiny fingerlike shapes, villi, about 0.04 in. (1mm) long.

- All of the villi joined end to end would stretch 248 mi. (400km).

- On each villus are even more microscopic fingerlike shapes called microvilli.

- Plicae, villi, and microvilli increase the surface area of the inside of the small intestine to about 6–12 sq. yd. (5–10m2) to absorb as many nutrients as possible from food.

There are about 500 million villi in the body.

PUSHING FOOD

- Without food inside, most of the digestive passageway would be squeezed flat by the natural pressure of parts, or organs, inside the body.

- Food has to be pushed through the passageway by waves of muscle action in its walls, called peristalsis.

In the gullet, peristalsis is so strong it works even if the body is upside down.

LEFTOVERS

- The average weight of waste (bowel movements, or feces) is 5.25 oz. (150g) per day.

- The weight varies greatly, increasing with the amount of fiber in food.

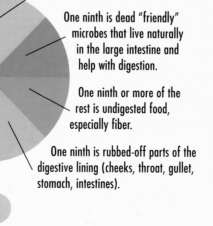

Two thirds water, about 3.5 oz. (100g).

One ninth is dead "friendly" microbes that live naturally in the large intestine and help with digestion.

One ninth or more of the rest is undigested food, especially fiber.

One ninth is rubbed-off parts of the digestive lining (cheeks, throat, gullet, stomach, intestines).

• See page 51 for information on fiber.

LARGE INTESTINE

- Average width 2–3 in. (6–7cm).

- Mainly takes back water and valuable body salts and minerals from leftover foods and wastes.

- First part, the cecum, is wider and has the appendix branching out from it.

- Second part is the ascending colon, going up the right side of the abdomen.

- Third part is the transverse colon, across the top of the abdomen.

- Fourth part is the sigmoid (S-shaped) colon, on the lower left of the abdomen.

Food can be divided into groups. This can help us plan a balanced diet.

Yellow: meat and fish
Green: cereals and grains
Red: fruit and vegetables
Blue: dairy products
Orange: sugary foods

We should eat foods from each of these groups in order to stay healthy. We should choose more grains, fruit, and vegetables and eat less sugary food.

MINERAL CHART

Iron
Needed for: red blood cells, skin, muscles, resisting stress, fighting disease.

Calcium
Needed for: bones, teeth, nerves, heartbeat, blood clotting, kidneys.

Sodium
Needed for: nerves and nerve signals, digestion, blood, chemical processes inside cells, kidneys.

Magnesium
Needed for: heartbeat and rhythm, energy use.

Iodine
Needed for: overall speed of the body's chemical processes, making thyroid hormones.

Zinc
Needed for: a healthy immune system, wound healing, maintaining senses of smell and taste.

Have you had plenty of lipids, complex carbohydrates, trace metallic elements, and cellulose today? These names may not be familiar, but they are all substances that your body needs to stay healthy. Usually we call these substances, and everything else the body needs to take in every day, by a simpler name—food. However, in your food there are six main groups of substances that you may have already heard about. They are proteins, carbohydrates, fats, vitamins, minerals, and fiber.

DAILY NEEDS

For an average adult with a typical job (not too inactive, nor overactive), the daily needs are:

Carbohydrates   10.5 oz. (300g)
(including 0.88 oz. (25g) or more of fiber)

Proteins   1.8 oz. (50g)

Fats   2.1 oz. (60g)
(mostly from plant sources)

Vitamins, examples:
Vitamin C 0.002 oz. (0.06g)
Vitamin K 0.000003 oz.
        (0.00008g)

Minerals, examples:
Calcium   0.04 oz. (1g)
Iron   0.00063 oz. (0.018g)
Chloride   0.12 oz. (3.4g)

CARBOHYDRATES

Carbohydrates are energy foods.

- Broken down by digestion into smaller, simpler pieces such as sugars.

- Taken in and used as the body's main source of energy, called glucose, or blood sugar, for the life processes of all of its microscopic cells.

- Also used for all muscle movements, from heartbeat and breathing to fast running.

- Foods with plenty of carbohydrates are starchy or sweet, such as rice, wheat, barley, and other cereals or grains; products made from these include pasta and bread; "starchy" vegetables include potatoes, turnips, and corn as well as many sweet fruit such as bananas and strawberries; sugary items include candy and chocolate.

Bread is made from wheat, a good source of carbohydrates.

FATS AND OILS

Fats are used for both building and energy.

- Broken down by digestion into smaller, simpler pieces called lipids.

- Foods with plenty of fats include red meats, oily fish, eggs, milk, and cheese, and other dairy products.

- Some plant foods also contain fats, such as avocados, olives, peanuts, and soybeans.

- Taken in and used for building parts, such as nerves, for making and repairing parts of microscopic cells, and for energy if carbohydrates are lacking.

- Too much fat from animal sources (fatty red meats and processed foods such as burgers and salami) is linked to various health problems such as heart disease and high blood pressure.

Fat is an important part of our diet, but we should get most of what we need from plant sources such as olive oil.

PROTEINS

Foods rich in protein are sometimes called "building foods," as they help build our body parts.

- Broken down by digestion into smaller, simpler pieces called amino acids.

- Amino acids are taken in and built back up into the body's own proteins that make up the main structure of muscles, bones, skin, and most of the other body parts.

- Foods with plenty of protein include all types of meats, poultry such as chicken, fish, eggs, dairy products such as milk and cheese, and some plant foods such as soybeans, nuts, and other beans and peas.

Dairy products, such as butter and sour cream, are a good source of protein.

FIBER

Fiber is needed to help food pass properly through the body.

- Sometimes called roughage.
- Is not really broken down or digested by the body, but passes through the digestive tract largely unaltered.
- Needed to give food "bulk" so that the intestines can grip it and make it move through them.
- Helps satisfy hunger, reducing the temptation to eat too much.
- Reduces the risk of wastes being too small and hard and getting "stuck," called constipation.

- Also reduces the risk of various intestinal diseases, including certain kinds of colon cancer.

Fresh fruit and vegetables are a good source of fiber, particularly if the skins are eaten.

FIVE-A-DAY GUIDE

"Five a day" means five helpings, portions, or servings of fresh fruit or vegetables each day.

This should provide the body with enough of all of the vitamins and minerals, as well as some energy and plenty of fiber.

VITAMINS

- Needed for various body processes to work, stay healthy, and ward off disease.

- Most are needed in small amounts, fractions of an ounce per day.

- Have chemical names and also letters such as A, B, and so on.

- The body can store some vitamins but needs regular supplies of others.

- Eating a wide range of foods, especially fresh fruit and vegetables, should provide all of the body's needs.

Snacking on fresh fruit and vegetables helps meet your body's vitamin requirements.

MINERALS

- Needed for various body processes to work, stay healthy, and ward off disease.

- Most are needed in small amounts, fractions of an ounce per day.

- Most are simple chemical substances — metal elements — such as iron, calcium, and sodium.

- The body can store some minerals but needs regular supplies of others.

- Eating a wide range of foods, especially fresh fruit and vegetables, should provide all the body's needs.

VITAMIN CHART

Vitamin A
Chemical name: carotene

Needed for: eyes, skin, teeth, bones, general health.

Vitamin B1
Chemical name: thiamine

Needed for: brain, nerves, muscles, heart, energy use, general health.

Vitamin B2
Chemical name: riboflavin

Needed for: blood, eyes, skin, hair, nails, fighting disease, general health.

Vitamin B3
Chemical name: niacin acid

Needed for: energy use, controlling blood contents.

Vitamin B6
Chemical name: pyridoxine

Needed for: chemical processes inside cells, brain, skin, muscles, energy use, general health.

Vitamin B12
Chemical name: cobalamin

Needed for: blood, brain, nerves, growing, energy use, general health.

Vitamin B9
Chemical name: folic acid

Needed for: blood, digestion, growth.

Vitamin C
Chemical name: ascorbic acid

Needed for: teeth, gums, bones, blood, fighting disease, skin, general health.

Vitamin D
Chemical name: calciferol

Needed for: bones, teeth, nerves, heart, general health.

Vitamin E
Chemical name: tocopherol

Needed for: blood, cell processes, muscles, nerves, general health.

Vitamin K
Chemical name: phylloquinone

Needed for: blood clotting, general health.

LIVER & PANCREAS

Your body cannot digest food with just its digestive tract (passageway), which is made up of the mouth, gullet, stomach, and intestines. The liver and pancreas are also needed. These organs are next to the stomach, and they are digestive glands, which means they make powerful substances that break down the food in the intestines. Together with the digestive tract, the liver and pancreas make up the whole digestive system.

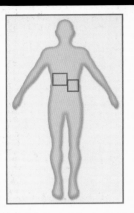

The liver is in the upper abdomen, behind the lower right ribs. The pancreas is in the upper left abdomen, behind the stomach.

WARM LIVER

The liver is so busy with chemical processes and tasks that it makes lots of heat.

- When the body is at rest and the muscles are still, the liver makes up to one fifth of the body's total warmth.

- The heat from the liver is not wasted. The blood spreads out the heat all around the body.

See pages 44–45 for information on the circulatory system.

GALLBLADDER AND BILE

liver

pancreas

gallbladder

THE LIVER'S TASKS

The liver has more than 500 known tasks in the body — and probably more that have not yet been discovered. Some of the main ones are:

- Breaking down nutrients and other substances from digestion, brought directly to the liver from the small intestine.

- Storing vitamins for times when they may be lacking in food.

- Making bile, a digestive juice.

- Breaking apart old, dead, worn-out red blood cells.

- Breaking down toxins or possibly harmful substances, such as alcohol and poisons.

- Helping control the amount of water in blood and body tissues.

Alcohol is a toxin that the liver breaks down and makes harmless. However, too much alcohol can overload the liver and cause a serious disease called cirrhosis.

- If levels of blood sugar (glucose) are too high, hormones from the pancreas tell the liver to change the glucose into glycogen and store it.

- If levels of blood sugar (glucose) are too low, hormones from the pancreas tell the liver to release the glycogen it has stored.

The gallbladder is a small storage bag under the liver.

- It is 3 in. (8cm) long and 1 in. (3cm) wide.

- Some of the bile fluid made in the liver is stored in the gallbladder.

- The gallbladder can hold up to 1.5 fl. oz. (50mL) of bile.

- After a meal, bile pours from the liver along the main bile duct (tube), and from the gallbladder along the cystic duct, into the small intestine.

- Bile helps break apart, or digest, the fats and oils in foods.

- The liver makes up to 2 pt. (1L) of bile each day.

HOW THE PANCREAS WORKS

Fatty foods, such as French fries, are broken apart by enzymes made in the pancreas.

- The pancreas has two main jobs. One is to make hormones; the other is to make digestive chemicals called pancreatic juices.

- These juices contain about 15 powerful enzymes that break apart many substances in foods, including proteins, carbohydrates, and fats.

- The pancreas makes about 3.2 pt. (1.5L) of digestive juices daily.

- During a meal, these pass along the pancreatic duct tubes into the small intestine to attack and digest foods there.

• See pages 62–63 for information on hormones.

WHEN THINGS GO WRONG

A yellowish tinge to the skin and eyes is known as jaundice, and it is often a sign of liver trouble.

Usually the liver breaks down old red blood cells and gets rid of the coloring substance in bile fluid. If something goes wrong, the coloring substance builds up in the blood and skin, causing jaundice. Hepatitis, an infection of the liver, can cause jaundice.

UNUSUAL SUPPLY

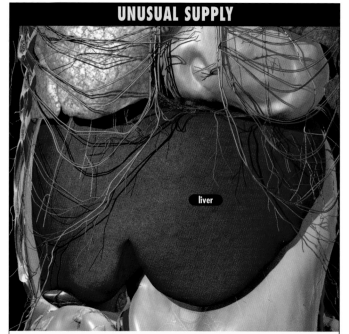

One of the liver's main functions is to break down nutrients for the body. This means the liver has a unique blood supply.

- Most body parts are supplied with blood flowing along one or a few main arteries.

- The liver has a main artery, the hepatic artery.

- The liver also has a second, much greater blood supply. This comes along a vessel called the hepatic portal vein.

- The hepatic portal vein is the only main vein that does not take blood straight back to the heart.

- This vein runs from the intestines to the liver, bringing blood full of nutrients from digestion.

• See pages 46–47 for information on blood.

BABY LIVER

Most babies and young children have big abdomens (stomachs). This is partly because their liver is much larger in proportion to their body's overall size when compared to the liver of an adult.

- An adult's liver is usually $\frac{1}{40}$ of their body weight.

- A baby's liver is closer to $\frac{1}{20}$ of their body weight.

By the time a baby becomes a toddler, their liver is not such a large proportion of the total body weight.

WHAT IS THE LIVER?

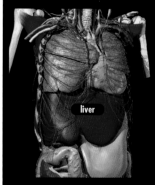

The liver is the largest single part, or organ, inside the body.

- Wedge shaped, dark red in color.
- Typical weight 3.3 lbs. (1.5kg).
- Depth at widest part on right side 6 in. (15cm).
- Has a larger right lobe and a smaller left lobe.
- Lobes separated by a strong layer, the falciform ligament.

WHAT IS THE PANCREAS?

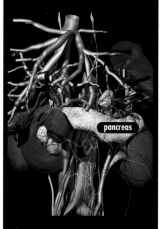

The pancreas is a long, slim wedge- or triangular-shaped part.

- It is soft and grayish pink in color.
- Typical weight 0.21 lbs. (0.1kg).
- Typical length 6 in. (15cm).
- Has three main parts: head (wide end), body (middle), and tail (tapering end).

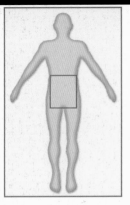

MAIN PARTS OF THE KIDNEYS

Cortex
Outer layer, formed mainly of microscopic blood vessels from the filtering units, or nephrons.

Medulla
Inner layer, formed mainly from the tiny tubes of the filtering units, or nephrons.

Renal pelvis
Space in the middle of the kidney where urine collects.

KIDNEYS & URINARY SYSTEM

You are a bit of a waste—that is, your body makes wastes and unwanted substances, which it must remove. Some of these wastes come out of the end of the digestive tube and are often called solid waste. The other main kind is liquid waste, sometimes called "water," but with the proper name of urine. This is very different from solid waste. It is not made from digestive leftovers, but by filtering the blood.

• See pages 48–49 for information on digestion.

KIDNEYS—SIZE AND SHAPE

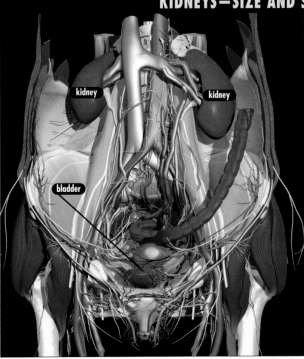

- The right kidney is usually about 0.30–0.59 in. (1–1.5cm) lower than the left one.

- Each kidney is shaped like a bean, with a slight hollow, or indent, on one side.

- Average kidney measurements are 4 in. (11cm) high, 2 in. (6cm) wide, and 1 in. (3cm) from front to back.

- In a woman, the typical weight of the kidneys is 4.6–5 oz. (130–140g).

- In a man, the typical weight is 5–5.3 oz. (140–150g).

The kidneys' huge blood supply can be seen by the size of the renal arteries (red) and veins (blue). The pale ureter tubes lead down to the bladder.

KIDNEY MICROFILTERS

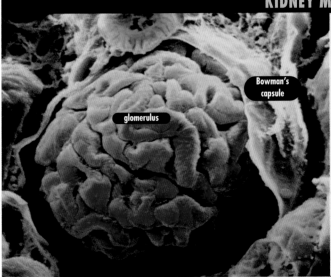

Each kidney contains about one million microscopic filters called nephrons.

- Each nephron begins with a tiny tangle, or knot, of the smallest blood vessels—capillaries—known as the glomerulus.

- Waste substances and water squeeze out of the glomerulus into a cup-shaped part around it called the Bowman's capsule.

It is in the nephrons that the work of the kidney takes place.

- The wastes and water then flow through a microscopic tube, the renal tubule, where some water, minerals, and salts are taken back into the blood.

- All of the tiny tubules of all of the nephrons in one kidney, straightened out and joined end to end, would stretch 62 mi. (100km).

- The end result is urine, which is mostly water that contains dissolved wastes such as urea and ammonia.

BLADDER—THE NEED TO GO

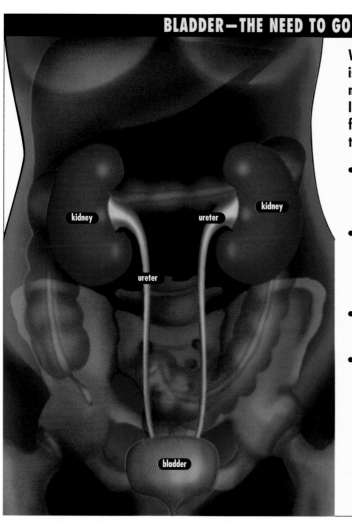

kidney

kidney

ureter

ureter

bladder

When empty, the bladder is pear shaped and not much bigger than a thumb. It gradually stretches and fills with urine until you feel the need to empty it.

- We can tell how much urine is inside the bladder by how much we need to urinate.

- 8–9 fl. oz. (250–300mL) of urine (about the amount in a coffee mug)—slight urge to urinate.

- 12–15 fl. oz. (400–500mL)— stronger urge to urinate.

- 15–18 fl. oz. (500–600mL)— desperate urge to urinate.

Bacteria can infect the bladder, causing cystitis. Symptoms include a burning sensation during urination and an urgent need to empty the bladder, although little urine comes out.

BLOOD TO URINE

The kidneys receive more blood for their size than any other body part.

Amount of blood
- Each minute at rest, the kidneys receive 2.5 pt. (1.2L) of blood.

- This is about one fifth of all of the blood pumped by the heart.

Quick flow
- This blood flows quickly through the kidneys, so they do not actually contain one fifth of all of the body's blood.

- Over 24 hours all of the blood in the body passes through the kidneys more than 300 times.

Amount of urine
- On an average day, about 3 pt. (1.5L) of urine is filtered from the bladder.

Variation of amount
- However, the amount of urine varies according to how much water is taken into the body in foods and drinks.

- The amount of urine also varies according to how much water is lost in hot conditions as sweat.

Hot and cold
- On a hot day with few drinks, urine volume may be less than 2 pt. (1L).

- On a cold day with many drinks, urine volume may be more than 11 pt. (5L).

• See pages 44–45 for information on the circulatory system.

FEMALE AND MALE

- The urethra, which takes urine from the bladder to the outside, is different in females and males. This is because, in males, the urethra forms part of the reproductive system as well as the urinary system.

- In females, the urethra is 1.5 in. (4cm) long and 0.24 in. (6mm) across.

- In males, it is 7 in. (18cm) long and runs along the inside of the penis.

Men and women have different systems for taking urine to the outside of the body.

• See pages 58–59 for information on the reproductive system.

MAIN URINARY PARTS

Kidneys
Filter the blood to make waste liquid, known as urine.

Ureters
Tubes about 10–12 in. (25–30cm) long that carry urine from the kidneys to the bladder.

Bladder
Properly called the urinary bladder, it stores urine until it is "convenient" to get rid of it.

Urethra
Tube that carries urine from the bladder to the outside.

MEAT EATER

When you eat lots of meat, your urine gets darker. This is because your body makes urea, which gives urine its color, from proteins.

• See page 51 for information on proteins.

WHERE IN THE BODY?

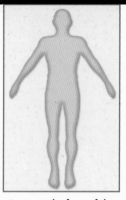

Genes, in the form of the chemical DNA, are present in almost all of the microscopic cells in the body. Only a few cell types, like red blood cells, lack them.

Most children look like their parents—and this is because of genetics. Genes are instructions for how a human body grows, develops, maintains and repairs itself, and usually keeps itself healthy. Genes are passed on from parents and inherited by their children. The instructions for building a mechanical machine are usually written down and drawn as diagrams. The genetic instructions for building and running the "human machine" are in the form of a chemical substance called DNA.

DNA

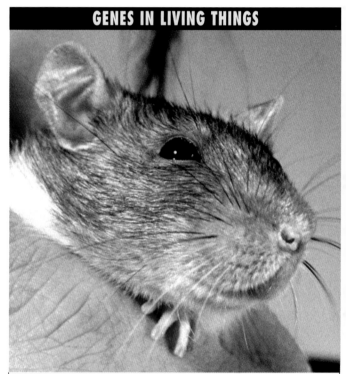

DNA is deoxyribonucleic acid. It is a chemical substance shaped like two ladders held together and twisted like a corkscrew. This is called a double helix.

- DNA contains four kinds of chemical subunits called bases: adenine (A), thymine (T), guanine (G), and cytosine (C).

- Like words in a sentence, these bases are in a certain order along DNA.

- The order of the bases is a code, the genetic code, that carries the genetic instructions.

- In a full set of DNA, there are over three billion sets of bases.

- This full set of DNA that contains all of the genes for the human body is called the human genome.

CHROMOSOMES

- There are 46 lengths of DNA in each cell in the body, in the cell's control center, or nucleus.

- Each length is tightly wound, or coiled, into a shorter, thicker item called a chromosome.

- The chromosomes are not all different; they are in 23 pairs.

- One chromosome from each pair comes from the mother and one from the father.

- Each time a cell divides as part of growth and normal body maintenance, all of the chromosomes are copied.

- Each of the two resulting cells has the complete set of 23 pairs.

- All 46 pieces of DNA in the chromosomes from a single cell, straightened out and joined together, would stretch almost 6.6 ft. (2m) in length.

- If the same was done to all of the DNA in the body, it would stretch from Earth to the Sun — and back — 100 times!

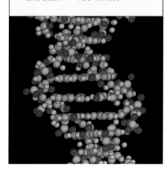

GENES IN LIVING THINGS

The genes that make a mouse are almost the same as those that make a person. Out of every 100 genes, a mouse has 92 that are the same as ours.

All humans have the same overall set of genes. Tiny differences, in less than one out of 500 genes, make each of us unique.

- The exact number of genes that humans have is still disputed.

- Scientists think people have somewhere between 30,000 and 35,000 genes.

- Almost all other living things have genes like humans that are formed of DNA.

- Often the same genes doing the same jobs occur in very different kinds of living things.

- The more similar living things are to humans, the more similar the sets of genes are.

- A chimp has 98 out of every 100 genes the same as ours.

- A fruit fly has 44 out of every 100 genes the same as ours.

- A tiny fungus (mold) called yeast has 26 out of every 100 genes the same as ours.

STRONG AND WEAK GENES

In any family the children usually look like at least one of their parents. Sometimes children look more like their grandparents, because some characteristics do not show up in every generation.

- Each gene can exist in several forms, or versions, called alleles.

- The blue allele for the eye-color gene tells the body how to make a blue coloring substance for the iris.

- The brown allele for the eye-color gene tells the body how to make a brown coloring substance for the iris.

- As mentioned before, each person has two copies of a gene, one inherited from the mother and one from the father.

- A person with two alleles for brown eyes has brown eyes.

- A person with two alleles for blue eyes has blue eyes.

- If a person has one allele for blue eyes and one for brown, the brown is stronger, or dominant, while the blue is weaker, or recessive, and the person has brown eyes.

- Many genes work in this way, with different alleles that are dominant or recessive when put together.

- See page 59 for information on making eggs and sperm.

A gene is a portion of DNA that contains the chemical code for making a part of the body or instructing how that part works.

For example, the gene for eye color tells the body how to make the colored substance, or pigment, for the colored part of the eye called the iris.

Number
- The human body has a total of about 30,000 genes.

- Sometimes several genes work together to control one feature.

Instructions for appearance
Genes instruct for skin color, hair color and type, overall adult height, earlobe shape, and many other features of the body.

Instructions for processes
Genes also control how the body's chemical processes, such as digesting food, work inside the body.

WHAT ARE CLONES?

Usually each person has a unique selection of genes possessed by no one else.

The exception is identical twins, who have exactly the same genes.

Animals with exactly the same genes are called clones.

Dolly the sheep is the most famous clone. Scientists took genes from an adult sheep and used them to create an identical copy—Dolly.

GENETIC FINGERPRINTING

The DNA from skin, hair, and blood can help the police in their inquiries. Genetic information can eliminate a suspect or help the police secure a conviction.

Police procedures have been revolutionized since reliable DNA fingerprinting became available.

- Small pieces of DNA—for example, from the white blood cells in a tiny speck of blood—can be copied millions of times.

- This is done by a laboratory process called PCR, polymerase chain reaction.

- PCR gives enough DNA for testers to look at various sets, or sequences, of genes.

- The main testing method is called gel electrophoresis.

- The results are flat layers of a jellylike substance containing dark stripes, or bands, like a supermarket bar code.

- The sequence of bands gives a genetic fingerprint.

- If two samples of DNA match exactly, the chances are millions to one that they came from the same body.

REPRODUCTION

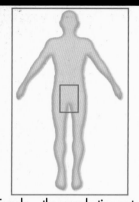

Female — the reproductive parts, or sex organs, are near the base of the lower body (abdomen).

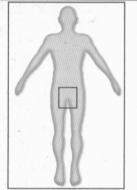

Male — the reproductive parts, or sex organs, are mostly below the abdomen, between the legs.

One of the main features of life is that all living things make more of their type through breeding, or reproduction. This happens in humans, too. The process of reproduction occurs in the same basic way in the human body as it does in other animals such as cats, mice, and whales. When a female and a male get together, the male's sperm fertilizes the female's egg. A tiny embryo then begins to grow inside the female. The body parts that do this are called the sexual, or reproductive, system.

FEMALE PARTS

Ovaries
Every 28 days or so one egg cell is released as a ripe egg, or ovum.

Oviducts
Also called fallopian tubes or egg tubes. These carry the ripe egg toward the womb.

Womb (uterus)
Where the new baby grows and develops from a fertilized egg during pregnancy.

Cervix
This is the neck of the womb. It stays closed during pregnancy, then opens at birth to allow the baby to be born.

Vagina (birth canal)
At birth the new baby passes along this from the womb to the outside world.

EGG CELLS

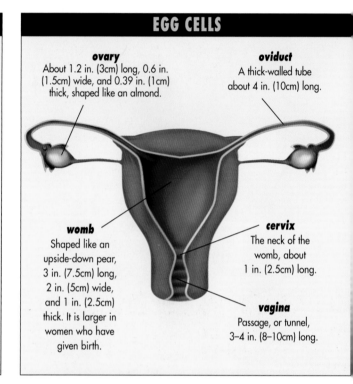

ovary
About 1.2 in. (3cm) long, 0.6 in. (1.5cm) wide, and 0.39 in. (1cm) thick, shaped like an almond.

oviduct
A thick-walled tube about 4 in. (10cm) long.

womb
Shaped like an upside-down pear, 3 in. (7.5cm) long, 2 in. (5cm) wide, and 1 in. (2.5cm) thick. It is larger in women who have given birth.

cervix
The neck of the womb, about 1 in. (2.5cm) long.

vagina
Passage, or tunnel, 3–4 in. (8–10cm) long.

EGG-RELEASE CYCLE

day 1
start of period

day 17–20
fertilized egg implants into lining of womb

day 14
egg released into oviduct

day 14–16
egg fertilized by sperm

The menstrual cycle lasts about 28 days. The cycle first begins when a girl is between 10–14 years old.

• Once every 28 days or so an egg cell ripens and is released from its ovary into the oviduct. This process is called ovulation.

• Before ovulation occurs the womb lining has become thick and rich with blood, ready to nourish the egg cell if it joins with a sperm cell and begins to develop into a baby.

• If the sperm cell does not join with the egg cell, the womb lining breaks down and is lost through the vagina as menstrual bleeding (a period). Then the whole process of egg ripening and womb changes begins again.

• This process is called the menstrual cycle and lasts about 28 days.

• This cycle is mainly controlled by sex hormones called estrogen and progesterone.

• See pages 60–61 for information on the stages of life.

• See pages 62–63 for information on hormones.

SPERM-PRODUCING CELLS

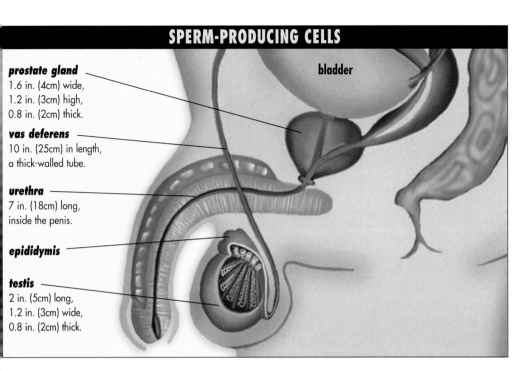

prostate gland
1.6 in. (4cm) wide,
1.2 in. (3cm) high,
0.8 in. (2cm) thick.

vas deferens
10 in. (25cm) in length,
a thick-walled tube.

urethra
7 in. (18cm) long,
inside the penis.

epididymis

testis
2 in. (5cm) long,
1.2 in. (3cm) wide,
0.8 in. (2cm) thick.

bladder

MALE PARTS

Penis
Contains the urethra tube along which sperm pass as they leave the body in a process called ejaculation.

Testes
Make millions of microscopic sperm cells every day.

Vas deferens
Also known as the ductus deferens or sperm tubes. Carry sperm cells from the testes and epididymis.

Epididymis
Stores sperm cells until they are released.

Scrotum
Bag of skin containing the testes and epididymis.

Prostate gland
Makes nourishing fluid for the sperm cells.

MAKING EGGS AND SPERM

When the body makes eggs or sperm, cells are copied in a unique way.

- Ordinary body cells divide in half to form more cells for growth, body maintenance, and repair.

- During this process all of the genes in all of the 23 pairs of chromosomes are copied, so each resulting cell receives a full set of 23 pairs. This type of cell division is called mitosis.

- Egg and sperm cells are made by a different type of cell division called meiosis.

- In meiosis the genes are not copied.

- Each egg or sperm receives just one of each pair of chromosomes, making 23 instead of 46.

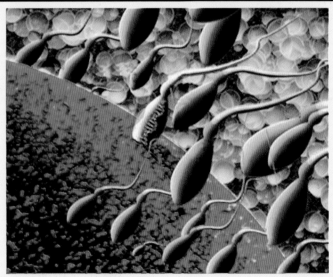

- When an egg joins with a sperm to create a new baby, the two sets of 23 chromosomes come together to form 23 pairs, which is back to the normal number.

Genes are carried by sperm and eggs. Each carries half of the genetic material needed to form a new baby. When they meet, the halves join together to make a new individual.

• See pages 56–57 for information on genetics.

Egg cells are about 0.004 in. (0.1mm) across, almost microscopic.

- At birth a new baby girl has 500,000 unripe egg cells in her ovaries. The number decreases as she gets older.

- By the time a girl has grown up and is ready to have children, the number of egg cells in her body is about 200,000.

- Over the years when she can have children, a woman's ovaries release about 400 egg cells.

MALE **SPERM**

Sperm are shaped like tiny tadpoles, with a rounded head and long whiplike tail.

- Among the smallest cells in the body, just 0.002 in. (0.05mm) in total length.

- Tens of millions are made every day in a massive tangle of tubes in the testes called seminiferous tubules.

- All of the tubules from one testis straightened out and joined end to end would stretch over 328 ft. (100m).

- Each sperm cell takes about two months to form.

- Sperm are then stored in the epididymis, which is folded and coiled next to the testes.

- Opened out straight, the epididymis would stretch 20 ft. (6m).

- When sperm are released, about 200–500 million pass in fluid along the vas deferens and urethra and out the end of the penis.

- If they are not released, sperm break down, and their parts are recycled within the body.

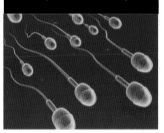

STAGES OF LIFE

In the beginning, every human being is a tiny speck smaller than the dot on this "i"—a fertilized egg cell. By the process of cell division (splitting), that single cell becomes two, four, eight, and so on. About 20 years later, by the time of adulthood, the body has 50 trillion cells of more than 200 different types. It is a fascinating story of amazing growth and development. At which stage are you?

GROWTH RATES

Growth is fastest during the early weeks in the womb and slows down toward birth.

- Speeds up slightly in first 2–3 years after birth.
- Slows down toward end of childhood.
- Sudden spurt during puberty, usually the early teens.
- Slows down toward late teens.
- Full height usually by 20 years of age.

IN THE WOMB: WEEK ONE

An egg cell is fertilized by a sperm cell, usually in the oviduct (fallopian tube) of the mother. The genes of egg and sperm (in the form of DNA) come together, and the genetic blueprint for a new body is formed.

24—36 hours
Fertilized egg cell splits into two smaller cells.

36—48 hours
Each of the two cells divides, forming four cells.

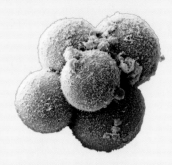

2—3 days
Cell division continues, forming a tiny ball of more than 20 cells moving slowly along the oviduct.

4 days
The ball of more than 100 cells, called a morula, reaches the inside of the womb.

5 days
The ball of hundreds of cells becomes hollow inside, called a blastocyst (early embryo).

6—7 days

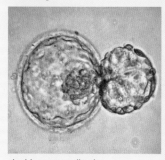

The blastocyst, still only 0.004–0.008 in. (0.1–0.2mm) across, settles, or implants, into the blood-rich lining of the womb.

The cells now take in nourishment from the lining and enlarge between divisions, so the early embryo starts to grow.

IN THE WOMB: EMBRYO

For the first eight weeks after fertilization the developing baby is called an embryo.

Week 2
The embryo becomes the shape of a flat disk, surrounded by fluid, within the womb lining. The disk lengthens and curls over at the edges.

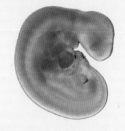

Week 3
The curled-over disk becomes longer and larger at one end, which begins to take the shape of the head and brain. Length 0.06 in. (1.5mm).

Week 4

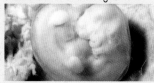

The embryo becomes C shaped. Simple tubes start to make the heart, and it begins pulsating. Arms and legs begin as small bulges on the body. Length 0.2 in (5mm).

Week 5
Head and brain grow rapidly. Inner organs such as the stomach and kidneys form. Nose begins to take shape. "Tail" is still present. Length 0.32 in. (8mm).

Week 6

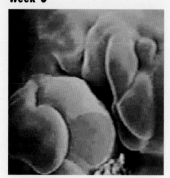

Heart and lungs are almost formed. Body becomes straighter. Eyes and ears are now obvious. Length 0.48 in. (12mm).

Week 7
Fingers and toes start to take shape. Neck becomes more visible. Tail shrinks. Length 0.6 in. (15mm).

This picture shows the embryo floating in its amniotic sac of fluid.

Week 8
Muscles and eyelids form. Tail has almost disappeared. All main body parts are present, even eyelids. Length 0.68 in. (17mm), about the size of a grape.

IN THE WOMB: FETUS

For the period between eight weeks (two months) after fertilization and birth the developing baby is called a fetus.

Month 3
Finishing touches are made, including folds for fingernails and toenails. Eyelids joined. Head still very large compared to body. Length 1.6 in. (40mm).

Month 4
Face looks much more human, first hair grows on head. First bones begin to harden. Length 2.2 in. (55mm).

Month 5
Reproductive parts begin to take shape, showing if the fetus is a girl or boy. Length 6 in. (150mm).

Month 6
Body becomes slimmer and is covered with fine hair, lanugo. Fetus can suck thumb, move arms, and kick legs; mother feels these movements.

Month 7
Body is lean and wrinkled. Fetus can swallow, eyes can detect light.

Month 8
Body puts on fat, becoming chubby.

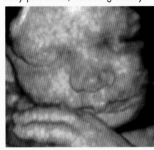

Nails grow to ends of both the fingers and toes.

Month 9
Baby is chubbier and fully formed. Average weight at birth 7–8 lbs. (3–3.5kg), average length 20–23 in. (50–60cm).

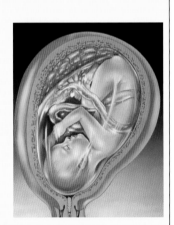

NEW BABY

By their first birthday most babies have almost tripled their birth weight, from just over 7 lbs. (3kg) to almost 22 lbs. (10kg). They have also grown in height from about 21 in. (55cm) to 29 in. (75cm).
Average times for movement and coordination skills (although there are wide variations):

4-8 weeks
Smiles in response to faces
2-4 months
Raises head and shoulders when lying on belly
5-7 months
Rolls over from belly onto back
6-8 months
Sits up perhaps with help, starts to make babbling noises
7-9 months
Begins to try to feed itself, puts items in mouth
8-10 months
Crawls
10-12 months
Stands up with support
12-15 months
Walks unaided

Most people are at peak physical fitness from their early 20s to mid 30s.

- Most men run their lifetime best between 27 and 29 years old.
- Most women run their lifetime best between 29 and 31 years old.
- Most marathon runners perform their best when aged between 30 and 37 years.

Certain reactions and body processes begin to slow down from the 40s in some people, but not until the 60s in others.

Signs of aging:
- Wrinkled skin
- Graying or whitening of hair
- Hair loss
- Less muscle power
- More brittle bones
- Less flexible joints
- Senses become less sharp
- The first sense to deteriorate is usually hearing, followed by sight. Touch and taste also become less sharp, and then smell.

PUBERTY

Puberty is the time when the body grows and develops rapidly from girl to woman or boy to man, and the reproductive (sex) parts start to work.

Puberty—girls
- Can occur any time between 9–16 years of age. It usually takes 2–3 years.
- First signs include rapid growth in height and enlarged breasts.
- Hair grows under arms and between legs (pubic hair).
- Hips increase in width.
- Pads of fat laid down under skin give a more rounded body outline.
- Voice deepens slightly.
- Menstrual cycle begins with first period, menarche.

Puberty—boys
- Can occur any time between 11–17 years of age. It usually takes 3–4 years.
- First signs include rapid growth in height, hair growing under arms and between legs (pubic hair) and on face (mustache and beard area).
- Shoulders increase in width.
- Muscle development increases, resulting in a more angular body outline.
- Voice deepens considerably, or "breaks."
- Reproductive (sex) parts enlarge and begin to make sperm.

HORMONES

Your brain is the boss of your body. It tells the muscles to pull, the lungs to breathe, and the heart to beat. It does this by sending out tiny electrical messages called nerve signals. But the brain also controls certain processes in another way, by natural body chemicals called hormones. These are made in hormone, or endocrine, glands. The hormones spread around the body in the blood and affect how various parts work. When you are frightened, your heart pounds and you feel "butterflies" fluttering inside—that is a hormone called adrenaline at work.

WHERE IN THE BODY?

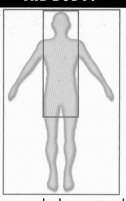

Hormone glands are scattered throughout the central body, from the head, down through the neck, and into the lower abdomen. The reproductive parts—known as the ovaries in women and the testes in men—are also hormonal glands.

THYROID

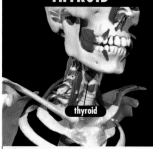

thyroid

Where
Under the skin of the neck just below the voice box, wrapped around the upper windpipe.

Shape
Like a bow tie or butterfly.

Size
3–4 in. (8–10cm) wide, 1.1 in. (3cm) high, 1.8 in. (2cm) thick, weight 0.88 oz. (25g).

Hormones made
Thyroxine (T4), triiodothyronine (T3), calcitonin.

Effects
T4 and T3 make all of the body's cells work faster, so the whole body chemistry, or metabolism, speeds up. Calcitonin lowers the level of the mineral calcium in the blood.

PARATHYROIDS

Where
Four glands, two embedded in each side of the thyroid.

Shape
Like tiny eggs.

Size
Each is 0.24 in. (6mm) high, 1.16 in (4mm) wide, 0.08 in. (2mm) thick, weight 0.002 oz. (0.05g).

Hormones made
Parathyroid hormone (PTH).

Effects
Controls the level of the mineral calcium in the blood.

As well as building bones, calcium is essential for our brains, muscles, and blood to work adequately.

• See page 50 for information on calcium.

PITUITARY

The pituitary gland helps children grow properly. It is sometimes called the "master gland" because it controls several other glands.

The pituitary is one of the smallest hormone glands, but it is almost the most important. It is controlled by the brain just above it and sends out hormones that affect the functions of other hormonal glands.

Where
Behind the eyes and below the central front of the brain, joined to it by a narrow stalk.

Shape
Beanlike.

Size
0.39 in. (1cm) high, 0.47 in. (1.2cm) wide, 0.31 in. (0.8cm) thick, weight 0.02 oz. (0.5g).

Hormones made
About ten, including growth hormone, vasopressin (AVP), and thyrotropin (TSH).

Effects
• Growth hormone makes the whole body increase in size and development.

• AVP makes the kidneys take back more water as they form urine.

• TSH makes the thyroid gland release more of its own hormones.

• See pages 54–55 for information on the kidneys.

PANCREAS

Where
In the upper left abdomen, behind the stomach.

Shape
Long, slim, wedge or triangular shaped.

Size
6 in. (15cm) long, about 0.22 lbs. (0.1kg) in weight.

Hormones made
Insulin and glucagon, made in about one million tiny cells called islets scattered throughout the pancreas.

Effects
Insulin lowers the level of blood sugar (glucose) by making body cells take in more of it; glucagon raises the level.

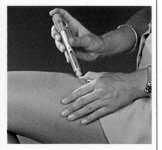

People with diabetes have a problem with the hormone insulin. They may have to inject insulin into their bodies.

• See page 53 for information on the role the pancreas plays in digestion.

THYMUS

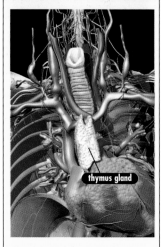
thymus gland

The thymus gland in the chest helps make white blood cells, which destroy germs.

Where
Behind the breastbone.

Shape
Two joined sausagelike blobs, or lobes.

Size
Relatively larger in young children, thumb sized and weighing up to 0.7 oz. (20g), shrinks slightly during adulthood.

Hormones made
Thymosin, thymopoietin, and others.

Effects
Helps white blood cells develop their germ-attacking powers.

• See pages 46–47 for information on blood.

ADRENALS

Where
Two glands, one on top of each kidney.

Shape
Like a small pyramid on the kidneys.

Size
Each is 2 in. (5cm) high, 1.2 in. (3cm) wide, 0.39 in. (1cm) thick, weight 0.18 oz. (5g).

Hormones made
Outer part, called the cortex, makes corticosteroids, or steroid hormones, including hydrocortisone and aldosterone; inner part, called the medulla, makes adrenaline and similar hormones.

Effects
Hydrocortisone decreases the effects of stress and helps control blood sugar and body repair. Aldosterone affects how the kidneys filter blood.

See box (right) for information on adrenaline.

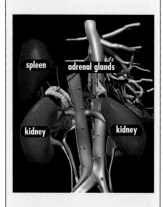
spleen
adrenal glands
kidney
kidney

FIGHT OR FLIGHT?

When the body is frightened or stressed and has to act fast, the adrenal glands release the hormone adrenaline (also called epinephrine).

This helps it get ready to face a threat and "fight," or escape and flee from the danger in "flight." The main effects of adrenaline are:

Blood vessels
• Widens blood vessels to body muscles and heart muscle.

Heart
• Increases heart rate.
• Increases amount of blood pumped by each heartbeat.

Breathing
• Increases breathing rate.
• Widens airways in lungs, allowing more air with each breath.

Digestion
• Decreases activity of inner parts such as stomach and intestines.

Sugar levels
• Raises level of blood sugar (glucose) to provide more energy for muscles.

Our ancestors would have had to act fast if they saw a potentially dangerous predator. Adrenaline prepares the body for the responses they would have made.

OTHER HORMONE-MAKING PARTS

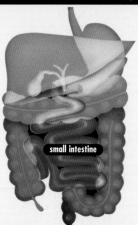
small intestine

Some body parts make hormones in addition to their main tasks.

Stomach
Gastrin makes the stomach lining release acid.

Testes
Testosterone gives men their male characteristics.

Ovaries
Estrogen and progesterone give women their female characteristics.

Heart
Atriopeptin affects blood pressure and the amounts of body salts and minerals.

• See pages 58–59 for information on reproduction.

The small intestine makes the hormone secretin, which tells the pancreas to release acid-neutralizing juices.

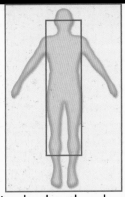

Lymph nodes and vessels are found in most body parts, especially in the neck, armpits, chest, central abdomen, and groin. They are also in the adenoids at the rear of the nasal chamber, the tonsils in the throat, the spleen behind the left kidney, and the thymus gland behind the breastbone.

LYMPHATIC & IMMUNE SYSTEMS

When people are sick, their "glands" often swell up—especially in the neck, armpits, and groin. But these are not really glands. They are called lymph nodes and are part of the lymphatic system. This system is the body's "alternative" circulation. Like blood, lymph fluid flows around the body in tubes known as lymph vessels. Also like blood, it carries nutrients to many parts and collects wastes. It is closely linked to the immune system, which is specialized to attack germs and fight disease.

LYMPH NODES

There are about 500 lymph nodes all over the body.

- The larger ones are in the neck, armpits, chest, central abdomen, and groin. There are others in the crooks of the elbows and the backs of the knees.
- Mostly shaped like balls, beans, or pears.
- Smallest ones less than 0.4 in. (1mm) across, larger ones 0.6–0.8 in. (15–20mm).
- Contain various types of white blood cells.
- Can double in size when fighting illness.
- Lymph flows into each node along several lymph vessels.
- Lymph flows away from each node along one vessel.

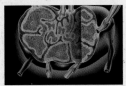

A typical lymph node contains lymph fluid and white blood cells.

LYMPH FLUID

Lymph fluid is usually pale or milky in color.

- The average amount in the human body is 2–4 pt. (1–2L).
- Mainly contains water, dissolved nutrients, disease-fighting white blood cells, and the antibodies they make.
- Forms from fluid that oozes out of and between cells and collects inside and between body tissues.
- Flows slowly along smaller lymph vessels, which join to form larger ones.
- The fluid has no pump of its own (like blood has the heart) but moves by general body pressure and the massaging effect of muscles and movements.
- Flows through lymph nodes on its journey.
- Lymph network gradually gathers lymph into two main lymph vessels in the chest. These are the right lymphatic duct and the thoracic duct.
- These ducts join the right and left subclavian veins, where lymph joins the blood.

SPECIALIST LYMPH PARTS

ADENOIDS
- Also called pharyngeal tonsils.
- Found at the rear of the nasal chamber in the uppermost throat.
- Consist of a gathering of small lymph nodes called nodules.
- Help kill germs in air that is breathed in.
- Swell when battling illness, causing problems with air flow through the nose, and may need removal if this happens too often.

TONSILS

Red, sore, swollen tonsils are a sign of tonsillitis.

- Also called palatine tonsils.
- Found at the sides of the throat, just below and on either side of the soft palate (rear of the roof of the mouth).
- Consist of a gathering of small lymph nodes called nodules.

- Help kill germs in breathed-in air, as well as foods and drinks.
- Swell when battling illness, causing a sore throat. They may need removal if this happens too often.

SPLEEN

The dark red spleen stores blood, recycles old red blood cells, and makes new white cells.

- Behind and above the left kidney.
- Largest collection of lymph tissue in the body.
- Length about 4.7 in. (12cm) (the size of a clenched fist).
- Weight about 5.25 oz. (150g), but can be half or twice this according to blood content and the body's state of health.

• See pages 40–41 for information on the airways.

IMMUNE SYSTEM

When we catch a cold, our immune system immediately begins fighting it. Colds usually last only a few days.

The immune system involves the lymphatic and blood systems and also many other body parts.

- Based on white blood cells of various types.

- Defends against harmful substances like toxins, or poisons.

- Also protects the body against invasion by germs such as bacteria, viruses, and microscopic parasites (called protists or protozoa).

- Helps clean away debris from normal body maintenance as old cells die and break down.

IMMUNITY

Once we have caught an illness and fought the infection, we have immunity to the germ in the future.

- After the body catches an infection, especially by a virus germ, white cells called memory cells "remember" the type of virus.

- If the germ invades again later, the immune system can recognize and fight against it right away and usually quickly defeat it. This is called being resistant, or immune, to that particular germ.

Viruses and bacteria are contagious, which means they spread between people in close contact with one another.

TYPES OF IMMUNITY

The body becomes immune to illnesses in several ways.

Innate, or native, immunity
Already in the body.

Acquired immunity
Occurs after exposure to antigens—for example, on the surface of a type of germ.

Natural acquired immunity
Happens when the body naturally catches the germ.

Artificial acquired immunity
When an altered form of the germ or its products is put into the body specially by vaccination.

Active immunity
When the body makes its own antigens.

Passive immunity
When ready-made antibodies are put into the body.

We are exposed to many germs in our everyday life. As we grow up our bodies naturally develop immunity to most of them. There are only a few diseases we need to be protected from artificially through immunizations.

MAIN DEFENDERS—LYMPHOCYTES

Lymphocytes are one of the main types of white blood cells.

The healthy body contains about two trillion lymphocytes. They are made in bone marrow, and there are two main types, B cells and T cells.

B CELLS
- B cells respond to the chemical messages from T cells.

- B cells are encouraged into activity by T cells.

- B cells change into plasma cells

that make defensive substances called antibodies.

- Different antibodies are made in response to different antigens, which are "foreign" substances on various invading microbes (or made by them).

- Antibodies spread around in the blood and lymph.

- Antibodies join to antigens and make them ineffective or destroy them.

T CELLS

- T cells are processed, or "trained," in the thymus in the chest.

- T cells attack and directly kill invading "foreign" cells such as bacteria.

- T cells also encourage white cells called macrophages to engulf, or "eat," invading microbes.

- T cells encourage B cells to make antibodies.

• See page 26 for information on bone marrow and page 46–47 for information on blood.

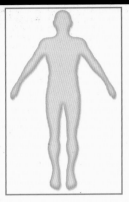

Any part of the body has the potential to stop functioning as well as it should.

DISEASES & MEDICINES

Most people are healthy most of the time. Almost everyone gets the occasional cold and cough. Some of us have a few bigger health problems, such as an infection like chickenpox or perhaps an injury such as a sprained joint or broken bone. A few people are less lucky and seem to be sick more frequently. But the basic rules for good health are the same: eat a nutritious and balanced diet, exercise often, do not smoke, and keep a positive approach, or attitude, to life.

TYPES OF MEDICINES

Anesthetic
Reduces or gets rid of sensations including pain.

Analgesic
Reduces or "kills" pain.

Betablocker
Slows heartbeat and makes it more regular, lowers blood pressure.

Bronchodilator
Widens (dilates) the small airways (bronchioles) in the lungs.

Cytotoxic
Destroys cells, especially malignant, or cancerous, ones in chemotherapy.

Diuretic
Reduces water content of the body by increasing the amount of urine.

Immunosuppressive
Reduces the actions of the body's immune defense system—for example, so it does not reject a body part transplanted from another person.

Steriod
Helps increase muscle size or dampen the action of the immune defense system.

Thrombolytic
Dissolves blood clots.

Vasoconstrictor
Makes the small arterial blood vessels narrower.

Vasodilator
Makes the small arterial blood vessels wider.

MEDICAL DRUGS

Many drugs have a name that begins "anti-." This shows which problem the drug fights against.

Antibiotic
Disables or destroys microbes, mainly bacteria.

Anticoagluant
Prevents blood clotting.

Anticonvulsant
Lessens the risk of convulsions or seizures.

Antidepressant
Reduces the effects of depressive illness by lifting mood and outlook.

Antiemetic
Reduces feelings of nausea.

Antifungal
Disables or destroys fungal microbes.

Antihistamine
Used against allergy-related illnesses such as hay fever, asthma, and food allergies.

Anti-inflammatory
Reducing inflammation (redness, swelling, soreness, pain).

Antipyretic
Lowers fever.

Antiseptic
Kills most kinds of germs, usually applied to the skin.

Antitoxin
Makes a poisonous, or toxic, substance harmless.

Antiviral
Disables or destroys virus microbes.

MAJOR CAUSES OF ILLNESS AND DISEASE

It can be quite difficult for young children to describe their symptoms. This can make diagnosis tricky for the doctor.

- Genetic problems, which can be passed on from parents or begin as a new case when genes are not correctly copied as cells multiply in the developing body.

- Congenital problems, which are present at birth.

- Infections caused by invading microbes.

- Infestations, due to worms, fleas, and similar animals.

- Malnutrition, due to not enough food and/or foods that are not balanced in their nutrients.

- Toxins, or poisons, from the surroundings, such as in water or breathed-in air.

- Physical harm through accidents and injuries.

- Radiation such as radioactivity, nuclear rays, or the sun's harmful ultraviolet rays.

- Cancers, when cells multiply out of control and spread to invade other body parts.

- Autoimmune problems, when the body's immune defense system mistakenly attacks its own parts (such as in rheumatoid arthritis).

- Allergic disorders, when the body's immune defense system mistakenly attacks harmless substances, such as plant pollen in hay fever.

- Metabolic conditions, when there is a problem with the inner processes of body chemistry.

BACTERIA

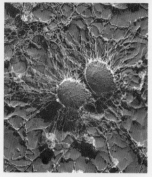

Two bacteria magnified 50,000 times

- Each bacteria is a single unit of life, a cell.

- Microscopic—about 100,000 would fit inside this "o."

- Different groups are known by their shapes, such as cocci (balls or spheres), bacilli (rods or sausages), and spirochetes (corkscrews).

- Many are disabled or killed by antibiotic drugs.

- Bacterial infections include many types of sore throats, skin boils, pertussis (whooping cough), tetanus, scarlet fever, most kinds of cholera and dysentery, plague, diphtheria, Legionnaires' disease, many kinds of bronchitis, most kinds of food poisoning (such as salmonella, listeria, and botulism), ear infections, anthrax.

MICROFUNGI

- Each microfungus is a single unit of life, a cell.

- Belong to the fungus group, which includes mushrooms, toadstools, and yeasts.

- Often grow and spread on the skin.

- Diseases caused include athlete's foot, ringworm, yeast infections (candida), fungal nail and hair infections.

PROTISTS (PROTOZOA)

The disease malaria is caused by a protist. It is transmitted to humans through mosquitoes.

- Each protist is a single unit of life, a cell.

- Sometimes called parasites or microparasites.

- Most are microscopic—about 1,000 would fit inside this "o."

- More common in warmer countries.

- Diseases caused include malaria (plasmodium), sleeping sickness or Chagas' disease (trypanosomiasis), and bilhartzia (schistosomiasis).

VIRUSES

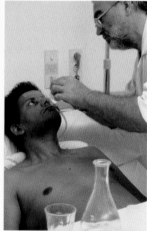

Scientists can treat only the symptoms of most viral infections, not the virus itself.

- Smallest known forms of life, if indeed they are truly alive.

- About 500,000 would fit on this period.

DISEASE-CAUSING MICROBES

- Several types of harmful microbes cause the illnesses known as infectious diseases, or infections.

- They are known in everyday terms as "germs" or sometimes "bugs."

- Most get into the body in breathed-in air, in foods or drinks, or through cuts and open wounds.

- When a harmful microbe spreads by direct or personal contact between people, rather than by indirect means such as air or water, this is known as a contagious infection.

- The time when the harmful microbe multiplies inside the body, but the person does not show signs of illness, is called the incubation period.

- Invade the body's own microscopic cells.

- Take over these cells and make them produce more copies of the virus.

- Viral infections include common colds, most types of flu (influenza), polio (poliomyelitis), warts, chickenpox, measles, mumps, rubella, yellow fever, most kinds of hepatitis, rabies, Ebola fever, AIDS (due to human immunodeficiency virus, HIV).

- Are not affected by antibiotic drugs.

- Several viral infections can be prevented by vaccinations to make the body resistant, or immune, to them (immunization).

• See page 65 for information on types of immunity.

MEDICAL SPECIALISTS

Anesthesiologist
Giving anesthesia to remove sensation and pain while patient is still conscious (local anesthesia) or to make the patient unconscious, too (general anesthesia).

Cardiologist
Heart and main blood vessels.

Dermatologist
Skin, hair, and nails.

Gynecologist
Female parts, usually sexual and urinary organs.

Geriatrics
Older people.

Hematologist
Blood and bodily fluids.

Neurologist
Brain and nerves.

Obstetrician
Pregnancy and birth.

Oncologist
Tumors, especially cancers and similar conditions.

Ophthalmologist
Eyes.

Orthopedic surgeon
Bones, joints, and the skeleton.

Pediatrician
Care of children.

Pathologist
The processes and changes of disease, such as laboratory studies of samples.

Physical therapist
Using physical measures such as massage, manipulation, exercise, heat.

Psychiatrist
Mental and behavioral problems.

Radiologist
X-rays and other imaging methods.

Thoracic surgeon
Chest, especially lungs and airways, and heart.

Urologist
Urinary system of kidneys, bladder, and their tubes.

MEDICAL TIMELINE

1796 — Vaccination
Edward Jenner performs the first vaccination against smallpox.

1851 — Ophthalmoscope
German scientist Hermann von Helmholtz invents the ophthalmoscope, a device for looking into and examining the inside of the eye.

1867 — Thermometer
English doctor Thomas Allbutt devises the first accurate clinical thermometer for measuring body temperature.

1882 — Tuberculosis
German doctor Robert Koch discovers the bacterium that causes the disease tuberculosis (TB).

1895 — X-rays
German physicist Wilhelm Röntgen discovers X-rays.

1896 — Sphygmomanometer
Italian doctor Scipione Riva-Rocci devises the first accurate sphygmomanometer, a device for measuring blood pressure.

1903 — Electrocardiograph
Dutch scientist Willem Einthoven devises the electrocardiograph (ECG), a machine that monitors heartbeats.

1910 — Arsphenamine
German scientist Paul Ehrlich discovers arsphenamine. It is used to treat syphilis and is the first drug to treat a specific disease.

1928 — Penicillin
Alexander Fleming discovers the antibiotic penicillin.

1943 — Kidney dialysis
Dutch doctor Willem Kolff invents the dialysis machine to treat people with kidney failure.

1958 — Ultrasound images
Ultrasound is used for the first time to produce images of a fetus in its mother's uterus.

• See pages 56–57 for information on DNA.
• See page 71 for information on genetic engineering.

MEDICINE

A disease or illness stops your body from working normally. Medicine involves finding out how a disease can be cured or prevented. Advances in medicine mean that today's doctors can diagnose and treat many illnesses. High-tech methods, such as CAT scans, allow doctors to look inside a living body for possible problems, while modern surgery removes, repairs, or replaces damaged body parts. Drugs, such as the germ-killing antibiotic penicillin, are being developed all the time to combat specific diseases.

An 18th-century case of surgical instruments. Many of the implements were used for amputations — a common remedy when little was known about bacterial infections.

THE STETHOSCOPE

In 1819, French doctor René Laennec invented the stethoscope, an instrument used by doctors to listen to a patient's breathing and heart rate.

Since 1819, Laennec's *cylindre*, a wooden tube, has been improved many times to produce the instrument used today.

ANTISEPTIC SURGERY

Joseph Lister was a British surgeon and the founder of antiseptic surgery.

• In 1867, Lister introduced dressings soaked in carbolic acid and strict rules of hygiene to kill bacteria.

• Lister's methods dramatically increased the survival rate from surgery. Prior to this, around half of all surgical patients died from gangrene or secondary infections.

Joseph Lister

ALEXANDER FLEMING 1881–1955

Sir Alexander Fleming at a microscope in his laboratory at St. Mary's Hospital, London (c. 1929)

Nationality: Scottish

Profession: Bacteriologist

Biographical information: Fleming trained as a doctor at St. Mary's Hospital, London, and served in the Medical Corps during World War I. He became interested in the problem of controlling infections caused by bacteria and continued his research after the war.

Most famous discovery: Fleming discovered penicillin, the first antibiotic. Antibiotics are drugs that kill bacteria. They are now used to treat many illnesses and diseases.

Eureka moment: One morning in 1928, Fleming was preparing a routine set of bacteria cultures when he noticed that something was killing the bacteria. When he investigated, he found that it was a bread mold called penicillin.

Scientists at work: Two other scientists, Howard Florey and Ernst Chain, helped perfect the manufacture of penicillin, and they shared the 1945 Nobel Prize for Medicine with Fleming.

DISCOVERING X-RAYS

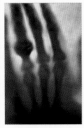

An x-ray of Röntgen's wife's hand (1895)

WILHELM RÖNTGEN

In November 1895, German physicist Wilhelm Röntgen found that by passing electricity through a vacuum he produced a new type of high-energy radiation that he called "x" (for unknown) rays.

SEEING BONES

Röntgen also discovered that a beam of x-rays could pass through the body to produce an image on a photographic plate. Röntgen found that while bones appeared as clear images on the plate, soft tissues, such as muscle and skin, were much less distinct.

LOOKING INSIDE THE BODY

Within weeks Röntgen's discovery was greeted as one of the most significant in the history of medicine. For the first time, doctors could look inside the living body without having to cut it open. Today, x-rays are routinely used to detect broken bones and other disorders.

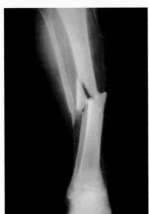

An x-ray showing a broken leg bone

CAT SCANNERS

X-rays are also used in combination with computers in computerized axial tomography (CAT) scanners. CAT scanners produce images in the form of body "slices" that show both hard and soft tissues. The idea of CAT scanners was first developed by British engineer Godfrey Hounsfield in 1967.

TIMELINE: FIRST TEST-TUBE BABY

British biologist Robert Edwards and British gynecologist Patrick Steptoe developed IVF (in vitro fertilization) as a way to help infertile women have babies.

Patrick Steptoe (left) and Robert Edwards

1966

Edwards and Steptoe remove ripe eggs from womens' ovaries and fertilize them with sperm outside the body.

1972

The doctors place eggs, fertilized in the laboratory, back inside the bodies of women with damaged fallopian tubes, hoping the eggs will implant. They make more than 80 unsuccessful attempts.

1977

British couple Lesley and John Brown begin IVF treatment. Lesley Brown conceives.

1978

Louise Joy Brown, the first test-tube baby, is born on July 25, 1978.

SURGICAL TIMELINE

1770s — Art of surgery
English doctor John Hunter transforms surgery (the process of cutting into the body to treat disease) from a lowly craft to a progressive medical science.

1846 — Anesthesia
The first public demonstration of ether anesthesia is carried out by anesthesiologist William Morton during a surgical operation in Boston, Massachusetts.

1865–1867 — Antiseptic surgery
Joseph Lister pioneers the use of germ-killing antiseptics during operations.

1937 — Hip replacement
In London, surgeon Philip Wiles performs the first hip-replacement surgery using a stainless-steel "ball and socket."

1940 — Plastic surgery
The first skin grafts, to repair burns suffered by WWII pilots, are carried out by English surgeon Archibald McIndoe.

1944 — Cardiac surgery
A pioneering operation by American doctors Alfred Blalock and Helen Taussig to treat heart disease in babies establishes the specialty of cardiac (heart) surgery.

1954 — Kidney transplant
The first successful kidney-transplant operation (transferring a healthy kidney from a donor to a recipient with a diseased kidney) is carried out in Boston, Massachusetts.

1967 — Heart transplant
The first heart-transplant operation is carried out by South African surgeon Christiaan Barnard.

1969 — Microsurgery
First use, in the U.S., of microsurgery in which a surgeon uses a binocular microscope to magnify tiny blood vessels or nerves so that they can be repaired.

1980 — Keyhole surgery
The introduction of keyhole surgery, which is carried out through small incisions in the skin.

1987 — Laser eye surgery
In the U.S., laser eye surgery, which uses intense heat to repair damaged tissues, is first performed.

2002 — Surgical robots
First robot-assisted cardiac operation in the U.S.

EDWARD JENNER 1749–1823

Nationality: British

Profession: Doctor

Biographical information: Edward Jenner was born in the town of Berkeley, England. He trained as a surgeon before studying medicine in London. He returned home as a doctor in 1773.

Most famous discovery: The discovery and initial development of vaccination.

Eureka moment: Milkmaid Sarah Nelmes boasted that she could not catch smallpox because she had earlier caught the less serious disease cowpox from the cows she milked. A smallpox outbreak in 1788 proved that she was right.

All of Jenner's patients who had caught cowpox did not get smallpox.

Scientist at work: In 1796, Jenner proved his theory by infecting a small boy first with cowpox and then with smallpox. He found that the boy was immune to smallpox. Jenner called his treatment a vaccination (from the Latin word for cowpox — *vaccina*).

1766 — Hydrogen (H)
In England, chemist Henry Cavendish discovers a gas (hydrogen) that he names phlogiston, or "inflammable air."

1772 — Nitrogen (N)
Daniel Rutherford, a medical student in Scotland, is the first to publish details of a new gas. The gas is named nitrogen in 1790.

1794 — Yttrium (Y)
Finnish chemist Johan Gadolin isolates a rare mineral that contains yttrium. This element gets its name from the Swedish town of Ytterby.

1807 — Potassium (K)
In England, scientist Humphry Davy discovers a new metal (potassium) when he applies electricity to a molten mixture of chemicals.

1811 — Iodine (I)
French chemist Bernard Courtois accidentally adds too much acid to a batch of seaweed in his father's saltpeter factory and discovers the element iodine.

1825 — Aluminum (A)
Danish physicist Hans Christian Orsted succeeds in producing a solid lump of the metal aluminum.

1868 — Helium (He)
Astronomers Pierre Janssen and Norman Lockyer independently identify a new element, helium, in the atmosphere of the Sun.

1886 — Germanium (Ge)
In Germany, chemist Clemens Winkler discovers the element germanium, which had been predicted by Dmitri Mendeleyev in his 1869 periodic table.

1894 — Argon (Ar)
English scientists John Strutt (Lord Rayleigh) and William Ramsay discover the gas argon.

1910 — Titanium (Ti)
In the U.S., metallurgist Matthew Hunter is the first to produce the element titanium in the form of a pure metal.

• See page 72 for information on discovering and inventing metal.

SCIENCE ALL AROUND

Science is simply the close observation of nature. Although many scientists now use sophisticated equipment, such as lasers and hadron colliders, their basic technique is the same as that taught in every school science class: observe, investigate, understand, and describe. Potential new discoveries are all around us. For example, an amazing new form of carbon, which scientists had previously thought impossible, was recently discovered in some residue that had built up around an old electric lamp!

THE PERIODIC TABLE

In 1869, Russian chemist Dmitri Mendeleyev discovered that the elements can be placed in ascending order of atomic size, arranged across a periodic table of rows and columns. Elements with similar physical or chemical properties are located close to one another.

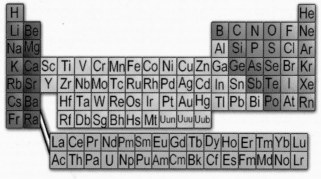

Mendeleyev's original periodic table had gaps that predicted the existence of undiscovered elements. These gaps have since been filled.

THE INVENTION OF THE MICROSCOPE

THE FIRST MICROSCOPE
The first working microscope was constructed in the Netherlands in 1668 by Anton van Leeuwenhoek. It had a small convex (bean-shaped) lens and could magnify around 200 times. The entire instrument was only 4 in. (10cm) long. The user held it up to the eye.

DISCOVERING BACTERIA
In 1674, van Leeuwenhoek was the first person to observe protozoa (from ponds). In 1676, he examined bacteria taken from his own mouth.

VAN LEEUWENHOEK'S MICROSCOPE

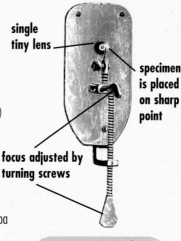

single tiny lens

specimen is placed on sharp point

focus adjusted by turning screws

• See page 103 for information on inventors and more microscope inventions.

A NEW CARBON

In 1985, three university professors jointly discovered an exciting new form of the carbon molecule.

Instead of just four atoms like other forms of carbon, it has 60 atoms arranged in a hollow, multisided geometric shape. The new substance, which is incredibly strong for its weight, has been named buckminsterfullerene, and the hollow shapes are known as buckyballs.

HIGH-ENERGY COLLISIONS

To study the structure of atoms, scientists build massive devices that use magnetism to accelerate bits of atomic nuclei so that they crash into one another at very high speeds and break apart.

The first such device, called a cyclotron, was built in the U.S. in 1933. The latest device, known as a Large Hadron Collider, is located on the border between France and Switzerland.

LASERS

THE FIRST LASER
In 1960, scientist Theodore Maiman built the first laser (light amplification by stimulated emission of radiation). It used a rod-shaped crystal of synthetic ruby to produce a very bright and narrow beam of light. Gas lasers were invented a few months after the ruby laser.

WHAT IS A LASER?
In a laser, a crystal or gas is energized so that its atoms start to emit light. The light produced by a laser is of almost uniform wavelength, and the light rays are almost perfectly parallel so that there is very little spreading of the beam.

An experiment showing an intense ruby laser beam penetrating two prisms

LASER BEAMS ON THE MOON
In the 1970s, lasers were used to measure the exact distance between Earth and the Moon. The narrow beam of a laser was bounced off reflectors that had been put on the Moon's surface by *Apollo* astronauts.

LASERS ALL AROUND
Today, tiny semiconductor devices, smaller than a pinhead, produce the laser light that reads the digital information encoded onto CDs and DVDs.

ELECTRICITY TIMELINE

ELECTRICITY TIMELINE

1800—First battery
Italian physicist Alessandro Volta invents the first electric battery. It uses chemical reactions to produce an electric current.

1807—Electrolysis
English scientist Humphry Davy invents the process of extracting metals from minerals by electrolysis. He heats the minerals to melting point and then applies an electric current to them.

1820—Ampère's law
French scientist André-Marie Ampère experiments with magnets and electricity and discovers the mathematical relationship (Ampère's law) between magnetism and the flow of electrical current.

1827—Ohm's law
In Germany, physicist Georg Ohm discovers the relationship (Ohm's law) between resistance and current in an electrical circuit.

1831—Induction
English scientist Michael Faraday discovers the laws of induction that explain how a variable magnetic field causes electrical current to flow through copper wires—the principle behind both the electric generator and the electric motor.

1864—Electricity and magnetism
Scottish mathematician James Maxwell discovers four basic equations that describe all of the relationships between electricity and magnetism.

1888—First generator
Croatian inventor Nikola Tesla designs the world's first successful alternating current (AC) generator. Alternating current (used for household electricity) is more powerful than the direct current (DC) produced by batteries.

1947—The transistor
In the U.S., electrical engineers invent the transistor, the world's first semiconductor device, marking the start of the electronic age.

• See the glossary for a detailed definition of a semiconductor.

THE STORY OF GENETIC ENGINEERING

• See page 12 timeline for Gregor Mendel's discovery of heredity.

1954—Genetic code
Russian physicist George Gamow is the first to suggest that the DNA bases T, G, C, and A form a genetic code that looks like CGCTGACATCGT, etc.

1966—Frog cloning
In England, biologist John Gurdon clones frogs from cells taken from the intestines of a tadpole.

1971—Restriction enzymes
In the U.S., molecular biologists Daniel Nathans and Hamilton Smith discover restriction enzymes that can be used to cut the DNA molecule into short strands.

1972—Recombinant DNA
American scientist Patrick Berg succeeds in splicing together strands of DNA to produce recombinant DNA (DNA that has been recombined from a number of different strands). This marks the beginning of true genetic engineering.

1994—GM crops
In the U.S., a rot-resistant tomato becomes the first genetically modified (GM) crop to be approved for sale to the public.

1996—A cloned mammal
In Scotland, a team of scientists led by Ian Wilmut succeeds in producing Dolly the sheep, the world's first cloned mammal.

Dolly the sheep had no immediate practical value, but the cloning technique is vital. If, for example, scientists can genetically engineer a cow to produce milk that contains lifesaving drugs, they can use the cloning technique to make thousands of identical cows.

• See pages 56–57 for information on DNA.
• See the glossary for scientific terms used in this timeline.

MAKING DOLLY THE SHEEP
• The nucleus was removed from an unfertilized egg.

• Next a cell from an adult sheep was fused with the egg by passing an electric current through the two.

• They became one cell that behaved like a fertilized egg and began to divide.

• Lastly the cell was implanted into another female sheep, where it developed normally into an embryo.

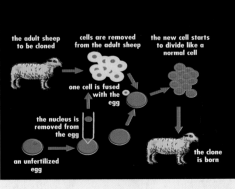

the adult sheep to be cloned

cells are removed from the adult sheep

the new cell starts to divide like a normal cell

one cell is fused with the egg

the nucleus is removed from the egg

an unfertilized egg

the clone is born

Dr. Ian Wilmut with Dolly the sheep

INVENTION TIMELINE

c. 35,000 B.C. — Advanced stone tools
Burins, engraving tools made from flints with a sharp edge, are used to decorate bone and wooden items.

Wooden handles are attached to stone tools for the first time, making it possible to hit things harder and to increase the amount of swing achieved with a tool such as an ax.

c. 30,000 B.C. — Rope
Rope braided from plant fibers is used for making nets and snares for catching animals.

c. 9000 B.C. — Ovens
The first known ovens, stone or clay chambers heated by a fire, are in use in Jericho in ancient Palestine.

c. 8000 B.C. — Flint mining
When people can no longer find enough flints on the ground around them for toolmaking, they begin to dig for stones under the surface—mining is invented.

c. 7000 B.C. — Flax and linen
The flax plant is cultivated for its fibers, which can be used to make ropes and linen.

c. 6000 B.C. — Ax heads
Stones are shaped to create ax heads (as we would recognize them today) with a straight, sharp edge and a heavy base.

c. 5500 B.C. — Weaving
The weaving of baskets develops: split bamboo is used in China, straw and flax in the Middle East, and willow in Europe.

c. 5000 B.C. — Leather
It is discovered that animal skins can be useful if they are dried and preserved using substances such as urine.

c. 5000 B.C. — Grindstones
Grindstones (two stones that fit together) are used to crush cereal grains. This produces flour, which is easier to digest than whole grains.

- See page 6 for information on stone tools.
- The timeline continues on page 73.

O ver thousands of years our earliest ancestors invented and discovered ways to make their lives both more comfortable and interesting. They developed farming to ensure a regular supply of food, they devised tools and simple machines to make work more efficient, and they conceived ways of recording their lives, such as painting and writing, without which it would be impossible to chart the history of human invention and discovery.

EARLY FARMING INVENTIONS AND DISCOVERIES

5000 B.C.—The scratch plow
The wooden scratch plow (for breaking up the soil) comes into use. It is probably pulled by donkeys.

4000 B.C.—The sickle
Bone-handled sickles with flint blades are used to reap wheat and barley.

3000 B.C.—The shadoof
The ancient Egyptians use a shadoof (a bucket on a weighted pole) to lift water from irrigation canals for their crops.

2000 B.C.—Pollination
The discovery that there are male and female plants makes it easier to select crops for size, taste, and disease resistance by artificial pollination.

A.D. 500—Three-piece plows
The development of heavy iron three-piece plows begins. They usually have wheels and are pulled by large farm horses. This type of plow enables farmers to work heavier soils and plow faster.

A.D. 500—The horse collar
The development of the horse collar enables a horse to pull a heavy plow without choking.

A.D. 800—Three-field system
In northeastern France, the three-field system is established. One field is planted in the fall with winter wheat or rye; the second field is planted the following spring with barley, peas, or oats (to feed horses); the third field is left fallow (to rest).

- See page 7 for information on the first farmers.

This ancient Egyptian wooden model dates to around 2000 B.C. It shows a farmer using a simple scratch plow pulled by oxen.

DISCOVERING AND INVENTING METAL

Archaeologists have studied metal artifacts to figure out when ancient civilizations first discovered metals such as bronze and iron.

COPPER 8000–6500 B.C.
The discovery of copper gave early humans a practical and more beautiful substitute for stone. Found naturally in its metallic state, copper's malleability made it easy to shape.

LEAD 6500 B.C.
Early metalworkers extracted lead by heating lead ore (stone containing lead) in a hot fire. Decorative lead beads, from around 6500 B.C., found in Turkey suggest that lead was considered a precious material.

BRONZE 3500 B.C.
Ancient metalworkers melted copper and tin together and created a new metal called bronze. This material could be cast to make weapons and decorative items.

IRON 2000 B.C.
Iron was extracted from iron ore (stone containing iron) by heating the ore in red-hot charcoal. Iron is difficult to melt, so early metalworkers developed new techniques such as hammering hot iron into the required shape.

THE INVENTION OF WRITING

THE FIRST WRITING

The Sumerians (who lived in what is now southern Iraq) had invented writing by around 3000 B.C. They used a piece of reed to make cuneiform symbols (wedge-shaped marks) on clay tablets. Then they baked the tablets to harden them. The symbols were used to keep records of trade and taxes.

HIEROGLYPHS

The ancient Egyptians also discovered writing soon after 3000 B.C. They used hundreds of pictures called hieroglyphs to represent words and sounds. They carved inscriptions on temple walls, painted on the walls of tombs, and wrote on papyrus paper.

CHINESE PICTOGRAMS

The ancient Chinese began writing around 1700 B.C. They used a different pictogram (symbol) to represent each word — there were thousands to learn! Scribes used a brush to paint ink onto wood, silk, and, in later times, paper.

- See page 7 for information on the Greek alphabet.

THE INVENTION OF PAINTING

Ancient paintings dating to around 30,000 B.C. have been found in caves in Western Europe.

Prehistoric artists not only invented painting; they also invented paint made from minerals such as chalk and red iron oxide, simple brushes made from chewed twigs or animal hair, and lamps that burned animal fat to light the dark interiors of the caves where they worked.

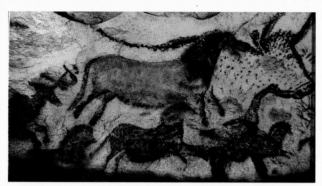

The artwork in the Lascaux caves, France, (above) have been dated to around 15,000 B.C.

LASCAUX CAVE PAINTINGS

Discovered:	September 12, 1940
Discovered by:	Marcel Ravidat, Jacques Marsal, Georges Agnel, and Simon Coencas, four teenage boys exploring in woods near the village of Montignac, France
The discovery:	Caves containing more than 2,000 prehistoric paintings and engravings

TIMELINE: INVENTION OF POTTERY

13,000 B.C.
The first potters discover they can make useful containers by shaping soft clay by hand, then heating it in a fire to bake it hard.

6500 B.C.
Thin layers of colored clay, called "slip," and natural pigments, such as red ocher, are used to decorate pottery. Examples of this innovation have been found in the ancient city of Çatalhöyük (now Cumra, Turkey).

4000–3000 B.C.
The potter's wheel is invented. Mesopotamian potters use a slowly spinning stone wheel to produce pots with a uniform shape.

A Mesopotamian vase from around 3400 B.C.

PAPYRUS

The ancient Egyptians invented papyrus, a type of paper made from papyrus reeds, which grew by the Nile River.

Fibers from the reeds were squashed together into flat sheets. Then the sheets were dried in the sun.

A papyrus reed

INVENTION TIMELINE

c. 4000 B.C. — Scales
Simple scales (a length of wood or metal balanced with pans hung from each end) are developed in Mesopotamia.

c. 4000 B.C. — Gold/silver
Gold and silver are discovered. They are used for making decorative ornaments and as a means of exchange.

c. 3500 B.C. — Bricks
In the Middle East, bricks are made from clay, then fired in a kiln to make them hard and waterproof. Prior to this bricks were made from mud and straw, but they sometimes dissolved in heavy rain.

c. 3000 B.C. — Cotton
Cotton fabric is invented when the people of the Indus Valley (in modern-day Pakistan) discover that the fibers attached to cotton-plant seeds can be woven into a fine fabric.

c. 2600 BCE — Chairs
The ancient Egyptians use chairs with padded seats and four legs. Ancient people had probably used many objects to sit on before this time, but chairs as we recognize them today were found in ancient Egyptian tombs from this period.

c. 2500 B.C. — Ink/mirrors
Ink for writing is made from soot mixed with glue.

Mirrors made from disks of polished bronze or copper are used in ancient Egypt.

c. 2000 B.C. — Wheel spokes
Mesopotamian craftsmen begin to produce wheels with a rim, hub, and spokes instead of the heavy solid plank used previously.

c. 1500 B.C. — Flags
Flags are invented in China and used in battles. If a leader's flag is captured by his enemy, it means the enemy has won the battle.

c. 600 B.C. — Rotary querns
The rotary quern is invented. For more than 4,000 years corn had been ground by hand, using two stones. The rotary quern comprises a circular stone that fits into a stone base. The top stone is turned by a wooden handle, crushing the grain between the two stones.

Appert, Nicolas
In 1810, French chef and inventor Nicolas Appert invented the bottling process for storing heat-sterilized food. In 1812, he opened the world's first commercial preserved foods factory, initially using glass jars and bottles. In 1822, the factory began using tin-plated metal cans.

Biró, Lásziò
The ballpoint pen was invented in the late 1930s by Hungarian brothers Lásziò and Georg Biró. Although the Biró brothers are credited with the invention of the ballpoint pen, a similar writing instrument had been invented in 1888 by American John Loud.

Celsius, Anders
In 1742, Swedish astronomer Anders Celsius invented the Celsius scale, using 0° (degrees) for the freezing point of water and 100° for the boiling point.

Cousteau, Jacques

In 1943, French explorer Jacques Cousteau and engineer Émile Gagnan connected portable compressed-air cylinders, via a pressure regulator, to a mouthpiece, inventing the Aqua-lung. This piece of apparatus gives divers complete freedom to explore the oceans.

Fahrenheit, Daniel
In 1714, German physicist Daniel Fahrenheit invented the mercury thermometer and devised the Fahrenheit temperature scale. In 1709, Fahrenheit had invented an alcohol thermometer.

INVENTORS

An inventor is anyone who thinks of something new to make or a new way to make or do something. We do not know the names of most of the inventors who have influenced our lives or exactly when they made their breakthroughs. But many inventors are famous, and we even know about the "eureka moment" when they had their brilliant idea.

ARCHIMEDES OF SYRACUSE 287–212 B.C.

The Archimedes Portrait by Domenico Fetti, painted in 1620

Nationality: Greek

Profession: Mathematician

Biographical information:
Archimedes was born and worked in the city of Syracuse in Sicily, Italy, although he studied in Alexandria, Egypt. He was killed when Roman soldiers conquered Syracuse.

Most famous invention: While wondering about how to test if a crown was made of pure gold, Archimedes discovered the principle of buoyancy—if an object is placed in a fluid, it will displace its own volume of fluid. This is now known as Archimedes' principle.

Eureka moment: Archimedes had the original "eureka" moment. Getting into a bathtub he noticed that the water rose up the sides— his body was displacing its own volume of water. He raced into the street, without any clothes, shouting, "Eureka!" (I've found it!)

• See page 102 for information on the Archimedian screw.

GALILEO GALILEI 1564–1642

Nationality: Italian

Profession: Mathematician

Biographical information:
The son of a musician, Galileo went to the University of Pisa to study medicine, but eventually became a professor of mathematics. During the 1630s, Galileo was arrested and imprisoned by the Catholic Church because of his scientific views.

Most famous invention:
Galileo is widely considered to be the founder of modern experimental science. He established the principle that scientific theories should be based on data (measurements) obtained from experiments.

Eureka moment: Galileo was able to devise a mathematical formula to describe the motion of falling objects. The story that he dropped identical weights of iron and feathers from the Leaning Tower of Pisa may not be true, but Galileo did establish that all objects fall at the same speed, no matter what they weigh.

Other discoveries: Galileo was also interested in astronomy. He did not invent the telescope, but in 1609 he built his own telescope. Galileo was able to observe the craters on our Moon, he discovered Jupiter's four largest moons, and he was the first person to describe the rings of Saturn.

• See page 75 for more information on Galileo's life and work.

Galileo on an Italian 2,000-lire banknote

LEONARDO DA VINCI 1452–1519

Leonardo da Vinci

Nationality: Italian

Profession: Artist

Biographical information: Da Vinci was apprenticed to a sculptor and worked as a painter for the rulers of Florence and Milan in Italy and France. He produced many famous paintings, including the *Mona Lisa.*

Da Vinci filled thousands of pages of notebooks with drawings and notes about everything he saw around him. He studied human anatomy, military engineering, the flight of birds, and the movement of water.

Most famous inventions: Da Vinci's notebooks contained drawings and ideas that would not be put into practice for hundreds of years, including parachutes, canals, armored cars, and submarines.

Da Vinci showed that by drawing what he imagines, an inventor can inspire future generations to make these visions real.

SIR ISAAC NEWTON 1642–1727

Nationality: English

Profession: Mathematician

Biographical information: Newton went to Cambridge University in 1661, but his studies were interrupted by an outbreak of the plague that closed the university for two years. During this period of enforced idleness, Newton did most of his best thinking. In 1667, he was appointed professor of mathematics at Cambridge. Most of his work is contained in his books *Principia Mathematica* (1687) and *Opticks* (1704).

Most famous discovery: Newton is best known for his theory of universal gravitation—that there is an attractive force between all of the objects in the universe, and this force is called gravity. Newton used his theory to discover the mathematical laws that govern the motion of all of the objects in the everyday universe. The movement of any object, be it a pickup truck or a planet, can be explained and predicted by what is known as Newtonian physics.

• See page 108 for information on the invention of the telescope.

Newton stories:

• Newton is supposed to have thought up the theory of gravitation after watching an apple fall from a tree.

• While studying light, Newton pushed blunt needles into the corners of his eyes to see what effect squashing his eyeballs had on his vision.

Other discoveries:

• A comprehensive theory of light that explained how lenses worked and how white light could be split into colors.

• A system of mathematics called calculus.

• A reflecting telescope with a curved mirror to give a better image.

Sir Isaac Newton

A TO Z INVENTORS

Franklin, Benjamin

American statesman, scientist, and writer Benjamin Franklin was fascinated by the new discovery of electricity. In 1752, convinced that thunderstorms were electric, he proved it by flying a special kite into a storm. Lightning struck the kite, and electricity traveled down the string. Franklin realized that buildings could be protected from thunderbolts if the electricity was conducted through a metal spike on the roof of a building to the ground via a thick wire. Franklin had invented a lightning conductor.

Galileo Galilei

Galileo was so intrigued by the swinging of the incense burner in Pisa's cathedral that he was inspired to work with pendulums. He measured the time it took to make a complete swing and discovered that it took the same amount of time to get back to where it started, even when the size of the swing changed. Galileo experimented with pendulums for many years, but by the time he thought of using a pendulum's even swing to keep a clock running smoothly, he was old and blind.

Gillette, King Camp

Advised by a colleague to invent "something that would be used and thrown away," American Gillette invented the disposable razorblade and new safety razor. Constantly having to buy new blades was not popular with customers, but never having to use a "cutthroat" razor again was. Gillette founded his razorblade company in 1903.

Halley, Edmond

In 1717, English astronomer Edmond Halley invented the first diving bell in which people could stay underwater for long periods of time. Earlier devices (that were primarily built for attempts to retrieve sunken treasure) had not been successful. Air was supplied to Halley's diving bell in barrels with weights to make them sink.

• See page 113 for more information on Edmond Halley.

INVENTORS

Kwolek, Stephanie

Pound for pound, Stephanie Kwolek's invention Kevlar is five times stronger than steel. It is also chemical and flame resistant. Kevlar, best known for its use in bulletproof vests and crash helmets, was developed in the 1960s when chemist Kwolek was working in the laboratory of U.S. company DuPont Textiles.

Leclanché, Georges

In 1866, French engineer Leclanché invented the sealed dry cell battery, which is still used in many flashlights today. Until the invention of the Leclanché cell, people were restricted to Alessândro Volta's battery, which contained a liquid that had to be constantly topped up.

Mars, Frank

In 1911, Frank Mars and his wife, Ethel, began making and selling butter-cream candy from their home in Tacoma, Washington. In 1920, Frank invented the Mars Bar when he came up with the idea of producing malted chocolate milk shakes in a solid form that could be carried and enjoyed anywhere.

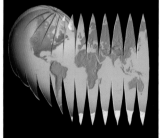

Mercator, Gerhard

In around 1568, Flemish cartographer Gerhard Mercator produced a map that gave sailors constant compass directions as straight lines. The Mercator projection provided a flat, "peeled" view of the globe. The map is very accurate for navigators, but showing the curved planet on flat paper causes distortions and makes countries at the poles look too big.

JOHANNES GUTENBERG 1400-1468

Nationality: German

Profession: Jeweler/craftsman

Biographical information: Gutenberg was born in Mainz and trained as a goldsmith. He lived and worked in Strasbourg, France, between 1430 and 1444; he then returned to Mainz.

Most famous inventions: The process of printing with movable type and a printing press based on existing screw presses used to crush juice from grapes and olives.

Inventor at work: After 20 years of secret work to perfect all of the necessary processes, Gutenberg printed and published his first book, a Latin Bible, in 1455. But money disputes with his financial backer, Johann Fust, caused him to lose his business.

• See page 8 for information on paper and printing.

JOSEPH AND JACQUES MONTGOLFIER

Joseph: 1740–1810

Jacques: 1745–1799

Nationality: French

Profession: Papermakers

Biographical information: The Montgolfier brothers worked in their father's paper factory in Annonay, France.

Most famous invention: The first hot-air balloon. On September 19, 1783, a sheep, a duck, and a rooster became the first living creatures to fly in free flight when they took off in a wicker basket suspended from a Montgolfier balloon.

On November 21, 1783, Jean-François Pilâtre de Rozier and the Marquis d'Arlandes flew over Paris for 23 minutes in a Montgolfier balloon— the first human flight.

Eureka moment: Joseph and Jacques had noticed how flames in their fireplace sent scraps of paper floating up the chimney. They became convinced that a large bag filled with hot air would rise.

The Montgolfier balloon was made of fabric lined with paper. It was 32.8 ft. (10m) across.

• See page 85 for a timeline of balloon inventors.

SAMUEL MORSE 1791-1872

Nationality: American

Profession: Artist and inventor

Biographical information: Morse was born in Massachusetts. His father worked in the church and wrote geography books. Morse went to Yale University when he was 14 years old. He earned money painting pictures of his friends and teachers and studied art in England, becoming a well-known painter.

Most famous inventions: Morse's interest in electricity led to his invention of the electrical telegraph and Morse code.

Eureka moment: Morse demonstrated his telegraph to U.S. Congress, and in 1843 they gave him $30,000 to build a telegraph line from Washington, D.C., to Baltimore, Maryland.

Other inventions: The bathometer, which was used to find out how deep rivers and lakes were.

• See page 86 for information on Morse code.

LOUIS BRAILLE 1809–1852

Nationality: French

Profession: Teacher

Biographical information: Braille was blinded at the age of three in an accident at his father's harness shop. In 1819, he went to the National Institute for Blind Children in Paris, and later he became a teacher there. He died from tuberculosis in 1852.

Most famous invention: A system of reading and writing for the blind using raised dots in a six-dot matrix system. Braille's system was first published in 1829.

Eureka moment: At school in Paris, Braille learned of a system called "night writing" invented by Captain Charles Barbier for nighttime battlefield communication.

In 1824, aged just 15, Braille developed his own system, using Barbier's as a starting point.

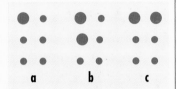

a   b   c

Braille is read by using the fingertips.

THOMAS ALVA EDISON 1847–1931

Nationality: American

Profession: Inventor

Biographical information: After being expelled from school for hyperactivity, Edison was educated at home by his mother. He began experimenting with batteries and electricity at the age of only ten. Edison built his own telegraph, and his first job was as a telegraph operator.

Most famous invention: Edison was already well known in the U.S., but his 1877 invention of the phonograph made him world famous. The phonograph was the first device that could play prerecorded music.

Inventor at work: In 1876, Edison decided to become a full-time inventor. He built the world's first industrial research laboratory, which he called an inventions factory, in Menlo Park, New Jersey.

Other inventions: The most famous is the electric light bulb. Edison sometimes made as many as 400 inventions a year, including the incandescent electric lamp, the microphone, and the kinetoscope.

Edison patented 1,093 inventions during his lifetime.

- See pages 87 and 92 for more information on Edison's inventing work.

GEORGE EASTMAN 1854–1932

Nationality: American

Profession: Photographic film manufacturer

Biographical information: After leaving school, Eastman worked in insurance and banking while pursuing his hobby of photography. In 1880, he perfected a method of making photographic plates and set up a factory where he soon developed transparent film.

Most famous inventions: The first Kodak camera (Eastman invented the name *Kodak*, and it became a trademark), which marked the beginning of amateur photography.

In 1900, Eastman launched the Brownie camera. It was so cheap, only one dollar including the film, that everybody could afford to buy one, making photography available to all.

George Eastman (left) and Thomas Edison introduce color motion pictures to the world in 1928.

- See page 9 for a timeline of the invention of photography.

- See pages 87 and 92 for more information on Edison's inventing work.

- See page 9 for a timeline of the invention of photography.

A TO Z INVENTORS

Perignon, Dom
Benedictine monk Dom Perignon is credited with inventing champagne in around 1670, but other winemakers of the Champagne region of France probably contributed to its development. The special method of fermentation, known as *méthode champenoise*, produces the carbon dioxide that creates the bubbles loved by all partygoers.

Richter, Charles F.
American seismologist Charles F. Richter developed his numbering system for measuring earthquakes in 1935. An earthquake measuring below 2 on the Richter scale would be recorded by equipment, but not felt by a person. An earthquake measuring 8 or more would be devastating.

Roosevelt, Theodore
While on a hunting expedition in 1902, U.S. President Theodore "Teddy" Roosevelt refused to shoot a defenseless bear cub. The story enhanced the popularity of the already popular president. Morris Michtom, a New York retailer, cashed in on the incident by selling plush-covered bears with button eyes and jointed limbs. He called them "Teddy's Bears." A huge success, they soon became known as teddy bears.

A TO Z INVENTORS

Rubik, Ernö
Hungarian design professor Ernö Rubik invented the Rubik's Cube. Popular during the early 1980s, more than 150 million cubes were sold (100 million authorized units and 50 million imitations). Once twisted from its original arrangement, the puzzle has 43 quintillion possible configurations!

Schueller, Eugène
In 1936, French chemist Eugène Schueller produced the first suntan oil at his company, L'Oréal. Designer Coco Chanel made sunbathing fashionable around this time. Today the oil is sold around the world as Garnier Ambre Solaire.

Semple, William Finley
On December 28, 1869, William Semple of Mt. Vernon, Ohio, became the first person to patent a chewing gum. It was U.S. Patent No. 98304.

Sinclair, Clive
In 1985, British inventor Clive Sinclair invented the C5, a battery-powered bike. The C5 had a top speed of 15 mph (24km/h), a range of 20 mi. (32km), and took eight hours to recharge the batteries. Unfortunately for Sinclair, consumers were not impressed with this new type of vehicle, and the invention flopped.

INVENTORS

MARIE CURIE 1867–1934

Nationality: Polish

Profession: Physicist

Biographical information: Marie Sklodowska worked as a nanny to support herself while she attended college in Paris. In 1895, she married French scientist Pierre Curie.

Most famous inventions: In 1898 the Curies discovered the radioactive elements radium, thorium, and polonium, named for Marie's homeland. In 1903 they shared the Nobel Prize for Physics with Henri Becquerel. In 1911,

Marie Curie was awarded the Nobel Prize for Chemistry for her continuing work on radium and radioactivity. Doctors found that radium could be used to treat cancer through radiotherapy.

Eureka moment: The discovery of radium involved breaking down and refining several tons of a mineral called pitchblende to locate less than one hundredth of a gram of pure radium.

Madame Curie poses in her Paris laboratory.

ALBERT EINSTEIN 1879–1955

Nationality: German–Swiss–American

Profession: Office clerk and mathematician

Biographical information: Einstein was born in Germany and attended college in Zurich, Switzerland. In 1901, he got a job at the Swiss Patent Office and became a Swiss citizen. In his spare time he worked on difficult mathematical problems. When his work became well known, he returned to Germany. In 1933, he went to the U.S., and in 1940, he became a U.S. citizen.

Most famous discovery: Somewhere among Einstein's math is the simple formula $E=mc^2$. This means that matter (m) can be converted into energy (e) and that the amount of energy will be equal to the amount of matter times the speed of light (c) squared. The speed of light is about 186,000 mi. (300,000km) per second, so mc^2

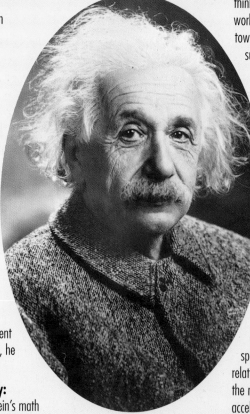

Albert Einstein

makes for a lot of energy. Einstein's formula summarizes what happens when an atom bomb explodes.

Eureka moment: The speed of light was central to Einstein's

thinking. One morning, traveling to work by bus, Einstein glanced at the town hall clock — if the bus suddenly accelerated to the speed of light, the clock would appear to stop. The relative motion between observer and observed is at the heart of Einstein's two theories of relativity.

Other discoveries: Newton's laws of motion do not work mathematically for objects moving very quickly (near the speed of light). Einstein's special theory of relativity (1905) extended the math to cover objects moving at a constant high speed. His general theory of relativity (1916) further extended the math to cover rapidly accelerating objects. As well as showing that matter and energy were interconnected, Einstein also showed that space and time were interconnected in a concept called space-time.

ENRICO FERMI 1901–1954

Nationality: Italian–American

Profession: Physicist

Biographical information: Fermi studied physics at the University of Pisa and was awarded a doctorate for research into x-rays. He worked in Italy until he was awarded the Nobel Prize for Physics in 1938. Fermi and his wife moved first to Sweden and then to the U.S.

Most famous invention: Fermi designed and supervised the construction of the world's first nuclear reactor. It was located in a basement racquetball court at the University of Chicago.

Eureka moment: In 1939, Fermi realized that an atom bomb was possible. Together with other scientists,

1951, University of Chicago—Fermi at the controls of the new synchrocyclotron built to study the origins of life

including Albert Einstein, he wrote to U.S. President Franklin D. Roosevelt about the discovery. Roosevelt ordered the Manhattan Project (see page 10).

Other inventions: Fermi discovered the first artificial element, neptunium

(No. 93), and the element fermium (No. 100). Fermium is named in his honor.

• See page 10 for more information on the work of Enrico Fermi.

FRANCIS CRICK & JAMES WATSON

Crick: 1916–2004

Watson: born 1928

Nationality: English (Crick); American (Watson)

Profession: Molecular biologist (Crick); biochemist (Watson)

Biographical information: Crick studied at Cambridge University in England and during World War II designed antishipping mines. Watson studied viruses at the University of Indiana, where he received a doctorate in 1950.

Most famous discovery:
In 1953, while working at the Cavendish Laboratory in Cambridge, Crick and Watson discovered that the three-dimensional structure of the DNA molecule was in the shape of a double helix.

• See page 13 for information on the story of DNA.

Crick (right) and Watson with their famous laboratory model of the DNA double helix

Eureka moment: By 1950 scientists knew what DNA was made from, but they had no idea of its shape. Crick and Watson made many models of what they thought it might look like. Finally they came up with a double helix, shaped like a long, twisted ladder.

In 1962, they shared the Nobel Prize for Medicine.

1733—Flying shuttle
In England, engineer John Kay invents the "flying shuttle," a mechanical attachment for hand looms that speeds up the weaving process by more than 100 percent.

1764—Spinning jenny
English cloth worker James Hargreaves invents the "spinning jenny," a hand-powered machine that can spin 16 threads at once.

1769—Waterpower
English inventor Richard Arkwright patents his water-powered spinning frame that can spin much stronger threads than is possible by hand.

1779—Spinning mule
In England, cloth worker Samuel Crompton perfects his "spinning mule," a water-powered machine that combines the advantages of the spinning jenny and the spinning frame.

1785—Power loom
In England, clergyman Edmund Cartwright patents the world's first power loom. Two years later he also invents a machine for combing wool.

1801—Jacquard loom
In France, weaver Joseph-Marie Jacquard invents an automatic mechanical loom that can weave patterns.

1851—Sewing machine
American inventor Isaac Singer produces the world's first lock-stitch sewing machine. The machine's secret is that it uses two threads— a needle pushes one thread through the cloth from above, while a second thread is pushed through the first by a shuttle moving back and forth underneath. This type of machine was also invented by American Walter Hunt in 1843, and had been patented by Elias Howe, but Singer's machine perfected the invention.

1856—Artificial dye
English chemist William Perkin discovers mauve, the first artificial dye.

• See page 91 for information on fashion inventions.

EARLY INDUSTRY

The process that we call the industrial revolution spread across 300 years and was the result of countless inventions, developments, and improvements. Two key factors were the widespread availability of metals, especially iron and steel, and the introduction of machinery. The textile industry was the first to be affected by the industrial revolution, and the first modern factories for spinning cotton were built in the 1700s in northern England.

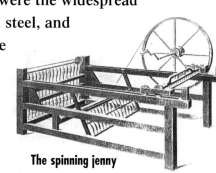

The spinning jenny

THE JACQUARD LOOM

• The first programmable machine was Joseph-Marie Jacquard's loom.

• The pattern woven by the loom was controlled by cards with holes punched into them. Changing the pattern of holes changed the pattern woven into the cloth.

MUNTZ METAL

In 1832, English businessman George Muntz invented an alloy of copper (60%) and zinc (40%); it was known as Muntz metal. This new alloy soon replaced pure copper in the process of sheathing the hulls of wooden ships.

MASS PRODUCTION

Mass production depends on three things: the use of machinery, interchangeable components, and the assembly line.

MADE BY HAND
The first machines were individually made by hand. The idea of interchangeable parts was first introduced in France in 1785 for making the firing mechanisms of sports guns.

MANUFACTURING FIREARMS
In 1801, inventor Eli Whitney demonstrated to the U.S. government his system of interchangeable parts for the manufacture of military firearms.

SAMUEL COLT
In 1855, American industrialist Samuel Colt set up a factory that used interchangeable parts and a production line to make handguns of his own design.

RANSOM OLDS
In 1901 in the U.S., inventor Ransom Olds introduced production-line methods into the newly established automobile industry for the manufacture of his Oldsmobile buggy.

MODEL T PRODUCTION LINE
In 1913, American industrialist Henry Ford built the world's first fully integrated factory assembly line for the production of the famous Model T Ford.

Workers added parts to cars as the cars moved by. The man-hours required to build a car dropped from 12 hours to 1.5 hours. A car was produced every 24 seconds.

• See page 82 for information on Henry Ford.

A line of Model T chassis. The car bodies were manufactured on the upper floor of the factory, then lowered onto the chassis, which were built on the lower floor.

THE CONSTRUCTION INDUSTRY

FIRST IRON BRIDGE
In 1777, the world's first iron bridge was constructed across the Severn River in Coalbrookdale in Shropshire, England.

PREFABRICATED BUILDING
In 1851, Crystal Palace was entirely built from iron and glass to accommodate the Great Exhibition in London, England. Engineer and botanist Joseph Paxton designed the building, based on the design of plant greenhouses. Paxton's revolutionary design contained more than 300,000 panes of glass and hundreds of ready-made cast-iron frames that simply bolted together on site—an instant building!

REINFORCED CONCRETE
In 1867 in France, amateur inventor Joseph Monier made the first successful reinforced concrete using lateral iron rods.

Crystal Palace under construction. Six million people visited the Great Exhibition to see the best of British industry, from steam trains to spinning machines.

IRON BUILDINGS
In 1889, the Eiffel Tower in Paris, France, was the last major building to be made from iron—in the future steel would be used instead.

STEEL-FRAMED SKYSCRAPER
By the second half of the 1800s, business space in U.S. cities was in demand. The refinement of the Bessemer steel-making process (1855) made it possible to construct very high buildings, because steel is both stronger and lighter than iron. The development of the first safety elevator also made skyscrapers (buildings of 10–20 stories high) possible.

PRESTRESSED CONCRETE
In 1928, French Engineer Eugéne Freyssinet was the first to use prestressed concrete.

DYNAMITE—AN EXPLOSIVE INVENTION

The invention: Dynamite—a type of nitroglycerine explosive that can be safely handled. Dynamite became widely used in the mining and construction industries.
Invented: 1866
Invented by: Swedish chemist Alfred Nobel
Other inventions: Blasting gelatin, smokeless powder for firearms, and explosives that were specifically used for military purposes (although Nobel later developed a conscience about this).
Inventor fact: When Nobel died in 1896, he bequeathed most of his fortune to establish Nobel Prizes for peace and scientific achievement.

OTIS SAFETY ELEVATOR

- Elisha Otis worked in a U.S. bed factory. Simple cargo elevators were used to move goods to upper floors. He invented a safety device that had arms that shot out from the elevator car and grabbed the side of the elevator shaft if the rope broke. To demonstrate his invention, he had the cable cut while he was in an elevator at the World's Fair of 1853.

- Skyscrapers would not have been built were it not for Otis's invention.

FANTASTIC PLASTIC

Plastics replaced a range of traditional materials used in industry such as wood, metal, glass, ceramics, natural fibers, ivory, and bone.

PARKESINE
In 1862, English chemist Alexander Parkes produced the world's first plastic, Parkesine. The material could be squeezed into a mold while soft and was made into small decorative items, such as hair clips.

CELLULOID
In the late 1860s, American inventor John Hyatt discovered how to make celluloid while looking for an ivory substitute for making billiard balls. Celluloid was made into combs, piano keys, dolls, knife handles, and film. However, it was highly flammable and caused many accidents.

BAKELITE
In 1910, Belgian-born American chemist Leo Baekeland invented the first thermosetting plastic (a plastic that sets permanently when heated). It was named Bakelite. Hard and chemically resistant, Bakelite is a nonconductor of electricity, so it was used in all sorts of electrical appliances.

POLYCARBONATE
In 1953, Dr. Daniel Fox, a chemist at General Electric, created a gooey substance that hardened in a beaker. He found he could not break or destroy the material. Lexan polycarbonate (PC) is now available in more than 35,000 colors. PC has been used in vehicle windows, helmets worn by the first men on the Moon, fighter-jet windshields, laptop computers, CDs, and DVDs.

IRON & STEEL TIMELINE

1709—Quality iron
In England, Abraham Darby first produces good-quality iron by smelting iron ore with coke (baked coal). Coke burns with a hotter flame than charcoal and can be used to fuel much larger furnaces.

1709—Iron bars
In Sweden, engineer Christopher Polhem invents a grooved roller that can be used for making iron bars.

1750—Crucible steel
In England, clock maker Benjamin Huntsman perfects a process for making steel by heating high-quality iron in a special reverbatory furnace. Called crucible steel, this new metal is so hard that knife makers at first refuse to use it.

1783—Puddling process
English iron maker Henry Cort patents his "puddling" process that converts pig iron, produced by smelting, into wrought iron that can be easily hammered and pressed into pots, pans, and other household items.

1847—Steel maker
American iron maker William Kelly discovers that he can convert iron to steel by blasting jets of air onto molten iron.

1855—Bessemer process
In England, inventor Henry Bessemer patents his own method of making steel using blasts of air.

1864—Siemens-Martin
The Martin ironworks in France begins producing steel in an open-hearth furnace invented by German engineer William Siemens. The Siemens-Martin process later becomes the world's leading method of steel production.

1866—Air boiling
In the U.S., Henry Kelly patents his "air boiling" method of steel making.

1877—Quality steel
In England, cousins Percy and Sidney Gilchrist invent a method of dephosphorizing steel to produce better quality metal.

- See page 72 for information on discovering and inventing metal.

1838—Pedal power
Kirkpatrick Macmillan, a Scottish blacksmith, invents the bicycle when he improves the recently invented "dandy horse" or "velocipede." He adds a pair of pedals to it, which drive the rear wheel.

1881—Electric vehicle
The world's first electric vehicle is driven around the streets of Paris, France. The electric power is supplied from storage batteries developed by Gaston Planté and Camille Faure.

1885—Automobile
In Germany, the mechanical engineer Karl Benz builds and test-drives the world's first automobile, a tricycle powered by an internal-combustion engine. Benz's motor tricycle has a top speed of 8 mph (13km/h).

1885—Motorcycle
Gottlieb Daimler (who also invented the gasoline engine) builds the world's first motorcycle in conjunction with German inventor Wilhelm Maybach.

1888—Pneumatic tire
Scottish veterinary surgeon John Dunlop patents the pneumatic tire. He invented the tire to give his son a more comfortable ride on his tricycle.

1904—Commercial success
The four-wheel curved-dash Oldsmobile designed by Ransom Olds becomes the world's first commercially successful automobile when some 4,000 are sold in the U.S. in a single year.

1908—Model T
American industrialist Henry Ford introduces the Model T—"the car you can have in any color, as long as it's black." The Model T marks the true beginning of the automobile age.

• See page 80 for information on mass production.

ENGINE POWER

For thousands of years people had to rely on muscle power for making overland journeys. They walked, rode on horseback, or sat in a wagon pulled by draft animals. Beginning in the 1700s, the traditional forms of transportation were transformed by the invention and development of new sources of mechanical power in the form of the steam engine and later the internal-combustion engine.

The blossoming movie industry of the 1920s was quick to see the potential of the automobile—Ford's Model Ts were soon in the movies!

INVENTION OF THE ENGINE

An engine is a device for transforming heat from burned fuel into motive power.

INTERNAL OR EXTERNAL?
Steam engines are external-combustion engines—the fuel is burned in a separate boiler (external from the engine) to make the steam that provides the motive force. Internal-combustion engines, such as gas and diesel engines, burn their fuel inside the engines.

THE FOUR-STROKE ENGINE
In 1876, German engineer Nikolaus Otto built the first four-stroke internal-combustion engine. It burned a mixture of air and coal gas. Four-stroke engines get their name because the piston goes through a repetitive cycle of four up-and-down movements, or strokes. Otto engines became widely used in European factories.

THE GASOLINE ENGINE
In Germany in 1885, Gottlieb Daimler invented the gas engine when he developed a carburetor—a device that allows a four-stroke engine to burn a mixture of air and gasoline. The advantage of gasoline is that it is much easier to store than coal gas.

THE DIESEL ENGINE
In 1893, German engineer Rudolf Diesel invented a four-stroke engine that burned a mixture of air and diesel oil.

A Nikolaus Otto four-stroke engine

HENRY FORD 1863–1947

Nationality: American

Profession: Engineer and businessman

Biographical information: Ford left school at 15 and apprenticed as a machinist. Later he set up a sawmill and engineering workshop on his father's farm. He built his first car in a workshop behind his home in Detroit, Michigan, in 1896. In 1903, he set up the Ford Motor Company.

Most famous invention: In 1913, Ford invented an efficient way of making cars—the assembly line. A car moves along a track in the factory, and each worker adds one part to the car as it passes him or her.

Eureka moment: Ford realized that if he could produce cars cheaply enough, he could sell them in huge numbers and make big profits.

Henry Ford

FIRST OIL WELL

- In 1859, Edwin Drake drilled the world's first oil well in Pennsylvania. He struck oil 69 ft. (21m) below the ground.

Edwin Drake (right) in 1866 in front of the first U.S. oil well

- At first oil refineries concentrated on producing lubricating oils and paraffin for lamps, but after 1900, with the development of the internal-combustion engine, gasoline and diesel fuel quickly became the most important refinery products.

SUPER STEAM

THE MALLARD

The fastest-ever steam locomotive was the *Mallard*. It achieved a maximum speed of 125 mph. (202km/h) in England in 1938. The locomotive was built by British engineer Sir Nigel Gresley.

TIMELINE: STEAM POWER

Cugnot's steam-powered tricycle had a top speed of 2 mph (3km/h).

At first steam power was mostly used to run stationary machines. It was only through the vision and determination of engineers and inventors that steam was eventually used to power the railroads.

1698—The steam pump
In England, engineer Thomas Savery invents a pump that uses condensed steam to create a vacuum that draws water up a pipe. The machine is used to pump water from underground mines.

1712—The beam engine
English engineer Thomas Newcomen invents the first true steam engine. It uses a pair of pistons in cylinders to tilt the ends of a centrally positioned horizontal beam that operates a pump.

1769—A steam wagon
French army engineer Nicholas Cugnot builds the world's first steam-powered land vehicle. Cugnot's prototype three-wheeled artillery tractor can pull loads of up to three tons. However, the weight of the huge copper boiler at the front makes it difficult to steer. On its first trip it runs into a wall.

1791—Rotary power
Scottish engineer James Watt perfects a steam engine that is capable of powering other machines. Watt's machine has a flywheel, which converts the up-and-down movement of a piston into rotary motion.

1801-1808—Railroad locomotives
Richard Trevithick builds a steam locomotive for an ironworks in Coalbrookdale in Shropshire, England. In 1808, he gives rides to passengers around a circular track built in London in his "catch-me-who-can" steam train.

1807—Steamboat service
In the U.S., engineer Robert Fulton starts a steamboat service on the Hudson River between the cities of New York and Albany. The service is reliable and successful.

1830—The Rocket
A 40-mi. (64-km) railroad line between the English cities of Liverpool and Manchester is primarily built to carry passengers. A locomotive named *Rocket*, designed by engineer Robert Stephenson, pulls the first train in 1830. For a short stretch, *Rocket* reaches a speed of 36 mph (58km/h).

Stephenson's *Rocket* locomotive sits next to a larger, more modern British steam locomotive.

FASTEST ON FOUR WHEELS

1899—62-mph (100-km/h) barrier
French engineer Camille Jenatzy builds an electric car that becomes the first vehicle to break the 62-mph (100-km/h) barrier.

1906—Stanley Steamer
A Stanley Steamer built by American brothers Francis and Freelan Stanley reaches a road speed of 127 mph (205km/h).

1921—207 mph (335km/h)
French driver Joseph Sadi-Lecointe reaches 207 mph (335km/h) in a gasoline-engine Nieuport-Delage racecar.

1988—Solar power
In the U.S., driver Molly Brennan achieves a top speed of 48 mph (78km/h) in a solar-powered vehicle called Sunraycer.

1997—Sound barrier
In Black Rock Desert, Nevada, Andy Green breaks the sound barrier in Thrust SSC, reaching a speed of 761 mph (1,228km/h).

ON THE ROAD TIMELINE

1952—Air bag
First patented in 1952 by American John W. Hetrick, and with a practical version developed in 1973, air bags were installed in most cars in the U.S. by 1988 and later added to European cars.

1959—Seat belt
First installed in a 1959 Volvo, Nils Bohlin's "lap-and-diagonal" seat belts anchor passengers to the car. Seat belts have since prevented millions of deaths and injuries.

1954—Breathalyzer
Chemicals that turn from orange to green, indicating the amount of alcohol in the breath, are the secret of the device invented by U.S. policeman Robert Borkenstein.

- *See pages 84–85 for more travel-related inventions.*

1485—Flapping design
Italian artist and inventor Leonardo da Vinci sketches a man-powered aircraft made of wood and fabric. Da Vinci's design is intended to imitate the flight of birds with flapping wings.

1804—Fixed wings
In England, amateur flight enthusiast and inventor George Cayley builds a model fixed-wing glider that establishes the basic configuration of the modern aircraft. The glider is strong enough to carry a boy, and later a stronger model carries Cayley's coachman across a narrow valley. Following the flight, the coachman resigns.

1896—Hang glider
In Germany, inventor Otto Lilienthal is killed after crashing into the ground while testing his latest design for a hang glider. Previously, Lilienthal had successfully flown distances of more than 656 ft. (200m) and had made more than 2,500 flights.

1903—Powered flight
Orville and Wilbur Wright achieve the world's first powered flight.

1907—First helicopter
French mechanic Paul Cornu becomes the first person to build and fly a helicopter. It hovers just off the ground for 20 seconds, then the fuselage rotates in the opposite direction to the rotor blades, causing the machine to crash to the ground.

1909—Cross-channel flight
French engineer and aviator Louis Blériot makes the first flight across the English Channel in the Type XI monoplane that he has designed and built.

1919—First across ocean
Setting off from Newfoundland and landing in Ireland, English pilots John Alcock and Arthur Brown fly a Vickers Vimy biplane across the Atlantic Ocean. The engines get blocked by ice several times, and Brown has to clamber along the wings to chip away the ice with a knife.

• The timeline continues on page 85.

PLANES & BOATS

Until the invention of powered flight, the only way to cross seas and oceans was by ship. Early sailors in wooden sailing ships were constantly at the mercy of the winds and high seas. During the 1800s, technological innovations, such as iron hulls and steam engines, made shipping faster, safer, and more reliable. Since the beginning of the 1900s, the development of aircraft has shrunk long-distance travel times from weeks to a matter of hours!

THE STORY OF THE FIRST FLIGHT

- On December 17, 1903, Wilbur and Orville Wright travel to sand dunes outside Kitty Hawk, North Carolina, with their plane, *Flyer*.

- Only five people witness the world's first powered flight.

- Wilbur runs alongside *Flyer*, holding one wing to balance the plane on the track.

- Orville operates the controls lying face-down on the lower wing.

- The flight lasts 12 seconds and covers a distance of 120 ft. (36.5m). The brothers make a further three successful flights that day.

ORVILLE AND WILBUR WRIGHT

Wilbur: 1867–1912

Orville: 1871–1948

Nationality: American

Profession: Engineers

Biographical information: Orville and Wilbur Wright were brothers. From an early age they were interested in engineering. They owned a business, manufacturing and designing bicycles.

Most famous invention: The airplane—they demonstrated the first powered, controlled, and sustained flight in their plane, *Flyer*.

Eureka moment: In 1899, Wilbur, while watching birds, realized that an airplane must be able to bank to one side or another to climb or descend and to steer left or right.

Inventors at work: The Wright brothers built gliders (to perfect the controls for their plane), a lightweight gas engine (to power it), and an efficient propeller. They even built a wind tunnel to aid their experiments. The brothers' approach to inventing was scientific. They thought about a machine's requirements in advance rather than "building the machine and seeing what happened" like their aviation predecessors.

The Wright brothers' plane, *Flyer*, in Kitty Hawk

INVENTING THE JET ENGINE

Invention of the jet engine
In 1930, Royal Air Force pilot Frank Whittle patented his idea for the jet engine—an aircraft engine that uses a jet of heated air to produce thrust.

Whittle recognized the potential for an aircraft that could fly at high speeds. He proved mathematically that his invention would work, but the British Air Ministry was not interested.

The first jet engine
Whittle built his jet engine, and on April 12, 1937, the turbojet engine had its maiden run on the ground. However, it was German inventors who developed the first operational jet aircraft in 1939.

Whittle's jet engine

TEST PILOTS

Test pilots make the invention of aircraft possible. They put new designs of air and spacecraft through maneuvers designed to test the machines' capabilities.

In 1947, the sound barrier was broken for the first time by American test pilot Chuck Yeager in the air-launched, rocket-powered Bell *X-1* aircraft. The *X-1* reached an amazing 668 mph (1,078km/h) at an altitude of 41,984 ft. (12,800m).

1783—First human flight
The first humans to fly take to the skies in a hot-air balloon invented and built by French brothers Joseph and Jacques Montgolfier.

• See page 76 for information on Joseph and Jacques Montgolfier.

1783—Hydrogen balloon
Shortly after the Montgolfiers' hot-air balloon flight, French scientist Jacques Alexandre César Charles makes the first flight in a balloon containing lighter-than-air hydrogen gas. Charles's balloon travels 29 mi. (46.5km).

1900—Zepplin
In Germany, LZ-1, the first large airship designed by engineer Ferdinand von Zeppelin, successfully takes to the air. Subsequently, Zeppelins are used both for warfare, as bombers, and for carrying passengers. In 1937, the Hindenburg airship disaster brings the airship era to an abrupt end.

1932—Auguste Piccard
Professor Auguste Piccard takes his hot-air balloon to a height of

Piccard (right) and Jones operated *Breitling Orbiter 3* from this pressurized capsule, which resembles a spacecraft.

55,750 ft. (17,000m). Piccard risks bursting blood vessels and his eardrums, and even blackouts, because his capsule is not pressurized as modern aircraft are today.

1961—Record breaker
A U.S. Navy research helium balloon carries two pilots, Malcolm Ross and Vic Parther, to an altitude of 113,711 ft. (34,668m) above Earth's surface.

1999—World circumnavigation
Balloon enthusiasts Bertrand Piccard and Brian Jones circumnavigate the world (25,305 mi./40,814km) in *Breitling Orbiter 3*. The helium balloon uses air currents to control its course. *Orbiter 3* is 180 ft. (55m) tall and is so large that it could contain the contents of seven Olympic-sized swimming pools!

THE FIRST SUBMARINE

The first submarine (a wooden rowboat with a watertight cover of greased leather) was designed in 1620 by Dutch engineer Cornelius van Drebbel.

The craft was powered by 12 oarsmen and reached depths of almost 16 ft. (5m) during tests on the Thames River, England. Passengers breathed through tubes that ran from the submarine to the surface of the water.

SHIP INNOVATIONS

1783
French engineers demonstrate that a steam engine can be used to propel a 150-ton riverboat.

1786
American engineer John Fitch designs and launches the world's first purpose-built steamboat on the Delaware River near the city of Philadelphia, Pennsylvania.

1838
Swedish engineer John Ericsson uses his ship *Archimedes* to demonstrate that a steam-driven screw (propeller) is more efficient than a steam-driven paddle wheel.

INVENTION OF THE HOVERCRAFT

- In 1955, British engineer Christopher Cockerell patented the hovercraft, a vehicle that moves on a cushion of air.

- In 1958, his prototype *SR.N1* crossed the English Channel (21 mi./34km) in 20 minutes.

- Cockerell patented around 70 inventions during his lifetime.

SR.N1 arrives in Dover after the first Channel crossing.

LONGITUDE

In the 1700s, sailors could tell their latitude (position north–south) by taking sightings of the sun. Longitude (position east–west) was difficult.

Using a clock to compare the time at home with the time at sea, according to the position of the Sun, was one way to calculate the distance traveled, but no pendulum clock could keep accurate time on rolling seas.

In 1761, clock maker John Harrison invented a chronometer (a large watchlike clock) with a mechanism and dials. Harrison's invention kept such accurate time, even at sea, that a navigator could figure out on a map where he was with an accuracy of less than 1 mi. (1.6km).

John Harrison's chronometer

FLIGHT TIMELINE

1927—Solo transatlantic
American aviator Charles Lindbergh makes the first solo flight across the Atlantic Ocean (from New York City to Paris, France) in the *Spirit of St. Louis*, a single-engine M62.

1930—Jet engine
In England, Royal Air Force pilot Frank Whittle patents his idea for a jet engine.

1939—Jet aircraft
In Germany, the He 178 monoplane, designed by Ernst Heinkel, makes its first flight powered by a jet engine developed by engineer Hans Pabst von Ohain.

1941—Sikorsky helicopter
Russian-born aviator Igor Sikorsky solves the problem of torque (the body of a helicopter turning in the opposite direction to the rotor blades) by installing a small rotor on the tail. His VS-300 hovers in the air for 102 minutes.

1952—Jet airliner
The world's first jet airliner, the de Havilland *Comet*, comes into service, carrying passengers between London, England, and Johannesburg, South Africa.

1970—Jumbo jet
The first Boeing 747 jumbo jet airliner comes into service between New York City and London. The jumbo jet can carry more than 360 passengers at a time.

1979—Human powered
American pilot Bryan Allen achieves the first human-powered cross-channel flight, flying the pedal-powered *Gossamer Albatross* aircraft designed by aeronautical engineer Paul MacCready.

1986—Around the world
American pilots Richard Rutan and Jeana Yeager fly nonstop around the world in the experimental *Voyager* aircraft. The flight, which lasts nine days, is made without refueling.

TELEGRAPH & TELEPHONE
TIMELINE

1794 — Chappe's telegraph
Claude Chappe begins the construction of his telegraph across France.

1825 — Electromagnet
The electromagnet is invented by Englishman William Sturgeon. This is vital for the later invention of the telegraph.

1837 — Five-needle telegraph
William Fothergill Cooke and Charles Wheatstone invent the five-needle telegraph. It works by sending an electric current along wires that move two of the five needles, either left or right, so that they both point to one letter at a time.

1843 — Morse telegraph
Samuel Morse demonstrates his telegraph to U.S. Congress, and they give him $30,000 to build a telegraph line from Washington, D.C., to Baltimore, Maryland, a distance of 40 mi. (64km).

1844 — Morse's message
Morse sends the first message on the new telegraph line. It reads, "What hath God wrought?"

1858 — Atlantic cable
A cable is laid between the U.S. and Great Britain so that telegraphs can be sent across the Atlantic. The cable fails within a month.

1860 — First telephone
A German teacher named Johann Philipp Reis invents a simple telephone. Reis builds just 12 telephones before he dies. One of Reis's telephones reaches Edinburgh University, and it inspires a student named Alexander Graham Bell.

• The timeline continues on page 87.

When the United States declared its independence in 1776, it took 48 days for the news to cross the Atlantic Ocean. The arrival of the telegraph in 1843 and the telephone in 1876 meant that news could get to anywhere in the world almost instantly. The arrival of radio communication in 1896 meant that sounds could travel vast distances without the need for cables. And in 1936, moving pictures and sounds could be seen by millions, at the same time, with the invention of television.

Wheatstone and Cooke's five-needle telegraph

CHAPPE'S TELEGRAPH

• In 1793, France was at war. A quick way to warn of an invasion was needed. In 1794, Claude Chappe invented the telegraph.

• Chappe's telegraph used two arms at the top of a tall tower. Ropes and pulleys moved the arms into different positions, each representing a letter.

• The towers were positioned 6–19 mi. (10–30km) apart, and the messages were read by people using telescopes.

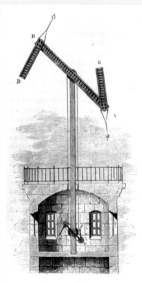

The main pole of the telegraph was about 20 ft. (6m) tall.

MORSE CODE

• Samuel Morse invented Morse code in 1838. He first got the idea for the code in 1832 when he was told about experiments with electricity.

• Morse's idea was to develop a code based on interrupting the flow of electricity so that a message could be heard.

• Morse code works very simply. Electricity is either turned on or off. When it is on, it travels along a wire. At the other end of the wire the electric current can either make a sound or be printed out.

• A short electric current, a "di," is printed as a dot, and a longer "dah" is printed as a dash.

A	•—	N	—•
B	—•••	O	———
C	—•—•	P	•——•
D	—••	Q	——•—
E	•	R	•—•
F	••—•	S	•••
G	——•	T	—
H	••••	U	••—
I	••	V	•••—
J	•———	W	•——
K	—•—	X	—••—
L	•—••	Y	—•——
M	——	Z	——••

The full Morse code is based on combining dots and dashes to represent the letters of the alphabet.

• See page 76 for information on Samuel Morse.

THE INVENTION OF THE POSTAGE STAMP

• In the early 1800s, postage in Great Britain was charged by distance and the number of sheets in a letter. The recipient paid for the postage, not the sender.

• In 1837, retired English schoolteacher Rowland Hill wrote a pamphlet calling for cheap standard postage rates, not charged by distance.

• The British Post Office took up Hill's ideas and, in May 1840, issued the first adhesive penny postage stamps.

• The stamps were printed with black ink and become known as "penny blacks."

ALEXANDER GRAHAM BELL 1847–1922

Nationality: Scottish-born American

Profession: Teacher and inventor

Biographical information:
Bell left school at 14 and trained in the family business of teaching elocution. His family moved to Canada in 1870. Bell trained people in his father's system of teaching deaf people to speak.

Most famous invention: Working at night with his assistant, Thomas Watson, Bell made the first working telephone in 1876.

Inventors at work: The telegraph already used electricity to convey messages over long distances. The telephone had to turn sound into electricity and back again. To make it work was a technical challenge that Bell and Watson solved by hard work over many months.

Eureka moment: The first words spoken down a telephone were, "Mr. Watson, come here, I want you!" Bell was testing out his newly invented telephone when he spilled some chemicals on his clothes and called his assistant for help.

Alexander Graham Bell opens the New York to Chicago telephone line in 1892.

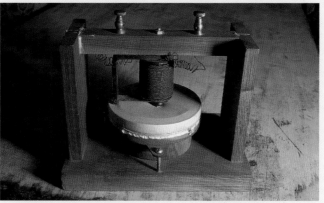

Bell experimented for many years with different ways of sending and receiving spoken messages. This "gallows frame" transmitter was one of his earliest machines.

THE INVENTION OF DIRECT DIALING

- At first telephone connections were made by operators pushing plugs into sockets.

- In 1889, in Kansas City, Missouri, undertaker Almon Strowger discovered that his local operator was married to a rival undertaker and was diverting his customers' calls to her husband.

- Strowger invented the first automatic telephone switch — a remote-controlled switch that could connect one phone to any of several others by electrical pulses without the need for an operator.

CELLULAR PHONES AND TEXT MESSAGING

1973—First cell-phone call
The first call on a cellular phone was made in April by Dr. Martin Cooper, general manager of Motorola. He called his rival, Joel Engel, head of research at Bell Laboratories.

1992—First text message
The first text message was sent. It is reported that the message was from Neil Papworth of Vodafone, and it said, "Merry Christmas."

2000—Camera phone
The camera phone was created by

Sharp Corporation in Japan. It was called the J-SH04.

2008—Texts skyrocketing
One trillion text messages were sent by cell phones in the U.S. alone.

VIDEOPHONES

- The first videophone with a screen for moving pictures was invented by AT&T in 1964. It allowed callers to see the people that they were calling.

- Using cell phones to record videos started with the creation of 3G cell phones by Dr. Irwin Jacobs in 2003.

TELEGRAPH & TELEPHONE TIMELINE

1861—The pantelegraph
The first fax machine is sold. It is called the pantelegraph.

Telegraphs can be sent from one end of the U.S. to the other.

1865—Public fax
The first fax service opens in France. It is used to send photographs to newspapers.

1866—Atlantic cable
The ship the *Great Eastern* lays a second cable along the floor of the Atlantic Ocean.

1876—Bell's telephone
Alexander Graham Bell invents the first successful telephone.

1878—Thomas Edison
American inventor Thomas Edison has also been working on a telephone, but Bell manages to beat him to it. Edison invents a microphone that makes the voice of the person speaking much clearer to the listener.

1880—First pay phone
The first pay phones open in New York City.

There are now nine separate cables between the U.S. and Great Britain.

1892—Direct dialing
The first direct-dial telephones become operational.

1915—First Atlantic calls
Telephone calls across the Atlantic can be made for the first time.

1936—Coaxial cable
The first coaxial cable is laid. This allows many telephone messages to pass along the same cable.

1963—160 million phones
The number of telephones in the world reaches 160 million.

1988—Fiber-optic cable
The first fiber-optic cable is laid across the Atlantic Ocean. Now telephone messages are carried on pulses of light.

• For more information on Thomas Edison see page 77, and for information on Edison's phonograph see page 92.

COMMUNICATION

1873—Electromagnetic waves
Scottish scientist James Clerk Maxwell prepares a paper in which he writes about electromagnetic waves that can travel through the air. He cannot prove that they exist.

1887—Heinrich Hertz
German scientist Heinrich Hertz transmits a spark using a tuned antenna. He also proves James Clerk Maxwell's theory about the existence of radio waves, which are one type of electromagnetic wave. However, the radio waves he created could not travel very far.

1894—Marconi's bell
Guglielmo Marconi makes a bell ring by using radio waves to activate it.

1897—Shore to ship
Marconi transmits a signal from land to a ship 18 mi. (29km) out at sea. The British Royal Navy shows great interest in this new invention.

1901—Atlantic signal
Marconi sends a radio signal across the Atlantic Ocean.

1906—Triode valve
The triode valve is invented by Lee de Forest. It makes radio signals more powerful.

1906—First voice and music
American scientist Reginald A. Fessenden transmits his voice and broadcasts music using radio waves. Before this, only Morse code could be carried on radio waves. Following his groundbreaking achievement, Fessenden does not pursue his radio experiments.

1920—First radio station
The world's first-ever commercially licensed radio station, KDKA Philadelphia, makes its first broadcast on November 2.

1923—Atlantic voice
The first-ever broadcast of a voice across the Atlantic Ocean travels from Pittsburgh, Pennsylvania, to Manchester, England.

1995—Digital radio
BBC radio stations begin digital broadcasting in the U.K.

GUGLIELMO MARCONI 1874–1937

Marconi in 1896 with some early apparatus

Nationality: Italian

Profession: Physicist

Biographical information: Marconi attended technical college in Italy, where he studied electricity and magnetism. After leaving college he continued his experiments at his family's farm, but could find little support for his work in Italy, so in 1896 he went to live in England.

Most famous invention: Marconi invented the first practical system of wireless communication using radio waves. In 1896, before leaving Italy, Marconi managed to transmit a radio signal over a distance of about 0.93 mi. (1.5km). In England, he quickly increased the range to about 62 mi. (100 km), and in 1899, he made radio contact between Great Britain and France.

Eureka moment: In 1901, Marconi successfully sent a radio message across the Atlantic Ocean, from Cornwall, England, to Newfoundland, Canada, a distance of more than 2,480 mi. (4,000km).

Inventor at work: Marconi continued to make numerous improvements to radio transmitting and receiving equipment. In 1909, he was awarded the Nobel Prize for Physics.

CLOCKWORK RADIO

- In 1991, British inventor Trevor Baylis invented the wind-up radio, enabling millions in the developing world with no permanent electricity supply to receive broadcasts.

- The radio works by winding up a spring that uncoils slowly and powers a small generator.

Inventor Trevor Baylis with his clockwork radio

RADIO ON THE MOVE

Invented in 1947, the transistor replaced the valves inside radios that picked up radio signals. Transistors were much smaller than valves, so it now became possible to make portable radios.

1954
The world's first pocket radio goes on sale on October 18. The Regency TR-1 is just 4.7 in. (12cm) tall. Around 100,000 TR1s are sold during the radio's only year of production.

1955
A Japanese company called Tokyo Tsushin Kogyo decides to build a portable radio for the U.S. market. Before it begins selling the radio, it changes the company's name to something Americans can easily say—Sony.

A 1962 Sony transistor radio with a wind-up watch and alarm

JOHN LOGIE BAIRD 1888–1946

Nationality: Scottish

Profession: Electrical engineer

Biographical information: Baird studied at the University of Glasgow, where he first became interested in the idea of using radio waves to transmit pictures. At the time most scientists considered such a system to be impossible.

Most famous invention: Television! In 1926, using equipment that he had made himself, Baird demonstrated the world's first working television system.

Eureka moment: Baird realized that pictures could be sent by radio if the images were broken down into a series of electronic impulses. He invented a mechanical scanner that, by 1926, was able to scan and transmit moving images.

Other inventions: Baird also demonstrated color television in 1928 and continued to research stereoscopic television.

In 1936, he demonstrated his mechanical system to the BBC, but instead they chose an electronic system from EMI.

televisor screen

This is a televisor, a mechanical television set devised by Baird. Viewers watched the first television broadcasts on these sets.

SATELLITES

Most of our long-distance communication relies on the hundreds of satellites that are in orbit around Earth.

• Each satellite receives a radio or television signal from one place and then transmits it onward.

• In the summer of 1962, the U.S. launched the *Telstar* satellite. *Telstar* provided a radio and television link between Europe and the U.S. for just a few hours every day.

• Most of the satellites in orbit today are geostationary—they are traveling at the same speed as Earth's rotation and will always be at the same point in the sky.

Telstar

ELECTRONIC TV PIONEERS

Vladimir Zworykin, vice president of RCA (c. 1951)

Baird is credited with the invention of television, but today the systems we use and the TVs we watch owe much to earlier inventors (see timeline, right) and to two pioneers of electronic television, Vladmir Zworykin and Isaac Shoenberg.

Vladimir Zworykin

• Russian-born Vladimir Zworykin emigrated to the U.S. in 1919.
• Zworykin was the first to take up the suggestion by Scottish engineer Alan Campbell-Swinton that it is possible to both create and display pictures using a cathode-ray tube.
• In 1931, heading a team at Radio Corporation of America (RCA), Zworykin created the first successful electronic camera tube, the iconoscope.

Isaac Shoenberg

• Russian-born Isaac Shoenberg emigrated to Great Britain in 1914.
• In 1936, working with a team at Electric and Musical Industries (EMI), Schoenberg used Zworykin's basic idea to develop the Emitron tube.

The winning system

In 1936, EMI's electronic television system (which used the Emitron tube) was demonstrated to the BBC. It was chosen over John Logie Baird's mechanical system. Except for some detailed differences, the EMI system is still in use today.

1740—Franklin stove
American Benjamin Franklin invents a simple cast-iron stove (similar to modern-day wood burners) for warming homes.

1792—Gas lighting
In 1792, Scottish engineer William Murdoch invents gas lighting. He heats coal in a closed vessel and then pumps the gas to lights around his cottage in Cornwall, England.

1830—Lawn mower
Patented in 1830, Edwin Budding's cylinder lawn mower makes maintaining a lawn possible for everyone. Before this only people with a gardener or flock of sheep could mow a lawn!

1844—Refrigerator
American doctor John Gorrie builds a machine that uses compressed air to provide cooling air for feverish patients in his hospital. In 1851, he receives the first U.S. patent for mechanical refrigeration.

c. 1860—Linoleum
British rubber manufacturer Frederick Walton invents linoleum, a washable floor covering made from cloth covered with a linseed oil and pine resin substance.

1907—Washing machine
U.S. inventor Alva Fisher invents the first electric washing machine. The machine has a drum that tumbles the clothes and water back and forth. The machine is called the "Thor."

1919—Pop-up toaster
U.S. inventor Charles Strite invents the first toaster to automatically stop toasting and pop out the toast when it is ready. However, it will be nine years before Otto Rohwedder invents sliced bread!

1946—Microwave oven
In 1945, U.S. engineer Percy LeBron Spencer invents the microwave oven. While working on radar, Spencer made the discovery that powerful microwaves had melted some candy in his pocket!

• See page 100 for information on domestic robots.

HOMES & FASHION

While most home- and fashion-related inventions could not claim to have changed our world, they have certainly made it more colorful, comfortable, and clean. Today, we wear clothes and shoes made from a variety of different materials. We also take it for granted that electric lights will illuminate our homes; that chilled foods and drinks are in the refrigerator; and that, when we need "to go," the toilet will flush and there will be a roll of toilet paper waiting for us!

THE INVENTION OF THE "DYSON"

- In 1978, British inventor James Dyson noticed that the dust bag in conventional vacuum cleaners clogged up quickly.

- Dyson had the idea of making a bagless cleaner. It used centrifugal force to suck dust into a plastic cylinder.

- Five years and 5,127 prototypes later, Dyson was finally making and selling the Dyson Dual Cyclone vacuum cleaner—the first real vacuuming breakthrough since the vacuum cleaner's invention in 1901.

The Dyson DC15

• See page 106 for more information on vacuum cleaners.

TOILET INVENTIONS

FIRST FLUSHING TOILET
- Sir John Harington was a British poet and humorist. He was a courtier to his godmother, Queen Elizabeth I.

- In 1596, he published *The Metamorphosis of Ajax* (a play on the word *jakes*, slang for *lavatory*). This humorous work included diagrams of a flushing toilet, or water closet (WC).

- Harington's toilet design had a bowl, a seat, and a tank of water for washing away the toilet's contents.

- He built just two of his toilets—one for himself and one for the queen at Richmond Palace.

THOMAS CRAPPER
- In the 1800s, toilet pioneers, such as Thomas Crapper, began to further develop the toilet and produce the style of items that we recognize today.

- Crapper registered a number of patents, including a spring-loaded toilet seat that sprang up as soon as the user stood, pulling rods that automatically flushed the pan.

TOILET PAPER
- American Joseph Gayetty is credited with inventing toilet paper in 1857. Before Gayetty's invention, people tore pages out of mail-order catalogs.

- In 1880, the British Perforated Paper Company invented a type of toilet paper. The shiny paper came in small sheets in a box.

THE LIGHT BULB

- Working independently, British inventor Sir Joseph Wilson Swan and American Thomas Edison each invented a light bulb.

- Swan is best known for his incandescent-filament electric lamp of 1879. It gave off light as an electric current passed through its carbon filament, contained in a glass bulb.

- In the United States, Edison had the same idea. By 1880 he and Swan had developed efficient, long-lasting light bulbs. In 1883, they formed the Edison & Swan United Electric Light Company.

THE INVENTION OF JEANS

The story of the invention of the pants that we now know as jeans is basically the story of Levi's 501 Jeans.

- Levi Strauss ran a dry goods business in San Francisco, California. Strauss supplied cloth to Jacob Davis, a local tailor.

- To cure the problem of his customers ripping their work pants, Davis came up with the idea of using metal rivets to strengthen the points of strain. This was a great success.

- Needing money to patent his invention, Davis teamed up with Strauss. On May 20, 1873, the two men received Patent No. 139121 from the U.S. Patent Office, and blue jeans were born.

- Around 1890 the "waist overalls," as they were called, were assigned the number 501.

- The name *jeans* was coined in around 1960.

Vintage Levi 501s

THE INVENTION OF SNEAKERS

The adidas Hyperride

Adolf (Adi) Dassler made his first shoes in 1920. He was just 20 years old. Dassler's vision was that every athlete should have the best footwear for his or her discipline.

- Athletes wore special shoes from Dassler's workshop for the first time at the 1928 Olympic Games held in Amsterdam, Netherlands.

- By the mid-1930s, Dassler was making 30 different shoes for 11 different sports, and his company was the world's leading sports-shoe manufacturer.

- In 1948, Dassler introduced adidas (a combination of his first and last name) as the company name, and a year later he registered the unmistakable "three stripes."

- In 1954, when Germany won the soccer World Cup, the team was wearing shoes — by adidas!

Adi Dassler in his sports-shoe factory

BABY FASHION

U.S. engineer Victor Mills did not like the cloth diapers worn by his grandaughter, so he challenged U.S. company Proctor & Gamble to find a solution to the problem.

In 1961, after years of testing, Pampers (disposable diapers) were launched — an important invention for babies (and parents) everywhere!

A truly practical invention

THE INVENTION OF NYLON

While a professor at Harvard University in 1928, Wallace Carothers was hired by the chemical company DuPont. Carothers' mission was to "get rid of the worms!"

1928—A silk substitute
Dupont wanted Carothers to make a substitute for silk, the fine and very costly fiber that is spun by silkworms. Carothers set to work with a team of eight people, including a scientist named Julian Hill.

1930—Inventing plastic
The team's first breakthrough was neoprene and then soon after a plastic nicknamed 3-16 polymer.

When Hill dipped a rod into 3-16, he could pull out a thread. The more he stretched the thread, the stronger it became.

The thread was as springy as silk, could be made from oil, water, and air, and no silkworms were required!

1934—Nylon
The 3-16 polymer was not suitable for cloth production because ironing melted it, but by tweaking the recipe, they produced the artificial silk required. Five more years of research, and the newly named *nylon* was ready to go.

INVENTION OF THE BRA

In 1913, New York partygoer Mary Jacob sewed together a few handkerchiefs and some ribbon to create the first bra — a garment that suited her slinky dress better than a corset.

In 1914, after changing her name to Caresse Crosby, she patented the brassiere. A large corset company purchased the idea, and within five years women everywhere were wearing bras.

THE RAINCOAT

In 1823, Scottish chemist Charles Macintosh invented a method of using rubber to produce waterproof cloth.

His name (misspelled as mackintosh, or shortened to "mac") became the popular name for a raincoat.

RECORDED MUSIC TIMELINE

1877—First recording
On December 6, the first sound recording is made by American inventor Thomas Edison on a machine called a phonograph at his Menlo Park laboratory in New Jersey.

1887—Going flat
The first recording machines use cylinders made from tinfoil or wax. In 1887, Emile Berliner invents the gramophone. The machine records sound as a wiggly groove on a flat metal disk.

1898—Magnetic recording
In Denmark, Valdemar Poulsen invents a new way of recording. His telegraphone records sound by magnetizing a steel wire.

1931—Tape recorder
The first tape recorders are built. Instead of steel wire, they use magnetic tape. The public sees tape recorders for the first time in Berlin, Germany, in 1935.

1963—Tape cassette
The first tape recorders use tape that has to be threaded through the machine by hand. Then, in 1963, electric company Philips produces the compact cassette. It is easier to use—you just slot it into a recorder and press the "play" button.

1960s—Portable music
Early tape recorders are the size of a suitcase. Then, in the 1960s, small battery-powered cassette recorders allow people to carry recorded music around with them. Soon recorders are not much bigger than the tape cassettes they play.

1982—Compact disk
Compact disks (CDs) go on sale. Music is recorded as microscopic pits on silver-colored disks.

1998—Downloading
The first MP3 player, the MPMan, lets people download music files from the World Wide Web.

2001—The iPod
Apple launches its own MP3 player, the iPod.

• See page 77 for information on Thomas Edison.

In the past, leisure pursuits were limited by the amount of free time available to people, and toys were primarily simple adaptations of everyday items. Nowadays we have far more leisure time and spending power. For the past 150 years, inventors and innovators have used their talents to entertain us and satisfy our demands, from simple toys such as LEGOs to the latest equipment for downloading music.

Edison's phonograph, the first sound-recording machine

MUSICAL INVENTIONS

c. 1700—Clarinet
German musician and instrument maker Johann Denner develops the clarinet from an earlier musical instrument called the chalumeau.

1709—Piano
Italian harpsichord builder Bartolomeo Cristofori invents a touch-sensitive harpsichord. This new instrument will eventually become the piano. Harpsichord players pluck their strings, but Cristofori's new instrument involves hitting the strings with hammers, so the harder the keyboard is struck, the louder it plays.

1948—Long-playing record (LP)
Engineer Peter Goldmark develops a flexible vinyl disk for Columbia Records that can play 25 minutes of sound on each side.

1949—45-rpm single
RCA Victor brings out the "single"—a 7-in. (17-cm) record that holds one song on each side.

EDISON'S PHONOGRAPH

- Shouting into the horn of Edison's phonograph (see above) made a needle vibrate and scratch a groove into tinfoil wrapped around a spinning cylinder.

- When the needle was moved back to the beginning of the cylinder, the groove made the needle vibrate.

- The tiny vibrations were made loud enough to hear by the machine's horn, recreating the original sound.

THE WALKMAN

- In 1979, Sony engineers took just four days to create a prototype pocket-sized tape player with earphones, an idea devised by Masura Ibuka, the head of Sony.

- Ibuka wanted something that businessmen could use to relieve the boredom of long plane journeys without disturbing other passengers.

- In June 1979, the Walkman was launched.

DIGITAL MUSIC

The iPod nano was introduced in 2005. It uses flash memory instead of a hard drive, so is smaller than the original iPod.

- Old recording machines made a copy of music on a tape or disk. If the recording was not perfect, crackles and hisses would spoil the listener's pleasure.

- Digital recording is different. The music is changed into a number code, and it is the code that is recorded.

- A CD player or MP3 player reads the code and uses it to create the music. Crackles and hisses that are not part of the code are ignored, so the music is perfect.

TOYS AND GAMES

Scrabble

When he lost his job as an architect during the Great Depression in 1931, Alfred Mosher Butts invented the game Scrabble. Butts calculated the letter frequency and point value for each letter by counting the frequency of letters on the front page of the *New York Times*.

Roller skates

In January 1863, James Leonard Plimpton patented a four-wheeled roller skate that was capable of turning. Plimpton built a roller-skating floor in the office of his New York City furniture business.

LEGOs

In 1955, under the leadership of Godfred Kirk Christiansen, LEGO launched the LEGO system of play, which included LEGO automatic-binding blocks. Christiansen's father, Ole Kirk, started the toy-making business in 1932. Approximately seven LEGO sets are sold each second!

Monopoly

Monopoly was invented by American Charles B. Darrow. He sold his idea to Parker Brothers in 1935. Monopoly was a similar concept to Lizzie G. Magie's "The Landlord's Game" (patented 1904). Magie's game was devised as a way to highlight the potential exploitation of tenants by greedy landlords.

Kaleidoscope

The kaleidoscope was patented by Scottish physicist Sir David Brewster in 1817. Kaleidoscopes use mirrors to reflect images of pieces of colored glass in geometric designs. The design can be endlessly changed by rotating the end of the kaleidoscope.

Barbie

Barbara Millicent Roberts, or "Barbie" as she is better known, was launched in 1959 by California toy company Mattel. Ruth Handler, cofounder of Mattel, spearheaded the doll's introduction. Mattel calculates that every second, two Barbies are sold somewhere in the world.

INVENTION OF BASKETBALL

Basketball was invented in December 1891 by James Naismith, a gym teacher at the International YMCA Training School in Springfield, Massachusetts. Basketball gets its name from the two-bushel baskets (used for collecting peaches) that Naismith used as the "hoops."

INVENTING MOVIE SPECIAL EFFECTS

- A new type of camera called a motion control camera was invented by George Lucas to make the first *Star Wars* movie in 1977.

- A motion control camera is a camera moved by a computer. The computer is programmed with the camera's movements, so the camera can go through exactly the same movements again and again.

- The camera filmed models of spaceships and planets, one by one. Then all of the separate images were combined to form one scene.

AT THE MOVIES TIMELINE

1882 — Camera gun
Frenchman Étienne-Jules Marey is the first person to quickly take a series of photographs with one camera. The gunlike camera takes 12 photographs on a paper disk in one second. It is the forerunner of the movie camera.

1887 — Paper to film
An American minister, Hannibal Goodwin, uses a strip of flexible film instead of light-sensitive paper to record images. Film quickly replaces paper.

1888 — First movie
The first film is shot in Leeds, England, by Frenchman Louis Aimé Augustin Le Prince. It shows traffic crossing a bridge.

1891 — Kinetoscope
American inventor Thomas Edison invents a machine called a kinetoscope for showing movies. Only one person can see the movie at a time!

1895 — Cinema is born
French brothers Auguste and Louis Lumière show movies to the public for the first time. Cinemas spread quickly throughout France and all over the world.

1927 — Talkies
Warner Brothers makes the first feature film with sound. It is called *The Jazz Singer*. Sound movies are called "talkies."

1993 — Computer characters
Jurassic Park features the most realistic computer-generated images (CGI) ever seen in a movie. CGI was used to create lifelike dinosaurs, which were blended with live action.

1995 — Computer movies
Disney and Pixar make the first totally computer-generated movie, *Toy Story*.

2001 — Digital movies
The first movie shot entirely using digital cameras is *Star Wars: Attack of the Clones*.

S ince our early ancestors wondered what would happen if they put meat on a fire, humans have enjoyed inventing with food and drink. We seek out new foods, create new tastes, and devise new ways to grow, prepare, and store our food. Today, because we know that too much fat and sugar is bad for us, scientists are hard at work making our favorite foods and treats more healthy!

GROWING FOOD TIMELINE

1492—New foods
Christopher Columbus discovers the New World. In the next 200 years, potatoes, corn, tomatoes, chilies, tobacco, and cocoa reach the rest of the world.

1701—Seed drill
Jethro Tull invents the seed drill in England. The drill sows seeds in straight lines.

1701—Fertilizer
The first guano (sea-bird manure) is brought to Europe from South America to use as fertilizer.

1834—Reaping machine
American Cyrus McCormick invents the horse-drawn reaping machine, which replaces men using sickles and scythes to cut corn and make hay.

1837—Steel plow
American John Deere invents the steel plow, which can plow the soil of the American Midwest without clogging. This makes it possible for people to settle and farm in this region.

1854—Threshing machine
An improved American threshing machine is made that can thresh 1,569 pt. (740L) of wheat in half an hour—six men can thresh only 127 pt. (60L).

1860—Milking machine
Modern improvements to the milking machine allow a farmer to milk six cows at once and milk an entire herd without help.

1873—Barbed wire
American Joseph Glidden perfects barbed wire. This invention makes fencing much cheaper for farmers.

1917—Ford tractor
The first mass-produced tractor made by Henry Ford goes on sale.

• See page 71 for information on genetic engineering.

INVENTING THE SANDWICH

• Everyone's favorite lunch was invented in the 1700s by Englishman John Montagu, the 4th Earl of Sandwich.

• The story goes that on one occasion in 1762, Montagu played cards for 24 hours nonstop. He ate beef between slices of toast so that one of his hands was free for playing cards at all times. Montagu's convenient snack was named *sandwich* after the inventive earl.

INVENTING COCA-COLA

• Described as the world's "best-known taste," the drink we now know as Coca-Cola was invented by pharmacist Dr. John Stith Pemberton in Atlanta, Georgia.

• On May 8, 1886, a pitcher of Dr. Pemberton's syrup was sampled at Jacob's Pharmacy and pronounced "excellent" by the lucky customers gathered there. Carbonated water was added to the syrup to produce a drink that was both "delicious and refreshing." The new product was immediately put on sale for five cents a glass.

• The inventor's partner, Frank M. Robertson, suggested the name Coca-Cola and correctly thought that "the two Cs would look well in advertising."

The famous Coca-Cola trademark was penned in Robertson's unique script.

LOUIS PASTEUR 1822–1895

Nationality: French

Profession: Scientist

Biographical information: The young Louis Pasteur did not impress as a student, but classes given by a brilliant chemistry teacher were to change his life. After studying at the famous École Normale Supérieure in Paris, he became dean of the Faculty of Science at the University of Lille.

Most famous discovery: Pasteur showed that invisible organisms can spoil food and cause disease. Pasteurization, the process he invented of making liquids hot enough to kill any harmful organisms without destroying their food value, is still used today, particularly in milk production. It is used to kill bacteria that can cause tuberculosis in humans.

Eureka moment: While studying the fermentation process of wine and vinegar, he made his greatest discovery: that fermentation and decay are caused by microscopic living organisms. By heating wine to about 140°F (60°C), he killed off the unwanted yeast cells that caused the product to spoil.

Other discoveries: Vaccinations,

including a vaccine for the killer disease rabies, developed from the brain tissue of infected animals. Pasteur was hailed as a hero when he cured a boy who had been bitten by a rabid dog.

• See page 69 for information on vaccinations.

CLARENCE BIRDSEYE 1886–1956

Nationality: American

Profession: Naturalist

Biographical information:
Clarence Birdseye was born in New York in 1886. He studied biology at college, but left to work as a field naturalist with the U.S. government in the frozen north of Canada.

Eureka moment: In Labrador in 1912, Birdseye watched Native Americans fishing through holes chipped in an icy lake. As fish were pulled out, they were immediately frozen by the intense cold air. Birdseye realized that speedy chilling solved the main problem with frozen food, which is ice!

Most famous invention: When food is frozen slowly, long, sharp crystals of ice are formed, which cut into the food, causing it to break up when defrosted. It took Birdseye eight years to figure out how to chill food quickly enough to stop the daggers of ice from forming. By 1930, Birdseye's machine, which squeezed prepacked food between two very cold plates, was ready to

Clarence Birdseye (in the white lab coat) experiments with a huge dehydration machine.

go into production. However, home freezers were still very rare.

It was not until 1955, following the launch of fish sticks, that Birdseye's invention of frozen food finally achieved fame and worldwide success.

INVENTING CORNFLAKES

- American Will Kellogg worked at his family's health resort, which was eager to promote healthy vegetarian food.

- In 1894, while experimenting with boiled wheat, Kellogg discovered that when crushed between rollers, wheat that had been previously soaked for a long time broke up into flakes.

- Toasted Corn Flakes were sold first by mail order and then at stores. In 1906, Will parted company with his brother John, who objected to the addition of sugar and salt to the cereal.

- Twenty years later, Will Kellogg was a cereal tycoon and one of the richest men in the U.S.

CHOCOLATE DISCOVERY & INVENTION
TIMELINE

c. 1000 B.C.
Chocolate is produced from cocoa beans. It is believed that the Olmec Indians of Central America are the first to grow cocoa beans as a crop.

Early A.D. 1500s
Christopher Columbus and later Spanish explorer Hernando Cortés record seeing cocoa being used and bought and sold during their explorations in the Americas.

1544
Mayan nobles bring gifts of ready-to-drink beaten chocolate to Prince Philip of Spain. It will be 100 years before Spain and Portugal export the drink to the rest of Europe.

The Spanish add sugar cane and vanilla to their cocoa drink, and cocoa becomes popular as a medicine.

Late 1600s
Eating solid chocolate is introduced in Europe in the form of rolls and cakes, served in chocolate emporiums.

1753
Swedish naturalist Carolus Linnaeus, dissatisfied with the word cocoa, renames it theobroma—Greek for "food of the gods."

1765
Irish chocolate maker John Hanan imports cocoa beans to the U.S. Hanan and fellow American Dr. James Baker build America's first chocolate mill, making "Baker's Chocolate."

1828
Coenraad van Houten invents the cocoa press.

1847
J. S. Fry & Sons create a paste that can be molded to produce the first modern chocolate bar.

1876
Milk chocolate is invented by Daniel Peter of Vevey, Switzerland, after eight years of experimenting!

THE INVENTION OF POTATO CHIPS

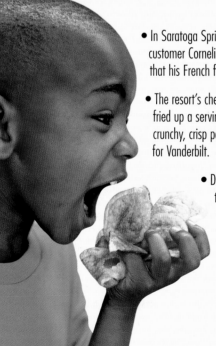

- In Saratoga Springs, New York, in 1853, customer Cornelius Vanderbilt complained that his French fries were too thick.

- The resort's chef, George Crum, fried up a serving of paper-thin, crunchy, crisp potatoes especially for Vanderbilt.

- Dubbed "Saratoga chips," this new way of cooking potatoes quickly became popular.

- George Crum had invented the potato chip!

CHOCOLATE CHIPS BY ACCIDENT!

- One day while preparing a batch of butter drop do cookies, American Ruth Wakefield substituted a semisweet Nestlé chocolate bar, cut up into pieces, for the usual cooking chocolate she used in her cookie recipe.

- Unlike the cooking chocolate, the pieces of Nestlé chocolate did not melt when they were baked; they only softened — the chocolate-chip cookie was born!

COMPUTERS TIMELINE

1822 — Charles Babbage
Charles Babbage (mathematician and inventor) draws up plans for his "difference engine," which will mechanize a whole series of calculations. Babbage also conceives a general-purpose machine called the analytical engine (a "real computer" by today's standards). Unfortunately, it is never completed.

1890 — U.S. Census
Government staff take seven years to analyze the 1880 U.S. Census results. Herman Hollerith patents a machine in 1884, the Hollerith census tabulator, which analyzes the 1890 census in just six weeks.

1937 — Programmable computer
Howard Aiken of Harvard University, in collaboration with IBM, develops "Harvard Mark 1." After experimenting with electromagnetic relay circuits and vacuum tubes (switches with no moving parts), Aiken is able to build something like Babbage's analytical engine.

1941 — Konrad Zuse
German engineer Zuse builds the first true computer. It is controlled by a program and uses binary form.

1943 — Colossus
As part of the wartime project to break enemy codes, the British government builds Colossus, the first electronic digital computer.

1946 — ENIAC
The first completely electronic computer is created. It is designed for the specific purpose of computing values for artillery range tables.

1947 — Transistor
The invention of the transistor leads IBM to reengineer its early machines from electromechanical, or vacuum tube, to transistor technology in the 1950s.

1954 — Business computers
IBM produces IBM 650, a magnetic drum computer costing $200,000. IBM eventually sells 1,800 models.

• The timeline continues on page 97.

THE COMPUTER

Computers are now used in almost every part of our lives, and yet the computer has been around for only a short time. One hundred years ago, mechanical machines that did calculations were used, but it was only at the end of the 1930s that electronic computers appeared. The first computers were large machines designed for use in laboratories, in industry, and for defense. In 1974, it became possible to have a computer in the home.

The Apple Macintosh, or Mac, was the first computer to have what is known as a desktop-type screen with icons.

ANCIENT COMPUTER

- The abacus was invented in the period 3000–1000 B.C. by the Babylonians (an ancient race of people living in the area that is modern-day Iraq).

- This early counting machine made up of beads on rods can be said to be the first step in the development of the computer.

THE POTENTIAL OF AN INVENTION

As with all of the greatest inventions, at first not everyone could see the computer's potential.

"I think there is a world market for maybe five computers."
Thomas Watson, chairman of IBM, 1943

"There is no reason anyone in the right state of mind will want a computer in their home."
Ken Olson, president of Digital Equipment Corp., 1977

THE FIRST COMPUTERS

ENIAC

1946 — ENIAC (Electronic Numerical Integrator and Computer) The first electronic and programmable computer. ENIAC contained over 17,000 vacuum tubes and occupied a room 49 ft. by 29 ft. (15m x 9m)!

1951 — UNIVAC 1
The world's first electronic computer to go on sale. It was created by John Eckert and John Mauchly. It was used by the U.S. government to help gather material for the national census.

UNIVAC

APPLE II

1977 — Apple II
The first successful personal computer to go on sale. It was made by Apple Computer Inc. It was the first computer to have a color screen and its own keyboard.

1983 — Apple Lisa
The first computer to use a mouse and pull-down menus goes on sale. Apple Lisa was also created by Apple Computer Inc.

KEY COMPUTER DEVELOPMENTS

A factory worker makes vacuum tubes.

Vacuum tubes
The main electronic parts of early computers were called vacuum tubes, or simply valves, because they controlled the flow of electricity.

Transistors are made of materials called semiconductors.

1947—Transistors
The first prototype transistor was invented at Bell Laboratories in the U.S. A transistor acts as an electronic switch, and once it was perfected in the 1950s, it quickly replaced the vacuum tube.

This microchip, held in the jaws of an ant, contains thousands of components.

1960s—Microchips
In the late 1960s, the integrated circuit was developed. Thousands of transistors and other electric components could be built onto a tiny silicon chip, or microchip.

1968—Microprocessors
In 1968, Ted Hoff of Intel was asked to come up with a design for a new calculator chip that could do several jobs at once. He devised the idea of the microprocessor. Launched in 1971, the microprocessor made it possible to build much smaller computers.

INVENTIONS FOR THE COMPUTER

1964—Ink-jet printer
The first ink-jet printer was invented in 1964. It was considered pretty amazing, but computer owners today would be very disappointed with the results.

1965—Computer mouse
U.S. engineer Doug Engelbart and his team at the Human Factors Research Center of Stanford Research Institute design and develop the computer mouse.

1976—Laser printer
First laser printer introduced.

1991—Digital camera
Kodak produces the first digital camera, the DCS 100. The photos have to be stored on a separate piece of equipment.

Today's digital cameras collect 4.1 billion separate pieces of information every time you take a picture.

Computer mouse

COMPUTERS ALL AROUND

Today, the computer is in almost every electrical item we use.

CELLULAR PHONE
The computer in a cell phone figures out where you are and which is the closest transmitter.

CAR
An in-car computer figures out the most economical use of gasoline in most modern cars.

VIDEO CAMERA
All modern video cameras include an "autofocus" function that examines what it can see, detects the edges of each item coming through the lens, and adjusts the focus to keep pictures sharp.

AIRLINER
There are probably more computers in an airliner than any other vehicle. Computers control everything from the speed and height at which the plane flies to the running of the in-flight movie and the cooking of your meal.

ALAN TURING 1912–1954

Nationality: British

Profession: Mathematician and computer expert

Biographical information: Turing was born in 1912. He had a gift for mathematics and studied this subject at Cambridge University.

Most famous invention: Turing's work as a mathematician was stopped by World War II. He was taken to Bletchley Park, England, where he led a team trying to find a way to crack the Enigma code used by Germany, Italy, and Japan. In 1943, Turing designed a computer called Colossus that helped decipher the German codes and win World War II.

Eureka moment: In 1924, university student Alan Turing wrote an essay in which he described a machine that is the basis of all computers in the world today. It was the first idea for a computer to include memory, a processor, and a way of storing information on tape.

Other inventions: After World War II, Turing continued working on computers. In 1950, he wrote an article in which he said that a computer could have the same intelligence as any person. Alan Turing died in 1954 after swallowing poison.

COMPUTERS TIMELINE

1959—First minicomputer
Digital Equipment Corporation produces an early mini computer, the PDP-1. It sells for $120,000—a fraction of the cost of mainframe computers. The later model PDP-8, in 1965, uses the recently invented integrated circuit and sells for $20,000.

1967—Computer keyboard
Keyboards are used for data entry.

1968—Intel
Intel is formed. The company grows to become one of the world's largest and most important computer-processor manufacturers.

1970—Floppy disk
The floppy disk is produced by IBM.

1971—Microprocessor
The first microprocessor is produced.

1974—Personal computer
The first personal computer, the Altair 8800, goes on sale. It is sold as a kit, so the customer has to put the computer together before he or she can use it.

1975—Microsoft
Bill Gates and Paul Allen form Microsoft and adapt BASIC language for use on the Altair PC.

1976—Apple Computer Inc.
Apple Computer Inc. is founded by Steve Wozniak and Steve Jobs.

1981—IBM PC
IBM launches its personal computer (IBM PC), which uses Microsoft Disk Operating System (MS-DOS).

1982—The CD
Philips Electronics and Sony Corporation work together to invent the CD.

1984—The Mac
Apple launches the Macintosh computer, designed to appeal to those who are not computer experts.

1985—Windows
Microsoft releases the first version of the Windows operating system.

1995—Windows 95
Microsoft releases Windows 95, which for the first time fully integrates MS-DOS with Windows.

2007—Windows Vista
The latest Microsoft release enables home computers to access and share digital media files.

INTERNET TIMELINE

1960s to 1980s — ARPANET

A team at the U.S. Advanced Research Projects Agency (ARPA) develops a communication network between researchers and scientists in the United States.

Other organizations join the network throughout the 1970s and early 1980s, and the network grows and grows.

1971 — First e-mail

The first e-mail is sent by computer engineer Ray Tomlinson.

1973 to 1974 — Inventing the Internet

Vinton Cerf and Bob Kahn design the Internet—a network of computers and cables. They also define IP (Internet Protocol), the way in which information is sent on the Internet.

1979 — Emoticons

Adding emotions to e-mail messages is suggested, such as –) to show that something is tongue-in-cheek. By the early 1980s, emoticons such as :-) and :-(are in widespread use.

1980 — First virus

The first virus is accidentally released onto ARPANET, bringing the whole network to a halt.

1983 — The Internet

The Internet is launched and made available to everyone.

The domain name system (DNS), which takes you where you need to be on the Internet using a Web address, is invented by Paul Mockapetris.

Computer expert Fred Cohen invents the term *computer virus*.

1987 — MP3 files

The development of the MP3 file format begins at the Fraunhofer Institute in Germany. It allows music and speech recordings to be compressed and is used by many people on the Internet to easily copy and swap their music collections.

• The timeline continues on page 99.

The Internet is a worldwide collection of computers connected by cables, telephone lines, and satellites. Anyone can be part of the Internet by connecting their computer to a telephone line. It allows people to send messages (e-mails) to anyone else who is connected, interact with other computer users wherever they are in the world, and look at information created by both large organizations and private individuals via the World Wide Web.

TIM BERNERS-LEE 1955–

Tim Berners-Lee

Nationality: English

Profession: Computer scientist

Biographical information:
Berners-Lee was born in London, England, in 1955. Interested in computers, he studied at Oxford University. While at Oxford he built his own computer from old electronic parts and bits of a TV. Both of his parents worked in the computer industry.

Eureka moment: Berners-Lee developed a program called Enquire to help him access varied pieces of information needed in his work. The information was stored in files that contained connections called hypertext links.

Most famous invention: The World Wide Web. In 1989, while working at CERN (European Organization for Nuclear Research) in Geneva, Switzerland, Berners-Lee wrote a program that allowed CERN's scientists to share their work through a global hypertext document system. The Web was released to the world via the Internet in 1991.

Other invention: In 1994, Berners-Lee founded the World Wide Web Consortium. The consortium's goal is to lead the Web to its full potential in the future.

INVENTING THE INTERNET

• Internet pioneers Vinton Cerf and Bob Kahn invented Internet Protocol (IP), a way of sending little "packages" of information through the Internet network.

• A "package" is like a postcard containing information.

• If the postcard has the right address, it can be given to any computer connected to the Internet, and the computer can figure out which cable to send the postcard ("package") down so that it gets to the right recipient.

INVENTION OF E-MAIL

In 1971, U.S. computer scientist Ray Tomlinson devised a computer program for sending messages on the ARPANET network. The program would become e-mail, one of the main ways of communicating on the Internet.

• The first test message was sent between two machines that were physically next to each other, but connected only by ARPANET. The test was successful — e-mail had been invented.

• Today, Tomlinson cannot remember what the first e-mail said, but he jokes it was probably just something like, "QWERTYUIOP."

• Probably the first e-mail message sent to another person on ARPANET was one announcing the new service and telling people to use @, the symbol that Tomlinson chose to separate user names from host-computer names.

@

MOSAIC

- In 1993, the world's first user-friendly Web browser was developed by American Mark Andreessen and a team at the U.S. National Center for Supercomputing Applications (NCSA).

- Mosaic used a point-and-click application that made it easy for people to navigate the World Wide Web.

- By 1994, Mosaic had several million users.

PONG

- In 1972, Atari Corporation was founded by U.S. computer engineers Nolan Bushnell, Ted Dabney, and Al Alcorn.

- In 1972, Bushnell and team invented the video game Pong, based on Ping-Pong (table tennis).

- Two onscreen paddles knocked a ball back and forth across the screen.

- Pong became hugely popular as an arcade-style coin-operated game and went on to be produced in a home version.

1970s poster advertising the revolutionary new game Pong

TIMELINE: INVENTION OF COMPUTER GAMES

1889—Nintendo
The Nintendo company is founded in Japan. It makes playing cards.

1958—First Computer game
William A. Higinbotham of Brookhaven National Laboratory in New York uses an analog computer, control boxes, and an oscilloscope to create "Tennis for Two," a game to amuse visitors to the laboratory.

1962—Spacewar!
A team at Massachusetts Institute of Technology (MIT) in the U.S. invents a game as part of a program to demonstrate the new PDP-1 computer. The game, which would now look extremely simple, involves players moving spaceships and firing torpedoes.

1972—Pong
Atari Corporation invents Pong.

1977—Missile Attack
Mattel releases the first hand-held game, but it uses small lights rather than a screen to display graphics.

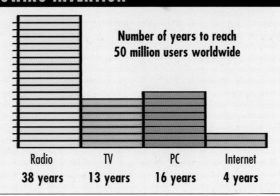

1980—Battlezone
The first 3-D game is produced. Battlezone is such a breakthrough that the U.S. government uses it to train troops.

1989—Nintendo Game Boy
Video games go hand held with the release of the first Nintendo Game Boy.

1994—PlayStation
Sony releases PlayStation, but only in Japan. It reaches the rest of the world the following year.

2000—PlayStation 2
This is even more successful than the original PlayStation, selling out worldwide within days.

In 2000, Nintendo sells its one hundred millionth Game Boy.

2002—Xbox
Microsoft enters the console market as it launches the Xbox.

2006—Wii
Microsoft launches their fifth—and most popular—home video game.

- See page 104 for more information on oscilloscopes.

A FAST-GROWING INVENTION

In 1998, the U.S. Department of Commerce report "The Emerging Digital Economy" stated, "The Internet's pace of adoption eclipses all other technologies that preceded it."

When radio was invented, it took 38 years to reach 50 million users. The Internet took just four years.

Number of years to reach 50 million users worldwide

Radio	TV	PC	Internet
38 years	13 years	16 years	4 years

See page 104 for more information on oscilloscopes.

INTERNET TIMELINE

1988—Internet worm
Robert Morris, a U.S. science student, unleashes an Internet worm (a program that propagates itself across a network) onto the Internet. The Morris worm brings 6,000 computers to a halt.

1989—Inventing the WWW
Tim Berners-Lee invents the World Wide Web—a way for computer users to access many different types of information from different sources.

1991—WWW on the Internet
The World Wide Web is launched and made available to the world via the Internet.

1992—Surfing
The term *surfing the Internet* is used for the first time by American librarian and Internet expert Jean Armour Polly.

1993—Mosaic
The first Web browser is created. It is called Mosaic.

1994—Yahoo!
The Yahoo! search engine is created in April 1994 by David Filo and Jerry Yang, two U.S. PhD students.

1995—Internet Explorer
Launched in July 1995 as part of the Windows 95 package, Internet Explorer 1.0 makes the Internet accessible to more people.

1995—Online music
RealAudio is launched. This software makes it possible for Internet users to listen to live music and radio online.

1995—Online bookshop
amazon.com is launched by U.S. computer scientist Jeff Bezos.

2000—Web movie
The science-fiction movie *Quantum Project* is the first movie made especially to be seen on the Internet instead of at a theater.

2003—iTunes
Apple debuts its iTunes music-download service.

2005—Video sharing
YouTube launches, allowing users to upload, view, and share video clips.

2009—Web usage
The number of Internet users is put at 6,710,029,070 worldwide.

ROBOTS

• The timeline continues on page 101.

The word *robot* was first used by Czech writer Karel Capek in 1921. The word means "forced labor," and it is a good way of describing what robots are used for. Robots can do many jobs that humans can do, but they can also tackle jobs that a human would find too difficult or dangerous. Robots are currently used in factories, they explore outer space and the inside of volcanoes, they carry out medical operations, and they appear in our homes as toys or cyber (robotic) pets.

RoboSapien

The AIBO robotic pet dog.
AIBO dogs can even play soccer.

CYBER PETS

A robot dog first made an appearance at the New York World's Fair in 1939. Today, cyber pets can behave just like real animals.

AIBO DOGS
The latest cyber dogs made by Sony can play, walk, obey spoken commands, and even recognize the voices and faces of their owners.

ROBOSAPIEN
This humanlike cyber pet can run, dance, throw things, pick things up, and do karate. Robosapien can even swear and break wind.

TAKARA AQUAROID FISH
This cyber pet can be put into an aquarium. It looks like a fish, moves away from strong light, and can swim at two different speeds.

i-SOBOT
This is the world's smallest humanoid robot, produced by Tomy.

MOSRO—THE ROBOT SECURITY GUARD

- MOSRO patrols factories and shopping centers.

- MOSRO can detect gas, smoke, and movement using a camera and infrared detectors.

- MOSRO issues warnings in more than 20 languages.

This is the MOSRO MINI mobile security robot. It is just 11 in. (28cm) tall.

DOMESTIC ROBOTS

Robomow RL1000 (2003)
Can mow lawns without any help. It can cut grass to six different heights. It is just over 12 in. (30cm) high.

Cye Robot (2003)
A robot butler. It can carry dishes, deliver letters, and help guests find their way around the house. It can be controlled through the Internet.

Maron-1 (2002)
Can be controlled with a cell phone. It can detect intruders in a house, take photographs, and operate dishwashers and video recorders.

Maron

INVENTING HAZBOTS

Robots that do dangerous jobs that cannot be done by people are sometimes called "hazbots."

RADIOACTIVITY

In 1999, a hazbot called Pioneer was used at the Chernobyl nuclear power plant in Ukraine, the site of the worst nuclear accident in history. Pioneer went into the burned-out radioactive power plant to determine levels of radioactivity and to test the structure of the remaining building.

Pioneer was built by a team from Carnegie Mellon University and Redzone Robotics.

BOMB DISPOSAL

The British army has used bomb-disposal robots since the early 1970s. The first was called Wheelbarrow.

NATURAL HAZARDS

Robots can be used to investigate volcanoes. A robot called Dante II explored an Alaskan volcano in 1994. Dante II can be remotely controlled or it can move by itself.

FIREFIGHTING

Robots are used in firefighting because they are not affected by heat and smoke. Robug III is a firefighting robot designed at Portsmouth University in the U.K. It has eight legs and suckers that allow it to climb walls and move across ceilings. Robug III can also pull very heavy weights.

THE INVENTION OF MINI ROBOTS

At the U.S. Department of Energy's Sandia National Laboratories, scientists are developing the world's smallest autonomous, untethered robot.

- The mini robot has eight kilobytes of memory, is 0.39 in. (1cm) high, and weighs less than 1.05 oz. (30g).

- It is powered by watch batteries, and future enhancements could include a miniature camera, a microphone, and chemical sniffers.

- The mini robot travels on two track wheels at a speed of 19.5 in. (50cm) per minute.

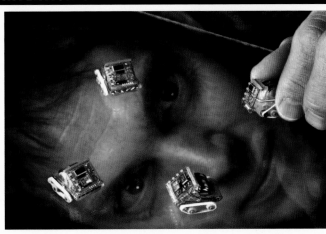

The mini robots can travel in swarms like insects and fit into tiny spaces such as pipes.

- Future uses could include detecting chemical or biological weapons, disabling land mines, or missions as a mini spy — taking photographs of secret papers without being seen.

ROBOTS IN SPACE

1997—CASSINI-HUYGENS
Studies the planet Saturn, its rings, and moons.

2003—SMART-1
Searched the Moon for frozen water and for new minerals and chemicals on its surface.

2003—BEAGLE 2
Designed to investigate the surface of Mars. However, there was no contact after touchdown.

2003—SPIRIT and OPPORTUNITY
Study the soil and rocks of Mars.

2004—ROSETTA
Will meet with a comet in 2014 and investigate the comet's surface.

GEORGE DEVOL 1912–

Nationality: American

Profession: Engineer and inventor

Biographical information: Devol was born in February 1912 in Louisville, Kentucky. In 1939, Devol designed and built an automatic counter at the New York World's Fair. The counter kept a record of the number of visitors.

Most famous invention: The first industrial robot. In 1954, Devol invented the first programmable robot. He did not use the word *robot*. Instead he called it *universal automation*. Devol founded the world's first robot-building company, Unimation, which built robots for lifting and stacking hot pieces of metal in car factories.

Other inventions: During World War II, Devol helped build systems that could protect aircraft from radar. They were used during the D-day landings in Europe in 1944.

ROBOTICS TIMELINE

1977—Voyagers
The deep-space explorers *Voyagers* 1 and 2 are launched from the Kennedy Space Center in Florida.

1981—Direct-drive arm
The first "direct-drive arms" are built. They have motors in the joints of the arms. This makes them faster and more accurate than older robotic arms. They are designed by Takeo Kanade, professor of robotics at Carnegie Mellon University in Pittsburgh, Pennsylvania.

1989—Genghis
A walking robot called Genghis is shown for the first time at Massachusetts Institute of Technology (MIT).

1992—Robot Wars
Combats between robots, sometimes called BattleBots, begin. The first "Robot Wars" takes place in 1994.

1994—Dante II
A robot called Dante II walks down a volcano in Alaska.

1996—Robotuna
The first robot fish is built. It is designed by Professor Michael Triantafyllou of Massachusetts Institute of Technology (MIT). It is hoped that underwater robots will be able to explore parts of the ocean where humans cannot reach.

1997—Sojourner
The robotic rover *Sojourner* begins its exploration of the surface of the planet Mars.

1998—Furby
Furby goes on sale. It is the first robot toy that can respond to commands.

2000—Asimo
The humanlike robot called Asimo is built by Honda. It is 3.94 ft. (1.2m) tall, walks on legs, and can even walk around corners. It is designed to help around the house.

2002—Heart surgery
The first robot-assisted coronary artery bypass surgery is performed in the U.S. on a 71-year-old retired businessman.

INVENTIONS

S ome inventions are the result of years of dedicated research. Others come as a flash of inspiration. An invention may solve a specific problem or be the byproduct of an inventor's irresistible urge to understand how things work and then improve on them. All inventions draw on the accumulation of human knowledge and the work of earlier inventors. In this section of the book we take a brief look at a wide range of inventions. Many may not have made the headlines, but they represent the work of inventive men and women from all around the world.

WORDS OF WISDOM

"To invent, you need a good imagination and a pile of junk."

Thomas Alva Edison
Inventor

ACUPUNCTURE

This ancient therapy is based on the idea that life force, or chi, flows in certain channels that can become blocked. The practice of twirling a needle in the right place to make the chi flow smoothly again has hardly changed since it was first used in China some 4,500 years ago. Thankfully steel needles have now replaced stone ones!

ARCHIMEDEAN SCREW

A means of raising water for irrigation, the Archimedean screw comprises a cylinder with a large screw inside. The bottom of the screw is dipped in water, and as the screw is turned water is pushed up the cylinder. We do not know for sure if Archimedes actually invented this or whether he saw it in use and wrote about it, but the device came to carry his name.

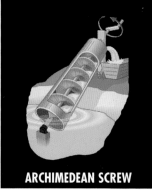

ARCHIMEDEAN SCREW

ADDER-LISTER

In 1888, U.S. inventor William Burroughs patented an adding machine that printed its calculations. With more than 80 keys and a handle to operate the printer, the "adder-lister" went on sale in 1892.

ADDING MACHINE

The arithmometer, patented in 1820 by Frenchman Thomas de Colmar, was the first calculating machine that really worked. It could add, subtract, multiply, and divide. It took awhile to catch on and underwent many developments, but from the middle of the 1800s, hundreds were in use.

AEROSOL CAN

Norwegian Erik Rothheim invented the aerosol can in the late 1920s for packaging paint and polish.

AIR CONDITIONING

In 1902, U.S. engineer Willis Carrier designed an "apparatus for treating air." Carrier's invention was based on cooling the temperature until the moisture condenses out, then draining away the water to produce pleasantly cool, dry air.

AMALGAM FILLING

Before the early 1800s, metal tooth fillings were made by heating metal to the boiling point before they were put into teeth. Around 1826, working independently, August Taveau in France and Thomas Bell in Great Britain mixed mercury and silver to form a paste that they found could be inserted cold into the mouth and that hardened quickly. The amalgam filling is still used today.

ASPIRIN

In 1899, German chemist Felix Hoffman rediscovered an old formula for a painkiller. The drug was aspirin, which contains salicylic acid (juice from willow tree bark). Hoffman developed and tested the aspirin and used it to treat his father's arthritis. He patented Acetyl Salicylic Acid in 1900.

1899: ASPIRIN

BIKINI

In 1946, the bikini was independently invented by two Frenchmen, Jacques Heim and Louis Reard. Heim designed a very small swimsuit he called the *atome* (French for "atom"), while

1946: BIKINI

Reard's creation was named the *bikini* after the Bikini Atoll in the Marshall Islands, which was in the news at the time because atom-bomb testing was taking place there.

BINGO

Originating in Europe, Beano, as it was first called, arrived in the U.S. in 1929. Toy salesman Edwin Lowe renamed the game Bingo after he heard someone accidentally call "Bingo" instead of "Beano." Lowe hired a math professor, Carl Leffler, to figure out combinations for the bingo cards. Leffler eventually invented 6,000 different combinations. The game went on to become a popular means of fundraising for churches.

BUBBLEGUM

In 1906, the first bubblegum, called Blibber-Blubber gum, was invented by Frank Fleer, but the chewy invention never went on sale. In 1928, Walter Diemer, an employee at Fleer's company, invented the pink-colored Double Bubble bubblegum.

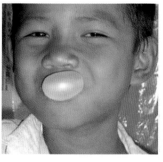

1906: BUBBLEGUM

BUBBLE PACK

Bubble pack appeared in 1960 in its earliest form as AirCap cellular cushioning. It consisted of two layers of soft plastic with bubbles trapped between them. Inventors Alfred Fielding and Marc Chavannes were originally trying to make textured wall covering!

CAMERA OBSCURA

The modern camera started as a darkened room with a tiny hole in one wall. It was called a camera obscura. On the opposite wall an upside-down image of the outside world would appear. In 1558, Italian physicist Giovanni Battista Della Porta changed the hole for a lens that, by letting in more light, produced a much sharper image. The Italian words *camera obscura* mean "a dark room."

CAN OPENER

Before 1855 a hammer and chisel were required to open cans. Then British inventor Robert Yeates invented his can opener—a sharp blade that was stuck in the top of a can and then worked around.

**1855:
CAN OPENER**

CAT'S-EYES

Flexible rubber housing is the key to British engineer Percy Shaw's 1934 invention of cat's-eyes. It enables the reflectors that light the center of roads to be cleaned by every car that crosses them.

CHAIN SAW

A gas-engine sawing machine was made by German Emil Lerp in 1927. Although similar to a modern saw, it was too heavy for one person to lift. In 1950, the Stihl company produced the first chain saw that was light enough for one person to use.

**1927:
CHAIN SAW**

COMPTOMETER

Displaying its results in a set of windows, U.S. engineer Dorr E. Felt's calculating machine was much faster than its rival William Burrough's adder-lister, which printed its results. Both of the machines were in use until the mid-1900s.

COTTON-TIPPED SWABS

This baby-cleaning aid was introduced in the U.S. in 1926. Q-tips™, as they are commonly called, were invented by Leo Gerstenzang after he saw his wife trying to use toothpicks and cotton balls.

DC06 ROBOT

Manufactured by Dyson, this robotic vacuum cleaner has sensors to help it avoid stairs and small children. It also remembers where it has cleaned.

DDT

The now little-used insecticide DDT, a chlorine-based chemical, had been known for years before, in 1939, Swiss chemist Paul Müller discovered that it killed insects but had little effect on warm-blooded animals.

DIVING SUIT

Augustus Siebe, a German engineer, invented the first practical diving suit in 1819. Siebe's suit comprised a jacket and an airtight helmet. Air was pumped into the helmet from the surface.

ELECTRON MICROSCOPE

Invented by Ernst Ruska in the 1930s, the electron microscope "sees" with electrons rather than photons of light. Today's electron microscopes make it possible to view items as small as atoms and then display their images on a computer screen.

1930s: ELECTRON MICROSCOPE

ESCALATOR

The escalator can be credited to two inventors in the late 1800s. Inventor George Wheeler sold his idea (because he had financial problems) to Charles Seeburger, a rival inventor. Seeburger then sold the patent to the Otis Elevator Company and the copyright to the name *escalator*, which he had created for the machine.

• See page 81 for information on the Otis safety elevator.

FERRIS WHEEL

American George W. Ferris designed the first Ferris wheel for the 1893 World's Fair in Chicago. Ferris was a bridge builder and owner of a company that tested iron and steel. The finished wheel had a diameter of over 246 ft. (75m). Thirty-six wooden cars held up to 60 riders each. The price of a ride was 50 cents.

1893: FERRIS WHEEL

FIELD-ION MICROSCOPE

Invented by Erwin Müller in 1956, the field-ion microscope has a magnification of more than 2.5 million times.

LAUGHING GAS

Although discovered earlier, in 1799 Humphry Davy found that nitrous oxide could make people laugh. He suggested it might be useful in surgery, but also used it to give party guests a good laugh.

LEMONADE

Lemon juice was probably used in drinks for many years before the first commercial lemonade was produced. In 1676, in Paris, France, vendors belonging to the Compagnie de Limonadiers sold glasses of a mixture of lemon juice, honey, and water. They dispensed the lemonade from tanks strapped to their backs.

LETTERBOX

On October 4, 1892, American George Becket patented a letterbox with a self-closing flap for houses.

LIE DETECTOR

Originally developed by Czech psychologist Max Wertheimer in 1904, the polygraph, or lie detector, monitors blood pressure, pulse, and breathing, all of which change when people lie.

INVENTIONS

LIQUID PAPER

American secretary Bette Nesmith Graham invented liquid paper by mixing some of her artists' materials in her kitchen blender. When other secretaries noticed Bette using her invention to hide typing errors, they wanted some, too! Bette started her "Mistake Out" company in 1956.

M&M's

M&M's were invented by snack-food genius Frank Mars (of Mars Bar fame) in the 1930s. Frank wanted to invent a chocolate that had a protective candy coating to stop it from melting.

1930s: M&M's

MACADAMIZED ROAD

In 1783, returning to his native Scotland after making his fortune in the U.S., John McAdam took an interest in the poor state of the roads. He experimented with different road surfaces, and by 1815, using a mixture of different-sized stones, he had perfected a waterproof, durable surface suitable for the coach traffic of the day.

MARGARINE

In 1869, French chemist Hippolyte Mége-Mouriés invented a butter substitute called margarine by bubbling hydrogen through a mixture of vegetable oils.

MATCH

As knowledge of chemicals improved in the early 1800s, inventors tried to create an improved means of light (or match, as we would call it today). In 1827, British chemist John Walker produced his "friction match," which lit up when rubbed on sandpaper.

MINER'S SAFETY LAMP

In the early 1800s, many lives were lost owing to explosions in mines. The explosions were caused by the flames from miners' lights making the methane gas under the ground explode. Mine owners commissioned three men to try to find a solution: chemist Humphry Davy, William Clanny, a doctor, and mechanic George Stephenson. The mine owners were pleased with Davy's design, but the miners preferred the lamp designed by Stephenson, who was "one of their own." Eventually most miners' lamps incorporated ideas from all three inventors.

NEON SIGN

Inventors had discovered that low-pressure gas in a tube could be lit up with electricity. In 1910, French physicist Georges Claude found that the gas neon produced an intense orange-red glow—not suitable for lighting, but great for advertising signs!

1910: NEON SIGN

NITROGLYCERINE

Discovered in 1846 by Italian chemist Ascanio Sobrero, nitroglycerine was the first "high explosive"—an explosive much more powerful than gunpowder. Just dropping a container of the chemical on the floor can cause a large explosion.

OFRO ROBOT

Built by Robowatch Technologies, Germany, OFRO robots are designed to carry out surveillance in high-security places, such as airports, nuclear power plants, and prisons.

OIL PAINT

Oil paint had been known about since Roman times, but until the early 1400s, artists used paints such as tempera, which is made with eggs. French and Flemish painters Robert Campin and Jan van Eyck perfected the use of oil paints in the 1400s. The graded tones that could be achieved with oil paints gave a greater sense of realism to their work.

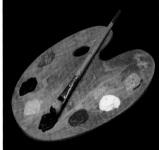

1400s: OIL PAINTS

OSCILLOSCOPE

A device that makes it possible to see electrical signals on a screen, the cathode-ray oscilloscope was invented in 1897 by German physicist Karl Ferdinand Braun.

PACKAGE VACATION

The first "package" vacation was in 1841—a train trip from Leicester to Loughborough in England. The excursion was a success. By 1855, the organizer, British missionary Thomas Cook, was organizing trips to Europe.

PAPER CUP

In 1908, U.S. inventor Hugh Moore designed a vending machine to deliver water in individual paper cups. Previously, thirsty consumers had to share a tin cup. Moore's paper cups became known as "Dixies," named after the company set up to make them in 1919.

PARACHUTE

Frenchman Louis Lenormand gave his invention its first serious trial in December 1783 by jumping from the Montpelier Observatory with a 14.1-ft. (4.3-m) chute. He landed safely. Although invented originally as a means of escaping a burning building, a parachute was used in 1797 by another Frenchman to jump to safety when his hot-air balloon burst over Paris.

PARKING METER

Businessman Carlton Magee's invention first appeared in Oklahoma City in 1935. Magee hoped his Park-O-Meter would stop all-day parkers from taking up spaces on the streets and make a little money for the city.

PENCIL

Having already identified graphite as a distinct mineral, in 1565 Conrad Gessner, a German-Swiss naturalist, had the idea of placing the carbon in a wooden holder to form a writing instrument. Modern pencils with a core of lead glued inside a thin tube of wood were first made in 1812.

1812: PENCILS

PEPSI-COLA

In 1893, Caleb Bradham, a pharmacist in New Bern, North Carolina, began to experiment with different soft-drink concoctions. Bradham's mixtures were sampled by customers at his pharmacy. In 1898, one of his formulations known as "Brad's Drink" proved popular, and on August 28, it was renamed "Pepsi-Cola."

In 1902 the trademark was registered, and the Pepsi-Cola Company was formed. In 1908, Pepsi was one of the first companies to start using motor vehicles instead of horse-drawn carts.

1893: PEPSI-COLA

PLASTIC BANDAGES

In 1920, Earle Dickson of U.S. surgical dressing manufacturer Johnson & Johnson invented plastic bandages. He stuck together adhesive tape, gauze, and fabric and then rolled them up for future use. Dickson's invention was soon on sale in the U.S. as Band-Aid™.

PICK-PROOF LOCK

In 1784, British engineer Joseph Bramah offered £210 ($400) to anyone who could pick the lock he had invented. It was 67 years before the reward was claimed by U.S. locksmith A. C. Hobbs, who took 51 hours to pick the lock.

POST-IT NOTE

U.S. company 3M's Post-it notes were launched in 1980. A company chemist, Spencer Silver, made a "not very sticky" adhesive, but it was his colleague Art Fry who suggested the use for it.

RAWLPLUG

Since 1919, when British builder John Rawlings devised his "plug," there has been no need to damage walls when installing them. Rawling's invention means you simply drill a hole, then insert a fiber wall plug, which expands to hold the screw.

RING-PULL CAN

The first drink cans required a separate opener. In 1965, U.S. engineer Ermal Fraze patented the convenient "ring-pull" can. The sharp-edged ring pulls could be dangerous if thrown away, so engineer Daniel Cudzik invented the "stay-on

ROBART III ROBOT

First made in 1992, ROBART III is used by the U.S. Navy. It has a camera, infrared sensor, and also a gun that can fire darts. ROBART III was built by Bart Everett of the Naval Oceans Systems Center.

RUBBER

French scientist Charles-Marie de La Condamine discovered rubber trees with their sticky sap while on an expedition to South America. Although other Europeans had come across the substance in their travels, it was La Condamine's samples, sent back to France in 1736, that put the product on the scientific map. Rubber was named when British chemist Joseph Priestley found that it could "rub out" pencil.

RUBBER BAND

In 1845, Stephen Perry of Messrs Perry and Co. of London, England, a rubber manufacturing company, invented the rubber band. Perry used it to hold his papers and envelopes together.

SAFETY PIN

U.S. mechanic Walter Hunt invented the modern safety pin in 1849. His design was actually very similar to one that was invented and worn by people 2,000 years ago. The clothing clasps were called fibulae, and they were used by the ancient Greeks and Romans for fastening their clothing.

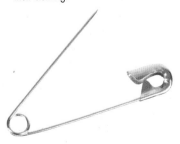

1849: SAFETY PIN

SCANNING TUNNELING MICROSCOPE

Invented in Switzerland in 1981 by Gerd Binnig and Heinrich Rohrer, the scanning tunneling microscope can be used to study and photograph individual atoms.

SCISSORS

The scissor principle was known in 3000 B.C., but scissors like those we use today, with two blades pivoted at the center, were invented by the Romans in about A.D. 100.

A.D. 100: SCISSORS

SHOPS

Ancient Greek historian Herodotus (c. 480–420 B.C.) stated, "The people who invented coins also invented shops." He may well have been referring to the Lydians (an ancient civilization from the area that is now Turkey). The first stores were probably running around 600 B.C.

SLICED BREAD

Inventor Otto Frederick Rohwedder began work on a bread slicer in 1912. In 1928, he finally invented a machine that could slice bread and then wrap it up to stop it from going stale.

SLINKY

In 1943, engineer Richard James invented the "Slinky" after he witnessed a long coil of metal (part of a U.S. Navy experiment) fall from a desk and appear to walk! He took the idea home to his wife, Betty, who named the toy "Slinky" after consulting her dictionary to find a word that described the spring's movement. To start off their new enterprise, Richard and Betty had just 400 springs made by a local machine shop. They soon needed to replenish their stock when the Slinky turned out to be a huge success!

SPECTACLES

The glass workers of Murano in Venice, Italy, invented eyeglasses some time around A.D. 1275.

A.D. 1275: SPECTACLES

STEREOSCOPE

By combining two slightly different pictures, one for each eye, a three-dimensional image is produced by a stereoscope. Invented before photography by Charles Wheatstone, stereoscopy became a craze after David Brewster showed a version of the stereoscope at the Great Exhibition in London in 1851.

SUPERGLUE

In 1951, U.S. researchers Harry Coover and Fred Joyner realized the potential of the chemical cyanoacrylate (discovered in 1942) for use in a superstrong glue. A trace of water is all that is needed to trigger a chemical reaction that turns the liquid glue into plastic.

TAPE

U.S. engineer Richard Drew's first sticky invention was masking tape, a sticky paper tape. In 1925, by coating cellophane with a similar adhesive, he produced what is known in the U.S. by the trade name Scotch Tape and in the U.K. as Sellotape.

SUPERMARKET

In 1916, in order to cut costs in his business, U.S. grocer Clarence Saunders invented "self-service" at his Piggly Wiggly store in Memphis, Tennessee. It was cheaper to let people take goods from the shelves than have staff members serve them. Saunders had invented the self-service supermarket.

1916: SUPERMARKET

SUPERMARKET CART

U.S. retailer Sylvan Goldman noticed that customers at his Humpty Dumpty supermarkets never purchased more than they could carry. In 1937, he had wheels and baskets welded to folding chairs, and the supermarket cart was born.

SURGICAL GLOVES

Convinced that germs were a threat to their patients, 19th-century surgeons needed to find a way to keep their hands sterile while operating. In 1890, U.S. surgeon William Halsted invented thin rubber surgeons' gloves, and the problem was solved.

THERMOS

Based on James Dewar's vacuum bottle, Rheinhold Burger's metal-cased flask was launched in 1904. The name *Thermos* was chosen after a competition.

TOOTHPASTE IN A TUBE

Crème Dentifrice, produced in 1892 by U.S. dentist Washington Sheffield, was the first toothpaste to come in a tube. Before Sheffield's innovation, toothpaste had come in a jar.

TRAFFIC SIGNAL

An early form of traffic lights appeared in London in 1868. In 1923, a system using three moving arms was patented in the U.S. by inventor Garrett Morgan.

TRAMPOLINE

Circus acrobat and Olympic medalist George Nissen invented the trampoline in 1936. He built a prototype in his garage and later patented the idea.

TRIVIAL PURSUIT

Described as "a party in a box" and a "revolt against television," the quiz game Trivial Pursuit was devised by four Canadian friends in 1979. After a slow start, the marketing took off when the game was launched in the U.S. In 1984 alone, more than 20 million games were sold!

TYPEWRITER

American mechanical engineer Christopher Sholes patented the first practical typewriter in 1868. Sholes laid the keyboard out in the pattern that is known as QWERTY—after the six letters that appear at the top left on the keyboard. This layout was designed to slow down the typist in order to stop the keys from jamming. Modern keyboards still have the same layout.

UMBRELLA

The steel-ribbed umbrella that we know today was invented in England in 1874 by Samuel Fox.

1874: UMBRELLA

VACUUM CLEANER

In 1901, British engineer and inventor Hubert Cecil Booth invented the vacuum cleaner. Booth's large horse-drawn machine went from house to house sucking out the dirt through hoses. Booth formed the British Vacuum Cleaner Company in 1903 and built his first canister-style machine in 1904.

1979: TRIVIAL PURSUIT

VELCRO

Patented in the 1950s, Swiss inventor George de Mestral's invention of Velcro came to him after tiny plant burs (seed pods) attached themselves to his clothes and his dog while they were hiking in the country. Under a microscope, the burs were discovered to have tiny hooks that got caught in the fabric of Mestral's pants. Mestral's idea was to produce a two-sided fastener with hooks on one side and soft loops on the other—Velcro. The name *Velcro* is a combination of two French words, *velours* (velvet) and *crochet* (hook).

VELOCIPEDE

The "draisienne" invented by Baron Karl von Drais de Sauerbrun in 1817 is recognized as the first two-wheeled rider-propelled machine. Although von Drais called his device a *Laufmaschine* ("running machine"), *draisienne* and *velocipede* became more popular names. Made of wood, the machine was propelled by the seated rider paddling his or her feet on the ground. Copies were soon being made in other countries, and in 1818, Denis Johnson of London patented a "pedestrian curricle," which was an improved version of the draisienne.

VENDING MACHINE

Drop in a coin and the machine releases a shot of holy water. Ancient Greek inventor Hero of Alexandria described this early type of vending machine in a book around A.D. 60. It is not known if the machine was ever built.

WINDSURFER

Norman Darby's passion for shipbuilding led to his invention of the sailboard, or Windsurfer. One day in 1943 while out sailing, Norman wanted to cross a stretch of very shallow water. First he removed the keel of his small boat and then the rudder. He found that he could steer by tilting the sail. From that moment he worked to perfect a purpose-built board.

ZODIAC

The Mesopotamians were avid stargazers. Around 500 B.C., astronomer-priests divided the night sky into 12 equal parts and identified each part by a different constellation. The constellations that they recognized are the basis of the modern-day zodiac signs and horoscopes.

500 B.C.: ZODIAC

WHAT IS A PATENT?

To prevent other people from making, using, or selling an invention without the inventor's permission, they must apply to a government patent office to take out a patent.

- If no one else has patented the same invention, a patent will be granted for a specific period of time. Patents usually cover the way things work, what they do, how they are made, and what they are made of.

- Today, most patents are granted to cover newly invented improvements to existing technology.

FAMOUS PATENTS

- U.S. Patent No. 1647
  June 20, 1840
  Samuel Morse
  Telegraph

- U.S. Patent No. 13661
  October 9, 1855
  Isaac Singer
  Sewing machine

- U.S. Patent No. 223898
  January 27, 1880
  Thomas Edison
  Electric light

- U.S. Patent No. 686046
  November 5, 1901
  Henry Ford
  Automobile

- U.S. Patent No. 821393
  May 22, 1906
  Orville & Wilbur Wright
  Airplane

- U.S. Patent No. 1773079
  August 12, 1930
  Clarence Birdseye
  Packaged frozen food

PATENT PROBLEMS

In theory, it should be very simple to patent your idea. However, in practice, it can sometimes be a long and expensive process if people try to steal your idea or claim they had it before you.

- Alexander Graham Bell filed his patent application for the telephone on March 7, 1876, only hours before his rival Elisha Gray.

- Gray pursued Bell with 600 lawsuits claiming the idea.

CONCRETE FURNITURE

In 1911, American inventor Thomas Edison proposed a new range of home furnishings made from concrete.

- Easy to manufacture and low in cost, Edison's special lightweight concrete would be used to produce phonograph cabinets, pianos, and even bedroom furniture.

- Unfortunately, when Edison shipped some phonograph cabinets to a trade show, they arrived in pieces—not good publicity for a product marketed as being able to withstand being dropped and abused!

- The world was not ready for Edison's new idea, and concrete furniture faded into history.

IT SEEMED LIKE A GOOD IDEA AT THE TIME . . .

Sometimes inventors are convinced that they *have* actually found the best thing since Otto Rohwedder's sliced bread—it is just that nobody else appreciates their genius!

Here are a selection of inventions that, for some reason, did not make it into production.

AIR-COOLED ROCKING CHAIR

On July 6, 1869, U.S. Patent No. 92379 was issued to Charles Singer for his innovative, breezy rocking chair. The chair was to have bellows (devices that were once used for blowing air onto fires) connected to a hose that blew air onto the sitter as he or she rocked.

THE VÉLO-DOUCHE

In 1897, an English bicycle manufacturer contemplated the idea of a "Vélo-douche shower bath"—an exercise bike combined with a shower to keep the rider clean and fit.

A CUTE INVENTION

On May 19, 1896, U.S. Patent No. 560351 was issued to inventor Martin Goetze for his device for producing and maintaining dimples on human skin.

SNOW TO AUSTRALIA

About 35 years ago, an intriguing idea was patented in the U.K. by inventor A. P. Pedrick. The idea was to irrigate the Australian desert by using the force from the spin of Earth to pipe snow and ice balls from Antarctica.

CHEWING-GUM LOCKET

On January 1, 1889, U.S. Patent No. 395515 was issued to Christopher W. Robertson for his invaluable invention, the chewing-gum locket. Conveniently stashed away in the locket, chewed gum could safely be carried by a person. Much better than leaving it around to get dirty or, more importantly, "found and chewed by someone with an ulcerous or diseased mouth"!

BLASTOFF!

In 1500, Chinese scientist Wan Hu tried to fly by tying 47 rockets to his sedan. The rockets exploded, and he was never seen again!

WORDS OF WISDOM

"Results . . .
I have gotten a lot of results. I know several thousand things that won't work."

Thomas Alva Edison
Inventor

EXPLORING SPACE

DISCOVERY TIMELINE

1543 — Sun-centered universe
Polish astronomer Nicolaus Copernicus publishes his *Six Books Concerning the Revolutions of the Heavenly Orbs*, presenting his discoveries and his theory of a universe with the Sun at the center.

1609 — Galileo's telescope
Galilei Galileo hears of Hans Lippershey's invention and builds his own telescope. He uses his new instrument to make many discoveries, including Jupiter's four largest moons and sunspots, from which he deduces that the Sun rotates.

1610 — Orion nebula
Frenchman Nicolas-Claude Fabri de Peiresc discovers the Orion nebula (or Great Nebula). This star "nursery" is visible with the naked eye. Stars are being born there right now.

1705 — Halley's comet
Edmond Halley discovers that comets observed in 1531, 1607, and 1682 are the same comet. He predicts the comet will return in 1758. The comet is sighted in that year (after Halley's death) and named in his honor.

1922–1924 — New galaxies
American astronomer Edwin Hubble discovers that there are other galaxies outside the Milky Way.

1931 — Radio waves from space
American engineer Karl Jansky is assigned by Bell Telephone Laboratories, New Jersey, to track down interference, which is causing problems with telephone communication. Jansky finds all of the sources except one. In 1931, after months of study, he establishes that the radio interference is coming from the stars.

1995 — Comet Hale-Bopp
U.S. amateur astronomers Alan Hale, in New Mexico, and Thomas Bopp, in Arizona, independently discover a new comet on July 23, 1995. At its brightest in 1997, Hale-Bopp was a thousand times brighter than Halley's comet.

The first sky watchers looked to the heavens and asked questions about the planets and stars they could see. When the telescope was invented in the 1600s, astronomers were finally able to study the stars and planets in more detail. In the early 1900s, pioneering rocket scientists such as Konstantin Tsiolkovsky, Robert Goddard, Herman Oberth, and Werner von Braun further expanded our horizons when they developed the means to blast a satellite, or a human, into space.

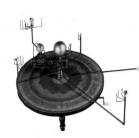

The orrery, a mechanical model of our solar system, invented in the mid-1700s

ROCKET PIONEERS

1150 — Chinese rockets
Gunpowder-propelled rockets are invented by the Chinese.

c. 1900 — Tsiolkovsky
Russian scientist Konstantin Tsiolkovsky suggests using rockets with stages that can be jettisoned to get large objects into space.

1926 — Goddard's rocket
American Robert Goddard experiments with different fuels. In 1926, the first rocket to use a liquid propellant is launched from Goddard's Aunt Effie's cabbage patch.

Goddard's work earned him the title the "the father of modern rocketry."

1920s–1930s
German Herman Oberth develops most of the modern theory for rockets and space flight. German scientist Werner von Braun produces the V-2 rocket (a weapon) for Germany in World War II, then goes to the U.S. to work on the space program.

INVENTION OF THE TELESCOPE

HANS LIPPERSHEY
Dutch eyeglass maker Hans Lippershey is credited with inventing the refracting telescope in 1608. Lippershey discovered that if you look through two lenses of the right type, they will enlarge distant objects.

Lippershey offered his new "looker" to the government for use in warfare, and was granted 900 florins for the instrument, but there was a requirement that it be modified into a binocular device.

Refracting telescopes
Refracting telescopes (below) work by having a convex lens that bends light rays from an object to form an upside-down image of the object. A second lens, the eyepiece, bends the rays again and magnifies the image.

convex lens

Refracting telescope   eyepiece

Reflecting telescopes
A reflecting telescope (below) uses a shaped primary mirror to reflect light to a smaller secondary mirror. The light is then reflected to the focus, and the image is viewed through an eyepiece.

primary mirror   focus

light

secondary mirror   eyepiece

Reflecting telescope

Newton's telescope

Newton's telescope
In 1668, English mathematician Isaac Newton developed the reflecting telescope. English astronomer John Gregory had thought up an alternative reflector design in 1663.

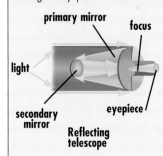

Radio telescopes
Radio telescopes receive the radio waves emitted by objects in space and, via a computer, convert those waves to images.
Radio waves can penetrate through dust clouds that block visible light.

• See timeline for information on radio waves from space.

SOLAR SYSTEM DISCOVERIES

Some of the planets and dwarf planets in our solar system have been known for many years; others were discovered more recently. Both astronomers on Earth and space probes have added to the long list of solar system discoveries.

JUPITER

Jupiter's Great Red Spot (GRS) was discovered by French astronomer Gian Domenico Cassini in 1665 using an early telescope.

Thanks to space probes, we now know the GRS measures around 7,440 mi. (12,000km) by 15,500 mi. (25,000km) and is a vast, violent storm.

VENUS

Following the mapping of Venus's surface by NASA's *Magellan* probe (1990–1994), scientists discovered that Venus is covered in volcanoes, including an active volcano, Maat Mons. Venus and Earth are the only two planets that are known to have active volcanoes.

MERCURY

When Mercury was first photographed by NASA probe *Mariner 10* in 1974, it was discovered that it has many deep craters. The largest, the Caloris Basin, is around 806 mi. (1,300km) across.

PLUTO

Pluto's existence had been predicted by astronomer Percival Lowell, but it was actually discovered by American Clyde Tombaugh at the Lowell Observatory, Arizona, in 1930.

In 1978, Pluto's close satellite, Charon, was discovered by James Walter Christy.

URANUS

Sir William Herschel discovered Uranus on March 13, 1781 using a homemade reflecting telescope that was 7 ft. (2m) long. Herschel originally thought Uranus was a comet.

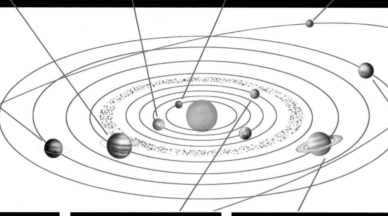

Pluto

Charon

NEPTUNE

Neptune was discovered in 1846 by astronomer J. G. Galle in Berlin, Germany. Neptune's position had been predicted by mathematicians John Couch Adams in England and Urbain Le Verrier in France.

MARS — CRATERS

In 1971, space probe *Mariner 9* discovered a system of canyons known as the Valles Marineris. The canyons stretch for around 2,480 mi. (4,000km). Some individual canyons are 62 mi. (100km) wide, and some are 5–6 mi. (8–10km) deep.

MARS

The largest volcano in the solar system, Olympus Mons, was discovered on Mars. It is 17 mi. (27km) high. The tallest volcano on Earth, Mauna Loa in Hawaii, rises 6 mi. (9km) above the ocean floor.

SATURN

Saturn's ring system was discovered by Galileo in 1610. Galileo's primitive telescope could not make out the structure of the rings. We now know that Saturn's rings are made of millions of small chunks of rock and ice.

MARS — MOONS

In 1877, American astronomer Asaph Hall discovered Mars's two moons. He named them Phobos and Deimos after the sons of Ares, the Greek counterpart of the Roman god Mars.

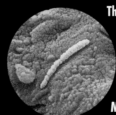

This is the rodlike structure that some scientists believe to be a fossilized microscopic Martian creature.

IT CAME FROM SPACE

We all benefit from inventions developed by NASA for their space missions.

- Battery-powered tools were invented for use in space, where there are no electrical sockets.

- The digital watch was invented to help astronauts keep accurate time.

- Plastic sandwich boxes were originally used to keep food for astronauts fresh.

HUBBLE SPACE TELESCOPE

The Hubble Space Telescope is a satellite built by NASA and ESA. It was launched in 1990 and orbits Earth at around 372 mi. (600km) above the planet's surface.

- The telescope is named after astronomer Edwin Hubble.

- Hubble is a reflecting telescope, and it also works in ultraviolet. It is powered by two solar panels.

- Hubble is designed to look a long way beyond the solar system. The volume of space it can cover is 350 times bigger than can be seen from Earth.

LIFE ON MARS

In 1996, U.S. geologist David S. McKay and a team from NASA's Johnson Space Center in Houston, Texas, reported that they had found evidence of microscopic life on Mars. The tiny microbes were found inside a meteorite that had traveled from Mars to Earth, possibly taking millions of years. At present many scientists do not agree with McKay's findings.

EARLY ASTRONOMERS

The earliest astronomers were not interested in how the universe worked. They needed to know when to plant or harvest crops and when rivers would flood, and they used the movements of bodies in the heavens to make calendars and to predict events in the future. Consequently, at one stage astrology and astronomy became intertwined. It was the ancient Greeks who first started to ask questions about the universe and how it worked. Their work was built on by the studies of great European astronomers from the 1400s onward.

HIPPARCHUS OF NICAEA C. 190–120 B.C.

Nationality: Greek

Major achievements:

- Hipparchus was believed to have cataloged more than 800 stars and also studied the motions of the Moon.

- He invented a brightness scale, subsequently developed by later generations of astronomers into a scale referred to as magnitude.

- Hipparchus calculated the length of Earth's year to within 6.5 minutes.

An illustration of early astonomer Hipparchus

• See page 144 for more information on magnitude.

PTOLEMY OF ALEXANDRIA C. A.D. 87–150

Nationality: Greek

Major achievements:

- Ptolemy wrote many books containing Greek ideas and observations collected throught history, including *Almagest* (*The Great Book*).

- Ptolemy described more than 1,000 stars in his books, including 48 different constellations.

- The astronomer also made early calculations of the size and distance of the Sun and Moon.

- Ptolemy devised a geocentric system with Earth at the center of the Sun, Moon, planets, and stars, although he did not distinguish the differences between them. His order for closest to farthest from Earth read: the Moon, Mercury, Venus; Sun, Mars, Jupiter, and Saturn.

Greek astronomer Ptolemy (center)

NICOLAUS COPERNICUS 1473–1543

Nationality: Polish

Major achievements:

- Copernicus realized the Earth-centered, or geocentric, system dating back to Ptolemy was inaccurate.

- He devised a new heliocentric (Sun-centered) system. Copernicus stated that Earth and all of the other planets revolved around a stationary central Sun.

- Copernicus's ideas were incorporated in his book *On the Revolution of the Heavenly Spheres,* completed in 1530.

- The book was not published until 1543, perhaps just a few days before he died.

**Polish astronomer
Nicolaus Copernicus**

TYCHO BRAHE 1546–1601

A bronze statue of Tycho Brahe in Prague, Czech Republic

Nationality: Danish

Major achievements:

- Brahe discovered a supernova (luminous star explosion) in Cassiopeia in 1572. It is now called Tycho's star. He suggested this was a "fixed" star outside the solar system.

- Brahe plotted the accurate positions of 780 stars over a period of 20 years.

- The astronomer employed German Johannes Kepler as his assistant to help him with his studies.

- Brahe's star catalog was not published until after his death.

The title page and an illustration from Brahe's *Rudolphine Tables,* completed by Kepler

JOHANNES KEPLER 1571–1630

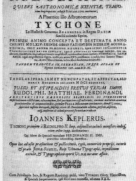

Nationality: German

Major achievements:

- Kepler became Brahe's assistant in 1600.

- He devised the laws of planetary motion, linking a planet's orbit and speed to the Sun.

- The astronomer wrote the first astronomy textbook, *Epitome Astronomiae Copernicanae* (*Epitome of Copernican Astronomy*). He also wrote a science-fiction book called *Somnium* (*The Dream*).

- Kepler completed and published Brahe's star catalog, *Rudolphine Tables,* in 1627.

ASTRONOMICAL DISCOVERIES TIMELINE

1619
Kepler's third law of planetary motion is published.

1632
An official observatory is set up in Leiden, Netherlands.

1668
Isaac Newton builds the first reflecting telescope in England.

1675
Danish astronomer Ole Romer measures the speed of light.

Great Britain's Royal Observatory is established in Greenwich, London.

1687
Newton publishes *Principia,* explaining the laws of motion and gravitation.

1705
Halley correctly predicts a comet seen in 1682 will return in 1758.

1781
William Herschel discovers Uranus, the seventh planet of the solar system.

French astronomer Messier discovers galaxies, nebulae, and star clusters and compiles a catalog of these objects.

1796
Pierre-Simon Laplace publishes his theory of the origin of the solar system.

1801
Giuseppe Piazzi discovers the first asteroid, Ceres, now classified as a dwarf planet.

1843
German astronomer Samuel Heinrich Schwabe describes the sunspot cycle.

1863
Sir William Huggins begins the first complete spectral analysis of stars.

1929
Hubble shows that there are galaxies outside our own galaxy that are moving apart.

1937
First radio telescope is built.

LATER ASTRONOMERS

After the telescope was invented many more people began gazing up at the night sky. Some had little science background or did it for a relaxing hobby, but they sometimes chanced upon an amazing discovery that put their name forever into the history books. Others were full-time professional astronomers who spent a lifetime observing and recording, yet their names are known to very few. This element of chance is smaller today, but it still exists and draws millions of people to watch the skies every night.

Astronomy
The general study of objects in space, including stars, planets, moons, galaxies and other bodies. Often includes observing and recording.

Astrophysics
The study of the physical nature of stars, planets, and other space bodies, including their makeup and contents, temperatures and pressures, densities, and conditions.

Cosmology
The study of the origins, history, makeup, and fate of the universe as a whole, often carried out using mathematics and physics rather than stargazing.

Space science
Often more concerned with spacecraft, probes, rockets, and other hardware, as well as the conditions for space travelers.

GALILEO GALILEI 1564–1642

Nationality: Italian

Major achievements:

- Galileo improved the first telescopes and was the first person to use them for scientific studies of the night skies.

- He observed mountains and craters on the Moon, many stars too faint to see with the unaided eye, and four moons orbiting Jupiter.

- Galileo recorded his early discoveries in his book *Sidereal Messenger* (1610).

- Galileo believed the ideas of Copernicus—that the Sun and not Earth was the center of the solar system as had been previously stated by Ptolemy.

- He put forward both sets of theories in his book *Dialogue on Two Chief World Systems* (1632). This work was heavily criticized, and the astronomer was put under house arrest by religious leaders for his views.

- Galileo made advances in many other areas of science, including the mechanics of moving objects such as pendulums, falling cannonballs, and bullets from guns.

• See page 110 for information on Ptolemy.

GIOVANNI DOMENICO CASSINI 1625–1712

Nationality: Italian-French

Major achievements:

- Cassini was appointed director of the Paris Observatory in 1669.

- He made many discoveries, including four satellites of Saturn and the gap in Saturn's rings (now named the Cassini Division).

- Cassini made many advances combining his observations with calculations, including the orbit times of Mars, Venus, and Jupiter, the paths of Jupiter's moons, and the first fairly accurate measurement from Earth to the Sun (the AU, astronomical unit).

JOHN FLAMSTEED 1646–1719

Nationality: British

Major achievements:

- Flamsteed became the first Astronomer Royal in 1675.

- He made the first extensive star charts using the telescope as part of work aimed at giving sailors a better method of navigation. The charts recorded positions of more than 2,935 stars.

- Due to a dispute with Isaac Newton and the Royal Society, the charts were not published until six years after Flamsteed's death.

EDMOND HALLEY 1656–1742

Nationality: British

Major achievements:

- Edmond Halley traveled to Saint Helena in the South Atlantic at the age of 20 to make the first telescopic chart of stars as seen in the Southern Hemisphere.

- Halley became interested in comets after the "Great Comet" of 1680. He figured out from historical records that a comet seen in 1531, 1607, and 1682 should return in 1758, which it did. The comet is now named after Halley.

- The astronomer was the first to suggest that nebulae were clouds of dust and gas inside which stars might form.

- Halley became Astronomer Royal in 1720 and began an 18-year study of the complete revolution of the Moon.

- Halley's other activities included studying archaeology, geophysics, and the history of astronomy.

WILLIAM HERSCHEL 1738–1822

Nationality: German–British

Major achievements:

- Herschel made many of his own telescopes.

- He discovered the planet Uranus in 1781 and some moons of Uranus and Saturn.

- During his lifetime Herschel cataloged more than 800 double stars.

- He also published a chart of more than 5,000 nebulae in 1820.

- Herschel recognized that the Milky Way was a flattened disk of stars.

PERCIVAL LOWELL 1855–1916

Nationality: American

Major achievements:

- Lowell became interested in astronomy after reports by Giovanni Schiaparelli of "channels" on Mars. "Channels" was misunderstood as "canals," and Lowell became convinced of the existence of Martians, even writing books on them.

- He established Lowell Observatory on a 7,216-ft. (2,200-m) peak in Arizona in 1894, mainly to study Mars.

- Lowell predicted the existence of another planet beyond Neptune. This was Pluto, and it was discovered in 1930 at Lowell Observatory.

STEPHEN HAWKING 1942–

Nationality: British

Major achievements:

- Hawking continued Einstein's ideas about time being a fourth dimension, and he worked on the origin of the universe at the big bang.

- He worked on a common theory for the four basic forces in the universe—gravity, electromagnetism, and strong and weak nuclear forces.

- Hawking made great advances to our understanding of black holes, detailed in his book *A Brief History of Time*.

EDWIN HUBBLE 1889–1953

Nationality: American

Major achievements:

- Working mostly at Mount Wilson Observatory, California, Hubble's studies of nebulae, such as parts of Andromeda, showed they were masses of stars.

- Hubble concluded that these star masses were galaxies outside our own Milky Way.

- He introduced a system of classifying galaxies by their shape.

- Hubble measured the speed of galaxies in 1929 and showed that farther ones move faster, leading to Hubble's law and the idea that the universe is expanding.

ASTRONOMICAL DISCOVERIES TIMELINE

1948
16-ft. (5-m) Hale reflector telescope comes into use at Mount Palomar, California.

1949
The first x-rays from space are detected.

1950
Jan Oort predicts the existence of the Oort cloud of comets.

1951
Gerard Kuiper proposes the existence of the Kuiper belt of comets.

1963
First quasar (quasistellar object) is discovered.

1967
First pulsar (spinning neutron star) is discovered.

1976
20-ft. (6-m) reflector telescope comes into use at Mount Semirodniki, U.S.S.R.

1986
Halley's comet passes Earth.

1987
SN 1987A becomes the first supernova to be seen with the unaided eye in modern times.

1990
Hubble Space Telescope is sent into Earth orbit by the space shuttle.

1992
COBE satellite detects microwave "echoes" of the big bang.

1998
Astronomers discover that the expansion of the universe appears to be speeding up.

2003
WMAP satellite makes first detailed map of minute temperature variations in the microwave echoes of the big bang.

2005
Astronomers announce the discovery of 2003 UB313, now renamed Eris, the largest object to be found in the outer solar system since Pluto in 1930. It is now classified as a dwarf planet.

The solar system is based around the Sun, our closest star, at the center.

- It is made up of eight planets that go around, or orbit, the Sun. They are (listed in order from closest to the Sun) Mercury, Venus, Earth, Mars, Jupiter, Saturn, Uranus, and Neptune.

- All of these planets apart from Mercury and Venus have orbiting objects called moons.

- Smaller space objects called asteroids that orbit in the wide gap between Mars and Jupiter known as the asteroid belt.

- Objects called comets also orbit the Sun, but their orbit streches farther out than any planet in our solar system.

- Space objects called KBOs (Kuiper belt objects) orbit in a wide region beyond Neptune called the Kuiper belt.

- The limits of the solar system are usually taken as the Oort cloud, which is beyond the Kuiper belt.

- Pluto used to be treated as the ninth planet in the solar system. However, in August 2006 it was redefined as a dwarf planet.

OUR HOME IN SPACE

A city may seem like a big place. But most cities are tiny compared to their whole countries. Many countries are small compared to their continents, and all of the continents together cover less than one third of our home planet—the huge globe of Earth. So when we try to imagine that Earth is just one of the smaller planets in the vastness of the solar system, it is very difficult indeed. Studying the solar system means attempting to understand incredible distances, sizes, and forces. And even then, the solar system is just one microscopic speck among the star clusters of our galaxy, the Milky Way, which is only one tiny . . .

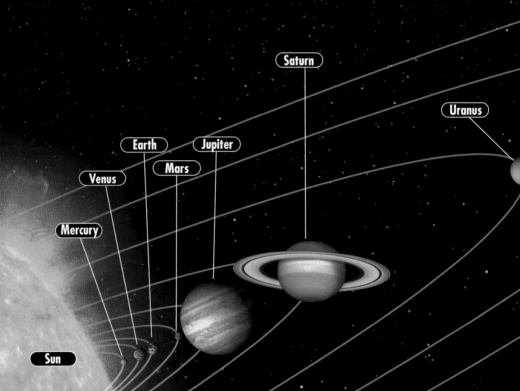

Saturn · Uranus · Earth · Jupiter · Mars · Venus · Mercury · Sun

HISTORY OF THE SOLAR SYSTEM

The solar system probably began to form about five billion years ago.

- A vast cloud of space gas and dust began to clump together under its own pull of gravity. The clump began to spin.

- The center of the clump became the Sun.
- Much smaller bits spinning around it became the planets and perhaps some moons.

- Most of the solar system, including Earth, was formed by 4.5 billion years ago.
- The solar system is probably only about one third as old as the universe itself.

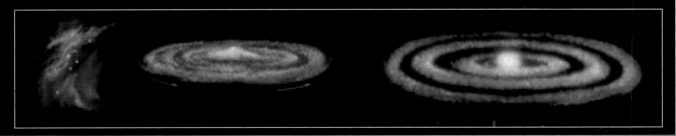

OUR CHANGING VIEWS

People's concepts of the solar system and the universe are constantly evolving.

- In ancient times people thought all objects seen in the day and night skies went around Earth.

- Gradually scientific observations showed that Earth and other planets went around the Sun.

- The invention of the telescope in about 1608 confirmed this idea and allowed the discovery of many more space objects.

- From the 1930s astronomers realized that some space objects gave out invisible radio waves, as well as or instead of light rays.

- Radio telescopes (right) allowed the discovery of yet more objects in space, many invisible to ordinary optical telescopes because they give out no light.

- More types of rays were discovered coming from space objects.

- Ever since 1990, the Hubble Space Telescope, far above the hazy blur of Earth's atmosphere, has discovered yet more stars and other space objects.

Pluto

Neptune

SOME SPACE UNITS

Space is so gigantic that ordinary Earth units such as feet and miles are far too small for convenient use.

Astronomical unit (AU)
The mean ("average") distance from Earth to the Sun—927,506 mi. (149,597,870km).

Light-year (lt.-yr.)
The distance that light (which has the fastest and most constant movement in the universe) travels in one year, usually taken as 5.865634×10^{12} mi. (9,460,528,404,846km).

Parsec (pc)
$1.91735281 \times 10^{13}$ mi. (30.86 million million km), defined by a star's apparent shift in position (parallax) when viewed from two points that are a distance apart equal to the distance from Earth to the Sun.

Million
1,000,000.

Billion
1,000,000,000.

Trillion
1,000,000,000,000.

Axial tilt
The angle at which the axis, the imaginary line joining the north and south poles of a planet, is tilted compared to the level of the solar plane.

ORBITS AND ECCENTRICITY

Most orbits, especially those of the planets around the Sun, are not exact circles.

- They are shaped more like ellipses, or ovals.

- The Sun is not in the center of the oval of most orbits, but slightly offset toward one end, occupying one of the points called the focus.

- The amount that a planet's orbit differs from a circle is called eccentricity.

- The bigger the eccentricity, the more elliptical the orbit.

Planet	Eccentricity
Mercury	0.205
Venus	0.006
Earth	0.016
Mars	0.093
Jupiter	0.048
Saturn	0.054
Uranus	0.047
Neptune	0.0097
[Pluto	0.248]

So, Venus has the most circular orbit, closely followed by Neptune, while Pluto's orbit is the most elliptical, followed by Mercury's.

Planet	Distance from Sun (AU)
Mercury	0.387
Venus	0.723
Earth	1.00
Mars	1.52
Jupiter	5.20
Saturn	9.54
Uranus	19.19
Neptune	30.01
[Pluto	39.48]

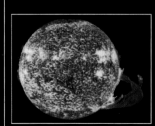

The Sun dwarfs all of the planets in the solar system.

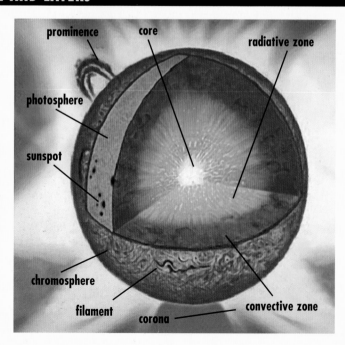

THE SUN

Our closest star, the Sun is the center of the solar system. All of the planets and asteroids are held in their orbits by its immense gravity. It also attracts visitors from the farthest reaches of the system, such as comets. For billions of years the Sun has been providing Earth with light that green plants use as an energy source for living and growing. Herbivorous animals eat the plants, carnivorous animals eat the herbivores, and in this way the Sun powers life on Earth—including our own.

ORBIT DETAILS

Average distance from center of Milky Way: 26,000 light-years

Time for one orbit around center: 225 million years

Average orbital speed: 135 miles per second (217km/sec)

Time to spin on axis: 25.38 days at equator

STAR PROFILE

Diameter at equator	**864,400 mi. (1,392,000km)**
Surface area	**2.3 trillion sq. mi. (6.1 trillion km²)**
Mass (Earth = 1)	**332,900**
Volume (Earth = 1)	**1.3 million**
Overall density (Earth = 1)	**0.255 (1.4g/cm³)**
Gravity (Earth = 1)	**28** (If you weigh 10 lbs./4.5kg on Earth, you would weigh 280 lbs./127kg on the Sun.)
Number of main planets	**8**

A NASA photograph
of the Sun

STRUCTURE AND LAYERS

CORE

- About 173,600 mi. (280,000km) across.
- Nuclear fusion reactions convert hydrogen to helium, producing immense amounts of light, heat, and other radiation.
- Energy output equivalent to 90 million billion tons of TNT per second.

RADIATIVE ZONE

- About 217,000 mi. (350,000km) deep.
- Conveys heat and light outward by photon transfer between ions.
- Temperature falls with distance to core.

CONVECTIVE ZONE

- About 217,000 mi. (200,000km) deep.
- Superhot material carries heat outward from radiative zone.
- Material cools at photosphere and sinks back to receive more heat, causing convection currents.

PHOTOSPHERE

- Visible surface of the Sun.
- Around 372 mi. (600km) deep.
- Emits photons of light and other energy forms into space.

CHROMOSPHERE

- About 1,550 mi. (2,500km) deep.
- Visible as a red-colored flash around the Sun at the start and end of a total solar eclipse.

CORONA

- Wispy outer atmosphere around the Sun.
- Extends many millions of miles into space.

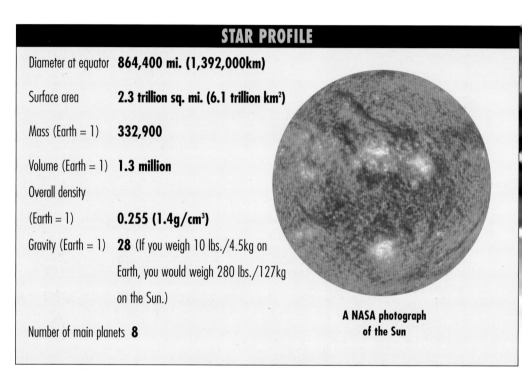

FLARES AND PROMINENCES

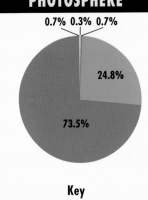

- Solar flares are massive explosions in the lower corona and chromosphere. They were first observed in 1859.

- They trigger huge solar eruptions called coronal mass ejections.

- Solar prominences are larger and longer lasting than flares.

- Many leap up, along, and down in a curved arc back to the Sun.

- Typically, prominences are thousands of miles long.

- The largest ones can be over 310,000 mi. (500,000km) long.

MAKEUP OF PHOTOSPHERE

0.7% 0.3% 0.7%

24.8%

73.5%

Key

- ■ Carbon
- ■ Oxygen
- ■ Helium
- ■ Hydrogen
- ■ Traces

SOLAR WIND

- Solar wind steams away from the Sun in all directions.

- It reaches speeds of up to 248 mi. (400km) per second and comes mainly from the corona.

- Solar wind consists of charged particles, mainly protons and electrons with a few heavier ions.

- Where solar wind interacts with Earth's magnetic fields, near the North and South poles, it creates auroras — shimmering "curtains" of light high in the sky — the northern lights (the aurora borealis) and southern lights (the aurora australis).

A diagram of solar wind; Earth (right) is protected by its magnetic field.

SUNSPOTS

Sunspots are cooler variable patches on the photosphere, probably caused by magnetic interactions.

- The inner umbra of each spot is around 7,200°F (4,000°C). The outer penumbra is about 9,932°F (5,500°C).

- They were first noticed to vary in a regular, or cyclic, way by Heinrich Schwabe between 1825 and 1843.

- Sunspots usually vary in an 11-year cycle. An average sunspot's "life" is two weeks.

- On March 30, 2001, SOHO (Solar and Heliospheric Observatory) recorded the largest sunspot group so far, covering more than 13 times the area of Earth.

NASA photo of a sunspot

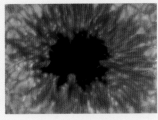

Close-up of a sunspot

TEMPERATURES

Corona 35.6 million°F (19.8 million°C)   **Surface** 10,472°F (5,800°C)   **Core** 59 million°F (32.8 million°C)

SUN TIMELINE

27,000 years ago
Depicted in rock carvings in Europe, North Africa, and Australia and cave paintings 10,000 years later.

From 7,000 years ago
The Sun is worshiped as a god by many ancient civilizations.

4,900 years ago
First phase of construction of Stonehenge, a Sun-aligned Stone Age temple in England.

From 4,000 years ago
The Sun is worshiped as the god Ra in ancient Egypt.

2,030 years ago
Chinese astronomers make the first mention of sunspots.

1300s
Aztec people make sacrifices to their Sun god, Huitzilopochtli.

1610–1611
Sunspots first seen through a telescope by Johannes and David Fabricius, then by Galileo Galilei.

1962
McMath-Pierce Solar Telescope is erected in Arizona, the largest telescope dedicated to Sun study.

1990
Ulysses probe is launched from the space shuttle to study the Sun's north and south poles and solar wind.

1995
Joint European/U.S. probe SOHO is launched on December 2.

1997
ACE (Advanced Composition Explorer) satellite is launched to study particles and materials from the Sun and elsewhere.

2001
Space probe Genesis is launched on August 8 in order to capture samples of solar wind.

2004
On September 8 Genesis returns but is damaged in a crash landing.

2004
Analysis begins on the hundreds of Sun samples retrieved from the Genesis probe.

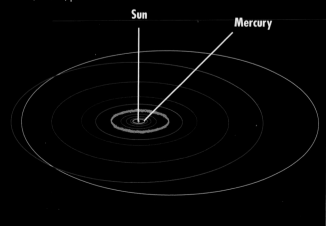

MERCURY

Known by most ancient people from its brief periods of visibility at dawn and dusk, Mercury was named after the Roman winged messenger of the gods—because it has the fastest orbital speed of any planet, averaging 300 miles per second (47km/sec). Being the closest planet to the Sun, Mercury is blasted by solar heat and other radiation. This has swept away all but the flimsiest atmosphere, and it heats Mercury's daytime side to incredible temperatures—yet the night side plunges to around –300°F (–183°C).

SURFACE CONDITIONS

ATMOSPHERE:
Almost zero—traces of potassium, argon, oxygen, argon.

NATURE OF SURFACE:
Bare iron-rich rocks pitted with hundreds of large craters.

AVERAGE SURFACE TEMPERATURE: 338°F (170°C)

LOWEST SURFACE TEMPERATURE: –300°F (–183°C)

HIGHEST SURFACE TEMPERATURE: 800°F (425°C)

WEATHER OR CLIMATE:
None, due to lack of atmosphere.

SEASONAL CHANGES:
None, due to almost zero tilt of axis.

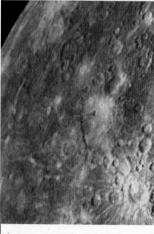

A color photograph of Mercury, showing the pitted iron-rich surface

PLANET PROFILE

Diameter at equator **3,031 mi. (4,879km)**
Surface area **28 million sq. mi. (75 million km²)**
Tilt of axis **0.01°**
Mass (Earth = 1) **0.055**
Volume (Earth = 1) **0.054**
Overall density (Earth = 1) **0.984 (5.42g/cm³)**
Gravity (Earth = 1) **0.377**
(If you weigh 100 lbs./4kg on Earth, you would weigh 38 lbs./17kg on Mercury.)

Number of moons **0**

A NASA photograph of the planet Mercury

ORBIT DETAILS

Average distance from Sun 36 million mi. (57.9 million km)
Average distance from Sun 0.387 AU (Earth =1)
Closest distance to Sun (perihelion) 28.6 million mi. (46 million km)
Farthest distance from Sun (aphelion) 43.3 million mi. (69.8 million km)
Average orbital speed 30 mi. (47.4km) per second

Slowest orbital speed 24.1 mi. (38.9km) per second
Fastest orbital speed 37 mi. (59km) per second
Time for one orbit (Mercury year) 87.9 Earth days
Axial rotation period 58.6 Earth days
Length of Mercury day 176 Earth days

Sun
Mercury

MAJOR FEATURES

Less than half of Mercury's surface has been mapped in any detail (by *Mariner 10*), so its surface features are less known than those of most other planets.

Caloris Basin
Massive crater made by asteroid/meteoroid impact, measuring 837 mi. (1,350km) across.

Caloris Montes
"Heat's Mountains," curved ranges with peaks rising to 9,840 ft. (3,000m) sited at one of the hottest places on Mercury, within the Caloris Basin crater.

Discovery Scarp
Joining two craters, this "cliff" is 217 mi. (350km) long, and its maximum height is around 9,184 ft. (2,800m).

The heavily pitted Caloris Basin crater

• See pages 138–141 for information on asteroids and meteors.

OTHER FEATURES

- **SCARPS (RUPES)** Long clifflike ridges with one steep side and one gradually sloping side, formed as below.

- **RIDGES (DORSA)** Long prominent ridges with two steep sides, formed as Mercury's core cooled and shrank and the already solid crust was cracked into wrinkles.

- **YOUNGER PLAINS** Uplands probably formed from hardened lava flows, less marked by craters from impacts.

- **OLDER PLAINS** Lowlands much more pockmarked with overlapping craters than the younger plains.

- **ARECIBO VALLIS** Valley named after the Arecibo Observatory, home to Earth's largest radio telescope, in Puerto Rico.

- **ICE** Despite Mercury's incredible heat, there is probably ice (frozen water) at its north pole in deep craters with permanent shade from the Sun.

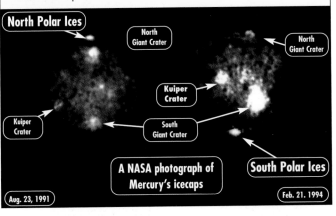

North Polar Ices

North Giant Crater

North Giant Crater

Kuiper Crater

Kuiper Crater

South Giant Crater

Kuiper Crater

South Polar Ices

A NASA photograph of Mercury's icecaps

Aug. 23, 1991

Feb. 21, 1994

SMALL AND CURIOUS

The minute size of Mercury is shown in the above picture of the planet (circled in red) in transit against the Sun.

- Mercury is the smallest planet in the solar system.

- It has a very "eccentric," or oval-shaped, orbit, much more so than most other planets. Only the dwarf planet Pluto is more "eccentric."

- Its axis is hardly tilted at all, being at right angles to the Sun, so the Sun is always directly over its equator all through its year.

MERCURY TIMELINE

5,000 years ago
The Sumerians mention Mercury, which they call Ubu-idim-gud-ud.

3,300 years ago
Earliest detailed observations of Mercury in ancient Babylon.

2,500 years ago
In ancient Greece, Mercury (like Venus) was thought to be two different planets with two names—Apollo in the dawn sky and Hermes at dusk.

2,470 years ago
Heraclitus believes that Mercury, along with Venus, orbits the Sun rather than Earth.

1,000 years ago
Ancient Chinese documents refer to Mercury as the "Water Star."

1639
Giovanni Zupi's telescope observations show different parts of Mercury are lit at different times by the Sun.

1965
Radar measurements show that Mercury spins three times for every two orbits.

1973
U.S. *Mariner 10* launched in November to fly past Venus and Mercury.

1974
Mariner 10 makes first flyby of Mercury on March 29.

1975
Mariner 10's third flyby in March returns information on Mercury's magnetic field.

2004
U.S. Mercury probe MESSENGER is launched in August.

2008–2009
MESSENGER makes three flybys of Mercury.

2011
MESSENGER due to enter Mercury orbit in March and survive for one year, studying the thin atmosphere and exploring the surface.

DISTINGUISHING FEATURES

Mercury has several features that mark it out from other planets.

Mercury has several hundred named craters, with names such as Dickens, Shakespeare, Chopin, Mark Twain, Beethoven, Degas, and Sibelius. All of its craters are named after famous artists and classical musicians.

In 1974 the *Mariner 10* spacecraft produced this image of the 37-mi. (60-km)- wide Degas crater.

TEMPERATURE

Mercury has the widest temperature range of any planet, spanning almost 1,112°F (600°C) between day on the sunny side and night on the shady side. (Earth's maximum range is less than 302°F/150°C.)

SPINNING MERCURY

Because of its proximity to the Sun and slow spinning speed, at certain places and times on Mercury an astronaut would see the Sun rise to just above the horizon, then go back and set, and then rise again, all on the same Mercury day.

MERCURY TRANSIT

Since Mercury is closer to the Sun than Earth, when the two planets are almost in line, Mercury appears to cross the disk of the Sun when viewed from Earth. This is called the transit of Mercury. There are about 14 transits every century.

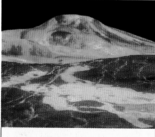

WHERE IN THE SOLAR SYSTEM?

The second planet from the Sun, Venus is named after the Roman goddess of love—and is shrouded in mystery. In fact, it is shrouded by thick swirling clouds of gases and droplets of acid that hide its surface from the gaze of outsiders. Although Venus is about the same size and mass (weight) as Earth, it could not be more different. It is the hottest of all the planets, partly because its thick atmosphere traps vast amounts of heat from the nearby Sun in a "runaway greenhouse effect" far more extreme than that experienced here on Earth.

SURFACE CONDITIONS

ATMOSPHERE:
Thick, dense, mainly carbon dioxide, also nitrogen and sulfur acids.

NATURE OF SURFACE:
Hard and rocky, with numerous volcanoes.

AVERAGE SURFACE TEMPERATURE:
900°F (470°C)

LOWEST SURFACE TEMPERATURE:
113°F (45°C) (at cloud tops)

HIGHEST SURFACE TEMPERATURE:
932°F (500°C) in valleys near the equator

WEATHER OR CLIMATE:
Thick, swirling deadly poisonous atmosphere. Winds reach 484 mph (300km/h) at the top of the clouds.

SEASONAL CHANGES:
Minimal on surface, due to dense atmosphere.

A *Magellan* radar image of the volcano Sif Mons on Venus.

PLANET PROFILE

Diameter at equator **7,520 mi. (12,103km)**

Surface area **177 million sq. mi. (460 million km²)**

Tilt of axis **177.3°**

Mass (Earth = 1) **0.815**

Volume (Earth = 1) **0.88**

Overall density **5.2g/cm³**
(comparable to Earth's average density)

Gravity (Earth = 1) **0.90**

Number of moons **0**

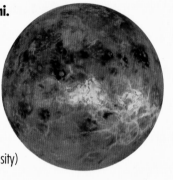

A NASA mosaic of the planet Venus

ORBIT DETAILS

Average distance from Sun
67.2 million mi. (108.2 million km)

Average distance from Sun
0.723 AU (Earth =1)

Closest distance to Sun (perihelion) 66.7 million mi. (107.4 million km).

Farthest distance from Sun (aphelion) 67.7 million mi. (108.9 million km)

Average orbital speed
21.7 mi. (35km) per second

Slowest orbital speed
21.6 mi. (34.8km) per second

Fastest orbital speed
21.9 mi. (35.3km) per second

Time for one orbit
(Venus year) 224.7 Earth days

Axial rotaton period
243 Earth days

Length of Venus day
117 Earth days

Sun

Venus

MAJOR FEATURES

Several probes have been sent to Venus, and radio waves have been used to map virtually the entire planet.

Ishtar Terra
Northern highlands about the size of Australia, bearing Venus's highest mountains.

Maxwell Montes
A range of mountains about 527 mi. (850km) long, with the highest peaks over 36,080 ft. (11,000m) tall.

Lakshmi Planum
Vast upland plain or plateau partly encircled by Maxwell Montes.

Aphrodite Terra
Southern uplands, roughly the size of South America.

Arachnoid volcanoes
Photographed by the space probe *Magellan*, these have unusual ridges around them. The central volcano with its surrounding ridges looks like a giant spider.

A NASA photograph of the sprawling Aphrodite Terra, shown in brown

OTHER FEATURES

- **CORONAE** Circular centers surrounded by ringlike ridges, the largest being Artemis Corona at 1,302 mi. (2,100km) across.

- **PLAINS** Flat and fairly smooth, these cover two thirds of the surface with low volcanoes up to 124 mi. (200km) across.

- **MOUNTAINS** Six main mountain ranges covering about one third of the surface.

- **UPLAND REGIONS** One of the largest is Beta Regio, dominated by Rhea Mons and Theia Mons.

- **LOWLAND DEPRESSIONS** Wide and low, these include Atalanta Planitia, Guinevere Planitia, and Lavinia Planitia.

- **ALL FEATURES** All of Venus's surface features are named after females (either real people or from myths and legends), with the exception of the Maxwell Montes, named after scientist James Clerk Maxwell.

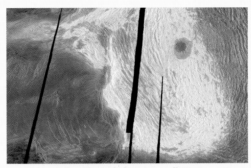

A radar shot of the Maxwell Montes

TRANSIT OF VENUS

Since Venus is closer to the Sun than Earth, when the two planets are almost in line, Venus appears to cross the disk of the Sun when viewed from Earth. This is called the transit of Venus. The date it occurs and the time Venus takes to cross the Sun's face have been used to estimate the distance between Earth and the Sun. Transits occur in pairs. The two in each pair are about eight years apart, but the time between pairs is more than 100 years.

The transit of Venus across the Sun

- See page 122 for information on Earth's orbit.

DAYTIME VIEWING

- Because of its closeness and bright reflection of sunlight, Venus is so bright that it is one of only two space bodies, other than the Sun, that can be seen during daylight from Earth—the other is the Moon.

- It is also often the first starlike body to appear at dusk and the last to fade at dawn, earning it the names "evening star" and "morning star."

REVERSE SPIN

Venus is one of only two planets with retrograde spin (the other one is Uranus). This means it spins on its axis in the opposite direction to the other planets. Seen from the side, its surface moves from east to west, or right to left—or clockwise if viewed from above its North Pole.

CLOSEST NEIGHBOR

No other planet comes closer to Earth than Venus. At its closest, it is 24 million mi. (38.2 million km) away.

SLOWPOKE

Venus takes longer to spin once on its axis than it takes to complete one orbit of the Sun.

CIRCULAR ORBIT

Most planets have an orbit that is an ellipse (oval). The journey of Venus around the Sun is the most circular of all of the planets—that is, it is the least "eccentric" orbit (especially compared to that of Venus's close neighbor Mercury).

UNDER PRESSURE

The atmosphere's pressing force, or pressure, on Venus (pictured below next to Earth) is incredible—90 times more than our own, and equivalent to the pressure 3,280 ft. (1,000m) under the sea on Earth.

VENUS TIMELINE

3,600 years ago
Astronomical records in Babylonia record appearances of Venus.

3,500 years ago
Ancient Babylonians record Venus as one of the brightest "stars."

2,500 years ago
In ancient Greece, Venus is thought to be two different planets—Phosphorus in the dawn sky and Hesperus at dusk.

2,000 years ago
Ancient Chinese observers refer to Venus as the "Metal Star."

1610
Galileo observes phases of Venus.

1639
First transit of Venus is observed.

1672
Giovanni Domenico Cassini claims to discover a moon of Venus.

1961
Russian space probe *Venera 1* aims at Venus, but fails.

1962
U.S. probe *Mariner 2* flies past Venus.

1966
Venera 3 probe crash-lands on the surface. *Venera 4* is more successful the following year and sends back information. *Veneras 5, 6,* and *7* send back information in subsequent years.

1970
Venera 7 makes the first successful landing.

1975
Venera 9 is the first spacecraft to send a picture back from the surface of Venus, on October 21.

1978
U.S. sends two *Pioneer* probes to Venus.

1990
The *Magellan* probe maps all but 1/50th of the surface.

1998–1999
Cassini-Huygens flys past Venus.

2004
First of a pair of transits is witnessed.

2006
European Space Agency's *Venus Express* reaches final orbit on May 9.

2012
Next transit of Venus due.

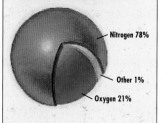

EARTH

We think of our home world as "average" for a planet. But the more we learn about the rest of the solar system, the more we see that Earth is very unusual. Earth is the only planet that has abundant water in liquid form. This is mainly because its average surface temperature is just 72°F (22°C). In fact, more than three fourths of Earth's surface is made up of rivers, lakes, seas, oceans, and frozen water in the form of glaciers and icecaps.

SURFACE CONDITIONS

ATMOSPHERE:
Almost four fifths nitrogen, one fifth oxygen, traces of carbon dioxide, water vapor, and other gases.

NATURE OF SURFACE:
Varied, from high rocky mountains to deep valleys and trenches, mostly covered with water.

AVERAGE SURFACE TEMPERATURE: 72°F (22°C)

LOWEST SURFACE TEMPERATURE: −128°F (−89°C)

HIGHEST SURFACE TEMPERATURE: 136°F (58°C)

WEATHER OR CLIMATE:
Varies owing to movement of atmosphere and its water vapor distributed by clouds and falling as rain. Generally conditions become colder from the equator (Tropics) to the poles.

SEASONAL CHANGES:
Marked seasons owing to considerable tilt of axis — cold, icy winters and hot summers.

COMPOSITION OF EARTH'S ATMOSPHERE

Nitrogen 78%
Other 1%
Oxygen 21%

PLANET PROFILE

Diameter at equator **7,926 mi. (12,756km)**

Surface area **196 million sq. mi. (510 million km^2)**

Tilt of axis **23.4°**

Mass **5.97 x 10^{24} kg**

Volume **260 billion mi. (1.08 trillion km^3)**

Overall density **5.517g/cm^3**

Gravity **32.04ft./s^2 (9.78m/s^2)**

Number of moons **1**

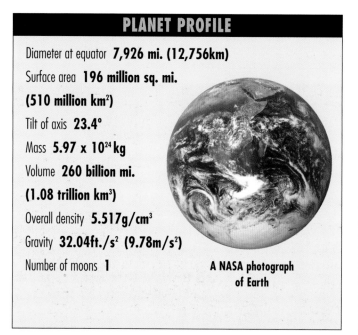

A NASA photograph of Earth

ORBIT DETAILS

Average distance from Sun
93 million mi. (149.6 million km)

Average distance from Sun
1 AU

Closest distance to Sun (perihelion) 91.4 million mi. (147.1 million km)

Farthest distance from Sun (aphelion) 152.1 million km

Average orbital speed
18.6 mi. (29.8km) per second

Slowest orbital speed
18.2 mi. (29.3km) per second

Fastest orbital speed
19 mi. (30.3km) per second

Time for one orbit
(Earth year) 365.256 Earth days

Axial rotation period
(Earth day) 23.93 Earth hours

Sun

Earth

MAJOR FEATURES

Earth has been extensively mapped.

Rivers
The Amazon River of South America carries more water than the next five biggest rivers combined, emptying 7 million cu. ft. (200,000m^3) per second into the Atlantic Ocean.

Oceans
The Pacific Ocean covers almost half (46%) of Earth's surface.

Mountains
The Himalayas of central Asia and northern India have eight of the world's ten tallest peaks.

Deserts
The Sahara Desert of North Africa is by far the greatest arid (very dry) area, covering more than 3.5 million sq. mi. (9 million km^2).

Lowest point
The bottom of the deep-sea Mariana Trench in the northwest Pacific Ocean is 35,788 ft. (10,911m) below the ocean's surface.

Highest point
The peak of Mount Everest in the Himalayas is 29.028 ft. (8,850m) above sea level.

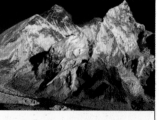

Earth's highest mountain, Everest

OTHER FEATURES

The outer reef of the Great Barrier Reef

- **LAKE SUPERIOR** The largest body of fresh water by area on Earth.

- **LAKE BAIKAL** The largest body of fresh water by volume on Earth.

- **THE LAMBERT GLACIER** Situated on Antarctica, it is the largest glacier on Earth, 310 mi. (500km) long and 50 mi. (80km) wide.

- **THE GRAND CANYON** This spectacular deep valley has been worn away by the Colorado River. It is 217 mi. (350km) long, up to 19 mi. (30km) wide, and in places 5,248 ft. (1,600m) deep between almost sheer cliffs.

- **THE GREAT BARRIER REEF** A long series of rocky reefs built over thousands of years by billions of tiny animals called coral polyps.

PLATE TECTONICS

- Earth's outer surface of thin rocky crust, plus a thin layer of semimelted rock below, is split into 12–15 giant curved pieces called lithospheric plates.

- Over millions of years, these slid or drifted around the globe, at the rate of about 0.39–1.2 in. (1–3cm) per year, carrying the major landmasses with them in a process called continental drift.

- At the edges of some plates new rock was added by a process called ocean-floor spreading.

- Where two plates rammed into each other, the crust buckled into mountains, such as the Himalayas and Andes.

- Where one plate slid below the other (subduction zone), there were earthquakes and volcanoes.

POLAR ICE

- Apart from large cloud systems, the glistening icecaps over the North and South poles are perhaps Earth's most noticeable features from space.

- Each shrinks in the summer, then spreads in the winter, due to Earth's seasonal changes and zoned climate from equator to pole.

- The Arctic icecap over the North Pole is a "raft" of ice up to 33 ft. (10m) thick floating in the Arctic Ocean, with a winter extent of 5.9 million sq. mi. (15 million km^2).

- The Antarctic icecap over the South Pole covers the vast southern landmass of Antarctica, with a winter extent of 7.4 million sq. mi. (19 million km^2).

LIFE

- Earth is the only body in the solar system known to support life. This life depends on liquid water and mostly occurs in the narrow temperature range of 32–104°F (0–40°C).

- The greatest variety of land life occurs in the tropical rain forests, which have nine out of ten of the 20-plus million species of plants, animals, and other life forms.

- The richest variety of marine life is found in coral reefs.

- Many areas of wildlife are being affected, polluted, and used for agriculture and industry by the dominant life form on Earth—Homo sapiens.

Prehistory
More than 10,000 years ago, people make maps of their areas carved on stone or ivory, scratched into tablets, or woven into hangings.

3,000 years ago
Early Greeks theorize Earth is a flat disk.

2,500 years ago
In ancient Greece, the idea grows that the world is round, or a globe, based on observations, such as how the stars vary at different places on Earth.

1519–1522
Ferdinand Magellan's expedition circles the globe to show that Earth is indeed a sphere.

1785
James Hutton proposes his principle of uniformitarianism, which means Earth's surface has been shaped over huge lengths of time by the same processes we see at work today—volcanoes, earthquakes, mountain building, and erosion by wind, rain, ice, and snow. He believes Earth is "immeasurably ancient."

1882
William Thomson (Lord Kelvin) figures out Earth's age from its cooling rate. His approximate age for Earth is one tenth of today's estimate.

1908
Frank Taylor and Howard Baker put forward a scientific explanation for continental drift.

1912
Alfred Wegener suggests a version of the modern theory of plate tectonics, which causes continental drift.

1956
Claire Patterson determines from amounts of radioactivity in rocks that Earth is 4.5 billion years old; today the accepted age is believed to be closer to 4.6 billion.

1960s
Earth scientists come to accept Weneger's basic ideas and develop the modern version of plate tectonics.

1989
The first of the 24 operational NAVSTAR satellites is launched, which from the 1990s provide GPS (Global Positioning System) for satellite navigation to locate any spot on Earth's surface within a few tens of feet.

WHERE IN THE SOLAR SYSTEM?

A moon is a natural object of reasonable size circling a planet. The one we call the Moon (usually with "the" and a capital "M") is Earth's single moon. It has also been known to scientists as Luna, and the word *lunar* has to do with the Moon. Seen from Earth, the Moon is about the same size as the Sun. It appears to change shape during its 29.5-day orbit because we can see only the sunlit part of its surface, creating the phases of the Moon. Its pull of gravity also makes the water in the seas and oceans rise and fall, which we call the tides.

ORBIT DETAILS

Average distance from Earth
238,855 mi. (384,400km)

Average distance from Earth
0.0026 AU (Earth = 1)

Closest distance to Earth (perigee) 225,700 mi. (363,100km)

Farthest distance from Sun (aphelion) 253,000 mi. (405,700km)

Average orbital speed
0.63 mi. (1.02km) per second

Slowest orbital speed
0.60 mi. (0.97km) per second

Fastest orbital speed
0.67 mi. (1.08km) per second

Time for one orbit
(Earth units) 29 days, 12 hours, 44 minutes

Axial rotation period
(Earth units) 27 days, 7 hours, 43 minutes

MOON PROFILE

Diameter at equator **2,160 mi. (3,476km)**

Surface area **14.6 million sq. mi. (37.9 million km²)**

Tilt of axis **3.6–6.7°**

Mass (Earth = 1) **0.0123**

Volume (Earth = 1) **0.020**

Overall density (Earth = 1) **0.606 (3.34g/cm³)**

Gravity (Earth = 1) **0.165**

Number of moons **None**

An artist's illustration of the Moon

LUNATICS

The Moon features greatly in many legends and stories. One superstition was that if a person stared at a full moon for too long, they would go crazy. This is where the word *lunatic* comes from. Another legend was that on a full moon certain people would grow hair, long teeth, and claws and become savage and deadly werewolves.

ORIGIN

It is thought the Moon was formed when a huge Mars-sized space lump of rock, provisionally named Theia, crashed into Earth some 4.5 billion years ago. This was when Earth was about 100 million years old. The loose matter and debris orbiting Earth after the impact came together to form the Moon.

MAJOR FEATURES

The Moon has been visited and mapped several times.

Largest crater
The largest-known crater in the solar system, the South Pole-Aitken basin is 1,396 mi. (2,250km) across and 8 mi. (13km) deep.

Sea of Tranquility
The site of the first *Apollo* Moon landing in 1969. It is 370 x 558 mi. (600 x 900km).

Sea of Serenity
Site of the last Moon landing in 1972, about 341 mi. (550km) wide.

The heavily pitted Copernicus crater

Sea of Crises
Main dark circular area near the upper eastern (right) edge.

Montes Apenninus
Peaks more than 14,760 ft. (4,500m) high.

Copernicus
Small, 12,500-ft. (3,800-m) deep crater (below).

Ocean of Storms
Largest lowland plain, covering 1.6 million sq. mi. (4 million km²).

• See page 159 for information on probes to the Moon.

SURFACE CONDITIONS

ATMOSPHERE:
Tiny traces of helium, neon, hydrogen, argon.

NATURE OF SURFACE:
Craters, mountains, valleys, plains called "seas."

AVERAGE SURFACE TEMPERATURE:
−9.4°F (−23°C)

LOWEST SURFACE TEMPERATURE:
−382°F (−230°C)

HIGHEST SURFACE TEMPERATURE: 255°F (124°C)

WEATHER OR CLIMATE: None.
SEASONAL CHANGES: None.

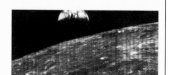
The barren surface of the Moon

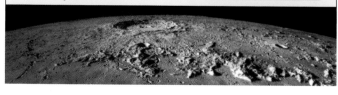

OTHER FEATURES

- **MARIA** Meaning "seas," these are dark lowland plains of hardened basalt rocks that once flowed as lava. They are completely dry, like the rest of the Moon, and occur mainly on the near side.

- **RILLS** Ancient lava channels. They include Hyginus rill and Hadley rill.

- **NAMES** Most of the craters are named after famous scientists, especially astronomers.

NEAR AND FAR

- The Moon turns around once in the same time it takes to go around Earth once.

- This means that it mainly keeps one side facing Earth.

- Due to the Moon's slight variations in orbit and the "wobble" on its axis, a total of almost three fifths of its surface is visible from Earth.

- The other two fifths is always hidden and has been seen only by spacecraft in lunar orbit.

- The far side is sometimes called the "dark side of the Moon," but it receives sunlight in the same pattern as the near side.

PHASES OF THE MOON

The Sun lights up only half the Moon at a time. As the Moon moves around Earth, we see varying amounts of the sunlit half of the Moon. This causes it to show changes of shape called phases. When the Moon is roughly between the Sun and Earth, its dark side is turned toward us, and we normally cannot see it. This is called the new moon. As the Moon moves around Earth, the sunlit side begins to show. First we see a thin crescent, then a half-moon, and then a full moon. At full moon, all of the sunlit side faces us. After full moon, the phase decreases slowly to half and back to a crescent as we see less and less of the sunlit side. Finally it is a new moon once again. The time from one new moon to the next new moon is 29.53 days.

THE MOON AND TIDES

Tides are the regular rising and falling of the surface of the oceans. Although the Sun has some influence, ocean tides are mainly caused by the gravitational interaction between Earth and the Moon. The gravitational pull of the Moon causes the oceans to bulge out in the direction of the Moon. Another bulge occurs on the opposite side, since Earth is also being pulled toward the Moon and away from the water on the far side. Since Earth is spinning on its axis, the tides rise and fall twice a day, with the interval between low tide and high tide being just over six hours.

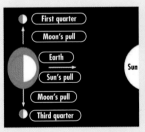

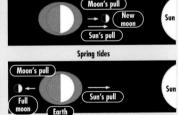

ECLIPSES

Solar eclipse
When the Moon comes between Earth and the Sun and blocks part (partial eclipse) or all (total eclipse) of the Sun's disk. The amount of the disk blotted out varies with the position on Earth. The area of shadow on Earth of a total eclipse is 167 mi. (270km) wide and moves across Earth as Earth spins and the Moon continues its orbit. On average there are two total eclipses every three years.

Lunar eclipse
When Earth comes between the Sun and Moon. The Moon seems to fade but stays a copper-red color as the Sun's rays are bent around the edge of Earth by the atmosphere.

THE MOON TIMELINE

1959
Russian space probe *Luna 2* crashes into the surface in September—the first human-made object to reach another world. The following month *Luna 3* goes around the Moon and sends back the first images of the unknown far side.

1966
Luna 9 soft-lands and sends back the first close-up images of the Moon's surface. *Lunar 10* becomes the first probe to go into steady Moon orbit.

1966
The first of the U.S. *Surveyor* missions touches down in June and sends back more than 11,000 images.

1968
In December, U.S. *Apollo 8* enters into Moon orbit but does not land, and the crew stays onboard the command module in lunar orbit.

1969
U.S. *Apollo 11* touches down on July 20, carrying the first humans to visit another world. Neil Armstrong is first to step out of the lunar module (lander), followed by Edwin "Buzz" Aldrin. Michael Collins stays in the command module in orbit.

1969
Apollo 12 lands to carry out scientific studies in November.

1971
Apollo 14 collects 95 lbs. (43kg) of Moon rocks in February.

1972
Apollo 16 collects nearly 221 lbs. (100kg) of Moon material.

1972
Eugene Cernan is the last person to step on the Moon.

1994
The *Clementine* space probe collects information that suggests there might be frozen water on the Moon.

2003
European spacecraft *Smart 1* is launched.

2004
In February, U.S. President George W. Bush announces plans for a new series of Moon missions.

2004
Smart 1 takes up lunar orbit on November 15 to study and map the surface using x-rays.

WHERE IN THE SOLAR SYSTEM?

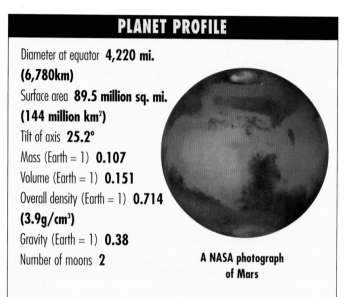

MARS

Named after the Roman god of war, Mars is also called the "red planet" because its surface rocks and dust contain large amounts of the substance iron oxide—better known here on Earth as rust. Like Earth, Mars has polar icecaps, volcanoes, canyons, winds, and swirling dust storms. Features resembling riverbeds, estuaries, and shorelines suggest that great rivers— probably of water—once flowed across Mars's surface. Despite many visits by space probes, landers, and rovers, no signs of life have ever been found.

SURFACE CONDITIONS

ATMOSPHERE:
Mostly carbon dioxide, small amounts of nitrogen and argon, traces of oxygen, carbon monoxide, and water vapor.

NATURE OF SURFACE:
Rocks and dust, including giant volcanoes, deep canyons, and dusty plains.

AVERAGE SURFACE TEMPERATURE:
−81ºF (−63ºC)

LOWEST SURFACE TEMPERATURE:
−220ºF (140ºC)

HIGHEST SURFACE TEMPERATURE:
77ºF (25ºC)

WEATHER OR CLIMATE: Clouds, fog, strong winds, dust storms, red sky.

SEASONAL CHANGES:
Marked (similar to Earth), with intensely cold winters.

A photograph of the surface of Mars taken by the *Viking* lander

PLANET PROFILE

Diameter at equator **4,220 mi. (6,780km)**

Surface area **89.5 million sq. mi. (144 million km²)**

Tilt of axis **25.2º**

Mass (Earth = 1) **0.107**

Volume (Earth = 1) **0.151**

Overall density (Earth = 1) **0.714 (3.9g/cm³)**

Gravity (Earth = 1) **0.38**

Number of moons **2**

A NASA photograph of Mars

ORBIT DETAILS

Average distance from Sun
141.6 million mi. (227.9 million km)

Average distance from Sun
1.52 AU (Earth = 1)

Closest distance to Sun (perihelion) 128.4 million mi. (206.6 million km)

Farthest distance from Sun (aphelion) 154.8 million mi. (249.2 million km)

Average orbital speed
15 mi. (24.1km) per second

Slowest orbital speed
13.6 mi. (21.9km) per second

Fastest orbital speed
16.4 mi. (26.5km) per second

Time for one orbit
(Mars year) 686.9 Earth days

Axial rotation period
(Mars day) 24.62 Earth hours

Sun

Mars

MAJOR FEATURES

North Polar Cap

- Water ice that remains through the summer.

- Sand dunes formed by wind.

- Approximately 682 mi. (1,100km) across.

South Polar Cap

- The frost contains frozen carbon dioxide.

- Carbon dioxide freezes at around −193ºF (−125˚C).

- Approximately 260 mi. (420km) across.

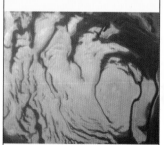

South Polar Cap

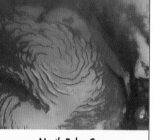

North Polar Cap

OTHER FEATURES

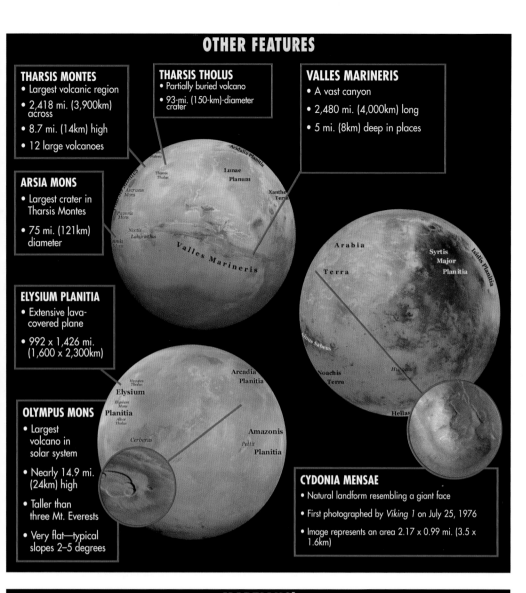

THARSIS MONTES
- Largest volcanic region
- 2,418 mi. (3,900km) across
- 8.7 mi. (14km) high
- 12 large volcanoes

ARSIA MONS
- Largest crater in Tharsis Montes
- 75 mi. (121km) diameter

ELYSIUM PLANITIA
- Extensive lava-covered plane
- 992 x 1,426 mi. (1,600 x 2,300km)

OLYMPUS MONS
- Largest volcano in solar system
- Nearly 14.9 mi. (24km) high
- Taller than three Mt. Everests
- Very flat—typical slopes 2–5 degrees

THARSIS THOLUS
- Partially buried volcano
- 93-mi. (150-km)-diameter crater

VALLES MARINERIS
- A vast canyon
- 2,480 mi. (4,000km) long
- 5 mi. (8km) deep in places

CYDONIA MENSAE
- Natural landform resembling a giant face
- First photographed by *Viking 1* on July 25, 1976
- Image represents an area 2.17 x 0.99 mi. (3.5 x 1.6km)

MARTIANS!

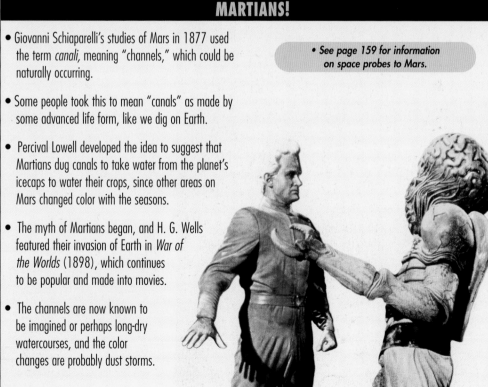

- Giovanni Schiaparelli's studies of Mars in 1877 used the term *canali*, meaning "channels," which could be naturally occurring.

- Some people took this to mean "canals" as made by some advanced life form, like we dig on Earth.

- Percival Lowell developed the idea to suggest that Martians dug canals to take water from the planet's icecaps to water their crops, since other areas on Mars changed color with the seasons.

- The myth of Martians began, and H. G. Wells featured their invasion of Earth in *War of the Worlds* (1898), which continues to be popular and made into movies.

- The channels are now known to be imagined or perhaps long-dry watercourses, and the color changes are probably dust storms.

- See page 159 for information on space probes to Mars.

MARS TIMELINE

4,000 years ago
Ancient Egyptian astronomers observe Mars.

3,000 years ago
The Babylonians call Mars Nirgal, the "Star of Death."

1610
Mars is studies by Galileo by telescope.

1877
Giovanni Schiaparelli produces maps and written studies of Mars. Mars's two moons are discovered by Asaph Hall.

1964–1965
Mariner 4 is the first craft to reach Mars, returning 21 photographs of the planet.

1969
Mariners 6 and *7* fly past, sending 175 close-up pictures, as two more Russian probes fail.

1971
Mariner 9 takes more than 7,300 close-up pictures of the Martian surface.

1976
U.S. *Vikings 1* and *2*, two-part spacecraft carrying orbiters and landers, land in July and September, carrying out many observations.

1997
Mars *Global Surveyor* enters Mars orbit and operates until 2006.

1997
Mars *Pathfinder* lands, and its rover Sojourner explores the Martian surface.

1999
The U.S. Mars *Climate Orbiter* and Mars *Polar Lander* reach the planet, but both fall silent.

2001
U.S. *Mars Odyssey* successfully reaches Mars orbit and sends back a wealth of scientific information.

2003
European *Mars Express* enters orbit, but its *Beagle 2* lander is lost.

2004
Mars exploration rovers *Spirit* and *Opportunity* touch down and begin to explore the Martian surface, sending back a great deal of information.

2009
Spirit and *Opportunity* continue to rove and send back data.

2025
Proposed end date for possible U.S. missions carrying astronauts to Mars.

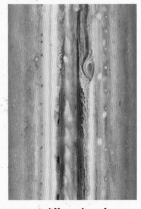

JUPITER

By far the biggest planet in the solar system, Jupiter is a vast world of swirling gases and storms of unimaginable fury. As the fifth planet out, it is the closest "gas giant" to the Sun. It is not much smaller than some of the stars called brown dwarfs, but it does not shine itself; instead it reflects sunlight as all planets do. Even so, its huge pull of gravity holds more than 60 moons in orbit around it. Jupiter is named after the Roman king of the gods, also called Jove.

ATMOSPHERIC CONDITIONS

ATMOSPHERE:
Mostly hydrogen, hydrogen sulfide, some helium, traces of methane, water vapor, ammonia, and other gases.

NATURE OF SURFACE:
Small core of molten rock that is surrounded by layers of metallic, liquid, and gaseous hydrogen. There is no clear surface.

AVERAGE TEMPERATURE:
−238°F (−150°C)

LOWEST TEMPERATURE:
−274°F (−170°C)

HIGHEST TEMPERATURE:
−202°F (−130°C)

WEATHER OR CLIMATE:
Complete cloud coverage, with storms and wind speeds over 248 mph (400km/h).

SEASONAL CHANGES:
Few, being so far from the Sun.

PLANET PROFILE

Diameter at equator **88,846 mi.**
(142,984km)

Surface area **24 billion sq. mi.**
(61.4 billion km²)

Tilt of axis **3.13°**

Mass (Earth = 1) **318**

Volume (Earth = 1) **1,321**

Overall density (Earth = 1) **0.24**
(1.33g/cm³)

Gravity (Earth = 1) **2.14**

Number of moons **60 plus and counting**

A NASA photograph of Jupiter

ORBIT DETAILS

Average distance from Sun
483.7 million mi. (778.4 million km)

Average distance from Sun
5.203 AU (Earth = 1)

Closest distance to Sun (perihelion) 460.3 million mi. (740.7 million km)

Farthest distance from Sun (aphelion) 507.1 million mi. (816.1 million km)

Average orbital speed
7.7 mi. (13.0km) per second

Slowest orbital speed
8.5 mi. (12.4km) per second

Fastest orbital speed
8.5 mi (13.7km) per second

Time for one orbit
(Jupiter year) 11.87 Earth years

Axial rotation period
(Jupiter day) 9.92 Earth hours

Sun

Jupiter

MAJOR FEATURES

Jupiter has several distinctive features mapped by astronomers.

Great Red Spot
A giant storm system three times wider than Earth that travels around Jupiter just south of the equator, once every six days.

White spots
Smaller circulatory storm systems in Jupiter's atmosphere, similar in size to Earth.

Brown spots
Stormy regions that are probably warmer than the surrounding clouds.

Rings
These consist of dust knocked from Jupiter's moons by meteor strikes.

Inner structure
Central small rocky core, then a layer of "metallic" hydrogen, then liquid hydrogen, and finally the outermost atmosphere of mainly hydrogen gas. These layers grade from one to another, with no sharp boundaries.

Jupiter's Great Red Spot

• See page 159 for information on probes to Jupiter.

A diffuse shot of Jupiter's surface

OTHER FEATURES

- **BELTS** The red-brown bands of warmer falling gas.

- **ZONES** Lengths of cooler light-colored clouds that change like the darker belts. Zones contain higher clouds than belts. Blue-tinted clouds are lowest and warmest.

- **TURBULENCE** Belts sometimes move in the opposite direction to their neighboring zones, creating swirling patterns of storms and turbulence along their edges.

MOON RECORDS

- Ganymede is the largest moon in the solar system.

- Callisto is the most heavily cratered object.

- Io probably has the most volcanic activity.

A NASA collage showing Io's red- and black-colored lava flows and yellow sulfur patches

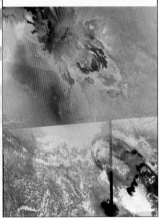

JUPITER'S RINGS

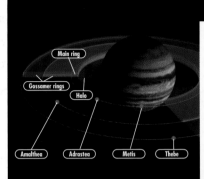

- **HALO** Faint inner ring 6,200 mi. (10,000km) thick.

- **MAIN RING** Dust from Adrastea and Metis, 62 mi. (100km) thick.

- **INNER GOSSAMER RING** Dust from Amalthea, 1,612 mi. (2,600km) thick.

- **OUTER GOSSAMER RING** Dust from Thebe, 5,456 mi. (8,800km) thick.

- **FAINT OUTER RING** Rings beyond Outer Gossamer Ring, 5,456 mi. (8,800km) thick.

TRUE GIANT

Jupiter has more than twice as much mass ("weight") than all of the other planets added together. However, it would probably need to be 50 times heavier to start burning like a true star.

SPEED SPIN

Jupiter is not only the largest planet, but it also spins around the fastest, once in less than ten Earth hours. The spinning speed of the upper atmosphere at the equator is five minutes faster than at the poles, so the atmosphere is continually being twisted and torn.

JUPITER'S MOONS

On January 7–11, 1610, Galileo discovered Jupiter's four main moons, now known as Galilean moons, following their orbits across the face of the planet. This was direct evidence that Earth was not at the center of everything and strengthened Galileo's idea that planets like Earth and Jupiter probably revolved around the Sun.

MOON (or group)	DIAMETER	DISTANCE FROM JUPITER
Inner group (Metis, Adrastea, Amalthea, Thebe)	Four small moons less than 124 mi. (200km) across	Less than 124,000 mi. (200,000km)
Io	2,258 mi. (3,634km)	261,454 mi. (420,769km)
Europa	1,936 mi. (3,116km)	415,958 mi. (669,420km)
Ganymede	3,262 mi. (5,250km)	663,400 mi. (1,067,639km)
Callisto	2,988 mi. (4,809km)	1.17 million mi. (1.88 million km)
Themisto	4.9 mi. (7.9km)	4.58 million mi. (7.37 million km)
Himalia group	Most under 62 mi. (100km)	6.2–7.4 million mi. (10–11.9 million km)
Ananke group	Most under 19 mi. (31km)	13 million mi. (21 million km)
Carme group	Most under 3.1 mi. (5km)	14.3–14.9 million mi. (23–24 million km)
Pasiphaë	Small outermost moons	14.3 million mi. (23 million km)

JUPITER
TIMELINE

3,000 years ago
Jupiter is known to the Greeks and then the Romans.

1,500 years ago
In ancient China, Jupiter is known as the "Wood Star."

1610
Galileo observes Jupiter's four largest moons.

1665
The Great Red Spot is first observed.

1690
Giovanni Domenico Cassini notices that the upper atmosphere takes longer to spin at the poles than around the equator.

1973
U.S. Pioneer 10 probe flies past Jupiter.

1979
Voyager 1 flies past, taking spectacular photographs. Voyager 2 achieves similar results.

1992
Ulysses probe passes by Jupiter on its way to the Sun, taking measurements.

1994
Parts of comet Shoemaker-Levy 9 hit Jupiter in July, photographed by the approaching Galileo space probe.

1995
Galileo becomes the first probe to go into orbit around Jupiter, starting on December 7. On the same day, an atmosphere probe it had already released parachutes 93 mi. (150km) into the atmosphere, collecting information.

1996–2003
Galileo continues its studies of Jupiter and its closer moons.

2000
The Great Red Spot has shrunk to about half the size it measured in 1900.

2000
Cassini probe passes on way to Saturn.

2003
Galileo finally plunges into the clouds in September.

2007
The New Horizons probe flew past on its way to Pluto.

2011
The U.S. Jupiter probe Juno is scheduled for launch. Juno will orbit over Jupiter's poles.

SATURN

Long famed for its glistening, breathtakingly beautiful rings, Saturn is the solar system's second-largest planet after its neighbor Jupiter. Saturn was the Roman god of farming, civilization, and prosperity—and also the name of the rockets that powered *Apollo* astronauts to the Moon. Due to its fast spin, "gas giant" makeup, and very light weight compared to its size, Saturn bulges around its middle, or equator, as it rotates. This means the planet is fatter than it is tall by almost 7,440 mi. (12,000km).

ATMOSPHERIC CONDITIONS

ATMOSPHERE:
Mostly hydrogen, small amount of helium, traces of methane, water vapor, ammonia.

NATURE OF SURFACE:
Molten core 32,240 mi. (52,000km) below the surface, surrounded by layers of metallic and molecular hydrogen.

AVERAGE TEMPERATURE:
−202°F (−130°C)

LOWEST TEMPERATURE:
−310°F (−190°C)

HIGHEST TEMPERATURE:
−184°F (−120°C)

WEATHER OR CLIMATE:
Clouds and storms of fast-moving gases, high winds.

SEASONAL CHANGES:
Few, being so far from the Sun.

Saturn's northern hemisphere is presently a serene blue, much like that of Uranus or Neptune.

PLANET PROFILE

Diameter at equator **74,901 mi. (120,536km)**

Surface area **16.8 billion sq. mi. (42.7 billion km²)**

Tilt of axis **26.7°**

Mass (Earth = 1) **95.2**

Volume (Earth = 1) **763.59**

Overall density (Earth = 1) **0.127 (0.70g/cm³)**

Gravity (Earth = 1) **0.91**

Number of moons **50 plus**

A NASA photograph of Saturn

ORBIT DETAILS

Average distance from Sun
885.9 million mi. (1.4 million km)

Average distance from Sun
9.54 AU (Earth = 1)

Closest distance to Sun (perihelion) 838.5 million mi. (1.4 million km)

Farthest distance from Sun (aphelion) 934 million mi. (1.5 million km)

Average orbital speed
6 mi. (9.6km) per second

Slowest orbital speed
5.6 mi. (9.1km) per second

Fastest orbital speed
6.3 mi. (10.1km) per second

Time for one orbit
(Saturn year) 29.46 Earth years

Axial rotation period
(Saturn day) 10.77 Earth hours

Sun

Saturn

MAJOR FEATURES

Saturn has been explored by a number of probes.

Rings
These are made of billions of fragments of ice and rock that reflect sunlight, glisten, and sparkle. The largest particles are car sized.

- Fainter, more distant rings
- Outermost main ring A
- Middle ring B
- Innermost main ring C
- Innermost ring D
- Cassini Division
- Encke Division

Equatorial zone
Rotates about 25 minutes faster per Saturn day than the polar zones, with wider cloud banding.

North and south temporate zones Clouds and winds of 1,116 mi. (1,800km/h).

South polar zone
Lighter colored clouds and a warm dark spot.

This false-color NASA image shows the aurora ovals at the north and south poles of Saturn.

OTHER FEATURES

- **CORE** Saturn's core is probably very hot, almost 21,632°F (12,000°C), and the planet gives out more heat energy than it receives from the Sun.

- **SOUTH POLE** A very hot region that glows bright on infrared (heat-ray) photographs.

- **BAND CLOUDS** Less marked than on Jupiter, consisting of stripes and zones of clouds at different temperatures. They tend to be wider closer to the equator.

- **WHITE SPOTS** Tend to come and go, probably areas of swirling gases.

MAIN MOONS

After the discovery of Titan by Huygens, the second to fifth moons were spotted by Giovanni Domenico Cassini.

YEAR	MOON	DIAMETER	DISTANCE
1684	Tethys	657 mi. (1,057km)	182,652 mi. (293,950km)
1684	Dione	694 mi. (1,117km)	233,988 mi. (376,567km)
1672	Rhea	949 mi. (1,527km)	326,802 mi (525,937km)
1671	Iapetus	890 mi. (1,432km)	2.2 million mi. (3.5 million km)

TITAN

A selection of shots of Titan from the European Southern Observatory

- Titan is the second-largest moon in the solar system after Jupiter's Ganymede.

- It has a thick atmosphere.

- Its atmosphere is mainly nitrogen (like Earth's), plus methane, ethane, acetylene, propane, carbon dioxide, carbon monoxide, hydrogen cyanide, and helium.

THE RINGS OF SATURN

The rings of Saturn were first noticed by Galileo, who could not quite make them out with his early telescope. He guessed they might be moons, one on each side, and called them "ears of Saturn." They appear to change shape when viewed from Earth, as they are tilted and turn slowly with Saturn's orbit, so we see them at different angles. Viewed edge on, they are at their thinnest about every 15 years. Each main ring is made of thousands of smaller ringlets.

Name	Inner-edge distance from Saturn (mi.)	Width (mi.)
D ring	3,720 (6,000km)	4,433 (7,150km)
C ring	8,990 (14,500km)	10,850 (17,500km)
Columbo Gap	11,036 (17,800km)	62 (100km)
Maxwell Gap	17,050 (27,500km)	167 (270km)
B ring	19,840 (32,000km)	15,810 (25,500km)
Cassini Division	35,650 (57,500km)	2,914 (4,700km)
A ring	38,564 (62,200km)	9,052 (14,600km)
Encke Division	45,613 (73,570km)	201 (325km)
F ring	49,724 (80,200km)	310 (500km)
G ring	64,480 (104,000km)	4,960 (8,000km)
E ring	74,400 (120,000km)	186,000 (300,000km)

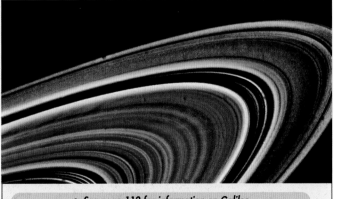

• See page 112 for information on Galileo.

VAST BUT LIGHT

Saturn is the only planet whose density, or mass per volume, is less than water. We would say it is "lighter than water," and if there were a tank of water big enough to run a bath for this enormous planet, Saturn would float in it!

2,500 years ago
Saturn is known to the Greeks and then the Romans.

1610
Galileo sees two shapes on either side of Saturn, the first observation of its rings.

1655
Christiaan Huygens discovers Titan and gives a true explanation of Saturn's ring system.

1789
William Herschel discovers that Saturn bulges at the equator and is flatterned at the poles.

1847
John Herschel (son of William Herschel) names the then-known seven moons of Saturn.

1979
Pioneer 2 is the first space probe to visit Saturn.

1980
Voyager 1 sends back the first clear pictures of the planet.

1981
Voyager 2 flies past in August and discovers further features, including darker "spoke" regions in Saturn's B ring, smaller gaps between rings, and more moons.

1997
Cassini-Huygens space probe is launched on October 15.

2004
Cassini-Huygens flies close to moon Phoebe in June and reaches Saturn's orbit on July 1.

2004
After two Titan flybys, the *Huygens* lander is released from the *Cassini* orbiter on December 25.

2005
Huygens plunges into Titan's atmosphere on January 14, sending information after touching down. *Cassini* continues to orbit and fly past many moons, especially Titan.

2010
Expected end of main mission for *Cassini* orbiter, but this may be extended.

URANUS

Uranus is the third "gas giant" and seventh planet from the Sun. It is very similar in size and structure to its next neighbor out, Neptune, being partly gas but also containing a lot of rocky and frozen material. The axis of Uranus is almost at right angles to the Sun, so Uranus seems to lie on its side and roll like a blue marble around the Sun. The planet is named after the Greek ruler of the heavens and the father of Saturn.

ATMOSPHERIC CONDITIONS

ATMOSPHERE:
Mostly hydrogen, about one sixth helium, also methane, traces of ammonia.

NATURE OF SURFACE:
Gassy, with any solid surface deep below; glows in sunlight as bright blue green or cyan.

AVERAGE TEMPERATURE:
–337°F (–205°C)

LOWEST TEMPERATURE:
–353°F (–214°C)

HIGHEST TEMPERATURE:
–328°F (–200°C)

WEATHER OR CLIMATE:
Swirling clouds, winds, and gases, despite smooth "glassy" appearance.

SEASONAL CHANGES:
Extreme, since Uranus lies on its side so that during each orbit, both poles and the equatorial regions face the Sun.

This rendered image shows the *Voyager* spacecraft in the sky above Uranus.

PLANET PROFILE

Diameter at equator **31,765 mi. (51,118km)**

Surface area **3.13 billion sq. mi. (8.08 billion km²)**

Tilt of axis **97.8° (almost at right angles to the Sun)**

Mass (Earth = 1) **14.37**

Volume (Earth = 1) **63.1**

Overall density (Earth = 1) **0.236 (1.30g/cm³)**

Gravity (Earth = 1) **0.86**

Number of moons **approaching 30 and counting**

A NASA photograph of Uranus

ORBIT DETAILS

Average distance from Sun
1.8 billion mi. (2.8 billion km)

Average distance from Sun
19.2 AU (Earth = 1)

Closest distance to Sun (perihelion) 1.7 billion mi. (2.7 billion km)

Farthest distance from Sun (aphelion) 1.9 billion mi. (3 billion km)

Average orbital speed
4.2 mi. (6.79km) per second

Slowest orbital speed
4.14 mi. (6.68km) per second

Fastest orbital speed
4.42 mi. (7.13km) per second

Time for one orbit
(Uranus year) 84.1 Earth years

Axial rotation period
(Uranus day) 17.24 Earth hours

Sun

Uranus

MAJOR FEATURES

Uranus has been mapped from Earth and by *Voyager 2*.

Inner structure
Uranus is probably quite similar in composition all the way through, with gases and intermingled particles of rock and ice.

Color
Uranus usually appears pale to mid blue green, a color known as cyan, probably because methane crystals in its atmosphere absorb most of the red light in sunlight, leaving it mainly blue.

Streaking
Hubble Space Telescope images reveal faint streaks that change slowly, perhaps owing to seasonal variations.

Warmer equator
Despite Uranus's extreme tilt, the equator is slightly warmer than the polar regions.

Artist's impression of the rings of Uranus

OTHER FEATURES

- **SURFACE FEATURES** There are few obvious features when Uranus is viewed through telescopes from Earth, with the surface being smooth with a "satin" glow, almost like a polished marble.

- **MAGNETIC FIELD** This invisible force field is "offset," with its center not in the middle of the planet (like Neptune), and it is also tilted at 60° compared to the planet's spinning axis.

ON ITS SIDE

The axis of Uranus is almost at right angles to the Sun and the other almost "upright" planets. So, Uranus spins as if lying on its side, rolling around the Sun. The axis of Uranus does not swing around as it orbits the Sun, as if a long piece of string joined it to the Sun, but points the same way. So the south pole of Uranus (pointing sideways) faces the Sun for a short time. Then as the orbit continues, the North Pole gradually comes around the face of the Sun in the opposite part of the orbit.

MAIN MOONS

MOON	DIAMETER	DISTANCE
Miranda	293 mi. (472km)	80,519 mi. (129,870km)
Ariel	718 mi. (1,158km)	118,364 mi. (190,910km)
Umbriel	725 mi. (1,170km)	164,920 mi. (266,000km)
Titania	978 mi. (1,578km)	270,506 mi. (436,300km)
Oberon	944 mi. (1,522km)	361,783 mi. (583,520km)

There are about 14 smaller moons inside the orbit of Miranda, most discovered by *Voyager 2*. The biggest is Puck, measuring about 99 mi. (160km) across.

RINGS OF URANUS

Ring	Distance from center of Uranus (mi.)	Width of ring (mi.)
1986U2R	23,560 (38,000km)	1,500 (2,500km)
6	25,940 (41,840km)	0.62–1.9 (1–3km)
5	26,183 (42,230km)	1.2–1.9 (2–3km)
4	26,400 (42,580km)	1.2–1.9 (2–3km)
Alpha	27,726 (44,720km)	2.5–6 (4–10km)
Beta	28,315 (45,670km)	3–6.8 (5–11km)
Eta	29,258 (47,190km)	0–1.24 (0–2km)
Gamma	29,531 (47,630km)	0.62–2.5 (1–4km)
Delta	29,940 (48,290km)	1.9–4.3 (3–7km)
Lambda	31,012 (50,020km)	0.62–1.24 (1–2km)
Epsilon	31,707 (51,140km)	12–62 (20–100km)

ODD LITTLE WORLD

- Uranus's principal innermost moon, Miranda, has one of the oddest appearances in the solar system.

- Massive canyons scar the surface, as well as mountains, cliffs, and craters.

- Three huge racetracklike shapes called ovoids are prominent, perhaps formed by upwelling of rocks from within.

- Miranda's Verona Rupes is a huge fault scarp. At 12 mi. (20km) high, it is the tallest cliff in the solar system.

- Miranda may have frozen water, methane-type substances, and rocks on its surface.

A composite image of Uranus's strange moon Miranda

• *See pages 122–123 for information on Earth.*

URANUS TIMELINE

Ancient times
Uranus is not known as a planet to ancient people.

1690
John Flamsteed records Uranus as a dim starlike object, 34 Tauri.

1748
James Bradley observes Uranus as a faint star and does the same in 1750 and 1753.

1764
Pierre Charles Le Monnier records Uranus a dozen times from this year to 1771.

1781
William Herschel discovers Uranus.

1787
Herschel discovers the moons Titania and Oberon.

1851
William Lassell discovers Ariel and Umbriel, Uranus's second- and third-closest "twin moons," on October 24.

1948
Gerard Kuiper discovers Miranda, Uranus's innermost moon, on February 16.

1977
Voyager 2 is launched on its great journey across the solar system.

1977
In March a system of rings is suspected as the planet blots out a faint star behind it in an odd manner.

1982
Voyager 2 passes Uranus at the time when its south pole points directly toward the Sun.

1986
Voyager 2 makes its closest flyby during January, some 68,200 mi. (110,000km) from its surface. It sees the rings in detail and discovers an extra one—and ten more moons in addition to the five visible from Earth with telescopes.

2007
The Sun is overhead at the equator of Uranus, halfway between its apparent journey from being directly over one pole to overhead at the other pole.

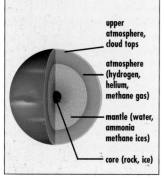

NEPTUNE

The deep blue color of this fourth "gas giant" inspired its name of Neptune, Roman god of the sea. Neptune's atmosphere is in fact ravaged by the fastest winds in the solar system. Although it is the fourth-largest planet, it is the third heaviest, being denser than its similar-sized neighbor Uranus. Also like Uranus, Neptune's atmosphere probably extends about one fifth of the way toward the center. Then it gives way to a mix of semiliquid ice, rock, methane, and ammonia, with a central core chiefly of part-molten rock and metal.

ATMOSPHERIC CONDITIONS

ATMOSPHERE:
Mostly hydrogen, one fifth helium, traces of methane, ethane.

NATURE OF SURFACE:
Gassy, with incredibly fast wind movements.

AVERAGE TEMPERATURE:
−373°F (−220°C)

LOWEST TEMPERATURE:
−369°F (−223°C)

HIGHEST TEMPERATURE:
−360°F (−218°C)

WEATHER OR CLIMATE:
Storms and swirling gases move at 1,240 mph (2,000km/h), more than four times quicker than Earth's fastest winds in tornadoes.

SEASONAL CHANGES:
Neptune has few seasonal changes. Since it is so far from the Sun, solar heat and light have little effect on this icy-cold planet.

upper atmosphere, cloud tops

atmosphere (hydrogen, helium, methane gas)

mantle (water, ammonia methane ices)

core (rock, ice)

PLANET PROFILE

Diameter at equator **30,775 mi. (49,528km)**

Surface area **2.9 billion sq. mi. (7.62 billion km²)**

Tilt of axis **28.3°**

Mass (Earth = 1) **17.15**

Volume (Earth = 1) **57.7**

Overall density (Earth = 1) **0.317 (1.76g/cm³)**

Gravity (Earth = 1) **1.14**

Number of moons **about 13**

A NASA photograph of Uranus. The Great Dark Spot is in the center.

ORBIT DETAILS

Average distance from Sun
2.79 billion mi. (4.498 million km)

Average distance from Sun
30.1 AU (Earth = 1)

Closest distance to Sun (perihelion) 2.77 billion mi. (4.46 million km)

Farthest distance from Sun (aphelion) 2.81 billion mi. (4.53 million km)

Average orbital speed
3.36 mi. (5.43km) per second

Slowest orbital speed
3.34 mi. (5.39km) per second

Fastest orbital speed
3.39 mi. (5.48km) per second

Time for one orbit
(Neptune year) 164.8 Earth years

Axial rotation period
(Neptune day) 16.1 Earth hours

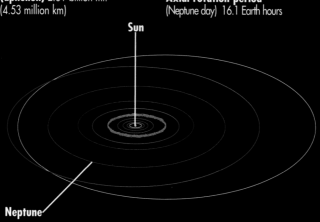

Sun

Neptune

MAJOR FEATURES

Neptune has been mapped from Earth and by probes.

Great Dark Spot
About as wide as Earth, this was probably a vast storm system of swirling gases. It faded in the mid-1990s, but another similar area, GDS2, appeared.

Color
Neptune is a dark blue green, probably because methane crystals in its atmosphere absorb most of the red light in sunlight, leaving it mainly blue.

Winds
Neptune has some of the fastest winds in the solar system, blasting along at over 1,426 mph (2,300km/h).

Inner structure
Outer atmosphere of hydrogen and helium, then lower down more methane and ammonia with more rock particles, merging into melted rock and metal in the central core.

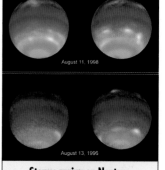

August 11, 1998

August 13, 1996

Storms raging on Neptune

OTHER FEATURES

- **MAGNETIC FIELD** Tilted at 47° to the axis around which Neptune spins, and also off center from the middle of the planet by more than 8,060 mi. (13,000km).

- **OUTER CLOUDS** Some clouds high above the main cloud layer cast shadows on those below, much as Earth's clouds cause shadows on the land.

- **RINGS** About nine faint rings surround Neptune, with a strange structure showing clumps and lumps of larger material rather than spread-out small particles.

- **ARCS** Curved arcs within the outermost ring, Adams, are probably owing to the movements and gravity of the moon Galatea on their inner side.

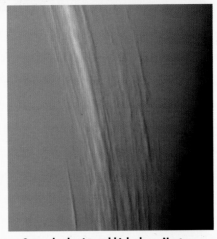

Outer clouds pictured high above Neptune

THE FIRST PAPER PLANET

Neptune was the first planet to be "discovered" on paper, from calculations of the orbit of Uranus that showed that another body beyond it affects its movements (see timeline, 1846).

NAMING NEPTUNE

Soon after Neptune was discovered, several astronomers suggested names, often inspired by its deep blue-green sealike color.

- Various experts, including François Arago, proposed Le Verrier after its codiscoverer.
- Others introduced Poseidon (right), a Greek sea god.
- Johann Galle proposed Janus.
- James Challis suggested Oceanus.
- Le Verrier himself proposed Neptune.
- The name Neptune was adopted by the end of 1946.

NEPTUNE'S RINGS

These are very faint, difficult to measure, and also seem to change rapidly.

Name	Distance from surface (mi.)	Width (mi.)
Galle (1989 N3R)	11,036 (17,100km)	9.3 (15km)
Le Verrier (1989 N2R)	17,639 (28,450km)	9.3 (15km)
Lassell (1989 N4R)	19,003 (30,650km)	3.7 (6km)
Arago	20,367 (32,850km)	not clear
Adams (1989 N1R)	23,653 (38,150km)	less than 31 (50km)
Liberty Arc	leading arc	not known
Equality Arc	middle arc	not known
Fraternity Arc	trailing arc	not known
Courage Arc	not known	not known

VOYAGER VISIT

- *Voyager 2* is the only probe to visit Neptune, and it got closer to this planet than to any other on its journey from Earth.

- Period of observation from June to October 1989.

- At its closest on August 25, the probe passed just 3,100 mi. (5,000km) above Neptune's north pole.

- A few hours later it passed within 24,800 mi. (40,000km) of the largest moon, Triton.

- Triton was *Voyager 2's* last studied object before it left the solar system.

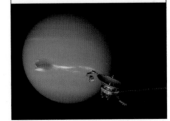

SIZE AND SHAPE

Neptune is the fourth-biggest planet in size, being slightly wider than its neighbor Uranus. But because Neptune is size-for-weight heavier, or more dense, than Uranus, it is the third-heaviest planet after Jupiter and Saturn.

NEPTUNE TIMELINE

1612
Galileo sees Neptune on December 28 but does not recognize it as a planet.

1843
Couch Adams calculates that probably another planet farther out than Uranus is affecting its orbit.

1846
In August, British astronomer James Challis twice observes Uranus using Adams's predictions but does not recognize the planet.

Neptune is officially discovered by Johann Galle at Berlin Observatory, Germany, on September 23. He uses calculations figured out by Urbain Le Verrier.

1846
Neptune's largest moon, Triton, is identified by William Lassell.

1880
Camille Flammarion proposes the name Triton for Neptune's main moon.

1949
Neptune's second moon, Nereid, is discovered by Gerard Kuiper.

1977
Voyager 2 is launched on its great journey across the solar system.

1989
The only space probe to visit, *Voyager 2* flies past on August 25—12 years after its launch.

1998
The "Neptune Papers," missing documents from the Royal Observatory, Greenwich, England, are found, and further evidence comes to light about who actually found Neptune first. The favorite is Le Verrier, but he did not search for the planet himself. The debate continues to rage on between groups of academics.

2011
Neptune will be in the same position in relation to the Sun as when it was discovered, having completed one orbit.

PLUTO

Since its discovery in 1930, Pluto had held the honor of being the smallest and farthest planet in the solar system. However, discoveries in 2003 and 2005 contributed to the change of this status. In August 2006, Pluto was officially redefined as a dwarf planet. Pluto is not very well known. All of our information comes only from telescopes, since no space probe has visited it. Pluto also has a highly unusual orbit, being very oval, or "eccentric." For part of its immensely long year, Pluto is actually closer to the Sun than to its neighbor Neptune.

ATMOSPHERIC CONDITIONS

ATMOSPHERE:
Not clearly known, very thin, probably nitrogen, carbon monoxide, and methane.

NATURE OF SURFACE:
Rock and various chemicals frozen as ice.

AVERAGE TEMPERATURE:
−390°F (−230°C)

LOWEST TEMPERATURE:
−403°F (−242°C)

HIGHEST TEMPERATURE:
−364°F (−220°C)

WEATHER OR CLIMATE:
Atmosphere may move as gases when Pluto is closer to the Sun, but then freeze as nitrogen ice at its farthest distance.

SEASONAL CHANGES:
As above.

An artist's impression of the surface of Pluto

PLUTO FACTS

Diameter at equator **1,440 mi. (2,274km)**
Surface area **6.4 million sq. mi. (17.9 million km²)**
Tilt of axis **122.5° to its orbit, 115° to orbits of other planets**
Mass (Earth = 1) **0.002**
Volume (Earth = 1) **0.007**
Overall density (Earth = 1) **−0.4 (2g/cm³)**
Gravity (Earth = 1) **0.06**
Number of moons **1**

A NASA photograph of Pluto

ORBIT DETAILS

Average distance from Sun
3.67 million mi. (5.9 million km)

Average distance from Sun
39.5 AU (Earth = 1)

Closest distance to Sun (perihelion) 2.7 billion mi. (4.4 billion km)

Farthest distance from Sun (aphelion) 4.6 billion mi. (7.4 billion km)

Average orbital speed
3 mi. (4.67km) per second

Slowest orbital speed
2.28 mi. (3.68km) per second

Fastest orbital speed
3.79 mi. (6.11km) per second

Time for one orbit
(Pluto year) 248.1 Earth years

Axial rotation period
(Pluto day) 6.39 Earth days

Sun

Pluto

PLUTO'S MOON

Charon is only half the size of Pluto, which makes the pair a double-planet system.

- Charon is the largest moon in the solar system compared to the object it orbits.

- It measures 747 mi. (1,205km) across, just under half of Pluto's diameter.

- Charon's orbit distance is 12,090 mi. (19,500km) across, and its orbit time is just 6.39 days.

- Charon's spin and orbit time, combined with Pluto's spin, mean that each keeps the same face toward the other at all times. This is called tidal locking.

- Charon's name was officially agreed in 1985—the "Ch" is pronounced "Sh" as in "Sharon."

- This moon has no atmosphere, but its surface is possibly coated in ice.

Artwork of Pluto and its moon, Charon (below), seen from space

PLUTO'S STATUS IN THE SOLAR SYSTEM

The year 2006 brought about a huge change in the way we classify our solar system.

On August 24, 2006, the International Astronomical Union (IAU) decided on a new category within our solar system. They agreed on the classification of dwarf planet. Presently this encompasses three solar system objects, but it is predicted that many more will join the category in the future. The current dwarf planets are:

• Pluto (location: Kuiper belt)

• Eris (location: Kuiper belt)

• Ceres (location: asteroid belt)

The term *dwarf planet* is slightly misleading, as this classification is not neccessarily dependant on the size of the respective object. Coincidentally, all three current dwarf planets are smaller than any planet. Dwarf planets are objects in the solar system that:

• orbit the Sun

• have an almost round shape

• have not cleared the neighborhood around their orbit

• are not a satellite

> • See page 138 for information on the Kuiper belt.

An artist's impression of one of the newly discovered trans-Neptunian objects

MANY NAMES

In the weeks following Pluto's discovery by Clyde Tombaugh (left), dozens of names were suggested, including:

Artemis, Athena, Atlas, Cosmos, Cronus, Hera, Hercules, Icarus, Idana, Minerva, Odin, Pax, Persephone, Perseus, Prometheus, Tantalus, Vulcan, Zymal

• Pluto was first suggested by Venetia Burney, an 11-year-old girl from Oxford, England.

• She suggested it was so cold and distant, it could be named after the Roman god of the underworld.

• Her grandfather mentioned this to an astronomer friend, who contacted the discovery committee in the U.S.

• The name Pluto was quickly agreed, perhaps for one good reason. Its first two letters are the initials of Percival Lowell, who founded the observatory where it was discovered.

PLUTINOS

From the 1990s many bodies similar to Pluto, but smaller, have been discovered in the Kuiper belt beyond Neptune. These Kuiper belt objects are called "Plutinos" if they complete two orbits of the Sun in the same time as Neptune takes to complete three orbits.

DOUBLE PLANETS

Pluto and its moon, Charon, are sometimes referred to as double planets, orbiting the Sun in tandem. If both objects were redefined as double planets, Charon would most likely be reclassified as a dwarf planet, too.

ODD ORBIT

• Pluto has by far the most elliptical, or oval, orbit of any object orbiting the Sun.

• From February 1979 to February 1999, Pluto was closer to the Sun than Neptune.

1902
Percival Lowell predicts another body, "Planet X," beyond Neptune.

1915
Lowell makes another prediction, this time fairly close to Pluto's actual size and position, but many experts say this is a coincidence (see below).

1930
Pluto is discovered by Clyde Tombaugh at Lowell Observatory, Arizona.

Pluto becomes the official name on May 30.

1977
Voyager 1 is launched and is originally due to visit Pluto, but is redirected to fly past Saturn's moon Titan.

1978
Pluto's moon, Charon, is discovered by James Christy.

1992
From September, hundreds of small icy objects are discovered beyond Neptune in a zone now known as the Kuiper belt.

1993
Debates begin as to whether Pluto is a true planet or a Kuiper belt object.

1995
New calculations show that Pluto has almost no effect on the orbits of Neptune and Uranus, so its original discovery was largely by chance.

2001
NASA begins to plan and build the *New Horizons* space probe.

2006
New Horizons probe is launched on January 19 to visit Pluto, Charon, and hopefully objects in the Kuiper belt.

On August 24, Pluto is reclassified as a dwarf planet.

2015
New Horizons is expected to fly within 6,200 mi. (10,000km) of Pluto in July, the first craft to visit the planet, and then within 18,600 mi (30,000km) of Charon.

2020
New Horizons may encounter objects in the Kuiper belt.

- There are three types of asteroids, all made of different materials.

- More than 90% of all known asteroids are called stony asteroids, because they contain stony materials called silicates.

- About another 5–6% of asteroids are made of metal. They contain mostly nickel and iron.

- The rest of the asteroids contain a mixture of silicates and metals.

- Metal asteroids may be from the smashed core of a small planet that was torn apart millions (or billions) of years ago.

- Some asteroids are very dark, because they are rich in carbon compounds.

THE TROJANS

If asteroids stray too close to the gas giant Jupiter, they can get trapped in its orbit. There are two groups of asteroids that circle around and around the solar system in front and behind Jupiter. Scientists have named these asteroids the Trojans. Sometimes they fall into Jupiter's gravitational pull and become satellites of Jupiter.

An artist's impression of a Trojan asteroid

ASTEROIDS

Asteroids are chunks of rock that orbit the Sun. They are pieces of rock left over from the formation of the planets and moons. Most asteroids are too far away and too faint to be seen clearly without using a telescope. Most orbit far away, beyond Mars, but occasionally one may come closer to the Sun or Earth. Asteroids have hit Earth in the past. A major impact about 65 million years ago may be linked to the extinction of the dinosaurs.

ASTEROID FACTS

Asteroids range in size from dust particles to objects almost 620 mi. (1,000km) across.

- The biggest asteroid, Ceres, is about 578 mi. (933km) across. It is now classified as a dwarf planet.

- Ceres was the first asteroid to be discovered. It was found by Italian astronomer Giuseppe Piazzi in 1801.

- Asteroids spin as they fly through space.

- Large asteroids are tracked in case any of them follow an orbit that may collide with Earth in the future.

- The biggest asteroids are ball shaped, like small planets, leading to their other names— minor planets or planetoids.

- Astronomers think the two moons of Mars, Phobos and Deimos, may be captured asteroids.

- The Moon's craters were caused by asteroid impacts.

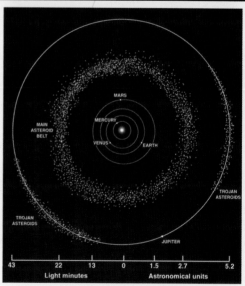

A stony asteroid

• See page 124 for information on the Moon and its craters.

WHERE DO ASTEROIDS COME FROM?

- Most asteroids orbit the Sun in a broad band called the asteroid belt between the orbits of Mars and Jupiter.

- The asteroid belt marks the end of the inner solar system and the beginning of the outer solar system.

- Asteroids that cross the orbit of Mars are called Amor asteroids.

- Asteroids that cross Earth's orbit are called Apollo asteroids.

- Aten asteroids have orbits that are inside Earth's orbit.

- The Trojans are asteroids that orbit ahead of, or behind, a planet. Mars, Jupiter, and Neptune have Trojan asteroids in their orbits.

- There are also rocky and icy bodies orbiting the Sun farther out than Neptune in a region called the Kuiper belt. These are known as Kuiper belt objects or trans-Neptune objects.

• See pages 126–129 for information on Mars and Jupiter

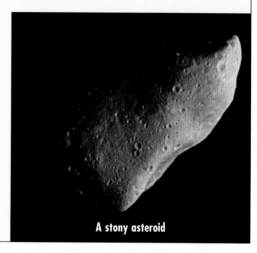

A NASA diagram showing the location of the main asteroid belt

FIRST DISCOVERIES

Below is a list of the first ten asteroids discovered.

Asteroid	Discovered	Size (mi.)
Ceres	1801	595 x 578 (960 x 932km)
Pallas	1802	354 x 326 x 299
		(571 x 525 x 482km)
Juno	1804	179 x 143 (288 x 230km)
Vesta	1807	326 (525km)
Astraea	1845	74 (120km)
Hebe	1847	126 (204km)
Iris	1847	129 (208km)
Flora	1847	100 (162km)
Metis	1848	98 (158km)
Hygeia	1849	267 (430km)

Ceres was discovered by Italian astronomer Giuseppe Piazzi.

STRANGEST ASTEROIDS

- Icarus is the asteroid with the strangest orbit. It comes closer to the Sun than the planet Mercury.

- The smallest asteroids are all sorts of odd shapes, because their pull of gravity is not strong enough to pull them into a ball shape.

- The asteroid with the strangest shape seen so far is probably Kleopatra. It is a 136-mi. (220-km)-long chunk of rock in the shape of a dog's bone!

ASTEROIDS WITH MOONS

- Asteroids have a very weak pull of gravity, but they are still able to attract and capture smaller asteroids as moons.

- The asteroid Ida has a small moon called Dactyl. Ida is 36 mi. (56km) across, and its moon, Dactyl, is only about 0.62 mi. (1km) across.

- An asteroid called 45 Eugenia may have a small moon, too.

- Some asteroids travel in pairs, called binaries, that orbit each other.

- An asteroid called 4179 Toutatis is thought to be two asteroids—one 1.5 mi. (2.5km) across and the other 0.93 mi. (1.5km) across—that may actually touch each other.

Nine photographs of Ida taken by the probe *Galileo*

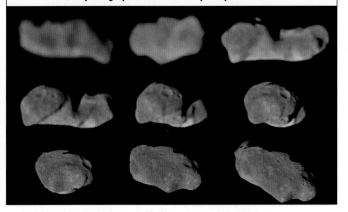

NEAR DISASTERS

In 1908 an asteroid slammed into a place called Tunguska in Siberia, flattening trees in an area 62 mi. (100km) across. If this happened today, the effect would be devastation. In 1991, there was a close shave when a small asteroid passed just 105,400 mi. (170,000km) over Earth. This is close in astronomical terms! Today, astronomers are looking for near-Earth objects like these. If they find them, there are various theories as to what they might be able to do to stop the threat. Some people think a nuclear missile could be launched into space to nudge the asteroid to one side.

SPACE PROBES TO ASTEROIDS

A series of probes has been sent into space to learn more about asteroids. Here is a list.

Space probe	Details
Galileo	On its way to Jupiter, *Galileo* passed asteroid Gaspra in 1991 and Ida in 1993.
Hayabusa	Met with asteroid 25143 Itokawa and is due to return particles from it to Earth in 2010.
NEAR Shoemaker	Passed asteroid 253 Mathilde on its way to 433 Eros. Orbited Eros 230 times and then landed—the first spacecraft ever to make a controlled landing on an asteroid—on February 12, 2001.
Deep Space 1	Flew past asteroid 9969 Braille (formerly known as 1992 KD) on its way to a comet.

NASA montage showing encounter between *Deep Space 1* and asteroid 9969 Braille

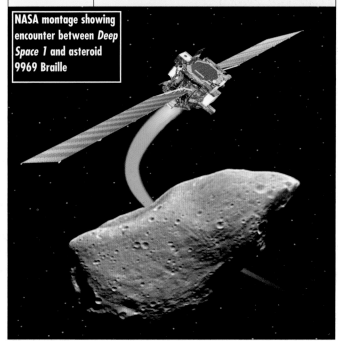

METEORS

Look up into a clear sky on any night and you might be lucky enough to see a streak of light. It appears for only a fraction of a second, and then it is gone. The bright streak is called a meteor, and it is made by a particle of dust entering Earth's atmosphere from space and burning up. Large meteors that survive their journey down through the atmosphere and hit the ground are called meteorites.

METEORITE FACTS

- About 500 baseball-sized rocks from space hit the ground every year.

- The largest meteorites hit the ground with such force that they make holes called impact craters.

- The biggest meteorite ever found is called the Hoba meteorite (after the place in Namibia where it landed). It weighs about 60 tons!

- A meteorite from Mars called ALH 84001 caused a stir in 1996 when some scientists thought they had found evidence of life inside it. However, most scientists now think the features seen in the meteorite are not signs of life.

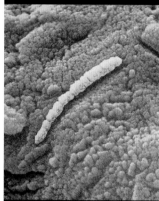

Close-up of structure found in meteorite from Mars

CRATERS

Large meteorites have struck Earth and left giant craters. One of the most famous of these is the Barringer Crater in Arizona (shown below), which measures more than 0.74 mi. (1.2km) across and 590 ft. (180m) deep. It was created 50,000 years ago by the impact of a 164-ft. (50-m)-wide meteorite.

METEORS

A spectacular meteor shoots to Earth

Meteors are also called shooting stars, although they are not stars.

- Most meteors are the size of a grain of sand.

- Some exceptionally bright meteors called bolides explode in the atmosphere with a sound like thunder.

- Meteoroids, the particles that become meteors, enter the Earth's atmosphere at up to about 43 mi. (70km) per second (155,000 mi./250,000km per hour).

- Scientists estimate that up to four billion meteors streak through Earth's atmosphere every day.

METEOR SHOWERS

There are a lot more meteors than usual at certain times of the year. These events are called meteor showers.

- Meteor showers occur when Earth flies through a trail of particles left behind by a comet.

- Earth passes through a comet's tail in the same part of every orbit, so meteor showers occur at the same times every year.

- All of the meteors in a meteor shower appear to come from the same point in the sky.

- Meteor showers are named after the constellations in the direction that the meteors appear to come from.

- Some meteor showers can produce hundreds of shooting stars an hour. Meteor showers last for anything from a few hours to several days.

• See pages 122–123 for information on Earth.

A NASA photograph showing a spectacular meteor shower

TYPES OF METEORITES

The three main types of meteorites are called irons, stony meteorites, and stony irons.

- Irons are made of an alloy (mixture) of iron and nickel.

- Stony irons contain rock and an iron-nickel alloy.

- There are three types of stony meteorites: chondrites, carbonaceous chondrites, and achondrites.

- Chondrites are made of small ball-shaped particles called chondrules, formed of minerals that have melted and fused together.

- Chondrites may be the oldest rocks in the solar system.

- Carbonaceous chondrites contain carbon.

- Achondrites are meteorites made from stone, but without the spherical chondrules found in chondrites.

- Most meteorites are chondrites.

- Achondrites may be rocks blasted out of the surface of the Moon or Mars by asteroid impacts.

stony iron

stony meteorite

iron meteorite

BEST METEOR SHOWERS

- Perseids (below) is named after the constellation Perseus. It can be seen between July 23 and August 22.

- Orionids is named after the constellation Orion. It can be seen between October 15–29.

- The meteor shower Geminids is named after the Gemini constellation. It can be seen between December 7–15.

THE TEN BIGGEST METEORITES

The largest meteorite ever found in the grounds of the Hoba farm close to Grootfontein, Namibia

Where found	When found	Weight
Hoba, Namibia	1920	60 tons
Campo del Cielo, Argentina	1969	37 tons
Cape York, Greenland	1894	31 tons
Armanty, Xinjiang, China	1898	28 tons
Bacubirito, Mexico	1863	22 tons
Cape York, Greenland	1963	20 tons
Mbosi, Tanzania	1930	16 tons
Campo del Cielo, Argentina	2005	15 tons
Willamette, Oregon, U.S.	1902	14 tons
Chupaderos, Mexico	1852	14 tons

PARENT COMETS

A comet whose trail produces a meteor shower is called the shower's parent comet.

Meteor shower	Parent comet/asteroid
Eta Aquarids	Halley's comet
Geminids	Asteroid 3200 (Phaethon)
Leonids	Tempel-Tuttle
Lyrids	Thatcher
Orionids	Halley's comet
Perseids	Swift-Tuttle
Taurids	Encke
Ursids	Mechain-Tuttle

The spectacular Eta Aquarids shower photographed in 1987

COMET FACTS

- About 850 comets have been spotted and listed by astronomers.

- Comets are named after their discoverers.

- Cometary nuclei (the center of comets) are typically only a few tens of miles across, although many are much smaller.

- If all of the known comets were added together, they would weigh less than the Moon.

- A comet's tail always points away from the Sun.

- The idea that a comet is made of dust and ice, like a dirty snowball, was suggested by Fred Whipple in 1950.

- If Earth passes through the trail of dust particles left behind by a comet, you may see lots of meteors (shooting stars) as the dust enters Earth's atmosphere and burns up.

Astronomer Fred Whipple, pictured in 1986

FAMOUS COMETS

- Halley's comet reappears every 76 years. It is named after astronomer Edmond Halley.

- Hale-Bopp is a long-period comet that is seen only once every few thousand years.

- Encke has the shortest period of all comets—it reappears every 3.3 years.

- See page 113 for information on Edmond Halley.

COMETS

Every few years, an object that looks like a fuzzy star with a long bright tail appears in the sky. These strange objects are not stars. They are comets. A comet is a chunk of gas, dust, and ice left over from the formation of the solar system. Comets orbit the Sun. When a comet nears the Sun, some of the ice on its surface evaporates and releases dust, forming a tail. Most comets are too dim to be seen with the naked eye, but every ten years or so an especially bright comet appears in the sky.

THE STRUCTURE OF A COMET

dust tail

coma

gas tail

nucleus (inside coma)

A comet has four parts: the nucleus, the coma, and two tails.

- The nucleus is the solid part of a comet in the middle of the comet's fuzzy head.

- The coma is the gassy atmosphere that surrounds the nucleus when the comet nears the Sun.

- The curved tail is formed of dust that is pushed away by solar radiation. The straight tail is ionized gas that

has been blown away by the solar wind.

- The coma and tail look bright only because they reflect sunlight.

WHERE DO COMETS COME FROM?

Comets originate from two places in the solar system.

- A belt of icy objects, called the Kuiper belt, begins at about the orbit of Neptune and stretches beyond the orbit of Pluto.

- A ball-shaped cloud of icy objects, called the Oort cloud, surrounds the entire solar system.

- The Oort cloud could be about 7 trillion mi. (11 trillion km) from the Sun.

- Scientists think the Oort cloud may contain trillions of comets.

- The Oort cloud is named after Dutch astronomer Jan Hendrik Oort (1900–1992), who suggested the idea of the distant cloud of comets in 1950.

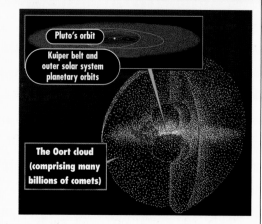

Pluto's orbit

Kuiper belt and outer solar system planetary orbits

The Oort cloud (comprising many billions of comets)

A diagram showing (inset) the location of the Kuiper belt in the solar system and (main picture) the Oort cloud, made up of billions of comets.

- See pages 134–137 for information on Neptune and Pluto.

COMET ORBITS

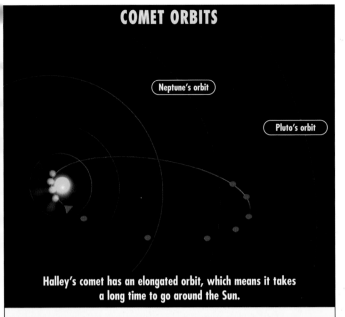

Neptune's orbit

Pluto's orbit

Halley's comet has an elongated orbit, which means it takes a long time to go around the Sun.

- Most comets orbit the Sun so far away that they cannot be seen.

- A passing planet can deflect a comet out of the Kuiper belt and send it on a new orbit closer to the Sun.

- Oort-cloud comets are so far away that passing stars can tug them into a new orbit that takes them toward the inner solar system.

- Comets from the Kuiper belt orbit the Sun faster than other comets. They are called short-period comets.

- Comets from farther away in the Oort cloud take longer to orbit the Sun, so they are called long-period comets.

COMET HISTORY

People in the ancient world feared comets as signs of coming disasters and recorded their sightings. Even recently any sightings are greeted with a sense of wonder.

- The "hairy star" that appears on the Bayeux tapestry is thought to be Halley's comet. The tapestry shows the Norman conquest of England in 1066.

- As recently as 1910, some people in Chicago, Illinois, were reported to have boarded up their windows to protect themselves from Halley's comet!

- Records of Halley's comet date back to 240 B.C. with certainty, and perhaps as far back as 1059 B.C.

- The Great March Comet of 1843 was clearly visible in daylight.

Halley's comet depicted on the Bayeux tapestry (top left)

SPACE PROBES AND COMETS

Space probe	Launched	Comet
ICE (U.S.)	6/10/85	Flew past comet Giacobini-Zinner
Vega 1 (Russia)	12/15/84	Flew past comet Halley
Vega 2 (Russia)	12/21/84	Flew past comet Halley
Sakigake (Japan)	1/8/85	Flew past comet Halley
Giotto (Europe)	7/2/85	Flew close to comet Halley and photographed its nucleus
Suisei (Japan)	8/18/85	Flew past comet Halley
Stardust (U.S.)	2/7/99	Flew past comet Wild 2 and collected particles for return to Earth in 2006
Rosetta (Europe)	3/2/04	Due to rendezvous with comet Churyumov-Gerasimenko in 2014
Deep Impact (U.S.)	12/21/04	Flew past comet Tempel 1 and smashed a mini probe into it

The *Deep Impact* spacecraft lifts off from launch pad 17-B, Cape Canaveral, Florida.

STARS

A star is a giant ball of glowing gas in space fueled by nuclear reactions in its core. You can see several thousand stars with the naked eye. But these are only the brightest stars. Astronomers have found tens of millions more stars by using powerful telescopes to probe the sky. The star at the center of our universe, the Sun, is an ordinary star. Compared to the Sun, some stars are giants. They each contain enough matter to make tens or hundreds of Suns.

STAR BRIGHTNESS

- How bright a star appears to be depends on how bright it really is, its size, temperature, and distance.

- The closer a star is to Earth and the larger it is, the brighter it looks.

- Astronomers call a star's brightness its magnitude.

- A star's magnitude (brightness) is given by a number.

- The brighter a star is, the smaller or lower its magnitude is.

- Stars of magnitudes +6 or more are too faint to be seen with the naked eye.

- The Sun is the brightest object in the sky, with a magnitude of −26.8.

• See pages 116–117 for information on the Sun.

STARS TOGETHER

- Most stars are not single stars like the Sun. They have at least one companion star.

- The two stars orbit each other.

- Some pairs of stars look close together only because they lie in the same direction from Earth, but their movements show that they are not orbiting each other.

- Sometimes two stars are so close together that one star sucks gas off the other star.

- Extra gas falling on a star may explode in a giant blast called a nova.

Mira A (right), with its companion star on the left

NAMES OF STARS

Artwork from an Egyptian temple showing the signs of the zodiac at the center

• See pages 110–111 for information on early astronomers.

- Some of the names we know stars by today were given to them by ancient Greek and Arab astronomers more than 2,000 years ago.

- In the 1600s, German astronomer Johann Bayer started naming stars using Greek letters.

- The brightest star in a constellation was called alpha, the next brightest beta, and so on. For example, the brightest star in the constellation Centaurus is called Alpha Centauri.

- When Greek letters ran out, astronomers named lots of fainter stars by adding "ordinary" numbers to their constellation names. For example, a faint star in Pegasus is called 51 Pegasi.

- Today, new stars are identified by numbers, often with the name of the person who discovered them and the year of discovery.

- The Hubble Space Telescope is pointed in the right direction using a catalog of 15 million stars whose positions are known with great accuracy.

BRIGHTEST STARS

After the Sun, the ten brightest stars seen from Earth are:

STAR	CONSTELLATION	MAGNITUDE
Sirius	Canis Major	−1.44
Canopus	Carina	−0.62
Arcturus	Boötes	−0.05
Alpha Centauri A	Centaurus	−0.01
Vega	Lyra	0.03
Capella	Auriga	0.08
Rigel	Orion	0.18
Procyon	Canis Minor	0.40
Achernar	Eridanus	0.45
Betelgeuse	Orion	0.45

The star Sirius in the constellation Canis Major (magnified image)

Stars are different colors. The color of a star shows its temperature in degrees Centigrade.

STAR TYPE	COLOR	TEMPERATURE (°C)
O	Blue	30,000–50,000 (54,032–90,032°F)
B	Blue-white	10,000–30,000 (18,032–54,032°F)
A	White	7,500–10,000 (18,032–10,832°F)
F	Yellow-white	6,000–7,500 (10,832–13,532°F)
G	Yellow	5,000–6,000 (9,032–10,832°F)
K	Orange	3,500–5,000 (6,332–9,032°F)
M	Red	Under 3,500 (6,332°F)

After the Sun, the ten closest stars to Earth are:

STAR	CONSTELLATION	DISTANCE
Proxima Centauri	Centaurus	4.2 light-years
Alpha Centauri	Centaurus	4.4 light-years
Barnard's Star	Ophiucus	6.0 light-years
Wolf 359	Leo	7.8 light-years
Lalande 21185	Ursa Major	8.3 light-years
Sirius	Canis Major	8.6 light-years
Luyten 726-8	Cetus	8.7 light-years
Ross 154	Sagittarius	9.7 light-years
Ross 248	Andromeda	10.3 light-years
Epsilon Eridani	Eridanus	10.5 light-years

BIRTH AND DEATH OF A STAR

All stars are born from clouds of dust, and they end their lives in violent circumstances. They begin life as dwarfs, before changing into giants or supergiants as they heat up. Depending on how much mass they start out with, they end their lives in a variety of different ways.

THE BIRTH OF A DWARF STAR

1. New stars come from giant clouds of dust and gas.

2. Knots begin to form in the gas cloud as gravity pulls it together. This compression causes the cloud to heat up.

3. Eventually the gas begins to spiral around. Jets of gas are expelled from the poles.

4. The star's brightness increases as nuclear fusion begins at its center. All of the gas and dust in the space surrounding the star is blown away, and eventually the star emerges from its dusty cocoon.

5. The process is complete. The new dwarf star begins to shine.

dwarf star's birth

THE DEATH OF A GIANT

1. If a star uses all of the hydrogen in its central core, hydrogen burning will start to occur in the surrounding shells, which then become heated and cause the outer envelope of the star to swell outward.

2. As a giant's interior gets hotter and hotter, eventually it puffs away its bloated outer shell. This is called a planetary nebula.

3. The hot remnant left behind after a giant has passed the planetary-nebula stage is called a white dwarf. The gravity of white dwarfs is so intense that the result is an Earth-sized remnant so dense that a matchbox full would weigh several tons.

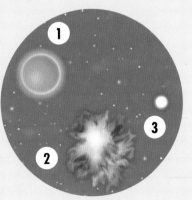

giant's death

THE DEATH OF A SUPERGIANT

1. Like a dwarf, a supergiant starts its life in the same way, but it is much hotter and brighter and can be hundreds of times the diameter of the Sun.

2. After a brilliant but short career, a supergiant commits cosmic suicide in a spectacular explosion called a supernova.

3. A supernova leaves behind an extremely dense remnant such as a neutron star or a black hole.

neutron star

black hole

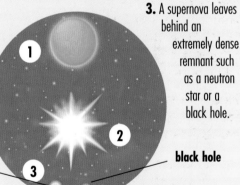

supergiant's death

Giants

A giant is a former dwarf that has cooled and expanded to a great size. In five billion years from now, this will be the fate of our Sun.

Supergiants

A supergiant starts its life as a main sequence dwarf, but it is much brighter, hotter, and more massive than the Sun and can be hundreds of times bigger. It has a hectic, but very short, life.

CONSTELLATIONS

HOW MANY CONSTELLATIONS?

- There are a total of 88 constellations.

- Ancient Egyptian astronomer Ptolemy listed 48 constellations in his book *The Almagest*, written in A.D. 150.

- European astronomers added 40 constellations in the 1600s and 1700s.

- In 1930, the International Astronomical Union mapped the boundaries between them all so that there were no gaps between the constellations, and so every star now belongs to a constellation.

- **See pages 110–113 for information on astronomers.**

FINDING NAMES

- Most constellations were named according to religious beliefs and mythological characters.

- The oldest constellations were probably named more than 4,000 years ago.

- The ancient Greeks had no names for constellations in the southernmost skies, because the stars there were not visible from Greece.

- European astronomers filled in the gaps between the northern constellations and began naming the southern constellations.

- The final gaps in the southern constellations were filled by French astronomer Nicolas Louis de Lacaille.

People have seen patterns in the stars since ancient times. The groups of stars that form these patterns are called constellations. The stars in a constellation rarely have any connection with one another. They simply lie in the same direction when viewed from Earth. Twelve of the most ancient constellations have special significance. They are the 12 constellations that the Sun, Moon, and planets pass through. They are also known as the signs of the zodiac. The ancient constellations are still used by astronomers as signposts to find their way around the night sky.

Winter sky

Orion, the Hunter, is a magnificent constellation visible during late evenings in the winter. The three stars in its belt can be used as a celestial signpost. Just below the belt is a shiny patch called the Orion nebula, which is a splendid sight through binoculars or a small telescope. The Orion nebula is actually a stellar nursery, where stars are being born right now.

GEMINI

A slightly curving line drawn upward through Rigel and Betelgeuse will get you to Gemini, with its two bright stars Castor and Pollux, the Heavenly Twins.

AURIGA

Over Orion's head is Auriga, the Charioteer. Near the bright star Capella is a distinctive triangle of stars called the Kids.

PERSEUS

Now follow a line northeast of Orion past Taurus and you will come to Perseus. This constellation contains a double open cluster, which is a great sight through binoculars.

CANIS MINOR

A line to the west of Orion takes you to the small constellation Canis Minor, the Little Dog. The three stars Procyon (in Canis Minor), Betelgeuse (in Orion), and Sirius (in Canis Major) form the prominent Winter Triangle.

TAURUS

Follow the three stars of Orion's Belt upward and you will come to the constellation Taurus, the Bull. Taurus contains the bright red star Aldebaran. This star appears to form part of the "V" of the Hyades, which is an open star cluster. In fact, Aldebaran is a foreground star and is not part of this distant group. Following the line from Orion's Belt yet farther, you will come to a close-knit bunch of stars called the Pleiades. These stars form yet another open cluster.

CANIS MAJOR

Canis Major, the Big Dog, is found by following Orion's Belt downward. It contains Sirius, the brightest star in the sky.

LEPUS

Beneath Orion is an undistinguished constellation called Lepus, the Hare.

ERIDANUS

Eridanus, the River, is another faint constellation that manages to meander a sixth of the way around the sky. It lies to the right of Orion, just past Rigel.

ORION

- Orion is one of the oldest constellations.

- More than 1,000 years ago, it was known as Tammuz to the Chaldeans.

- Tammuz was the name of the month when the three stars across its middle rose before sunrise.

- The Syrians knew it as Al Jabbar (the Giant).

- The ancient Egyptians knew it as Sahu, the soul of the god Osiris.

- The name we know it by (Orion) comes from the ancient Greeks.

- In Greek mythology, Orion was a giant hunter.

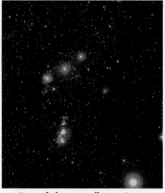

Part of the constellation Orion

SIGNS OF THE ZODIAC

The 12 constellations of the zodiac and the dates when the Sun passes through them are:

CONSTELLATION	DATES
Aries (The Ram)	3/21–4/19
Taurus (The Bull)	4/20–5/20
Gemini (The Twins)	5/21–6/21
Cancer (The Crab)	6/22–7/22
Leo (The Lion)	7/23–8/22
Virgo (The Virgin)	8/23–9/22
Libra (The Scales)	9/23–10/23
Scorpius (The Scorpion)	10/24–11/21
Sagittarius (The Archer)	11/22–12/21
Capricornus (The Goat)	12/22–1/19
Aquarius (The Water Bearer)	1/21–2/18
Pisces (The Fish)	2/19–3/20

Spring sky

When you look up at the late evening sky in the spring, you should be able to see the seven stars of the Big Dipper. Use the Big Dipper (marked below in red) to navigate your way around the sky.

CEPHEUS

A straight line through Merak and Dubhe in the Big Dipper and Polaris will take you to Cepheus, a dim constellation.

CASSIOPEIA

A line from Mizar in the Big Dipper through Polaris takes you to the constellation Cassiopeia, a beautiful W-shaped constellation that lies in the band of the Milky Way.

DRACO

Between Ursa Major and Ursa Minor is long, winding Draco, the Dragon, a fairly dim constellation.

URSA MINOR

Follow the two stars Merak and Dubhe in the Big Dipper northward and you will come to Polaris, the polestar, in the constellation Ursa Minor, the Little Bear.

BOÖTES

The three left-hand stars of the Big Dipper can be used to trace a gentle curve downward to the bright orange star Arcturus in the constellation Boötes, the Herdsman.

URSA MAJOR & THE BIG DIPPER

The Big Dipper, or Seven Stars, is not actually a constellation but the brightest part of the constellation Ursa Major, the Big Bear. The most important thing about the Big Dipper is that some of its stars make useful signposts to other parts of the sky.

LEO

Directly underneath the Big Dipper is the constellation Leo, the Lion. It is one of the few constellations that bears even the slightest resemblance to its name. Its bright star, Regulus, is the dot in an inverted question mark of stars known as the Sickle.

BRIGHTEST CONSTELLATIONS

The ten brightest stars lie in the following constellations:

STAR	CONSTELLATION
Sirius	Canis Major
Canopus	Carina
Arcturus	Boötes
Alpha Centauri	Centaurus
Vega	Lyra
Capella	Auriga
Rigel	Orion
Procyon	Canis Major
Achernar	Eridanus
Betelgeuse	Orion

LARGEST CONSTELLATIONS

1. Hydra (The Sea Serpent)
2. Virgo (The Virgin)
3. Ursa Major (The Great Bear)
4. Cetus (The Sea Monster)
5. Hercules (Hercules)

SMALLEST CONSTELLATIONS

1. Crux (The Southern Cross)
2. Equuleus (The Little Horse)
3. Sagittarius (The Archer)
4. Circinus (The Compass)

TELESCOPES

Astronomers have used telescopes to study the sky for more than 400 years. The first telescopes magnified images of distant objects by means of lenses. Later a new type of telescope had curved mirrors instead of lenses. Astronomers use telescopes to collect all sorts of waves and rays, including visible light from space, and this helps them learn more about stars, galaxies, and other objects.

TYPES OF LIGHT

Light is a form of radiation that is transported in waves. Each of the colors of the rainbow has its own wavelength. The entire range of wavelengths is called the electromagnetic spectrum. The protective atmosphere of Earth cuts out many of the wavelengths, but from space, the entire spectrum is detectable. By studying what kind of radiation is emitted from objects such as stars, astronomers can learn about an object's density, temperature, chemical composition, and how it moves.

visible light

radio waves — infrared — x-rays
microwaves — ultraviolet — gamma rays
wavelength increases

TELESCOPE PARTS

- A refracting telescope, or refractor, collects light with a large objective lens. The image is viewed through a smaller eyepiece lens.

- A reflecting telescope collects light with a large primary, or main, mirror and reflects it to an eyepiece, cameras, or other instruments by means of a smaller secondary mirror.

- Large mirrors sag under their own weight, so the biggest reflecting telescopes have mirrors made in smaller sections joined together.

- Each of the two Keck telescopes on Mauna Kea, Hawaii, has a 33-ft. (10-m) primary mirror made from 36 segments.

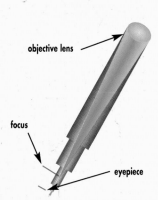

objective lens

focus

eyepiece

REFRACTING TELESCOPE

1. The objective lens catches the light and brings it into focus.

2. The eyepiece magnifies the focused image.

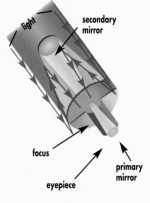

light

secondary mirror

focus

eyepiece

primary mirror

REFLECTING TELESCOPE

1. Light falls through the top of the open-frame tube and heads toward the primary mirror.

2. It is then reflected up the tube to the smaller secondary mirror.

3. The light is then reflected back down the tube, through a hole in the primary, to the focus.

TYPES OF TELESCOPES

radio telescope

refractors

reflector

Telescopes are classified in different ways. They can be divided according to the way they produce a magnified image.

- Refractors use lenses to form an image.

- Reflectors use curved mirrors to form an image.

- Refractors and reflectors collect and magnify light, but telescopes can make use of other types of energy.

- Radio telescopes use radio waves; infrared telescopes use infrared rays; x-ray telescopes use x-rays; ultraviolet (UV) telescopes use UV waves; and gamma-ray telescopes use gamma rays.

• See pages 112–113 for information on later astronomers.

MAKING SHARP IMAGES

The California Extremely Large Telescope in the United States

- Starlight is distorted as it travels down through Earth's atmosphere to the ground.

- The distorting effect of the atmosphere makes stars appear to twinkle and also makes it difficult for astronomers to take clear photographs of them.

- Astronomers avoid the distorting effect of the atmosphere by placing their telescopes on top of mountains, above the thickest part of the atmosphere.

- Telescopes in space, above all of Earth's atmosphere, have the clearest view of all.

- Some reflecting telescopes have "adaptive optics" — the mirror flexes (changes shape) continually to cancel the effect of the atmosphere and produce sharper images.

- Some telescopes work only in space, because the energy they use to make images is blocked by Earth's atmosphere.

SPACE TELESCOPES

TELESCOPE	LAUNCHED	USED TO STUDY
BeppoSAX	1996	x-rays
Chandra X-ray Observatory	1999	x-rays
Compton Gamma Ray Observatory	1991	gamma rays
Einstein (HEAO 22)	1978	x-rays
Herschel Space Telescope	2009	infrared waves
Hipparcos	1989	star positions
Hubble Space Telescope	1990	stars, galaxies, nebulae
Infrared Astronomical Satellite	1983	infrared waves
International Ultraviolet Explorer	1978	ultraviolet waves
Solar and Heliospheric Observatory	1995	the Sun
Spitzer Space Telescope	2003	infrared waves
Uhuru	1970	x-rays

LINKING TELESCOPES

The amount of detail a telescope can see depends on how much light or other energy it collects.

- When several telescopes are pointed in the same direction and linked together, they behave like a bigger telescope.

- The twin Keck telescopes in Hawaii have mirrors 33 ft. (10m) across, but when they are linked together, they behave like one telescope with a mirror 280 ft. (85m) across.

- The European Very Large Telescope (VLT) has four mirrors, each 27 ft. (8.2m) across. When linked together, they mimic a telescope with a 656-ft. (200-m) mirror.

TELESCOPES OF THE FUTURE

- The Giant Magellan Telescope will be almost 72 ft. (22m) across, and it will have seven huge 28-ft. (8.4-m) mirrors.

- The Thirty-meter Telescope, with a mirror 98 ft. (30m) across, will be sited in Hawaii, Chile, or Mexico.

- The Overwhelmingly Large Telescope (OWL) will have a mirror 328 ft. (100m) across, about ten times the size of the biggest telescope mirrors today.

- The Hubble Space Telescope's successor, the James Webb Space Telescope, will be launched in about 2013.

The Hubble Space Telescope

TELESCOPE TIMELINE

1609
Thomas Harriot becomes the first person to study the night sky through a telescope.

1668
Sir Isaac Newton builds the first reflecting telescope.

1845
Lord Rosse builds a giant 72-in. (183-cm) telescope at Birr Castle in Parsonstown, Irleand.

1897
The Yerkes 40-in. (102-cm) refractor is built in Williams Bay, Wisconsin.

1917
The Mount Wilson 100-in. (254-cm) reflecting telescope is first used in California.

1937
Karl Jansky builds the first radio telescope.

Grote Reber builds a 31-ft. (9.5-m) radio telescope.

1957
The 250-ft. (76-m) Jodrell Bank steerable radio telescope is completed.

1963
The 1,000-ft. (305-m) Arecibo radio telescope in Puerto Rico begins operating.

1974
The 153-in. (389-cm) Anglo-Australian Telescope in Australia opens.

1979
The 150-in. (381-cm) UKIRT, 140-in. (356-cm) optical reflector, and NASA Infrared Telescope Facility begin work on Mauna Kea, Hawaii.

1990
The Hubble Space Telescope is launched by the space shuttle.

1993
The first 33-ft. (10-m) Keck telescope begins work on Mauna Kea, Hawaii.

1996
Keck II begins operating on Mauna Kea, Hawaii.

2003
The Spitzer Space Telescope is launched in August.

2009
The Herschel Space Telescope is launched in May.

THE MILKY WAY

- The Milky Way is a thin disk of stars with a thicker bulge in the middle.

- It is sometimes described as looking like two fried eggs back to back!

- Stars are packed more closely together in the central bulge than in the rest of the disk.

- Stars are not evenly spread across the disk. They form arms that curl away from the center in a spiral shape.

- A beam of light would take about 100,000 years to cross the Milky Way from one side to the other. So we say the Milky Way measures 100,000 light-years across.

- The disk is surrounded by a ball-shaped "halo" of globular clusters containing very old stars.

- The halo shows that the Milky Way may once have been ball shaped before it became a disk.

- Astronomers know there is a lot more matter in the halo than they can see. They know it is there, because they can measure the effect of its gravity. This invisible matter is called dark matter.

- No one is certain what dark matter is.

Our star, the Sun, is one of billions of stars that travel through space together. This vast collection of stars is called the Milky Way galaxy. On a clear dark night, you may be able to see the hazy band of the Milky Way stretching across the sky. The stars are held together by the pull of their gravity.

GALAXY PROFILE

Shape	**Barred spiral**
Diameter of disk	**100,000 light-years**
Average thickness of disk	**2,000 light-years**
Diameter of central bulge	**12,000 light-years**
Thickness of central bulge	**6,000 light-years**
Number of stars	**200–400 billion**

A NASA photograph of the Milky Way

AGE OF THE MILKY WAY

- Astronomers think the Milky Way formed soon after the universe began.

- The Milky Way probably formed when the universe was only about 200–300 million years old.

- This means the age of the Milky Way is between 13 and 13.6 billion years.

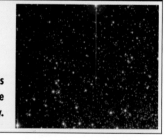

Globular cluster NGC 6397 contains some of the oldest stars in the Milky Way.

MILKY WAY CENTER

- We cannot see the center of the Milky Way because it is surrounded by thick clouds of gas and dust.

- Astronomers think there may be a giant black hole in the center, containing as much matter as one million Suns.

- We are in no danger of falling into the Milky Way's black hole.

- The Sun is located about two thirds of the way out from the center of the Milky Way toward its edge.

- The center is about 25,000 light-years away from us.

An artist's impression of the Milky Way

• See pages 152–153 for information on galaxies.

MANY ARMS

The Milky Way has many main spiral arms that curl out from the center of the galaxy. These include the Norma arm, the Scutum-Crux arm, the Sagittarius arm, and the Perseus arm. The Sun lies in a small arm called the Orion arm (also called the Local arm).

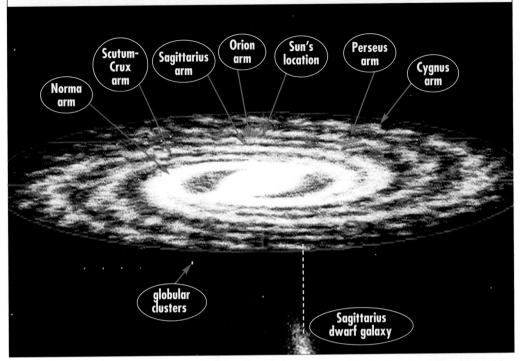

- Norma arm
- Scutum-Crux arm
- Sagittarius arm
- Orion arm
- Sun's location
- Perseus arm
- Cygnus arm
- globular clusters
- Sagittarius dwarf galaxy

IN A SPIN

Sun's path around the galaxy

- The Milky Way spins as it moves through space, like a giant cartwheel.

- The Sun takes about 226 million years to complete one orbit.

- The Sun moves around the Milky Way at a speed of 136 mi. (220km) per second.

- The Sun has orbited the center of the Milky Way about 50 times since its formation.

• See pages 116–117 for information on the Sun.

SPEEDING STARS

The majority of the stars in the Sun's vicinity in the Milky Way move around the galaxy at around 6–62 mi. (10–100km) per second. There are, however, some stars that travel around twice as fast as that speed.

CLOSEST GALAXIES

GALAXY	DISTANCE FROM EARTH
Canis Major dwarf galaxy	25,000 light-years
Sagittarius dwarf elliptical galaxy	88,000 light-years
Large Magellanic cloud	160,000 light-years
Small Magellanic cloud	190,000 light-years
Ursa Minor dwarf galaxy	240,000 light-years

The Sagittarius dwarf elliptical galaxy

FUTURE FATE

The Milky Way and another galaxy called the Andromeda galaxy are moving toward each other.

- Andromeda is bigger than the Milky Way.

- One day the two galaxies will collide, but they will not meet for several billion years.

- The two galaxies will probably merge and form a new galaxy.

- The new galaxy will not be spiral like the Milky Way, but it will probably be elliptical in shape.

- The Milky Way has already swallowed up many small nearby galaxies.

The two illustrations below simulate what might happen when the Andromeda galaxy hits ours. The central regions will merge into a single galaxy.

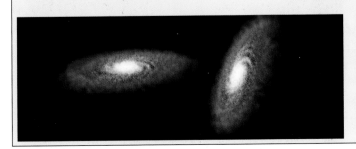

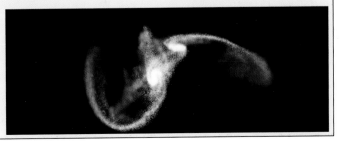

GALAXIES

• See page 113 for more information on Edwin Hubble.

There are billions of giant star groups like the Milky Way. They are called galaxies. Some galaxies are spiral in shape like the Milky Way. Others are different shapes. Galaxies are not evenly spread through space. They bunch together in groups, or clusters. The clusters themselves bunch together in bigger groups called superclusters. Our galaxy, the Milky Way, belongs to a cluster of about 30 galaxies called the Local Group. This is one of about 400 clusters of galaxies that form a grouping called the Local Supercluster.

GALAXY NAMES

- Galaxies known for a long time were named after their discoverer.

- The Large Magellanic cloud is named after the explorer Ferdinand Magellan, whose crew discovered it during the first voyage around the world in the 1520s.

- Some galaxies are named after the constellation in which they are found.

- The Sagittarius galaxy is named after the constellation Sagittarius that it appears in.

- Today, galaxies are named differently. They are usually known by the name of a catalog they are listed in and their number in the catalog.

- The New General Catalog (NGC) lists hundreds of galaxies. They all have an NGC number.

- Some galaxies are also known by an "M" number. They are galaxies that appear in a list drawn up in 1781 by French astronomer Charles Messier. In this list, the Andromeda galaxy is M31.

- Some galaxies appear in more than one list, so they have more than one name or number. For example, NGC 598 is also known as M33.

GALAXY SHAPES

irregular

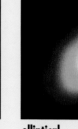

elliptical

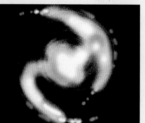

barred spiral

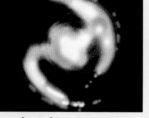

spiral

All galaxies have one of three basic shapes—spiral, elliptical, or irregular.

- Almost all galaxies are either spiral or elliptical in shape.

- Elliptical galaxies may be perfectly ball shaped or they may be flattened, stretched-oval shapes.

- Spiral galaxies usually have a central bulge of older stars surrounded by a disk of matter where new stars are forming.

- Stars in a spiral galaxy's disk trace out the shapes of spiral arms.

- Most spiral galaxies have a straight bar of stars through the central bulge. These galaxies are called barred spirals.

- Irregular galaxies have no definite shape.

- Some irregular galaxies look as if they were once spirals. They may have changed shape when they collided with other galaxies.

- Other irregular galaxies are confused jumbles of stars.

- This way of dividing galaxies into groups according to their shape was devised by American astronomer Edwin Hubble in the 1920s.

ACTIVE GALAXIES

Active galaxies are galaxies that give out far more light and other energy than their stars should produce.

- In the 1960s, astronomers discovered objects that looked like stars, but they were distant galaxies with a brilliant core 100 times brighter than a normal galaxy.

- At the center of these active galaxies there are quasistellar objects, or quasars.

- The blindingly bright core of a quasar is only about the size of our solar system, but brighter than scores of Milky Way galaxies.

- The huge amount of light pouring out of a quasar seems to be coming from matter falling into a black hole.

- The black hole at the center of a quasar is massive, perhaps one billion times the mass of the Sun.

The Chandra X-ray Observatory (model shown here) will allow researchers to obtain better x-ray images of quasars.

HOW GALAXIES MOVE

Astronomers can tell a lot about a distant galaxy by studying the light and other energy that it gives out.

- A galaxy gives out known patterns of light according to the chemical elements it contains.

- When astronomers analyze light from distant galaxies, these distinctive patterns look wrong. The colors seem to have been shifted toward the red end of the rainbow spectrum of visible light. This is called red shift.

- Red shift happens because the light waves have been stretched. Stretching light waves changes the colors that they make.

- Light waves are stretched like this when they come from something that is rushing away from us. This indicates that all of the galaxies we can see are flying away from us.

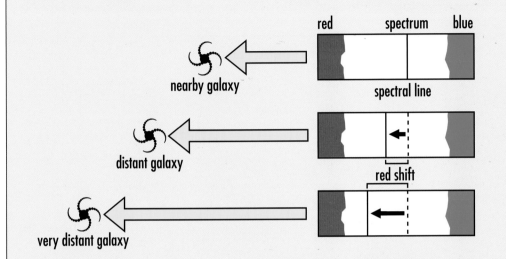

nearby galaxy

distant galaxy

very distant galaxy

red   spectrum   blue

spectral line

red shift

HOW MANY GALAXIES?

- No one knows the exact number of galaxies that exist today.

- Astronomers see galaxies wherever they look in the sky.

- When astronomers point their most powerful telescopes and most sensitive cameras at a tiny part of the sky, they can see 10,000 galaxies there.

- Astronomers believe there are billions of galaxies in total.

• See pages 148–149 for information on telescopes.

FARTHEST GALAXIES

- The farthest galaxies observed so far are about 13 billion light-years away from us.

- These galaxies are so far away that light from them has traveled across the universe for 13 billion years in order to reach us.

- Astronomers are seeing these distant galaxies as they looked 13 billion years ago when the light left them. This was only just after the universe formed, so even if there are farther galaxies, light from them would not have time to reach us. These distant galaxies may not be there anymore. Even if they still exist, they probably look very different today.

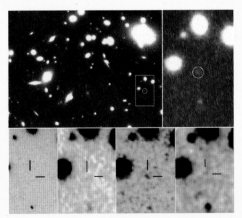

European Southern Observatory image of Abell 1835 IR1916, the most distant galaxy yet discovered, located about 13.2 billion light-years away

LARGEST LOCAL GALAXIES

Galaxy	Type	Diameter	Distance
Andromeda (below)	Spiral	150,000 light-years	2.5 million light-years
Milky Way	Barred spiral	100,000 light-years	-
NGC 598	Spiral	60,000 light-years	2.7 million light-years
Large Magellanic cloud	Irregular	20,000 light-years	160,000 light-years
Small Magellanic cloud	Irregular	10,000 light-years	200,000 light-years

THE UNIVERSE

The universe is all the matter, energy, space, and time that exists everywhere. Scientists have tried many theories to explain how and when the universe began. Today, most scientists agree that the universe burst into existence about 13.7 billion years ago in a huge explosion called the big bang. It flung matter and energy in all directions and produced the universe we know today.

DARK MATTER

- Scientists believe that there is a lot more matter in the universe than we can see.

- Most of the matter in the universe is invisible, but scientists can detect the effect of its gravity, which is how we know it exists.

- This invisible matter is called dark matter.

- No one yet knows what dark matter is made of.

EXPANSION OF THE UNIVERSE

Galaxies appear to be shooting away from us at very great speeds.

This is not because we occupy any special position in the universe—exactly the same thing would be observed from any other galaxy. In fact, it is not the galaxies that are moving but the space between them that is expanding. Imagine sticking stars on a balloon and then blowing up the balloon. The stars would seem to move apart as the balloon inflates. The expansion of the universe is a process that has been occurring over billions of years.

COSMOLOGY

- The branch of science concerned with studying the origin and development of the universe is called cosmology.

- Scientists who study cosmology are called cosmologists.

- Cosmologists may never look through telescopes. They often rely on information about stars, galaxies, and other objects from the people who actually observe them—astronomers.

Cosmologist Albert Einstein

- See pages 110–113 for information on astronomers.

NEW THEORIES

Scientists are still developing new theories to explain the origin and evolution of the universe.

- According to string theory, particles of matter are actually tiny vibrating loops and strands of energy.

- The strings may lie on sheets or tubes of space called membranes, or branes.

- String theory predicts that there are another six dimensions in addition to the three dimensions in space and one in time that we already know about.

- Another prediction of string theory is that there may be many more universes in addition to ours.

- These parallel universes are called multiverses.

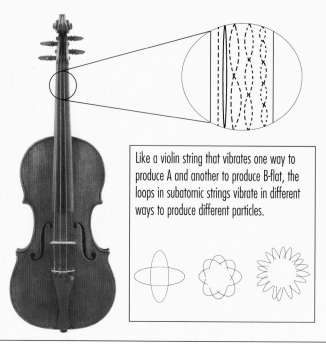

Like a violin string that vibrates one way to produce A and another to produce B-flat, the loops in subatomic strings vibrate in different ways to produce different particles.

THE BIG BANG

Most scientists think the universe began from a tiny speck that exploded at the start of space and time called the big bang.

- In its first moment of existence, the universe was unimaginably hot.

- It expanded rapidly during a stage called inflation.

- As the universe expanded, it cooled.

- Within a fraction of a second, the first particles were produced.

- One second after the big bang, the temperature had fallen to 50 billion degrees Fahrenheit (28 billion degrees Celsius).

- After three minutes, the temperature was one billion degrees Fahrenheit (555 million degrees Celsius) — cool enough for particles of matter to join together.

- About 300,000 years after the explosion, it was cool enough for whole atoms to form.

- Hydrogen, helium, and other simple elements formed.

- Matter was not evenly spread through the early universe.

- Denser clumps of matter developed into the first stars and galaxies only about 200 million years after the big bang.

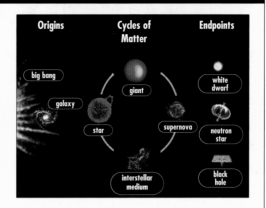

Origins   Cycles of Matter   Endpoints

big bang, galaxy, star, giant, supernova, interstellar medium, white dwarf, neutron star, black hole

- The big bang produced an expanding universe, which we see today.

- The big bang also led to the creation of hydrogen and helium in the proportions we see today.

- In the 1950s, scientists suggested that if the big bang really happened, its echo should still exist.

- As the universe expanded, the superhot radiation that filled it spread out and cooled. This radiation still exists today. It is called cosmic background radiation or cosmic microwave background.

- Two astronomers, Arno Penzias and Robert Wilson, detected cosmic background radiation in 1965.

- In 1992, the *Cosmic Background Explorer* (COBE) satellite made a map of the background radiation.

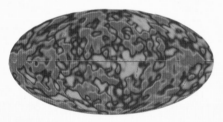

An image of the universe taken by the *COBE* satellite (left), confirming a temperature of 270 degrees below zero Fahrenheit (−168°C)

THE FUTURE OF THE UNIVERSE

What will be the eventual fate of the universe? Everything depends on how dense the universe is. There are three possibilities.

- If the density is higher than a certain value (the "critical density"), the universe will eventually stop expanding and collapse in on itself. This is called the big crunch scenario.

- If the density is less than critical, the universe will just keep on expanding, and the temperature of everything in the universe will plummet. Everything will become even colder. This scenario is called heat death.

- Finally, if the density is just borderline, the universe will expand less and less but will not collapse. This is called the flat universe scenario.

A balloon experiment, Boomerang, was sent high into the atmosphere above the Antarctic to measure the "bumpiness" in the cosmic background. This showed that the universe is flat — neither the big crunch nor the heat death scenario will happen.

The balloon experiment Boomerang, with a projection of its results superimposed behind

HUMANS IN SPACE

People have been traveling into space since 1961. The first manned spacecraft were just big enough to fit one person inside. Later spacecraft could fly three people around the world or take them all the way to the Moon and back. At first all of these spacecraft were used for only one space mission each. The U.S. space shuttle is different. It can be flown again and again. Until 2003, Russia and the U.S. were the only countries with a manned space program, but in that year China launched its first manned space mission. *Shenzhou 5* carried Yang Liwei into space on October 13. He safely returned home after orbiting Earth 14 times.

VOSTOK (U.S.S.R./RUSSIA)

Vostok was the first manned spacecraft and the culmination of a space race between the United States and the Soviet Union.

- The *Vostok* capsule was a small sphere only 8.2 ft. (2.5m) across.

- The Soviet Union called its space travelers cosmonauts.

- Each capsule carried one cosmonaut into space for missions lasting up to five days.

- The first cosmonaut was Yuri Gagarin.

- He made the first-ever manned space flight on April 12, 1961.

- On the way back, Gagarin was ejected from his capsule at a height of 22,960 ft. (7,000m) and landed by parachute.

- The first manned space flight lasted less than two hours from launch to landing.

- *Vostok 6* launched Valentina Tereshkova, the first woman in space, on June 16, 1963.

The *Vostok 1* space capsule

Cosmonaut Yuri Gagarin

GEMINI (U.S.)

Gemini 4 astronaut Ed White during his space walk over El Paso, Texas

- *Gemini* was a two-person spacecraft launched by the *Titan* rocket. There were ten manned *Gemini* space flights between 1965 and 1966.

- Ed White made the first space walk by an American astronaut during the *Gemini 4* mission.

- *Gemini* allowed astronauts to practice all of the maneuvers that would be needed for a Moon-landing mission.

- The longest *Gemini* mission was *Gemini 7*, which lasted for 13 days, 18 hours.

MERCURY (U.S.)

The U.S. answered *Vostok* with its own one-person space capsule, *Mercury*.

- After reentry, *Mercury* capsules landed in the sea.

- The first American astronaut was Alan Shepard. He made a 15-minute suborbital flight (into space but not around Earth) in *Mercury 3* on May 5, 1961.

- Alan Shepard was the only *Mercury* astronaut who would later walk on the Moon.

The recovered Mercury space capsule

- Virgil Grissom's *Mercury 4* capsule sank soon after it splashed down. Grissom was rescued.

- *Mercury 6* carried the first American to go into orbit, John Glenn, on February 20, 1962.

- There was an emergency during Glenn's flight when ground controllers thought his spacecraft's heat shield had come loose, but he landed safely.

- There were six manned *Mercury* missions between 1961 and 1963.

APOLLO (U.S.)

The *Apollo* spacecraft were designed to take three astronauts to the Moon and land two of them.

- The *Apollo* spacecraft were made of three modules—the command module, the service module, and the lunar excursion module (LEM).

- The crew spent most of their time in the command module, supplied with air, electricity, and rocket power by the service module.

- The LEM was the part of the spacecraft that landed on the Moon.

- The tiny command module was the only part of the spacecraft to return to Earth and splash down in the Pacific Ocean.

- The spacecraft were launched by the giant *Saturn V* rocket, except for *Apollo 7*.

- The crew of *Apollo 8* were the first humans to orbit the Moon.

- After four manned test flights, *Apollo 11* landed Neil Armstrong and Buzz Aldrin on the Moon's surface in 1969, while Michael Collins circled the Moon.

- The *Apollo 13* spacecraft suffered a serious explosion on its way to the Moon. The crew returned safely to Earth.

- The *Apollo 13* crew traveled farther from Earth than anyone else—248,106 mi. (400,171km).

- The last three *Apollo* missions carried an electric car called the *Lunar Rover*, used to travel across the Moon's surface.

- The last *Apollo* Moon-landing mission was *Apollo 17* in 1972. The *Apollo 17* crew stayed on the Moon for the longest time—75 hours.

- Over six missions, 12 *Apollo* astronauts landed on the Moon and brought Moon rocks back to Earth. They left packages of scientific instruments on the surface.

- Leftover *Apollo* hardware was used for a joint U.S.-Soviet mission called the Apollo-Soyuz Test Project and also for the Skylab space station.

• See pages 124–125 for information on the Moon.

SOYUZ (U.S.S.R./RUSSIA)

Soyuz was initially designed as part of the U.S.S.R.'s Moon mission, and it is the longest-serving manned spacecraft in the world.

- A *Soyuz* spacecraft has three modules—an instrument module, a reentry module, and an orbital module. The spacecraft is 23 ft. (7.0m) long and 8.86 ft. (2.7m) in diameter.

- The reentry module lands by parachute on the ground. It fires rockets just before touchdown to cushion the impact.

- The first manned *Soyuz* mission took place in 1967. Unfortunately the spacecraft crashed and killed the pilot, Vladimir Komarov. Since then, however, *Soyuz* has been a highly successful and reliable spacecraft.

- *Soyuz* spacecraft ferry cosmonauts and astronauts to and from the new International Space Station.

- A type of unmanned *Soyuz* spacecraft called *Progress* was developed to deliver supplies to space stations.

SPACE SHUTTLE (U.S.)

The development of a reusable space launcher was the next stage in the exploration of space.

- The space shuttle orbiter is the size of a small airliner. It is 121.4 ft. (37m) long, with a wingspan of 78.7 ft. (24m).

- A payload bay carries satellites, laboratories, and scientific instruments into space.

- The space shuttle has a crew of two pilots and up to five other astronauts.

- It is launched with the help of two solid rocket boosters and an external fuel tank that supplies fuel to the three big engines in the orbiter's tail.

- The first space shuttle was launched in 1981, crewed by John Young and Bob Crippen.

- Since 1981, there have been more than 100 space shuttle missions.

- The oldest shuttle astronaut was John Glenn, at the age of 77. He was the same John Glenn who made the first U.S. orbital flight in 1962.

- There are currently three orbiters— *Discovery, Atlantis,* and *Endeavour*.

- Two other orbiters, *Columbia* and *Challenger*, were lost along with their crews in accidents.

SPACE PROBES

A model of *Sputnik 1*, the first space satellite

People have traveled only as far as the Moon, but unmanned space probes have toured almost the entire solar system. The first probes were blasted into space toward the end of the 1950s when the cold war between the United States and the U.S.S.R. was at its height. These probes have explored the surface of Mars, created maps of Venus, taken close-up photographs of nearly all the planets and many of their moons, orbited Saturn, and even left the solar system altogether. There are too many space probes to list in full, but details of a few of the most important probes are given on these pages.

SPUTNIK (U.S.S.R./RUSSIA)

PROBE	LAUNCHED	DETAILS
Sputnik 1	Oct. 4, 1957	The world's first artificial satellite
Sputnik 2	Nov. 3, 1957	Carried dog Laika, the first living space traveler
Sputnik 3	May 15, 1958	Studied Earth's atmosphere and solar radiation
Sputnik 4	May 15, 1960	Unmanned test flight for *Vostok 1*
Sputnik 5	Aug. 19, 1960	Carried two dogs, Belka and Strelka
Sputnik 6	Dec. 1, 1960	The second test flight for *Vostok*. Recovery failed.
Sputnik 7	Feb. 4, 1961	A test flight for Venus probe *Sputnik 8*
Sputnik 8	Feb. 12, 1961	Launched Russia's first *Venus* probe
Sputnik 9	Mar. 9, 1961	Carried a dog named Chernushka
Sputnik 10	Mar. 25, 1961	Carried a dog named Zvezdochka

Laika, the first animal in space

PIONEER (U.S.)

The *Pioneer Venus Orbiter*, launched in May 1978

PROBE	LAUNCHED	DETAILS
Pioneer 1	Oct. 11, 1958	Intended to reach the Moon but failed
Pioneer 2	Nov. 8, 1958	Intended to reach the Moon but failed
Pioneer 3	Dec. 6, 1958	Failed to reach the Moon
Pioneer 4	Mar. 3, 1959	Passed within 37,200 mi. (60,000km) of the Moon
Pioneer 5	Mar. 11, 1960	Entered solar orbit; sent solar flare and solar wind data
Pioneer 6	Dec. 16, 1965	Entered solar orbit and studied the Sun's atmosphere
Pioneer 7	Aug. 17, 1966	Combined with *Pioneer 6* to study the Sun
Pioneer 8	Dec. 13, 1967	Joined *Pioneers 6* and *7* to study the Sun
Pioneer 9	Nov. 8, 1968	Joined *Pioneers 6, 7,* and *8* to study the Sun
Pioneer 10	Mar. 3, 1972	Passed within about 80,600 mi. (130,000km) of Jupiter's cloud tops
Pioneer 11	Apr. 6, 1973	Photographed Jupiter's south pole
Pioneer Venus Orbiter	May 20, 1978	Orbited Venus, studying its atmosphere
Pioneer Venus Multiprobe	Aug. 8, 1978	Dropped five probes into Venus's atmosphere before entering the atmosphere and burning up

VENERA (U.S.S.R./RUSSIA)

PROBE	LAUNCHED	DETAILS
Venera 1	Feb. 12, 1961	First interplanetary flight passed within 62,000 mi. (100,000km) of Venus
Venera 2	Nov. 12, 1965	Passed within 14,880 mi. (24,000km) of Venus
Venera 3	Nov. 16, 1965	First spacecraft to land on another planet
Venera 4	Jun. 12, 1967	Transmitted data during descent through atmosphere
Venera 5	Jan. 5, 1969	Transmitted data during descent through atmosphere
Venera 6	Jan. 10, 1969	Transmitted data during descent through atmosphere
Venera 7	Aug. 17, 1970	Transmitted data from the surface of Venus
Venera 8	Mar. 27, 1972	Transmitted data from the surface of Venus
Venera 9	Jun. 8, 1975	First spacecraft to send pictures from the surface of another planet
Venera 10	Jun. 14, 1975	Transmitted pictures from the surface of Venus
Venera 11	Sep. 9, 1978	Flyby probe dropped a lander onto Venus
Venera 12	Sep. 14, 1978	Flyby probe dropped a lander onto Venus
Venera 13	Oct. 30, 1981	Landed using radar maps made by *Pioneer-Venus* spacecraft
Venera 14	Nov. 4, 1981	Flyby probe dropped a lander onto Venus
Venera 15	Jun. 2, 1983	Orbited Venus and mapped surface by radar
Venera 16	Jun. 6, 1983	Orbited Venus and mapped surface by radar

Venera 13 replica at the Cosmos Pavilion in Moscow

• See pages 120–121 for information on Venus.

VIKINGS TO MARS (U.S)

In 1976, the U.S. landed two *Viking* spacecraft on the red planet.

PROBE	LAUNCHED
Viking 1	Aug. 20, 1975
Viking 2	Sep. 9, 1975

- After the U.S. *Mariner* Mars probes in the 1960s and 1970s had revealed Mars to be a cratered Moonlike world, scientists were eager to land a spacecraft on the surface.
- Both of the *Viking* missions placed an orbiter in orbit around Mars while a lander descended to the surface.
- The landers tested the Martian soil and atmosphere, and they sent data back to Earth via the orbiters, but found no definite signs of life.
- The *Vikings* also took the first high-quality close-up color photographs of the Martian surface (see below).

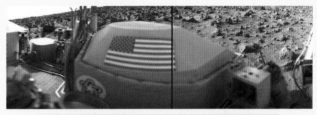

• See pages 126–127 for information on Mars.

RECENT PLANETERY PROBES

PROBE	LAUNCHED	DETAILS
Magellan	1989	Orbited Venus and produced detailed maps of its surface by radar
Galileo	1989	Surveyed Jupiter and its moons before plunging into Jupiter's atmosphere in 2003
Mars Pathfinder	1996	Landed the rover *Sojourner* on Mars in 1997
Cassini-Huygens	1997	Currently touring Saturn and its moons; landed the *Huygens* mini probe on Saturn's moon Titan in 2005
Mars Exploration	2003	Rovers *Spirit* and *Opportunity* landed on Mars in 2004 and found evidence of water
Mars Scout	2008	*Phoenix* rover collected soil samples and searched for water

EARLY MOON PROBES

The Moon has been visited by a series of probes, some manned and some robotic.

In 1959, *Luna 2* became the first space probe to reach the Moon, while its successor took the first photographs of the Moon's far side. In 1966, *Luna 9* made the first controlled landing on the Moon, and in 1967, *Surveyor 3* (pictured right in 1969 with Charles Conrad Jr. from *Apollo 12*) dug a trench in the Moon's soil. *Luna 16* brought back a sample of Moon dust to Earth in 1970, while in the same year its successor landed a rover vehicle, *Lunokhod 1*.

LIVING IN SPACE

People can stay in space for months or years at a time by living on orbiting space stations. Russia has launched eight space stations—seven Salyut stations and Mir. Meanwhile the U.S. used rockets and spacecraft left over from the *Apollo* Moon missions to create the Skylab space station. Now Russia, the U.S., and more than a dozen other countries have come together to built the ISS, the International Space Station (*Freedom*). Space stations allow scientists to carry out long-term experiments and observations and to study how people adapt to long periods in space.

SALYUT SPACE STATIONS

Salyut 1 was launched by the Soviet Union in 1971. It was the world's first space station.

- Most Salyut space stations measured 42.6 ft. (13m) long by 13.8 ft. (4.2m) across.

- Salyuts 1–5 had one docking port, where a transfer spacecraft could attach.

- Salyuts 6 and 7 had two docking ports.

- A Salyut space station weighed about 19 tons.

- Salyut 6 and 7 could be refueled, which enabled them to stay in orbit for longer.

- Salyut 7 spent almost nine years in orbit.

The 52.5-ft. (16-m)-long Salyut 7 on display in 1984 in Helsinki, Finland

SKYLAB MISSIONS

MISSION	LAUNCHED	LENGTH
Skylab 1	5/14/73	n/a
Skylab 2	5/25/73	28 days
Skylab 3	7/28/73	59 days
Skylab 4	11/16/73	84 days

Skylab astronaut Alan Bean

SKYLAB SPACE STATION

Skylab was the United States' only space station.

- Launched on May 14, 1973, it spent more than six years in orbit, but Skylab was shaken so much during launch that one of its solar panels was torn off.

- Skylab was 118 ft. (36m) long with a spacecraft docked and up to 22 ft. (6.6m) wide.

- Three three-man Skylab crews took tens of thousands of photographs of Earth and studied the Sun using Skylab's solar observatory.

- Skylab reentered Earth's atmosphere on July 11, 1979.

Skylab in orbit at the end of its mission

MIR SPACE STATION

The space station Mir with the shuttle _Atlantis_

In 1986, the Soviet Union launched the first core module of a new space station called Mir (Peace).

- Five more modules were added until the mid-1990s (see below).

- Mir spent just over 15 years in orbit.

- The U.S. space shuttle was able to dock with Mir.

- Seven shuttle astronauts spent a total of 28 months on Mir.

- In 1997, an unmanned _Progress_ supply craft crashed into Mir, damaging its hull and solar panels.

- The longest time spent in space at one time is 437 days, achieved by Russian cosmonaut Valeri Polyakov on Mir from January 8, 1994 to March 22, 1995.

- Toward its end, Mir had many breakdowns, and mold was growing on its equipment.

- Mir reentered Earth's atmosphere on March 23, 2001.

- Several large pieces of the 130-ton space station survived reentry and splashed down in the South Pacific Ocean, east of New Zealand.

MIR MODULES

MODULE	LAUNCHED	USED FOR
Core module	1986	Command center and accommodation
Kvant-1	1987	Astronomical observatory
Kvant-2	1989	Air lock for space walks
Kristall	1990	Processing materials
Spektr	1995	Remote sensing
Piroda	1996	Remote sensing

INTERNATIONAL SPACE STATION

ISS—HISTORY

In 1998, the first two modules of the International Space Station were launched and joined together in orbit.

- The first parts were called the Zarya module. Zarya was launched by a Russian proton rocket in November 1998.

- In December 1998, the space shuttle added the Unity Node connecting segment.

- In July 2000, the Zvezda service module was added.

- The first crew, called Expedition 1, arrived in November 2000.

- The Destiny module was added in February 2001.

- Air locks, docking ports for spacecraft, and connecting frames have been added, too.

• See pages 156–157 for information on the space shuttle.

The International Space Station

ISS—FUTURE

- Its solar panels will have a span of 239.4 ft. (73m), almost the length of a soccer field.

- The living space inside will be bigger than a jumbo jet.

- It will be about four times the size of Mir or five times the size of Skylab.

- It will have six laboratories, two habitation modules, and two logistics modules.

- The ISS orbits at a height of 250 mi. (400km) above the surface of Earth.

- NASA has built a humanlike robot, Robonaut, to help ISS astronauts.

- Shuttle problems from 2003 have delayed the probable completion of the main ISS units until at least 2010.

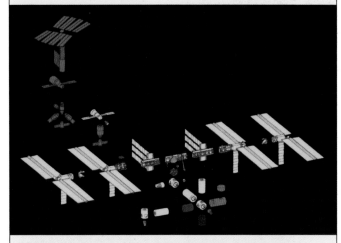

This ISS configuration shows the level of international participation.

☐ United States	■ Europe	■ Brazil
■ Russia	■ Italy	
■ Japan	■ Canada	

GLOSSARY

Abdomen The lower part of the main body, or torso, below the chest that contains mostly digestive and excretory (waste-disposal) parts and, in females, reproductive parts.

AIDS (acquired immune deficiency syndrome) A fatal disease caused by HIV (human immunodeficiency virus) that renders victims susceptible to infections and cancers. AIDS can be slowed, but not cured, by expensive drugs.

Alternating current The flow of electricity supplied to homes and offices through electrical power. It reverses direction about 50 or 60 times per second.

Anatomist A medical scientist who studies the bones, organs, and other structures that make up an animal body.

Anthropologist Someone who studies the traditional human societies and cultures that still exist in the modern world.

Arachnoid A type of volcano with ridges around it that resembles a spider's body and legs when seen from above. First discovered and named on planet Venus.

Archaeologist Someone who seeks out and studies nonwritten evidence of past human cultures and civilizations.

Artery A blood vessel (tube) that carries blood away from the heart.

Asteroid A lump of rock or metal, usually smaller than a planet, that does not have an atmosphere or moons orbiting it. It is larger than a meteoroid. Most asteroids orbit the Sun. They are sometimes called minor planets.

Asteroid belt The zone between the outermost inner planet, Mars, and the innermost outer planet, Jupiter, where millions of asteroids orbit the Sun.

Astronomer Someone who studies planets, stars, moons, and other bodies and objects in space.

Astronomy The study of planets, stars, moons, and other space bodies, as well as space itself and all of the universe. Astronomy is partly a practical science that involves observing and cataloging.

Atmosphere The layer of gases that surrounds a planet, star, or moon.

Atom The smallest possible unit of a chemically pure element. All materials and substances are composed of atoms and combinations of atoms known as molecules.

Atom bomb A device that uses the chain reaction of uranium or plutonium to produce an extremely powerful, destructive explosion. A single atom bomb is equivalent to one million tons of ordinary explosive.

Atomic size The atomic size of an element depends on the number of protons and neutrons in the nucleus. An atom of hydrogen has only one proton in the nucleus; an atom of uranium has 92 protons and even more neutrons.

Australopithecus (southern ape) One of a group of bipedal (using two legs) primates that lived in Africa about four million years ago. *Australopithecus* may have been the ancestor of modern human beings.

Axis An imaginary line passing through the middle of a star or planet around which it spins, or rotates.

Axon The very long, thin part of a nerve cell, or neuron; also called a nerve fiber.

Bacteria A group of single-celled organisms that are similar to the earliest forms of life. Bacteria do not have a nucleus or use DNA. Some cause diseases.

Base pair One of four nucleotide bases—thymine (T), guanine (G), cytosine (C), and adenine (A). Always arranged in pairs, they make up the genetic code.

BASIC (Beginners All-purpose Symbolic Instruction Code) A computer language that is used to write operating programs for a computer.

Big bang An unimaginably gigantic explosion thought to have happened at the beginning of the universe, more than 13 billion years ago, perhaps when space, time, and matter began.

Binary Using only two digits, 1 and 0. Computers operate according to instructions written in binary numbers. Text and other information (such as sound and video) can be digitized (converted into binary numbers) for storage or transmission.

Black hole A very small, dense dark area of space with immensely powerful gravity that is created when a star collapses to "less than nothing" and pulls in everything around it, including light.

Bladder A baglike sac or container for storing fluids. The body has several, including the urinary bladder (often just called "the bladder") and gallbladder.

Blood sugar Also called glucose, this is the body's main energy source, used by all of its microscopic cells to carry out life processes and functions.

Botanist A scientist who studies plants and their habitats.

Calculus A type of arithmetic used to find the solution to problems where there are two variable quantities, as in the complex motion of a cannonball through the air or a planet through space.

Capillary The smallest type of blood vessel in the body. It is usually less than one millimeter long and too thin to see except by using a microscope.

Cardiac Having to do with the heart.

Cartilage Tough, light, slightly flexible and compressible body substance, often called gristle, that forms parts of the skeleton, such as the ears and nose, and also covers the ends of bones in joints.

Cathode-ray tube A hollow glass device that "fires" a stream of electrons from one end so that they form an image on the flattened surface of the other end. The cathode-ray tube is the basis for ordinary TV sets.

Cell The basic microscopic building block of the body, a single living unit, with most cells 0.0004–0.002 in. (0.01–0.05mm) across. The human body contains more than 50 trillion cells.

Census A count of the total population of a country. Many governments conduct a census every ten years.

Central nervous system The brain and spinal cord.

Centrifugal force The force that appears to make objects on a rotating body move toward the outer edge.

Cerebral Having to do with the cerebrum, the largest part of the brain, which forms its wrinkled domed shape.

Cerebrospinal fluid The liquid surrounding the brain and spinal cord that protects and cushions them, as well as helps provide nourishment and take away wastes.

Cermis The inner layer of skin under the epidermis that contains touch sensors, hair follicles, and sweat glands.

Cilium A microscopic hair, usually sticking out from the surface of a cell, that can wave or bend, and perhaps sense substances, as in the olfactory epithelium of the nose and in the taste buds on the tongue. (Plural: cilia)

Clone A plant or animal produced from a single cell that is an identical copy of the plant or animal from which the cell was taken. A clone has exactly the same DNA as the "parent."

Coaxial cable An electrical communication cable with an insulated central strand of thick metal wire surrounded by a woven mesh of fine wires.

Collagen Tiny, tough, strong fibers found in body parts such as skin and bones.

Coma A bright glowing cloud, or "halo," around a body such as a comet.

Comet A relatively small ball of rock and ice, a "dirty snowball," orbiting the Sun on a lopsided path that may take it far beyond Pluto to the Oort cloud.

Constellation A pattern or picture seen in a group, or cluster, of stars viewed from the surface of Earth.

Core The central part of a planet, moon, star, or other space object.

Corona The glowing ring, or "halo," around the Sun, best seen during a solar eclipse when the Moon passes in front of the Sun.

Cortex The outer layer of a body part, such as the renal cortex of the kidney or the cerebral cortex of the brain.

Cosmology The development of astronomy dealing with the origin and evolution of the universe as a whole and how its parts work.

Cranium The upper domed part of the skull, or braincase, that covers and protects the brain.

Crater A bowl- or dish-shaped hollow on a planet, moon, or asteroid, caused by another object crashing into it.

Crust The hard, rocky outer layer of a planet such as Earth.

Current The flow of electricity around a circuit.

Cyclotron A device used to accelerate subatomic particles (such as protons, neutrons, or electrons) so that they crash into one another to produce other subatomic particles.

Dark matter Invisible material that we cannot detect using scientific methods but that is thought to make up a large percentage of the universe.

Day The amount of time it takes a planet or moon to spin around once on its axis so that its closest star returns to the same point in its sky.

Dialysis A medical technique for removing harmful chemicals from the blood of patients who have kidney failure.

Digital Stored or transmitted in digital form—as a series of binary numbers.

Direct current (DC) Electricity, produced by batteries and dynamos, that flows unidirectionally from a positive anode to a negative cathode.

DNA (deoxyribonucleic acid) The substance that contains the genetic code used to pass on characteristics to offspring. All living things except bacteria use DNA, and every species has its own type of DNA molecule.

Dwarf planet An object orbiting the Sun that is not a satellite, has not cleared the neighborhood around its orbit, and has a closed or round shape.

Dwarf star A star that is of average or low mass, luminosity, and size.

Eclipse When one space object, such as a moon, passes between another object and a star, as when the Moon moves between the Sun and Earth, casting a shadow on Earth.

Electromagnet A device that exhibits magnetism only when an electrical current is applied to it.

Electron A subatomic particle with a negative electrical charge. Electrons orbit the nucleus of an atom. An atom usually has the same number of electrons as protons in its nucleus.

Electron shell The orbit of electrons around an atomic nucleus forms a series of hollow spherical "shells," one inside the other, with the nucleus at the center.

Element One of the pure chemical substances. There are 92 naturally occurring elements and about 20 short-lived artificial elements that have been made in laboratories.

Embryo The name for a developing human body from fertilization as a single cell to eight weeks later.

Endocrine Having to do with hormones and the hormonal system (*see* Hormone).

Enzyme A substance that alters the speed of a chemical change or reaction, usually speeding it up. However, enzymes remain unchanged themselves at the end of the reaction.

Epidermis The protective outer layer of skin that is always being worn away but replaces itself constantly.

Equator An imaginary line around the middle of a planet or moon, at right angles to its axis of rotation (spin).

ESA (European Space Agency) A multinational organization concerned with space exploration and research.

Excretory Having to do with removing waste substances from the body. The main excretory system is made up of the kidneys, bladder, and their linking tubes.

Exposure time The length of time a camera shutter remains open in order to produce an image of the desired quality.

Fertilization When an egg cell joins a sperm cell to start the development of a new human being.

Fetus A developing human being from eight weeks after fertilization until birth.

Fiber-optic cable A communication cable made from woven strands of glass, designed to carry messages as pulses of laser light.

Font A set of the letters of the alphabet and numerals in matching size and style. Printers use many fonts when producing books and magazines—several fonts have been used in this glossary.

Fovea The small area in the retina of the eye where vision is most detailed and clear, due to the large number of cone cells.

Galaxy A huge group, or cluster, of stars, planets, and other objects held together in space by gravity and with immense distances of almost empty space to the next galaxies.

Gas giants Jupiter, Saturn, Uranus, and Neptune, the four largest outer planets in the solar system, which are made mostly of gases.

Gastric Having to do with the stomach.

Gene A means by which characteristics are inherited through DNA. A gene is a section of the genetic code that contains the instructions for one specific thing, such as making a particular protein.

Genome The complete genetic code for a particular species.

Giant star A star that is bigger and more luminous than the Sun.

Gland A body part that makes a substance or product that it then releases, such as the tear glands, which make tear fluid for the eyes, and the sweat glands in the skin.

Glucose *See* **Blood sugar**

Gravity A force that makes any object or matter pull, or attract, other objects toward it. *Gravity* often refers to Earth's gravity and *gravitational force* to the general name of the force that acts everywhere throughout the universe. Gravitational force is one of only four fundamental forces in the universe (the others are electromagnetic force, strong nuclear force, and weak nuclear force).

Gustatory Having to do with the tongue and taste.

Hemisphere One half of a star, planet, moon, or similar object, usually either above (north) or below (south) of its equator.

Hepatic Having to do with the liver.

HIV (human immunodeficiency virus) The microscopically small substance that causes AIDS (acquired immune deficiency syndrome). HIV is spread from person to person through sexual contact and blood.

Homo erectus An early type of human that lived between one and two million years ago. Some scientists believe that Homo erectus was a direct ancestor of modern humans.

Hormone A natural chemical messenger that circulates in the blood and affects how certain body parts work, helping the nervous system control and coordinate all body processes.

Humor An old word used to describe various bodily fluids, still used in some cases—for example, to describe the fluids inside the eye, the vitreous ("glassy") humor and aqueous ("watery") humor.

Immunity The protection or resistance to microbial germs and other harmful substances.

Inner planets Mercury, Venus, Earth, and Mars, the four smaller and mostly rocky planets of the inner solar system that are closest to the Sun.

Integumentary Concerning the skin and other body coverings, including nails and hair.

Internet An international network of computers developed in the 1970s. The Internet is now commercially used and can be accessed by all computer users.

Kuiper belt A zone of orbiting asteroid or cometlike objects in the outer solar system, circling the Sun beyond Neptune. The existence of the Kuiper belt was first proposed in 1951 by U.S. astronomer Gerard Kuiper.

Lander A spacecraft, or part of one, designed to land on a space object like a planet or moon or to plunge into the atmosphere of a gassy object like Jupiter. It can be crewed by astronauts or unmanned and controlled remotely.

Lens A curved piece of glass that bends, or refracts, light, as used in telescopes, binoculars, and microscopes.

Ligament A stretchy, straplike part that joins the bones around a joint so that the bones do not move too far apart.

Lunar Having to do with the Moon (Earth's moon).

Lunar eclipse When Earth passes between the Sun and the Moon, casting a shadow on the latter.

Mantle A layer of rock or other material that lies between the core and the outer surface of a planet or moon.

Mass The amount of matter in an object—the numbers and types of atoms or their subatomic particles, independent of any gravity acting on them.

Medulla The inner, or central, region of a body part, such as the renal medulla of the kidney or the adrenal medulla of the adrenal gland.

Meiosis A part of a special type of cell division when the chromosomes are not copied and only one set (not a double set) moves into each resulting cell.

Meninges Three thin layers covering the brain and spinal cord, which also make and contain cerebrospinal fluid. They are known as the dura mater, arachnoid mater, and pia mater.

Metabolism All of the body's thousands of chemical processes, changes, and reactions, such as breaking apart blood sugar to release energy and building up amino acids into proteins.

Meteor A meteoroid that enters Earth's atmosphere and burns up, appearing as a bright streak of light; also called a shooting star or a falling star.

Meteorite A meteoroid that falls all the way to Earth's surface.

Meteoroid A small chunk of rock, metal, ice, or a mixture of these, usually broken off a comet or asteroid.

Meteorologist A scientist who studies the weather.

Microchip A component of electronic devices; also known as an integrated circuit or silicon chip. A microchip is a small wafer of silicon with thousands of tiny electrical circuits on its surface.

Microprocessor A component of electronic devices. It is a self-contained microchip that can perform several electronic tasks at the same time.

Milky Way Our "home" galaxy that contains the solar system.

Mineral A simple chemical substance, usually a metal such as iron or calcium or a salt-type chemical such as phosphate, that the body needs in small quantities in food to stay healthy.

Minoan An ancient inhabitant of the island of Crete who developed the first civilization in Europe around 2500 B.C. The Minoan capital was the great palace at Knossos.

Mitosis A part of normal cell division when the chromosomes have been copied and one full double set moves into each resulting cell.

Moon A space object that orbits a planet.

Morse code The sequence of dots and dashes representing letters and numbers invented by Samuel Morse; used to transmit messages by flashes of sunlight on a mirror (heliograph) or along electrical wires (telegraph).

Motor nerve A nerve that carries messages from the brain to a muscle, telling it when to contract, or to a gland, telling it when to release its content.

Mucus The thickish, sticky, slimy substance made by many body parts, often for protection and lubrication, such as inside the nose and within the stomach.

Myo- Having to do with muscles—for example, the myocardium, or heart muscle.

NASA (National Aeronautics and Space Administration) The U.S. government agency responsible for space exploration and research.

Nebula A huge cloud of gas and dust in space where new stars are often forming. A planetary nebula is a "shroud" of gas thrown off by an overheating or fading star.

Negative In photography, a negative is an intermediate stage produced from exposed film. In a negative image, the colors and tones of the original scene are reversed so that light is dark and dark is light. A bright light is then shone through the negative onto light-sensitive paper to produce a positive image.

Neolithic (New Stone Age) The period of human prehistory when people developed farming and pottery. In Europe and Asia, the Neolithic period lasted from 12,000 to 7,000 years ago.

Nephron A microscopic filtering unit in the kidney for cleaning the blood.

Neuron A nerve cell—the basic unit of the nervous system.

Neutron star The small, incredibly dense, or "heavy," remnant of a star that has exploded and collapsed into a ball of subatomic particles called neutrons.

Nuclear reactor A device that uses radioactive material (such as uranium or plutonium) to produce a slow, heat-generating chain reaction. Nuclear reactors are used in atomic power plants.

Nucleotide base One of four chemical substances—thymine (T), guanine (G), cytosine (C), and adenine (A)—that are linked one after the other to form the long strands of a DNA molecule. The genetic code is often written in just four letters: T, G, C, and A.

Nucleus The central part of an atom or cell. In atoms, the nucleus is formed of protons and neutrons. In a cell, the nucleus normally contains DNA.

Observatory A building or site where telescopes are used to observe (watch) objects in space.

Olfactory Having to do with the nose and smell.

Oort cloud A huge ball-shaped cloud of comets and similar objects surrounding the entire solar system.

Optic Having to do with the eye, especially the optic nerve, which carries messages from the eye to the brain.

Orbit To go around and around another object. The orbit of a planet or moon is its path around another object, such as the Sun. Most orbits are not circular. They are elliptical, or oval.

Orbiter A spacecraft or part of one that orbits its destination rather than carrying out a flyby or trying to land on the surface.

Oscilloscope A device that uses a cathode-ray tube to show electrical signals as glowing lines on a glass screen. Oscilloscopes are used to monitor frequency, wavelength, signal strength, etc.

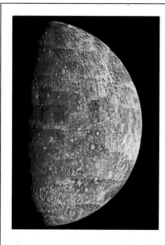

Ozone A form of the gas oxygen normally found in the upper levels of Earth's atmosphere, where it forms a barrier against ultraviolet radiation.

Paleolithic (Early Stone Age) The period of human prehistory when people made cutting implements and other tools from stone. The Palaeolithic period lasted from around 2.5 million to 20,000 years ago.

Paleontologist Someone who studies the fossilized remains of prehistoric animals.

Papilla A small lump, bump, or "pimple" on a body part such as the tongue. (Plural: papillae)

Peripheral nerves The body-wide network of nerves, but not the central nervous system of the brain and spinal cord.

Peristalsis Wavelike contractions of muscles in the wall of a body tube, such as the small intestine, ureter (from kidney to bladder), or oviduct (from ovary to womb).

Phoenician A person who lived along the eastern coast of the Mediterranean about 3,000 years ago. Phoenicians were traders and seafarers, and in around 800 B.C., they founded the city of Carthage in present-day Tunisia.

Photograph An image of reality captured by a light-sensitive medium (for example, photographic film) that can be printed onto a sheet of paper.

Photographic plate A sheet of metal or glass coated with light-sensitive chemicals that was used in cameras before the invention of transparent plastic film.

Physicist A scientist who studies the physical properties of substances and the way that objects of all sizes are affected by forces and energy.

Physiologist A medical scientist who studies the operation and activity of the organs in a healthy body.

Planet A large spherical rocky and/or gassy object orbiting a star. Planets can be defined and distinguished from other objects such as asteroids by their size, whether they orbit a star, whether they have an atmosphere, and other features.

Plate tectonics The natural mechanism by which the large plates of solid rock that make up Earth's outer crust "float" on the semisolid rock beneath and gradually change their position.

Pole The point on a rotating space object where the imaginary line around which it spins (the axis of rotation) passes through its surface.

Positive In photography, a positive image is one in which color tones have the same values as the original scene.

Primeval atom The phrase invented to name the unknown and incredibly small state of the universe immediately preceding the big bang that created the universe, as we know it, around 15 billion years ago.

Protein A type of substance produced by living things. Proteins are used to build the structures of cells and tissues.

Proton A subatomic particle. A component of atomic nuclei that has a positive electrical charge.

Prototype A trial version of a device intended for manufacture.

Protozoan A single-celled animal living in soil and water that is much more highly developed than bacteria.

Pulmonary Having to do with the lungs.

Pulsar A rapidly rotating neutron star that sends out "beams" of radio and other energy as it spins like a lighthouse and so appears to flash or blink on and off.

Radar Radio detection and ranging—a way of measuring shapes and distances of objects by bouncing or reflecting radio waves off them and detecting and analyzing the reflections.

Radioactivity Harmful emissions from certain substances, such as radium, uranium, and plutonium, that are said to be radioactive. There are three types of radioactivity: alpha rays, beta rays, and gamma rays. They are composed of subatomic particles such as neutrons, protons, and high-energy photons.

Radiometric dating The method of establishing the age of rocks by measuring the rate at which radioactive substances lose their radioactivity.

Renal Having to do with the kidneys.

Resistance The degree to which a material allows electricity to flow through it without losing energy in the form of heat.

Restriction enzyme A substance used to cut a long-stranded DNA molecule into short strands that each contains just a few genes.

Satellite Any object that orbits another object in space, whether it is natural, such as a moon, or artificial (manufactured), such as a space station. The term is often used for artificial objects that orbit Earth, such as communication satellite, and weather satellites.

Sebum The natural waxy-oily substance made in sebaceous glands (associated with hair follicles) that keeps skin supple and fairly waterproof.

Semiconductor A substance such as silicon that conducts electricity in a variable and controllable manner. Semiconductors are widely used to make transistors and microchips.

Sensory nerve A nerve that carries messages to the brain from a sense organ, or part, such as the eye, the ear, the tiny stretch sensors in muscles and joints, and the blood pressure sensors in the main arteries.

Shadowgraph The outline, or silhouette, image produced by blocking light from reaching a photoreactive surface.

Skeletal Having to do with the skeleton, the 206 bones that form the body's supporting inner framework.

Sol The Latin name for the Sun.

Solar Having to do with the Sun.

Solar eclipse When the Moon passes between the Sun and Earth, blocking the Sun's light.

Solar powered Driven by electricity produced from sunlight.

Solar system The Sun and all of the planets, moons, and other objects that orbit around it or one another.

Spacecraft Any kind of vehicle or vessel built for travel in space. This name is often used for a crewed vehicle—one that carries astronauts.

Space probe A small crewless spacecraft that is sent from Earth to explore space and send information or data back.

Space station A relatively large space base, orbiting Earth, where people can stay for long periods.

Speed of light Approximately 186,000 mi. (300,000km) per second. Light travels at slightly different speeds through different media—for example, a vacuum, air, or water. The speed of light through a vacuum is a constant throughout the universe.

Star A relatively large space object that for part of its existence contains nuclear-fusion reactions that produce heat and light, making it shine, or "burn." There are many types of stars, including white dwarfs, red giants, and neutron stars.

Stereoscopic Providing images that have depth (like those provided by a pair of eyes) as opposed to the flat images produced by cameras with a single lens.

Sunspot A darker, cooler area that is visible on the surface of the Sun.

Supergiant star A very big, bright giant star.

Supernova The massive explosion at the end of a supergiant star's life.

System In the body, a set of major parts, or organs, that all work together to fulfill one main task, such as the respiratory system, which transfers oxygen from the air to the blood.

Telescope Used for studying space, a device that makes faraway things seem bigger. Optical telescopes detect light rays, while other kinds of telescopes detect other forms of electromagnetic rays or radiation, such as radio waves, IR (infrared), UV (ultraviolet), and x-rays.

Tendon The stringy, fibrous, ropelike end of a muscle, where it tapers and joins to a bone.

Thoracic Having to do with the chest, which is also called the thorax.

Thrombosis The process of blood getting lumpy to form a clot, which is also known as a thrombus.

Tissue A group of very similar cells all doing the same job, such as muscle tissue, adipose (fat) tissue, epithelial (covering or lining) tissue, and connective tissue (joining and filling in gaps between other parts).

Transistor A component of an electronic circuit that depends on the variable conductivity of a semiconductor. Transistors are very small compared to the triode valves and vacuum tubes that they have replaced.

Transit The event that occurs when one relatively small space object is seen passing across the face of a larger, farther one, such as the transit of Venus, when the planet passes across the face of the Sun when seen from Earth.

Triode valve A fragile glass and metal device used in radios and other electronic devices before the invention of the transistor.

Trojans Two groups of asteroids following the same orbit as Jupiter around the Sun, one group in front of the planet and one behind.

Ultrasound imaging A medical technique that is used to provide images of the inside of a living body by using reflected sound waves.

Universe Everything that has ever existed, is existing, and could ever exist, including all of space and its contents.

Vacuum tube A component of early electronic circuits. A vacuum tube was a hollow glass device that contained complex arrangements of bare wires. The air inside the tube was evacuated, or sucked out, leaving a vacuum so that the wires did not burn out when they became hot during use.

Valve A flap, pocket, or similar part that allows a substance to pass one way but not the other.

Vein A blood vessel (tube) that conveys blood toward the heart.

Vertebra A single bone on the row of bones called the backbone, spine, or vertebral column.

Villus A tiny fingerlike projection from the microscopic cells in various body parts, including the inner lining of the small intestine.

Visceral Having to do with the main parts, or organs, inside the abdomen (the lower part of the main body, or torso), mostly the stomach and intestines, kidneys and bladder, and, in females, reproductive parts.

Vitamin A substance needed in fairly small amounts in food in order for the body to work well and stay healthy.

Year The amount of time a planet takes to complete one full orbit around its star.

White light Sunlight that can be split into the colors of the rainbow by refraction through a glass prism and raindrops.

INDEX